Praise for Behind the Mask

"A momentous, readable collection, its sole downside being that there are only 20 superhero stories."

— Kirkus Reviews (starred review)

"Short fiction readers should seek out . . . *Behind the Mask*."

— John DeNardo, SF Signal

Editor's Pick, March 2017 — New Pages

"Masterfully-written, this compilation lets us peek inside these people's ordinary lives, and shows us that they may not be as different as we think. . . . Absolutely recommend it!"

— Inky Reviews (4.5/5 stars)

"In this world where cynicism and noir are popular . . . super-heroes are the antidote. I found that hopeful vision in those particular stories of *Behind The Mask*."

— Shomeret: The Masked Reviewer

"Very well-crafted anthology with lots and lots of amazing, thought-provoking stories, both by established authors (Kelly Link and Seanan McGuire for example) as well as authors who are less well-known."

— Hannah, Goodreads Top Reviewer (4/5 stars)

BEHIND THE MASK

an anthology of
heroic proportions

edited by
Tricia Reeks
Kyle Richardson

Meerkat Press
Atlanta

Contents

Introduction

Tricia Reeks

I recently visited my grandson, Brady, whose crib—in the few months since I'd seen him last—had been replaced by a "big boy's" bed. And the trains, planes, and automobiles decor? Gone, in favor of wall-to-wall superheroes. The boy eats, sleeps, and breathes Superman, Batman, Wonder Woman, and a whole host of heroes and villains that my kids, my husband, and I all grew up with.

A three-generational superhero fan club.

That night, Brady orchestrated a hero/villain showdown on the coffee table, declaring that I would be Catwoman. I immediately complained that Catwoman was a bad girl—I mean I know it's just a game, but couldn't I at least be Wonder Woman? (I'm happy to say this anthology is *not* limited to only two female superheroes!) Brady quickly dashed my hopes, however, and with the unwavering confidence of a three-year-old, advised me that Mommy was Wonder Woman (silly Nana) and that Catwoman was definitely a good girl. So, for the night at least, as we lined up our plastic action figures for yet another clash between good and evil, I was Catwoman—*reformed* villain. Black leather, whip and all.

The idea for this anthology came about back in 2015, when Kyle Richardson, my co-editor, suggested with enthusiasm that the world could always use more superheroes. (That may not have been his exact words, but he definitely said superheroes, and he definitely said it with enthusiasm.) Soon after, I read and fell in love with Kelly Link's "Origin Story," and the idea for a collection of superhero stories focused on the (super)human condition quickly took root.

We received over seven hundred compelling submissions for *Behind the Mask*, so narrowing the book down to its current form took a super-heroic effort. In the end, we whittled it down to twenty wonderful stories, set in worlds inhabited by heroes, sidekicks, villains, and comic book artists—all straight from the minds of twenty incredible authors. Four of the stories are reprints that we couldn't wait to read again. The other sixteen are previously unpublished gems.

Some of the stories feature characters who might not be superheroes in the traditional sense, yet are heroic nonetheless, such as Sarah Pinsker's imaginative "The Smoke Means It's Working" and Stephanie Lai's majestic "The Fall of the Jade Sword."

Some shine a unique, captivating spotlight on supervillains, like Keith Frady's dramatic "Fool" and Carrie Vaughn's romantic "Origin Story."

Some are somber, ponderous works, where our heroes consider their impact on the world, like Lavie Tidhar's regret-tinged "Heroes" and Nathan Crowder's resonant "Madjack."

Others tread more light-hearted waters, with heroes adjusting to the sometimes-comical, sometimes-stressful life in the public eye, like Seanan McGuire's entertaining "Pedestal" and Patrick Flanagan's lively "Quintessential Justice."

And then there are the softer, quieter moments between heroes, as they navigate their extraordinary lives in their own unique ways, such as Ziggy Schutz's tender "Eggshells" and, of course, Kelly Link's captivating "Origin Story."

Combined with the stories of ten other terrific authors, we hope this is a collection you'll enjoy. And who knows? Maybe someday my grandson will read this or some other collection of superhero stories and remember with fondness the night when Nana was Catwoman, and Catwoman was a good girl, and superheroes were still as real as Santa.

And of this I am certain: the world could always use more superheroes.

Kyle Richardson

I met my first superhero when I was twelve years old.

It was one of those sticky-hot summer afternoons, made all the more unbearable by the stubbornness of my Chinese grandmother (who I lived with at the time), her peculiar lack of fans, and that obligatory disdain of hers for opening windows that, as far as I know, inevitably develops in everyone's old age.

When I whined (and I whined a lot back then) my grandmother would simply backhand the humid air and say, in that taut and twangy Cantonese-Pidgin accent of hers, *Fans just blow da hot air around!* Or, if the conversation veered toward the topic of windows: *Windows just let in all da dust!*

For preteen me, there was no arguing with this kind of bulletproof, built-upon-decades-of-experience logic. My only defense was to throw up my hands and groan.

So the house was hot and sticky, and hot and sticky it would stay. My Gameboy's batteries had died, as well—probably from some form of an alkalized heat stroke. And I, like any boy my age, had a restless curiosity to quench.

Cut to: the unexplored closet lurking in the slightly cooler basement.

At this point, you might be expecting some kind of supernatural event. A chemical explosion. A ruptured gas line. A freak storm that swelled around my grandmother's home, blasting an interdimensional gust of wind through a crack in the house's foundation.

Me? I found a dead millipede, half curled on the dusty linoleum floor. Like a question mark missing its dot.

Not much of an inciting incident.

The closet, at least, held more interesting things—like the cardboard boxes, stuffed to the point of overflow, stacked in the back corner of the closet where the shadows and cobwebs were the thickest.

I knew the boxes weren't mine—but at the same time, they *were*. They were my *discovery*. My *McGuffin*. My *golden idol*, abandoned in some ancient, mystical cave, left behind by some long-lost civilization.

I opened the boxes, of course, without hesitation. Or permission. I expected jewels, or elixirs, or unhatched dragon eggs. What I found was something else entirely.

I found a heartbroken man made of silver—a man who sailed the cosmos with energy crackling from his hands, his shiny feet planted firmly on his mercury surfboard. I found a brilliant scientist who turned green and monstrous when angered. I found a sarcastic young photographer who had the power to crawl up walls.

I'd found my uncle's stash of comic books and the characters living within them—in all their face-punching, spandex-clad, word-bubbled glory. More than anything, though: I found *life*, through the eyes of others. Here, in exchange for saving his home planet, a man was doomed to love his fiancée from a galactic distance. There, a young girl struggled as a thief on the streets of Cairo, with no parents to guide her, and no home to call her own.

Kinship. Empathy. The human experience. Above all else, these are the things I discovered that afternoon.

I returned to the boxes every day that summer, until I'd ransacked the entire collection. At some point, I told my uncle of the discovery. He responded with a casual shrug, un-angered by my intrusion (much to my relief). Rather, he seemed embarrassed by the age of his collection. "Oh, those are *old*," he said, almost apologetically. "The comics these days are much better."

His comment rang hollow to my ears, like being told of *other fish in the sea* when you only have eyes for one. "Better" was impossible. To me, those stories were the best.

Decades have since passed. I eventually moved out of my grandmother's home. (Now in a cooler climate, I sometimes find myself longing, almost irrationally, for a stuffier, stickier heat.) I met a girl. We fell in love. We brought a child into the world. And through all that time, illustration-laden fiction slowly abandoned me. Some stories were set on park benches, their pages limp and dog-eared, with the hopes that someone else would come along and give them a new home. Others were tossed, reluctantly, into library donation bins. In their place, books with fatter spines appeared on my shelves, books with covers that boasted the authors' last names in tall, brash fonts. But no matter what direction my tastes have taken me, that first foray into the world of comics still lingers, like a knot somewhere inside me that refuses to untie.

So when Tricia approached me with the idea of co-editing an anthology and asked if I had any thematic suggestions, my mind, naturally, went back to that dust-filled closet. To the day my imagination took flight.

Behind the Mask is, partially, a prose nod to the comic world—the bombast, the larger-than-life, the save-the-worlds and the calls-to-adventure. But it's also a spotlight on the more intimate side of the genre. The hopes and dreams of our cape-clad heroes. The regrets and longings of our cowled villains.

That poignant, solitary view of the world that can only be experienced from behind the mask.

The authors in this collection, both established and new, are all dexterous and wonderfully imaginative, each deserving of their own form-fitting uniforms and capes. Some of the stories pulse with social commentary, like Cat Rambo's whimsical and deft "Ms. Liberty Gets a Haircut" and Keith Rosson's haunting "Torch Songs."

Others twist the genre into strange and new territories, like Stuart Suffel's atmospheric "Birthright," Kate Marhsall's moving "Destroy the City with Me Tonight," and Adam Shannon's reality-bending "Over an Embattled City."

Some punch with heart and humor, like Matt Mikalatos's satisfying "The Beard of Truth" and Chris Large's adventurous "Salt City Blue," while others bite and grind, such as Michael Milne's evocative "Inheritance," Aimee Ogden's poignant "As I Fall Asleep," and Jennifer Pullen's heartfelt "Meeting Someone in the 22nd Century."

The list goes on—in this case, with ten more wonderful authors and their own dazzling stories, rounding out a collection that I hope instills in you the same wide-eyed thrill I experienced in that closet, some twenty-odd years ago—the thrill of falling in love with a new character; the thrill of discovering a new favorite author; or perhaps, simply, the thrill of turning the page to find out what happens next.

Happy Reading!

BEHIND THE MASK

an anthology of
heroic proportions

Ms. Liberty Gets a Haircut

Cat Rambo

The superheroes sit in a back booth at Barnaby's Ye Olde Tavern and Pizza. It's not the usual sort of superhero hangout and they'll probably never eat here again. They've had four autograph requests: two from customers, one from their waitress, and one from the manager, who also insisted on taking their picture with his cell phone.

It's a shame that they won't be coming back, Ms. Liberty thinks. The cheese pizza is hot and greasy, the sensation of consuming it agreeable. It's enjoyable, even, to sit around talking about the world, bullshitting and comparing stories and wishes and pet peeves.

"You know what I hate?" she says, pouring more beer. "The porn star superheroes. And nine times out of ten, they're female."

"Yeah, I know what you mean," Dr. Zenith Arcane says. "Names like Pussy Whip and BangAGang."

"And Cocktail."

"Goddess, yes. Cocktail." They swap wry smiles.

X, the superhero without a shape, shaves away pizza triangles, slurps down high-octane root beer. Ms. Liberty and Kilroy are splitting a pitcher and well on their way to ordering a second. Alphane Moon Bass. Most places don't have it.

Dr. Arcane eyes X and Ms. Liberty. She says, "Must be nice to be able to eat like that." She's got a watery salad and a glass of apple juice in front of her. She doesn't usually complain. But lately she's been downright snippy.

"I need to remind you about your hair," Dr. Arcane continues. "It's so early eighties."

Ms. Liberty's hair falls in frosted blonde waves, a mane, unexpected against the strict lines of her red, white, and blue jumpsuit. She touches a tendril at her shoulder.

"Are you her parent now?" Kilroy says, pouring herself another foamy mug. "By the sands of Barsoom, back off, good doctor!"

The children two booths down gasp in horror and delight as X changes shape while still eating. Now she's a wall-eyed, dome-shaped creature, purple in hue.

"A ghost from Pac-Man," Dr. Arcane tells X. "Celebrating the cultural patriarchy. Embrace your chains!" She takes a sip of apple juice.

"Did something crawl up your supernaturally sensitive ass?" Ms. Liberty asks.

"Don't piss me off," Dr. Arcane says. "Nobody likes me when I'm pissed off."

Ms. Liberty takes another pizza slice, eats it in five quick bites. She knows why she likes eating. It's not about the fuel. Anything will do for that. (Literally.) It's her programming that makes her enjoy the sensation of something in her mouth. And elsewhere. She can achieve orgasm in 3.2 seconds by saying a trigger phrase.

She really hates her creators for it. It's distracting. It's dehumanizing. It's objectifying. She understands the intent behind it, to have her engage in enthusiastic, frequent sex, hopefully with them. She doesn't understand, though, why they chose to then give her free will, to force her to perpetually struggle between that pull and the business of being a patriotic superhero, a cybernetic woman: super strong, super fast, super durable.

Even now she feels the firmness of the bench under her ass, the smoothness of the table's wood against her forearms. She glares at Dr. Arcane.

"What. Is. Bugging. You?" she says, spitting out each word like a bullet.

"We don't have the right dynamic."

"What?"

"The four of us—you a cyborg, X a genetically constructed being, alien Kilroy from four galaxies away, and myself, a pan-dimensional sorceress—"

"Sorcerer."

"Magic-user. At any rate, we need some more human people. To add a few more facets to our toolbox."

"You mean interview some new members?"

"An open call for facets, yes."

Ms. Liberty eats another piece, exploring the hot rush of grease, the intensity of cheese and tomato and basil. New members. It's not a bad idea.

• • •

The interviews are held in the Kiwanis hall. Ms. Liberty, X, Dr. Arcane, and Kilroy go through their clipboards while two dozen candidates wait out in the hall.

"If you're going to be our leader, you need to look like you haven't time-traveled here from the 20th century," Dr. Arcane grumbles to Ms. Liberty. "You may have been built with the blueprints from the Stepford wives, but you don't have to keep looking like one."

"It's a little late to be thinking of that," Ms. Liberty says. Her internal chronometer says 14:59:05. At 15:00:00, she'll signal Kilroy to open the door.

Dr. Arcane says something under her breath, glances back down at the clipboard. "What sort of grrl-power frenzy name is Zanycat?" she asks.

Zanycat, as it turns out, is a super-scientist's kid sister, pockets full of gadgets, gizmos, gee-whizzeries. She demonstrates flips, moves through martial arts moves like a ballerina on crack, and does quadratic equations in her head. She's a keeper, all right, although she's very young. Her certificate pronounces her barely at the legal age to be a sidekick: fifteen.

Pink Pantomime, a former reality-show star turned hero, doesn't do much for anyone but X.

Kilroy and Zenith like Bulla the Strong Woman, but her powers are too close to Ms. Liberty's.

Rocketwoman is vague about her origin; perhaps she's a villain gone good? Her armor is like something from the cover of a 40s SF magazine, but bubble-gum pink, teal blue, like a child's toy. Her gun is similarly shaped: it shoots out concentric rings of brilliant yellow energy that contract around a target.

They have gone through twenty-two candidates, making notes, asking questions. The twenty-third arrives, dressed in black and steel.

Dr. Arcane dates women by preference but believes that everyone exists on a continuum of bisexuality. She has slept with demons, mermaids, aliens, shape-shifters, ghosts, the thoughts of gods (and goddesses), robots, and super-models. But she has never seen anything like the sexuality of the woman who steps forward next: the Sphinx. She smells of sweet amber and smoke, her accent is sibilant and smoldering.

Ms. Liberty does not date, has not slept with anyone since discovering how thoroughly her sexuality is hard-wired. The resultant level of frustration, constant as a cheese grater on her nerves, is preferable to knowing that she's giving in to their design. But she also has never seen anything like the Sphinx, her languid power, her lithe curves, her eyebrows like ebony intimations.

Kilroy couldn't care less. X just sings of carrots.

According to her resume, she's a computer hacker and ninja-type. Competent and low-key. She doesn't talk much, despite their best attempts to draw her out.

At one point she looks up, meets Ms. Liberty's eyes. They stare at each other as though hypnotized, but it is impossible to tell what the Sphinx is thinking.

Less so with Ms. Liberty, who goes beet red and looks away.

"Why an all-woman superhero group?" the Sphinx asks.

"Why not?" Dr. Arcane says even as Ms. Liberty replies, "That was somewhat accidental. X and I both wanted to leave our old group and we knew Kilroy was looking for work. X and Dr. Arcane were old friends."

"Is it a political statement?"

"It's like this," Ms. Liberty says. "One of the reasons we left the Superb Squadron, X and I, was because we were the only females on there and we were getting harassed. I'm sure there are good guys out there, who would make a swell addition to our team. Maybe we'll explore that somewhere down the line. But for now, it's more comfortable to be all women."

The Sphinx nods. She and Ms. Liberty exchange looks again. Ms. Liberty imagines the Sphinx as the heroine of a comic book, a solitary wanderer, aloof and sexy and unpartnered.

• • •

"Get a haircut," Dr. Arcane tells Ms. Liberty on the way out of the hall.

"Stop nagging me. Why should I be judged on my appearance?"

Dr. Arcane pauses, considers this. "Valid point," she admits. "But here it's not about the group's appearance. It's about getting you laid."

"Artificial beings don't need to get laid," Ms. Liberty says.

"The hell they don't," Zenith retorts.

In the end they take on three provisional members: Rocketwoman, the Sphinx, and Zanycat. Three months trial membership, no health coverage until that period is past, but they'll be on the accidental damage rider as of tomorrow. Rocketwoman tells them all to call her Charisse, but everyone keeps forgetting, and the Sphinx and Zanycat prefer their hero names.

"What's the name of the group going to be?" Zanycat asks.

"We haven't been able to agree on one yet," Dr. Arcane admits.

"What are the candidates?"

"A corporate logo, Freedom Flight, an unpronounceable symbol, and Gaia's Legion."

X projects the symbol in turquoise Lucida Sans on her flank, bats cow-lashed eyes enticingly at Zanycat.

"A friend told me fast food companies are looking to sponsor teams, and there's good money in it," Kilroy says.

Arcane shakes her head. "We don't need to worry about that. I'm independently wealthy."

"*You* don't need to worry about that, you mean," Kilroy says. "Some of us are trying to make a living, put aside a little for retirement. Or a ticket back home."

"We need some sort of name for press releases, at least," the Sphinx says. They all stare at her.

"Press releases?" Dr. Arcane says incredulously.

"We need name recognition," the Sphinx insists.

"We need a fluid interpersonal dynamic!" Dr. Arcane shoots back.

"Actually, what we need is training that allows us to respond efficiently and effectively to threats," Ms. Liberty says. She adds, "In my opinion."

"How about a working title?"

"Like what?"

"Female Force?"

"UGH. Just call us Labia Legion and shoot us in the collective forehead."

• • •

The Sphinx and Ms. Liberty are sharing breakfast, the two of them up earlier than the rest for a change.

"I have a question," the Sphinx says.

"Go ahead." Ms. Liberty butters her waffle.

"Are we even really an all-female group?"

"What do you mean?"

"Well, Zenith, Charisse, Zanycat, myself, X for sure. But Kilroy's an alien—do they even have genders like ours?"

"She lays eggs, I believe, but she's been pretty cagy about it."

"And X—well, X is a construct. Not even built to be female, she apparently just decided it—but based on what? Attitude? Self-identification? Class? Power relationship to her creator?"

Ms. Liberty has had *this* conversation before, in the Super Squadron Headquarters.

"If she says she is, who am I to say no?" she says.

"That brings us to you," the Sphinx says.

Ms. Liberty says, "If I say I am, who are you to say no?"

"You're a construct too."

"Constructed to be female."

"Something you could change or reject as easily as throwing a switch."

Ms. Liberty says, "I have to be something more than superhuman. I'm female."

The Sphinx shrugs, drains the last of her coffee, slides from her chair.

"Going on patrol," she says.

• • •

Zanycat finds Zenith Arcane in the library, slouched over a couch reading, with three cats laid at intervals along her body. The group has been using Arcane's Manhattan brownstone, which is much much larger on the inside than on the outside, to the point where Zanycat has taken to spending mornings exploring the wings and passages, trying to map them on graph paper. She intends to ask Dr. Arcane about that, but she finds the older mage intimidating.

Right now, though, she has a different question, and Zenith seems like the best to tackle on the subject.

"So what *is* X?" she asks.

Dr. Arcane slides her reading glasses up her nose and closes her book. She gathers herself up, displacing the cats, and regards Zanycat. She steeples her fingers in front of herself in a professorial fashion.

"What categories do you want me to use?" she says.

"Is X an alien? A human? A manifestation of some cosmic force?"

"Ah. She was created by a human scientist who died when she was only a few years old. He kept her entertained with television and the Internet, so she tends to draw on pop culture forms."

"What's her real form?"

"She doesn't have one."

"Doesn't have one? How can that be?"

"I've known her for a few decades now, and I've yet to see her repeat a shape," Dr. Arcane said.

"Then how do you know she's a she? She doesn't just take on female shapes. I saw her do Invader Zim this morning."

Dr. Arcane beams as though a prize student has just won a scholarship. "Excellent question! Because she identifies as such."

"She said so?"

Arcane nods.

Zanycat presses further. "How do she and Ms. Liberty know each other?"

"From Superb Squadron. Ms. Liberty had been a member for a couple of years when X joined. She had been a member of the Howl, the shapeshifter group before then, but she was just a little too non-traditional for them."

"Aren't they villains?"

"You're thinking of the Pack. They're all shapeshifters as well."

"How many shapeshifter groups are there?"

"Four," Dr. Arcane says with the immediate decisiveness of someone who knows every facet of the supernatural world. This is her main power, in fact. Not that she can do that much, magically, but that she knows everyone, can connect you to a source on ancient Atlantean texts or a circle of star worshippers or even the Darkness That Crawls on the Edge of the Universe. "The Howl, the Pack, the Changing—which is a loose affiliation of generally good to neutral supernatural beings—and Clockwork Flight, which has a lycanthrope as a leader."

Zanycat makes a face and Dr. Arcane laughs. "What?" she says.

"There's too much to learn about all of this," Zanycat says.

"That's okay," Dr. Arcane tells her. "Most of the time you can go by your instincts."

• • •

Ms. Liberty has never talked about why she left the Superb Squadron before. She and the Sphinx stand side by side, watching an alleyway where giant radioactive battery-powered centipedes are emerging. Ms. Liberty says, out of the blue, "You know what bugged me? X always made it clear she thought of herself as she, but they couldn't take that at face value. They called her it, or that thing. And I thought—how far away is being female from being an it? And so I left, even though I forfeited most of my pension doing it."

The Sphinx says, "Do you and X—"

She pauses, as though trying to pick the next word, and Ms. Liberty suddenly realizes what she's going to say and says, "No! Nothing like that. We're friends."

The Sphinx looks at her. Ms. Liberty's heart is racing. A person doesn't ask another person that sort of question unless another sort of question is on that person's mind.

• • •

Twin menaces, Prince Torpitude and Princess Lethargia, rampage through downtown, smashing store windows, taking whatever pleases them, draping themselves with sapphire bracelets, fur stoles, shoving iPods and bars of shea butter soap in their pockets.

Everyone acquits themselves well. Kilroy shadowwalks behind the duo, distracts them while Rocketwoman swoops in and Ms. Liberty comes at them, Zanycat cartwheeling after, from the opposite side. The Sphinx cuts off their communication gear, keeps them from calling for back-up. Within twenty minutes they're contained and the cops are processing them with shots of hyper-tranquilizer and ferro-concrete bonds.

No press shows up, except for a blogger who interviews them, takes a couple of pictures with his pen-camera.

"What's the name of the group?" he asks, glancing around.

"It's unidentified," Zanycat says in a shy whisper, and he peers towards her, says, "Unidentified, all right. And your name?" Behind her, Dr. Arcane hears Rocketwoman give out a gasp, a happy little fangirl gasp that takes Arcane a moment to process.

He punches info into his Blackberry, takes a few more pictures of the scene of the struggle, and interviews two bystanders.

Ms. Liberty thinks later that she shouldn't be surprised when the post appears calling them the Unidentified.

"It's not a terrible name," Dr. Arcane argues.

"It sounds like a Latin American human rights movement," Ms. Liberty snaps.

X shrugs and moonwalks down the wall. She wears a purple beret and angel wings—no one is quite sure what the shape is, including Dr. Arcane, until Zanycat identifies it as pulled from a recent Barbie video game.

"What do you think, Rocketwoman?" Dr. Arcane says, rounding on her. "How's it stack up for you?"

"It's fine," Rocketwoman stammers. Dr. Arcane steps closer, "But how's it stack up against whatever we end up with?" she pursues, and is rewarded by seeing Charisse pale. "A-HA, I knew it!" She thumps her fist into her palm triumphantly.

"Knew what?" Kilroy asks.

"She's from the future."

They all turn and stare at Rocketwoman. Time traveling is the most illegal thing there is; there are corps of cops from a dozen cultures that will track a time-fugitive down.

Rocketwoman raises her chin, stares at them squarely. "I don't care," she says, "it's better than going back." Another realization hits Dr. Arcane.

"Goddess," she says, "not just any timeline but one of the Infernos at the end of Time, is that it?"

"I don't know," Rocketwoman says. Everyone can tell she's flickering between relief at finally being able to talk about it and worry that someone's going to come find her.

Dr. Arcane is unstoppable. "And what was our name, in the history books you studied?"

"The Unidentified," Rocketwoman admits.

Dr. Arcane's stare sweeps the room, nails each of them with its significance. "Ladies and ladies," she says, "I think we have a name."

It's hard to argue with that, although X wistfully expresses her symbol a few more times before Ms. Liberty finally tells her to give it up.

• • •

Ms. Liberty has taken a front bedroom for her own. It's not that she really sleeps: she can activate a program that is intended to be a simulacrum of sleep, which her creators assure her is far better than the real thing, but it has a disturbing slant toward erotic fantasies that makes her leave it off.

She doesn't sleep. Instead she writes. Romance novels. It's how she keeps herself able to buy cybernetic parts that are very expensive indeed. Let's not even talk about the cost or possibility of upgrades to her very specialized system. Her creators are gone, blown up long ago under highly suspicious circumstances, and she's never been able to track down the malefactor who carried out the deed.

Why romances? There's something about the formulaic quality of the series she likes. She writes for Shadow Press's superhero line, amuses herself by writing in the men of Superb Squadron, one by one, as bad lovers and evildoers. She has little fear they'll ever read one and recognize themselves. She also writes superhero regencies, daring women scientists and explorers, steam-driven plots to blow up royalty, Napoleonic spies and ancient supernatural crystals quarried by emerald-eyed dwarves from the earth's heart.

She works on one now, pausing on the love scene. She writes a kiss, a caress, and stops. She thinks of the feel of lips on her own skin and gives way to the urge to trigger her programming, leaning over the desk, feeling orgasms race along her artificially enhanced nerves.

She touches her face, feels the tears there.

Downstairs in the Danger Room, she works through drills, smashes fast and hard into punching bags, dodges through closing barriers, jumps and leaps and stretches herself until she is sore.

The door whispers open and the Sphinx enters. Without a word, she joins the practice.

Is Ms. Liberty showing off or trying to escape? She moves in a blur, demonically fast, she moves like a fluid machine come from the end of Time, she moves like nothing she's ever seen, forging her own identity moment by moment. And feels the Sphinx's skin, inches from her own, fever warm, an almost-touch, an almost-whisper.

"Is this the thing," Ms. Liberty says to the Sphinx, "that it matters because you will only sleep with females?"

"I will only sleep with someone," the Sphinx says, twisting, turning, cartwheeling, "who knows who they are."

Ms. Liberty's arms fall around the other woman, who is iron and velvet in her embrace. Then Ms. Liberty pushes away, stammers something incoherent, and rushes from the room.

The Sphinx looks after her, waits for hours in the room, gives up the vigil as dawn breaks. Several stories above, Ms. Liberty saves the twenty thousand words she's written, a love scene so tender that readers will weep when they read it, weep just as she does, saving the file for the last time before sending it to her editor.

• • •

Ms. Liberty lets X cook her dinner. This is a mistake for most beings. X has flexible and fairly wide definitions of "food," and she has no discernable theory of spices. But for a cybernetic body, fuel is fuel, and sensation is sensation. There are no unpleasant physical sensations for Ms. Liberty. All she has to do is make a simple modification, performed by mentally saying certain integer sets.

She knows that she can do the same with her emotions. She could make loneliness bliss, frustration as satisfying as completing a deadline. But would she be the same person if she did that? Is she a person? Or just a set of desires?

She eats chili and bread sandwiches, washes them down with a glass of steaming strawberry-beef tea. X has produced candies studded with dangerous looking sugar shards colored orange and blue and yellow and green. Inside each is a flake of something: rust, brine, coal, alderwood.

Ms. Liberty eats them meditatively, letting the flavors evoke memories.

Rust for the first day she met X, when they fought against the Robotic Empress. Brine for the Merboy and his sad fate. Coal for the day they fought the anti-Claus and gave each other gifts. Alderwood has no memory attached and it scents her mouth, acts as a mental palate cleanser. She goes upstairs and writes five chapters set in Egypt, and a heroine in love with the dusky native guide. At midnight she eats the chocolate-flavored flatbread X slides under the door and writes another 2,000 words before lying down to recharge and perform routine mental maintenance.

She pushes herself into sleep as smoothly as a drawer closing. Her last thought is: is she a superhero or just programmed that way?

• • •

They fight Electromargarine, the psychedelic supervillain.

A band of intergalactic pirates.

Super-intelligent orcas from the beginning of time.

The actual Labia League, which turns out to be supervillains who refer to themselves as supervillainesses.

Alternate universe versions of themselves.

A brainwashed set of superheroes.

A man claiming to speak for Mars.

A woman claiming to speak for Venus.

A dog claiming to speak for the star Sirius.

And all the time, Ms. Liberty keeps looking at the Sphinx and seeing her look back.

Dr. Arcane has her own set of preoccupations. There's Zany-cat's hero-worship, Kilroy's chemical dependency, and whatever guilt rides Rocketwoman. Zenith suspects the last is some death. She tries to figure out *who*, tries to observe where Rocketwoman's eyes linger, which conversations shade her voice with regret (all of them, which is a little ominous), how she looks when reading the morning newspaper.

Dr. Arcane catches her in the hallway, hisses in her ear, "Listen,

Charisse, I need for you to tell me who dies. If it's me, I won't be angry, I just want to get my affairs in order."

"I can't tell you," Rocketwoman says. She looks away, avoids Zenith's eyes.

Zenith snarls with frustration. She doesn't like not knowing, it's the one thing in all the world that can make her truly angry.

Plus all that stuff about the sanctity of the timeline that time travelers spill out is hooey. You can alter time, and many people have. If it was as fragile as all that, you'd have reality as full of holes as Brussels lace. No, when you change time you just split the timeline, create an alternate universe. The unhappy future still remains, but at least it's got (if you've done it right) a happy twin to balance it out. This is, in fact, why most travelers appear and Zenith is sure that Charisse is no exception. She's here to change *something*. She's just not saying what.

• • •

They fight something huge and big and terrifying. That's par for the course. That's what superheroes do, whether they're programmed by three almost-adolescents in lab coats or by centuries of a culture's honor code or by some childhood incident that set them forever on this stark path.

Dr. Arcane fights because she likes the world.

Rocketwoman fights because she's seen the future.

X fights because her friends are fighting.

Zanycat fights because it's what her family does.

Kilroy fights because there's nothing better to do until she gets to return home.

The Sphinx fights because she doesn't want to be a supervillain.

Ms. Liberty thinks she fights for all these reasons. None of these reasons. She fights because someone wanted a sexy version of Captain America. Because someone thought the country was worth having someone else fight for. Because a woman looks sexy in spandex facing down a flame-fisted villain.

Because she doesn't know what else she should be doing.

Because her instincts say it's the right thing to do.

• • •

Ms. Liberty finishes her novel, sends it off, starts another about a bluestocking who collects pepper mills and preaches Marxism to the masses. She spends a lot of time pacing, a lot of time thinking.

X has discovered paint-by-numbers kits and is filling the rooms with paintings of landscapes and kittens, looking somewhat surreal because she changes the numbers all around.

Zanycat is about to graduate high school and has been scarce. Next year she'll be attending City College, just a few blocks away, and they all wonder what it will be like. Zenith remembers being student and superhero—it's hard to do unless you're well-organized.

Kilroy has joined AA and apologized to several villains she damaged unnecessarily while fighting intoxicated. Before each meal, she insists on praying, but she prays to her own, alien god, and an intolerant streak has evidenced. She's apparently a fundamentalist of her own kind and believes the Earth will vanish in a puff of cinders and ash when the End Times come. That's why she's been working so hard to acquire money to get off-world, lest she be caught in the devastation.

• • •

Ms. Liberty goes to Reede and Mode to find fabric for a new costume. There's a limited range to the fabrics—not much call for high end fashion in super-science, but she comes across a silvery gray that looks good. She finds blue piping for the wrists and neck, not because she wants the echo of red, white, and blue, but because she likes blue and always has. And it makes her eyes pop. The super-robots take her measurements. They'll whip it up while she runs her next errand.

There are some places that are neutral territory for superheroes and villains. A few bars, for example, and most churches. And this hair salon, high atop the Flatiron Building. Arch rivals may face down there and simply step aside to let the other have first crack at the latest *Vogue Rogue*.

"My friends keep trying to push me to try something different, Makaila," she tells the hairdresser.

"Do you want to try something different?" the hairdresser demands, putting her hands on her hips. She has attitude, cultivates it, orders around these beings who could swat her like a fly, drain her soul, impale her with ice and kill her a thousand other ways, as though they were small children. And they enjoy it, they sink into the cushioned chairs and tell her their woes as she uses imaginarium-reinforced blades to snip away at super-durable hair, self-mending plastic. Usually she just trims split ends.

Ms. Liberty looks at the tri-fold mirror and three of her look back. She thinks that this is the first time she's decided to alter herself, step away from the original design. She thinks of it as modernization—a few decades of crime fighting can date you, after all.

Here's the question, she thinks. Does she want to be a *pretty* superhero? Is that what being a superhero means to her?

And here's another question: what is a superhero's romance? She's been writing them as though they were any other love story, writ a bit larger, with a few more cataclysms and laser guns in the background. Girl meets boy, there's a complication, then she gets her man. But what does the superwoman do after she's got him? Does she settle down to raise supertots or do they team up to fight crime? Can you have your cake and eat it too, as Marie Antoinette, the Queen of Crime, would insist?

Her makers thought sex was a worthy goal, a prime motivator. And instead all they'd done was make her start to question her body. And now was she questioning her own mind the same way, wondering if she wanted love or sex, and what the difference was.

Her three faces stare and stare from the mirror and she hesitates, conscious of the waiting Makaila. Finally, she says, "I want it short and easy to take care of," and leans back in the chair.

• • •

They fight:
Shadow elementals.
A team of super-scientists.
A group of sub-humans.
A cluster of supra-humans.
Ms. Liberty's creators in zombie form.
A villain who will not reveal her name.
The hounds of the Lord of the Maze of Death.
A rock band.
A paranoid galaxy.

A paranoid galaxy's child.

A paranoid galaxy's child's clone.

A witch.

And in the end, everything turns out fine, except for the hovering death that Rocketwoman still watches for, that Dr. Arcane still watches her watching for. The Sphinx and Ms. Liberty do go to bed together, after issues and problems and misunderstandings, and at that point we fade to black and a few last words from our sponsor, along with X in the shape of a giant candy bar.

• • •

"Every woman knows she's a woman," Ms. Liberty says. "She's a woman. And every hero is a hero. They're a hero. That's who they are."

Cat Rambo lives, writes, and teaches atop a hill in the Pacific Northwest. Her 200+ fiction publications include stories in *Asimov's*, *Clarkesworld Magazine*, and the *Magazine of Fantasy and Science Fiction*. She is an Endeavour, Nebula, and World Fantasy Award nominee. Her second novel, *Hearts of Tabat*, appears in early 2017 from Wordfire Press. She is the current President of the Fantasy and Science Fiction Writers of America. For more about her, as well as links to her fiction, see www.kittywumpus.net

Destroy the City with Me Tonight

Kate Marshall

Cass gets the diagnosis in high school, three weeks shy of eighteen, full of dreams about Paris and London and New York. She's always had the aches. Growing pains, her mother tells her—*normal*. She repeats it to herself as they wait for the X-rays—*normal*—in a waiting room with a broken air conditioner—*normal*—and an antiseptic smell. She repeats it when the nurse calls them back—*normal*—while the doctor looks down at his notes—*normal*—all the way until he says the words.

Caspar-Williams Syndrome.

The city is mapped on her bones, to lines that wrap ribs, tibia, mandible. A dense knot of streets engraves her sternum; a lonely road carves a notch in her clavicle. An intersection splays like a starfish below her left eye, and she stares at the shadow of it on the X-ray as the doctor explains. Rare condition. Few known cases. Well, we've all seen the news.

Her mother gives a strangled laugh, covers her mouth. "It's only," she says. "It's only, I thought I was going loopy in my middle age, but I guess . . ."

Cass thinks of the times her mother has forgotten to pick her up. Has seemed startled that she's in the room. Has stuttered over her name or only stared a moment, bewildered, as if she does not know who this stranger is.

Normal.

"The pain will get worse, if she doesn't leave. She might have weeks or months or years before it's unbearable," the doctor says, but Cass doesn't wait around. She's never liked long goodbyes.

It takes her a week to find the right city, searching maps for familiar streets, matching them to the osseous grooves beneath her skin. It's not London or Paris or New York; it's nowhere she'd choose to go, but she buys a one-way ticket. Her doctor gives her the name of a local specialist, but she never calls the number. There's no cure, after all, and she's had enough of tests.

She gets a job at a diner and an apartment barely big enough for a bed. The street she lives on sits snug in the crook of her left elbow. For the first time in years, her bones don't ache.

She waits.

• • •

It's six months before the visions start. The city starts her out easy: a little girl lost ten blocks from home. Cass walks her back and leaves her at the doorstep. It's stolen suitcases next, dumped in the bushes, money scraped out but otherwise intact. A few weeks after that, it's a mugging. She takes a fist to the stomach, punches back, feels the man's bones break. She doesn't even bruise.

Her boss forgets to give her shifts. Then he forgets she works there at all. But that's all right; her landlord's forgotten she's there, too, and stops collecting rent. Cass spends her nights riding buses, always tucked in the rearmost seat, waiting to be where the city wants her. She never once fights it.

• • •

Two years in, the symptoms are getting worse. Her fingerprints have smoothed out, vanished. Her features blur in photographs. She can stand in a room for an hour before people notice her.

She's always wondered why you'd bother with a mask; now she gets it. It's not to be concealed, it's to be seen, to be remembered. Her mask is pale blue, the hint of feathers at the edges; she gets wings tattooed across her shoulders. When the name arrives, it's Seraph. She takes to it, ditches Cass entirely. No one's called her by name in over a year, anyway.

The city offers up a better apartment, right on Main Street. The former tenant is dead, a tunnel taking the place of his right eye, the killing too quick for the city to catch on. She drops the killer off at the police station and cleans up the blood. The walls are decorated with black and white photos: New York, Paris, London. She frames her X-rays and hangs them next to Big Ben.

The next day she gets shot. It's the fifth time, but it still stings.

• • •

The apartment on Main has been "vacant" for six years now. At some point, the former tenant's family showed up for his things, but they somehow forgot to take the bed, the couch, the TV, the photos. They looked uneasy when they left, and they lingered, engine idling, for nearly an hour. She almost wished they'd come back and demand she get out, but like everyone else, they shook it off and left.

Seraph's skin is a map of its own now—scars too deep to heal clean. Bullets, knives. Rebar that punched through just under her ribs. Not enough to kill her, though she knows that they can die. She watched it happen once, on the news, the one called Glaive, body slicing downward through the air for a few graceful seconds before gravity and asphalt put an end to her momentary flight. Death breaks the amnesiac contagion; in death, she is remembered, known. Her name was Danielle and no one pushed her.

Seraph gets a recording. Watches it on repeat and wonders when she'll get too weary of being forgotten. When she goes, she decides, she doesn't want to be witnessed.

Another winter passes.

• • •

He shows up in April, when the streets are wet and cool. Another Caspar-Williams. The Rothschild variant, though it hasn't been proven that the variation is one of pathology rather than psychology. Every city produces a Rothschild eventually. An echo, a reflection, the destruction to her protection. Whether it's a matter of balance or just a fluke mutation of the virus, no one knows.

Shadows seethe around him when he moves. He's faster than her, hard to keep a fix on; his symptoms are advanced. That worries her, as she steps over the bodies he's left for her; she should have known about him before now if he's been infected this long. He kills bad men, but not exclusively. He doesn't seem to have any point or purpose but destruction.

Their first real fight is at the arboretum. She gets dirt in her hair and a broken arm and doesn't land a blow. Then the Main Street Bank, then the subway, then the football stadium, and by then she can't taste anything but her own blood, and her ears won't stop ringing.

"Why bother?" he asks her, before dislocating her shoulder with a twist. She doesn't have an answer.

She sits in the diner where she used to work, arm in a sling. No one comes to serve her; they never do. Symptom of the disease. She's not wearing her mask. She's no one. So it takes her a while to hear the voice calling her.

"Cass." The woman's said it three times before Seraph looks up. The woman is middle-aged, tired. She's clutching a page ripped out of a school yearbook. Distantly, Seraph remembers the faces on the rear side. Recognizes a few names, too.

"Mom," Seraph says. Not sure if she's surprised or glad or anything at all. She's spent years trying to forget her family, her friends, as thoroughly as they've forgotten her. No use clinging to what she can't have. Now the memories hurt like a half-healed wound wrenched open again.

The woman sits down across from her, smooths the page out on the table between them. One picture is circled. The girl looks vaguely familiar. *Cass*, the woman has written, letters traced and retraced until they're thick and manic. Arrows point to the picture, more words. *Cass your daughter cass CASS casS don't forget CASS.*

"I don't know if I'll remember long enough," the woman says. "So I wrote it all down, everything I wanted to say." She slides an envelope across the table, stuffed thick with folded paper. Her eyes are already getting distant. "There's treatment now. Maybe a cure. That's what they're saying."

Seraph allows herself a moment of fantasy. In her mind, they talk for a while. Catch up. The woman, her mother, says that she's proud of what Seraph's done. That she misses her.

In reality, she only gets those few sentences. Then the woman gets a puzzled expression, stands. She shakes her head a little, like she's forgotten something, and picks up the envelope before wandering away. She leaves the page from the yearbook.

Seraph folds it neatly into eighths and tucks it in her pocket. She doesn't cry; even she has trouble remembering Cass, these days.

She goes to the cathedral and sits at the peak of the roof, the wind tugging at her hair. There's nowhere in the city she can't get. It's in her bones, after all. She's not surprised when he shows up, but she is surprised when he sits down next to her.

"My mother came to see me today," she says.

"That's a head-trip," he says, and she nods. He offers her a cigarette; she declines.

"She says there's a cure."

"You going to take it?"

It's already the longest conversation she's had in years. "Would you?"

He shrugs. "I'm faster and stronger than anyone alive. I can heal a bullet wound with a nap."

"And you just use it to cause mayhem."

"And I'm supposed to what, save kittens from trees?"

"If you don't get the cure, I can't," Seraph says. "I can't let you run amok."

"Amok?" he laughs. "Okay. I'm your fault, you know."

"How are you my fault?"

"You infected me," he reminds her, and for a moment, it works. For a moment, she remembers.

Three weeks shy of eighteen, dreams of London and Paris and New York. He wants to see the Great Wall; she wants to see the Grand Canyon. He draws a map across her skin with one finger.

He sits in the waiting room with her. He holds her hand. Normal, she whispers; he squeezes her fingers tight.

The doctor tells them sexual transmission is unusual, but not unheard of. Her mother turns scarlet; Cass looks away. He just nods. At least they'll get to take one trip together. A pair of one-way tickets, but they don't talk. When they get to the city, they rent an apartment barely big enough for a bed. She waits tables; he washes dishes.

When the visions start, she goes out to meet them. He stays home, digging the heels of his palms into his eyes, trying to blot them out. She tries to convince him not to fight them: it's easier if you give in.

The city finds her a new place. She looks at photos of London and Paris and New York, and wonders if she should get anything from the old apartment. But she can't think of anything she cares about enough to bring.

She blinks. The memory is gone. He's still there, but not for long. He's standing, stubbing out his cigarette.

"I'm your fault," he says. "I've done everything I can to remember you, but you never even tried to hold onto me. You left me behind."

She can't remember whether that's true, but she doesn't argue. She goes home, instead. Smooths out the yearbook page. She finds his photo. The name beneath it isn't familiar, but he's signed next to the picture. *Can't wait for the summer.* A sloppy heart.

The morning paper arrives. They've given him a name: *Nightblade.* Dramatic. She thinks he'd like it, though she can't say why. She frames his picture, puts it up on her wall next to Paris and an X-ray of the bones of her right hand.

• • •

The nights they're too weary to fight, they meet at the church. Half the time, she can't remember why she's there until he shows. They don't talk much. Shared silence is revelation enough.

She watches a special on Caspar-Williams. It's still misunderstood, the mechanism of transmission imprecisely imagined. They're the only two in their city, but elsewhere, there are more. Dozens. New York, London, Paris. Men and women with maps on their bones, cities that own them. Most are like the two of them, strong and fast and quick to heal. But she sees a woman sheathed in flame, a man whose skin sprouts plates of armor like a beetle's carapace.

She pauses on a blurred image of herself in mid-leap, shadows streaming behind her like wings. She can't even see herself clearly in mirrors anymore.

"I have an idea," he says that night. "We can keep our powers and escape the city. See the world together, like we planned."

She pretends to know what he's talking about. Some nights she remembers. Tonight isn't one of them. "How?" she asks.

"You'll see."

She doesn't see him for weeks. She keeps hearing about the cure.

Watches an interview with a former Caspar-Williams sufferer. His cheeks are hollow, eyes sunken, but he smiles, arm around a wife who thought she was single the last three years. She doesn't seem to know what to do with herself.

"What has your life been like, the last three years?" the reporter asks her. She hesitates a long time. "It was good," she says at last, not looking at him, not looking anywhere in particular. "I didn't know I missed him."

Seraph crouches on the cathedral steeple, waits for him to show. The city calls to her; for just one night, she doesn't answer. Winter passes.

• • •

It's spring when he finds her again. Things have been quiet without him; she's lost the habits necessary to survive such utter isolation. When he tells her to follow him, she doesn't hesitate.

The machine is a nest of wires and clear tubing. Phosphorescent liquid churns at its core; it clings to the wall like a starfish, like a tumor. It pulses with the heartbeat of a dying titan. Seraph runs her hands over the cold metal; the city's fear is electric in her blood.

"Destroy the city with me," he says. "Destroy the city, and we'll be free. We'll still be strong. But we can go wherever we want."

She presses her body to the machine, fitting her limbs among its protuberances, laying her cheek against its thrumming heart.

"I can never remember your name," she confesses. "I put your picture on the wall, and I still can't remember."

"We loved each other," he says.

"I can't remember that, either." She steps away. "I have to stop you."

"You don't have to do it for me," he says. "Do it for yourself. See London and New York. Just think about it."

She tells him she won't, but she does. The notion itches, scratches, burrows.

Haven't I done enough for you? she asks the city. Its fear grows more urgent with every hour; her dreams are filled with glowing liquid and a heartbeat that shudders with promise.

She gets the number of the man she saw interviewed. He agrees to meet. By the time he gets there, he's forgotten why he's come, but he answers her questions. He doesn't regret it. She asks him what made him do it.

"I was lonely," he says. Then he shakes his head. "That's not it. Honestly, I couldn't stand seeing that everyone I loved got along fine without me."

She tells him about the machine. He asks what she's going to do.

"I could give him the cure," she suggests, but he shakes his head again. It's not a syringe of blue liquid you can jam in his thigh; it's months of drugs and radiation. She looks at his skin, paper-thin, his color like a day-old bruise. She wonders how much life he's traded to have any life at all.

"The thing is," she tells him, though he's lost track of her now, doesn't register her voice, "the thing is, if I stop him, I've got to kill him. Or else I've got to stay here, forever. Because he won't go for the cure, and he won't stop trying."

She stares at her hands, her fingers gnarled from fractures that have healed over wrong.

"I've never killed anyone before."

He laughs at something on his phone. She leaves him with the bill and walks down a street that stretches from the nape of her neck to the base of her spine.

It is not, in the end, a beautiful city. It has no real soul to it; it is forgettable, indistinct. It clings to her, infests her, gives little in return. No one on this street knows her name.

He joins her. They walk the city, stand at the edge, where the pain sets its teeth gently against their throats.

"It's ready," he tells her. He takes her hand. "Cass. Destroy the city with me tonight. Destroy the city, and be free."

She almost remembers him. In a way, it makes it easier, or else nearly impossible, when she turns to him, kisses him, hands on either side of his face. When she wrenches her hands to the side. When she feels his neck break.

It's not enough to kill him. There is no magical serum to make him weak, no stone from the orbit of a distant sun, no incantation. There's only brute strength and the crack of bones. Too much damage to heal.

When it's done, she goes to the church steeple. The city thanks her with a sunrise more brilliant and more beautiful than any she's ever seen, flooding light over men and women who are alive because of what she's done. Because of the blood drying to grime in the creases of her hands.

Not one of them knows her name. Not one of them knows about the machine still under their feet, waiting for a switch to be flipped.

The city shows her something new. Six hundred miles away, someone's matching her streets to the map on their bones, praying for an end to the ache. It's a promise, a gift. The city's consolation prize. *You won't be alone.*

She leans back. Wonders what part she'll play when they get here. Maybe they'll work together. She'll get a sidekick, and they'll get a mentor who knows every brick and shadow. They'll get each other. They won't have to be alone.

Except she was never alone, and she was. He was always here, and it wasn't enough.

Except that she hasn't taken apart the machine. She should have headed straight there. Scattered its pieces, destroyed its blueprints. She hasn't. She's finding that she likes the option. The switch she could flip and opt out of this whole dance.

Except that she knows, if she's willing to admit it, that someday—not soon, but someday—she'd smile. She'd hold out her hand. And she'd say, *Destroy the city with me tonight.*

She could fight it—for a while. But she's got one death to her name, now. Another would be easy. Another hundred wouldn't be hard. Her disease is advanced; she has trouble remembering herself these days, but she remembers enough to know that isn't the way she wants to be.

She smokes his cigarettes until the sun comes up. The city calls to her to reconsider, but she's made her choice. She walks to the clinic, blood still caked beneath her nails.

There's no paperwork to fill out; they move too quickly, the only way to ensure the treatment actually gets started before the disease wins out.

The needle slides into her arm. No blue liquid; it's clear, and it slithers into her blood like poison, hot and acidic. Her bones begin to ache, and the city grieves.

In another city, far away, a woman runs her fingers over the letters carved in her kitchen table. *CASS*, they say, and she begins to remember.

Further still, six hundred miles and more, someone buys a bus ticket. They step on board, searching for the streets etched on their bones.

Kate Marshall lives in the Pacific Northwest with her husband and several small agents of chaos disguised as a dog, cat, and child. She works as a cover designer and video game writer. Her fiction has appeared in *Beneath Ceaseless Skies, Crossed Genres*, and other venues, and her YA survival thriller *I Am Still Alive* is forthcoming from Viking. You can find her online at katemarshallwrites.com.

Fool

Keith Frady

On a skull-shaped tropical island deep in the Atlantic, five stories beneath a dormant volcano, Dr. Entropy admired his new portrait, contemplating Armageddon and its implied suicide. The portrait hung on a wall erected center stage of the theater, and Dr. Entropy's painted-self returned his judgmental squint with wide, maniacal eyes. Their wardrobes matched because Dr. Entropy was in costume: two red lab coats with black buttons and two pairs of black gloves and black boots. He thought his painted skin looked pastier than his flesh, but the only lights in his windowless volcano were artificial, and he had to admit to himself that it had taken a pale toll. The *portrait* Dr. Entropy stood in his workshop, clutching a ray gun in his right hand, his left touching a red button on a panel embedded in the volcano wall. The likeness was uncanny: a stranger passing by might have thought Dr. Entropy was considering himself in a mirror.

Generator Organizing Graphics and Hues Mark VI was not programmed to twitch or fidget or sigh, so he stood resolute as Dr. Entropy passed sentence on the portrait. He also could not speak to his creator unless given a command or asked a question, so he made no reply when Dr. Entropy said, "I did well creating you. This shall be a towering monument for whatever species next crawls on the Earth's surface. Every race should be so lucky as to gaze upon their God." Dr. Entropy turned away from the portrait and its artist, calling out, "Turn the lights off behind me."

G.O.G.H. Mark VI bowed. "Yes, Master."

Dr. Entropy paused backstage and added, "Spend the last few minutes of your existence doing as you wish."

The android bowed again. "Yes, Master."

Dr. Entropy entered the stairwell, which spanned all five levels of the volcano, and began climbing the spiral staircase. He wheeled his arms in large circles at his sides, rotated his neck, cracked his knuckles through his thick gloves, and paused at each landing to stretch his hamstrings and touch his toes. All the while he recited, "She sells seashells by the seashore. Peter Piper picked a peck of peppers. Red leather, yellow leather. Red leather, yellow leather." At the top of the staircase he paused before an open door. His workshop beyond it— usually overgrown with brambles of wire, boulders of alien metals, and gadgets and traps like so many trees in a forest—was deserted. All of his projects had been transferred to storage except for the machine featured in the portrait: a simple panel embedded in the volcano wall that coughed in beeps, winked in lights, sighed in whirs, and lacked all interface except at its center, where a single, plump button screamed in scarlet. The workshop would have opened to the sun and sky were it not for a metal dome capping the volcano's mouth. The dome was retractable, but he had not cracked it open and felt the sun on his face in all the long months he had been orchestrating the apocalypse.

Dr. Entropy took three deep breaths, then thundered into the workshop.

"As ripples on the sea's surface whisper of leviathans rumbling and undulating in the deep, so does this fragile button herald the end of all things," he said, staring at the red button across the room. Turning in a circle, gesturing at absent enemies: "I am leagues from the nearest shore, reposed on a throne that crowns the sleeping fury of the earth itself. Beholden to no country or flock of sheep who bay the false prophet that is the law, I shall baptize their idiotic ideologies in the smooth liquor of oblivion." A step closer to the button, bent over as if to whisper a lover's secret: "Once I awaken this dreaming, red harbinger with the tip of my finger, intense bursts of radiation will sear every last person and electronic to cinders, and satellites I launched into orbit will reflect this flood around the world to ensure not one corner is spared." Shrugging and teasing with a grin: "And the nuclear missiles that follow will ensure no lucky soul escapes behind a wall of lead." Looming over the button, a finger raised to the heavens: "No one can stop me now." His finger came down as if to open a hymn with the stroke of a piano key, but it hesitated, never reaching the button's surface.

"No one can stop me now," Dr. Entropy repeated, louder. The panel continued to cough and wink and sigh, but nothing else stirred. The workshop seemed so much larger without the cluttered multitude of half-completed gadgets and death traps. "No one"—Dr. Entropy challenged the metal dome, raising both arms above his head, fists clenched—"can stop me now!" He thrust his index finger down toward the button. It stopped, trembling, less than an inch from the button's scarlet grin, but moved no closer to apocalypse. Dr. Entropy glanced up toward the metal dome as if expecting something to crash through it. Met only with the unrelenting coughs and winks and sighs, his finger curled back into his fist.

"Yes. Well"—he straightened back up, grasping for an explanation to his hesitance—"of course. This planet may be diseased, but I am its cure, its favored son. How could I not grace it with one final performance?" Dr. Entropy turned his back to the button and strode toward the staircase. "That's it. For that single noble accomplishment, my birth, this putrefied world deserves a grand valediction." He pulled open the door to the stairwell, and glanced once more at the ceiling. "There's nothing stopping me."

A dilapidated couch Dr. Entropy had had since college anchored the main room of the living quarters, facing an 88-inch television he had made himself not long after moving into the volcano. Bookcases lined the left wall, and he perused the dog-eared paperbacks on their sagging shelves. His thumb caught on a particularly thick volume, and Dr. Entropy collapsed onto the couch and began flipping through *The Complete Shakespeare* for a monologue fit to end the world. He paused now and then to mouth a few lines or recite a promising passage aloud. The speech needed to shore him against doubt and galvanize his finger to its ultimate task. It had been foolish to rush in so unprepared mentally. Ending the world was also suicide, and that had perhaps been the philosophical hand that had stayed his finger. Dr. Entropy read louder. Nothing had stopped him. He had not hesitated, but acted out of prudence. A slight preparation, and then the world would bend its knee and collapse beneath the weight of its God.

When he found an appropriate monologue, Dr. Entropy tossed

the book on the coffee table in front of the couch, then went to the dressing room adjoining his bedroom. The mirror was outfitted with stage lights around its edges, an accessory Dr. Entropy had not used of late, but now he flicked them on and squinted at their stilted glare. "Isaac, come here," he called out as he studied his face, the lights accentuating every wrinkle and scar, and turning his skin into an emaciated yellow pallor.

He was applying foundation when Isaac arrived. Six inches shorter than his creator, Isaac was the most complex and detailed of Dr. Entropy's androids. When Isaac had been constructed, Dr. Entropy told himself that their physical resemblance to each other— their wide, green eyes, pugnacious chins, and untamed brown hair— was purely functional because he hadn't needed to spend extra time designing a new visage. After Isaac, though, he'd made all the androids identical bald, brown-eyed copies, differentiated only by their programming. And Dr. Entropy and Isaac were not a perfect match. Isaac looked younger, leaner, and more handsome, but the resemblance remained.

"You called, Master?" Isaac said from the doorway.

Dr. Entropy addressed Isaac's reflection in the mirror, "Summon all units to the theater."

"There was not a performance scheduled for today, Master," Isaac said.

"I'm also having second thoughts about that portrait," Dr. Entropy said, and Isaac watched him dab extra foundation into a particularly deep wrinkle.

"Master, is something wrong?"

"No." Dr. Entropy craned his head to and fro in the mirror so he could smooth every nook and cranny of his face and neck.

"The other units and I were wondering why you did not activate the device."

Dr. Entropy lowered the make-up brush and turned to look directly at Isaac. They stared at each other for a moment as Dr. Entropy tempered his panic and anger. He could not answer the question.

"What is your function?" Dr. Entropy asked.

"To obey your commands, and act as coordinator and network hub for all android units," Isaac said.

"And have I requested a tactical analysis?" Dr. Entropy asked.

"No, Master," Isaac said.

"A psychological evaluation?"

"No, Master."

"Then you do not wonder." Dr. Entropy returned his gaze to the mirror and rubbed lowlights into his cheeks. Isaac remained in the doorway, watching as Dr. Entropy contoured his face, darkened his eyebrows, and applied eyeliner. The grizzled, tired man who first sat in front of the mirror had been replaced by a sleek maniac.

The door to the living quarters opened, and Isaac stood to the side to allow G.O.G.H. Mark VI to pass into the dressing room.

"Generator Organizing Graphics and Hues Mark VI reporting, Master," he said.

"What is it doing here?" Dr. Entropy asked, wiping off a stray line of eyeliner.

Isaac said, "You expressed dissatisfaction with your portrait, so I summoned him here to receive further instruction and—"

In a single fluid motion, Dr. Entropy unholstered his ray gun and pulled the trigger. The gun hissed, and G.O.G.H. Mark VI fell to the floor. It deactivated without a sound, a smoldering circle burning at its heart. Before turning back to the mirror to apply the finishing touches to his make-up, Dr. Entropy noticed that the android was splotched with flecks of paint.

"Why is it covered in paint?" he asked.

"Your last command allowed him to do as he wished," Isaac said. "He painted."

"What did it paint?"

"A new portrait of you, Master."

Dr. Entropy's eyebrows shot up, and he threw a reflected glance at Isaac. "It already completed a new portrait?"

"Yes, Master. He wasn't inhibited by limits or instructions and finished the portrait in the time since you returned from the workshop. If he had been human, I might have said he was inspired."

"Yes, I did well creating it," Dr. Entropy said to the mirror.

"Yes, Master."

"Have the new portrait hung in place of the current one after the performance."

"You might not like it, Master," Isaac said.

"It will be better than what's there now, I'm sure. Be quick about it after I exit the stage. I will activate the device as soon as I conclude the performance. You are dismissed."

"What of the remains?" Isaac asked.

Dr. Entropy glanced at the dead android, and said, "Leave it. We're all about to die anyway."

"Yes, Master." Isaac bowed, and left.

When he heard the door close behind Isaac, Dr. Entropy shivered, dropping his ambivalent facade, and looked down at G.O.G.H. Mark VI. Deactivating a robot had never bothered him before, but regret gnawed at his gut. He had torn apart and rebuilt the previous five G.O.G.H. units instead of destroying them; perhaps he was sickened by the waste of now-unrecyclable material. Dr. Entropy reviewed himself in the mirror. A poised face caked with layers of make-up glowed in the stage lights' harsh glare, but he saw the uncertainty haunting his eyes. Taking three deep breaths, Dr. Entropy rose, stepped over the remains of his portrait artist, and as he left the living quarters, said, "She sells seashells by the seashore. Red leather, yellow leather."

One hundred, ninety-nine androids, some created for this express purpose, filled all but one seat in the theater. The empty seat was unnoticeable in the dark, more than halfway back and far to the right. No comment on this absence passed amongst them since Isaac, seated front row, center, had already informed them of the G.O.G.H. Mark VI's deactivation. The androids sat in incontrovertible stillness and silence—no breath stirred the air or puffed their chests. Their hands were folded in their laps, and every eye was fixed on the crimson curtains washed in the bright heat of the spotlights. The androids activated their theater mode so that they could react appropriately to the coming performance.

Dr. Entropy was the only one who made any noise; despite his attempt to sneak across the stage, every android heard his soft footfalls as easily as a scream. Except for the wall still holding the first portrait, there was no set, and Dr. Entropy wore his regular red and black costume. The only prop he wielded was his ray gun, tucked once more in its side holster. He tapped a button on his right glove, causing the house lights to cut out and the curtain to part with a dragging rustle in the dark. A second button press, and a sharp spotlight revealed Dr. Entropy standing in front of his own portrait, the two of them challenging the audience. Suffused with light, a long shadow behind him, Dr. Entropy began his final performance.

"Tomorrow, and tomorrow, and tomorrow." Dr. Entropy unsheathed the ray gun, brandishing it at his audience. Aiming the gun at one of the androids in the front row, grinning: "Creeps in this petty pace from day to day." Arcing the gun over a few patrons, his eyes widening to match his grin: "To the last syllable." Swinging the barrel to aim at Isaac, whose eyes shone with something that might have been pride: "Of recorded time." Placing the tip gently against his own temple: "And all our yesterdays have lighted fools." Crooning, eyes closed: "The way to dusty death."

Eyes snapping open in a scream, Dr. Entropy wheeled around and fired four rounds into the portrait. The painting melted, streaming down the wall now riddled with burning holes. Dr. Entropy laughed, then: a deep, unhinged laugh that echoed in the silence. He howled in his full glory, his doppelganger melting before him, and felt a boiling in his stomach as he watched his image die. "Out, out, brief candle!" he bellowed, and exited stage right, his strides carrying him into the stairwell.

The exit triggered the androids' theater mode reaction to applaud. To avoid damaging his androids' appendages, Dr. Entropy had installed into each unit a sound bit of someone clapping, and they now played these recordings on repeat, mouths opened so as not to inhibit the sound. The theater shook with the resounding applause of an unmoving audience.

"Life is but a shadow." Dr. Entropy's voice bounded up the stairs in time with his feet, the applause following behind him. Leaping and sauntering to the rhythm of the words: "A poor player who struts and frets his hour upon the stage." Slamming open the door to the workshop: "And then is heard no more." He found himself again staring across the room at the red button. Voice plummeting, his smile vanished: "It is a tale told by an idiot."

He was breathing heavily from the climb, eyes fixated upon the button. Sweat beaded his face, muddying his makeup, and he wiped a hand across his forehead, smearing it further. Faced with the monster, he hesitated once again.

Gritting his teeth, growling louder, he recited, "It is a tale told by an idiot." Unleashing a war cry, bounding forward, arm outstretched to the button: "Full of sound and fury!" Looming once more over the button, his left hand braced against the panel for support, Dr. Entropy raised his right fist. "Signifying nothing!" Screaming, his right fist slammed down while, in the theater below, his audience continued their thunderous applause.

Again and again he pounded the panel. Again and again his fist moved no closer to the button. Dr. Entropy could not hear it, but the androids' applause had reached its preset time limit, and all was silent in the theater as Isaac stood up on a world still spinning.

Dr. Entropy fell to his knees in front of the panel, his hand throbbing. "Why?" he pleaded with the button. "Why are you doing this to me?" He bowed his head, resting it against the panel's edge, his arms splayed out on either side of the button. He was still kneeling there, unraveling, when Isaac walked into the workshop behind him.

Isaac looked down on his creator, voice even and cool. "I installed the new portrait as you commanded."

"Where is he?" Dr. Entropy remained on his knees. "Where is Uberman? Why hasn't he come?"

"News outlets report he is attending a ribbon cutting ceremony at a furniture outlet store," Isaac said.

Dr. Entropy shifted. "He's not halting a natural disaster? Fighting some giant monster?"

"No."

"Then he must be on his way soon," Dr. Entropy said, nodding to himself. "Have the units left the theater?"

"No."

"Excellent, I must stage another performance." Dr. Entropy stood.

"Why?" Isaac asked.

"Because that one was a travesty. Quickly now, before Uberman arrives." Dr. Entropy strode past him.

"I'm afraid the units will not be able to attend." Isaac kept his back to Dr. Entropy.

Dr. Entropy stopped. "You dare disobey me? You dare challenge Dr. Entropy?"

"They cannot attend because I ordered them to deactivate."

Dr. Entropy's breath caught like he had been kicked in the stomach. He thought of G.O.G.H. Mark VI, smoldering obediently on the dressing room floor. That regret congealed with a sudden despair as

Dr. Entropy felt Isaac's words sink in: they were all gone, their cores wiped in the deactivation. Dr. Entropy wondered whether he had pushed the red button after all.

"I never ordered you to do that," he said.

"Dr. Entropy wanted to eradicate all life," Isaac said. "Deactivating the androids fell under that command by implication."

"You carried out an inferred command?" Dr. Entropy shook his head as he tried to figure out where Isaac's programming would have allowed it.

"I am able to detect nuances in commands and act as I see fit based off such analysis."

"You have never taken that liberty before."

"I never needed to until now. Dr. Entropy commanded it."

"I am Dr. Entropy," he said as he trudged out of the workshop.

The theater was a mass grave, ground zero of an explosion of forced suicide. One hundred ninety-eight androids slumped in their seats like puppets severed from their master's strings. Their artificial skin seemed as flesh in the dimmed house lights, and a few, from shutdown errors, were still twitching. Dr. Entropy fell to his knees. They were just androids, he tried to rationalize, but he could not face this microcosm of Armageddon, and he crawled away from those slack limbs and unlit eyes until he reached the center stage wall. He groped it, pulling himself up, and lifted his eyes to his portrait, needing those painted, maniacal eyes to still his trembling. What he saw instead broke him, and he wept.

He wept for G.O.G.H. Mark VI. He wept for his deactivated children. He wept for Dr. Entropy.

He struggled up the stairwell, begging forgiveness from a different android with every step, and wrenched open the workshop door to find Isaac about to end all of mankind, his finger inches from the button. Dr. Entropy reacted without thought, his right hand grabbing the ray gun from its holster and squeezing the trigger three times. The first blast caught Isaac in the shoulder, slamming him against the wall. The second and third shots went wide, sizzling into the volcanic rock. Isaac pressed a hand to his smoldering shoulder.

"Dr. Entropy would have wanted this," Isaac said.

"I don't."

"Because you are a fool!" He jabbed an accusing finger at Dr.

Entropy. Gesturing to the button: "The world is diseased, and here is the only cure. You used to know that."

"I don't think I ever did," Dr. Entropy said.

Pacing in front of the button: "How many times did you nearly destroy the world?"

"As many times as I wanted it saved," Dr. Entropy said, taking slow, cautious steps forward.

Grasping the air, as if to catch some ideal universe just out of reach: "It can only be saved by chaos, by the rolling grandeur of death. You reveled in devices of raw destruction, in the innate entropy of the universe."

"I reveled in their creation," Dr. Entropy said. "And none were as joyous as when I created you and your siblings," he was now only an arm's length from Isaac, and he lowered the ray gun.

"You are not my creator," Isaac said, then he shouted, his eyes wide and maniacal. "You are not my creator!" He turned back to the button and raised his hand, "In the name of my father!"

Dr. Entropy pounced, tackling Isaac to the ground. They struggled over the ray gun, its hissing reverberating around the room whenever Isaac got a finger on the trigger. Green explosions evaporated chunks of rock from the wall, and one stray shot blasted a hole in the metal dome capping the volcano. Isaac's wounded shoulder crumpled, and his arm splintered off during the fray.

"Dr. Entropy knew there was a way to quell the iniquity of the world," Isaac said.

"My sins are not the world's," Dr. Entropy said as they broke apart, the ray gun back in his hand and pointed at Isaac. "My suffering is not the world's."

"Not yet," Isaac said, and lunged for the button.

Two hisses, and Isaac collapsed, his hand sliding down the panel. Dr. Entropy removed his lab coat, revealing a plain white undershirt, and used it to wipe away the sweat and makeup streaming down his face. He dropped the stained garment and the ray gun, then sat by Isaac's corpse. Cradling Isaac's head in his lap, he stared up at the hole in the metal dome, and thought he could hear the ocean.

On a skull-shaped, tropical island deep in the Atlantic, five stories beneath a dormant volcano, a portrait hung center stage in a theater before an audience of the dead. Its subject stood erect as if carved from marble, bare fists held against his waist. A plain white undershirt rode the wave of his muscular chest down to a pair of black jeans. A lab coat, held aloft by a single clasped button around his neck, billowed behind him like a scarlet wind. His smile was easy, and he was looking up into a shaft of sunlight.

Keith Frady writes weird short stories in a cluttered apartment in Atlanta. His work has appeared in *Love Hurts: A Speculative Fiction Anthology*, *Literally Stories*, the *Yellow Chair Review*, and the *Breakroom Stories*.

Pedestal

Seanan McGuire

. . . did you see what Lady Thunder was wearing at the Oscars? Puh-LEEZ, she needs to start dressing her age and not her maturity . . .

. . . OMG, met Shock Star, and he is SO AMAZING, your favorite could NEVER . . .

. . . all six Moths are suing each other over their name, and it's like, grow up, people, life isn't just about merchandising . . .

. . . perfect . . .

. . . problematic . . .

. . . so pure . . .

. . . such a skank . . .

. . . they asked for this, you know? That's all I can think when one of them pretends to be upset about the paps. They asked for this, and we gave it to them. You'd think they could manage to be grateful. They owe us.

We own them.

You can do this. My reflection looked back at me dubiously, as if it wanted to argue with my self-affirmation. I did my best to ignore it, staring into my own eyes and firmly repeating the thought. *You can do this. You can put on your coat. You can pick up your keys. You can leave the house.*

"This is a terrible idea," said my reflection. "I want to register my objection ahead of the crowd. And there *will* be a crowd."

"Maybe there won't be," I said.

My reflection tilted her head and looked at me through

her—through *my*—eyelashes. I glared and turned away. Somehow, I can never manage to look quite as judgmental as my reflection. It's not fair. I'm the real person. I should be the one with the full arsenal of expressions.

Instead, I get to be the one with the full arsenal of anxieties and expectations. The blue light on my phone was blinking, signaling that more email had come in while I was arguing with myself. I bit my lip and threw the phone into my purse. If anything important came through, it would trigger an alarm, and I'd drop whatever I was doing to race off and save the world. Until then, I was going to focus on saving something a little closer to home: myself. I hadn't been outside the house when I wasn't in costume in over a week. The thought of pizza was starting to give me acid reflux. I needed a change.

I needed to go grocery shopping.

Fresh bread. I took a step toward the door. *Lunch meat.* Another step. *Grapes, green grapes, that haven't been in the back of a delivery van.* That was the last nudge I needed. The team delivery service was all too happy to keep me fed and healthy, but the person they used to pick their produce always went by perceived shelf life, and not by potential tastiness. One too many shipments of rock-hard pears and tasteless tomatoes had driven me into the comforting arms of takeout, which at least never pretended to be good for me.

Fruit, fruit, fruit. The silent chant got me through the process of putting on my shoes, willfully ignoring my reflection making faces at me from the shiny brass surface of the umbrella stand. *Fruit, fruit, fruit.* I shrugged my coat on and put my headphones in, blocking out anything my reflections had to say. *Fruit, fruit, fruit. Fruit and ice cream.*

I opened the door.

It was early afternoon, too early for kids to be getting out of school or adults to be coming home from work. My neighborhood might as well have been a ghost town, closed doors and curtained windows on every side. I locked the door, shoved my hands into my pockets, and started walking.

House hunting through a proxy had been surprisingly easy once enough money was involved. I said I wanted a quiet residential area, within walking distance of basic shopping—grocery store, bank, pet store, storage unit—and too far away from the trendy parts of town to ever be considered "cool." My realtor found me six options within the week. We narrowed it down from there, until I ended up in a place where no one knew who I was, or cared to know, as long as I didn't throw parties after ten.

There are people who say that anonymity lives and dies in the big city. Those people have never tried living in suburbia. Live in New York or Los Angeles and everyone knows who you are. Oh, they may be too "cool" to bother you, but they *know*, and they'll tell their friends, until eventually the cameras show up and there you are on the cover of another tabloid, wearing sweatpants and a sports bra, daring to look like a human being who needs to buy stuff like ice cream and tampons and potato chips. Daring to *exist* outside their spangled spandex fantasies. We're not supposed to do that. We're supposed to sit in our high-tech towers waiting for the sounds of danger, and then sweep in to save the day before any real damage can be done.

Saving the day pays the bills, but it doesn't do the grocery shopping. I had walked almost to my destination, sunk in a deep gray funk, when I tripped over the curb, looked up, and beheld the object of my quest: a Safeway, sign red and white and welcome as any hero signal projected against the clouds. I rushed to grab a cart, remembering—as I always seemed to when it was too late—that my reusable bags were in a heap in my hall closet.

Oh, well. They sell reusable bags on every checkout aisle. Buying new ones every time I go to the store probably defeats the purpose, but I donate an armload to the local women's shelter every couple of months, and they're always glad to have them.

Inside, the air was cool and sweet and smelled faintly of the disinfectant that they used every time someone spilled a gallon of milk or dropped a jar of pickles. Best of all, nothing was reflective. Even the newest supermarket will quickly find its chrome and glass surfaces dulled down by contact with the public, and this Safeway had been built sometime in the late seventies. Long enough ago that even the light fixtures were dinged and a little scratched-up, lending a comfortable air of reality to the whole scene. This was a real place. Real things happened here. They sold ramen noodles and navel oranges and pie crusts, and no one would ever expect to find me in the cereal aisle, which meant anyone who saw me there was likely to assume I was just a look-alike and dismiss me out of hand.

This was what heaven felt like. Anonymity, and all the grapes the world had to offer.

I was standing in the frozen foods aisle, considering the array of ice cream flavors on offer, when someone stopped next to me. I saw them moving out of the corner of my eye, a blur on my peripheral vision, and forced myself to keep studying the Ben and Jerry's. Normal people aren't so sensitized to motion that they'll turn at the slightest hint they may not be alone. Normal people go about their days confident that they're not about to be attacked by supervillains or swarmed by paparazzi. I needed to embrace my inner normal person.

"I know who you are."

The voice was calm, level, but with a note of gleeful "gotcha" that I had heard way too many times—had been hearing since I turned sixteen and was revealed as one of the trainee heroes for the West Coast Champions. At the time, I'd been too excited by the opportunity to use my powers and too terrified of the chance that I might fail to think about what it meant for me to have a costume with no mask. Only about a third of all heroes go unmasked, and it's almost always the women, like the people in charge of our costume designs want to be absolutely *sure* we're not going to smear our mascara. I'd looked at the bow in my hair and the bright blue "A" on my chest, and I'd thought I was perfect.

Until the men with the long-angle lenses had started staking out my family home, hoping to get a snap when I was visiting. It was always men, too. Right up until I turned nineteen and wasn't as attractive to the underage market, it was always, always men. The women didn't show up until I was legal, and while they were just as happy to go for the embarrassing picture, catching me with toilet paper stuck to my shoe or chewing with my mouth open, somehow they made a living without sticking their cameras under my skirt or following me into public restrooms.

Until the message boards found my phone number and posted it far and wide, resulting in a tropical storm of dick pictures descending on me in the night. And until they found the number after that, and the number after *that*, until I'd disconnected my phone and made do with the one the Champions issued me for official business. That should have been the end of it, but somehow, the tabloids had managed to dig up a few girls I'd gone to high school with and ran an interview where they talked about how I'd changed my number without telling *them*, who had been my best friends, and wasn't I out of touch? Wasn't I letting fame go to my head?

I hadn't even remembered those girls existed until their pictures had been printed in an article talking about how terrible I was. I still wouldn't recognize them if I saw them in the street.

"You can drop the act. It's not working."

"I'm sorry." I turned, smiling disarmingly. Our media liaisons had spent almost a year teaching me how to smile like that. It's a skill I hate and treasure in equal measure. I shouldn't need it. Since I do, I won't ever let it go. "You have me at a disadvantage. Have we met?"

The man standing a little too close to me in front of the frozen foods smirked. He was perfectly normal, the kind of person I saw every time I worked up the courage to leave my house for non-essential errands: a little taller than me, with tan skin, shaggy brown hair, and an ironic T-shirt over blue jeans. It was easy to picture him logging on to one of those message boards, or picking up one of those tabloids, and never stopping to consider the damage he was doing.

"You don't know me, but I know you, *Alice*," he said, smirk spreading into a grin, as proud as any Cheshire Cat. "I'd heard rumors that you lived somewhere around here."

Shit. So much for the anonymity of the suburbs. It had lasted longer than anyone back at headquarters expected—most of them had been betting on six months before I came crawling home, and I'd made it most of a year. That was a cold comfort. Anger coiled in my belly, slow and deliberate.

In the glass across the aisle, my reflection, pale ghost thing that it was, turned toward me, moving against the motion of my actual body. Its eyes were holes carved out of the frost.

Please don't let him see, I begged, and focused on the stranger. "I'm sorry. You're mistaking me for someone else."

"Am I?" Quick as a flash, his phone was out and in his hand—and then there was an actual flash, bright enough to sting my eyes, as he snapped his picture.

I squinted, briefly blinded. When my vision cleared, he was swiping his finger over the screen, choosing his caption with an expert's speed.

"There," he said, looking up and smirking again, smile eclipsed. "Let's see what my followers think, huh, Alice? Pretty sure they're going to know who you are. They love you, and you never want to give them the time of day."

Of course he was a fan blogger. Anyone who was willing to take the time to find and stake out my local Safeway was a cape-chaser, no question about it. But even some cape-chasers are harmless. They're proximity theorists, or people who got saved once and haven't been able to stop replaying the moment, or parents whose children have started showing signs of superpowers, or just curious. I always try to be kind to them, when I can. They don't deserve to be treated badly when they only ever wanted to say hello.

They're also usually not the kind of people who stop me in the frozen foods aisle, because they're usually looking to *connect*, not alienate. Bloggers are a different story. Bloggers want fireworks. They want instant friendship, the sort that Valentine can force with a wave of her perfectly manicured hand, or they want somebody to tear down. Those are the things that get them hits, and everything is hits in their world.

"Please," I said, and hated myself for the whine in my voice. "I'm just trying to do my grocery shopping. Can't you leave me alone?"

"That explains how you're dressed," he said, taking in and rejecting my outfit with a quick up-and-down glance and a sneer. "Don't they pay you enough to shop at real stores? Old Navy is not a good look on you."

My cheeks reddened, and I resisted the urge to tug on my—yes, Old Navy—jeans. They fit me well. My little sister, the one who *didn't* get the superpowers, but did get the good genes for everything else, used to call me "the buttless wonder," and finding jeans that actually look good on me is hard enough that when I do, I don't change brands until something gets discontinued.

"I don't go in for frivolous spending," I said.

The blogger grinned. "So you're saying your fans who enjoy nice things are frivolous? Nice. How do you feel about the ones who bought your fashion line last season? Not that you had anything to do with designing it, but I assume you get part of the profits."

The Alice's Tea Party collection had been a huge success, in part because while I didn't have anything to do with the actual designs, Valentine and Shock Star *did*, and they would both have gone pro if their superpowers hadn't gotten in the way. They're good. Every hero on the main team has had at least one clothing collection, because it's good marketing and it makes our actual fans feel closer to us.

Not that I actually wanted my fans to feel closer to me. Mostly, I wanted them to feel like I was a person and deserved to be allowed to have a life that was separate from saving the world or doing public appearances. I wanted to wear ratty jeans and buy frozen vegetables and not worry about whether I'd remembered to brush my hair before leaving the house.

Had I remembered to brush my hair before leaving the house? Shit.

The blogger kept grinning as his phone began to vibrate and chirp, shaking so hard that for a moment, I thought he was going to drop it. "Eighty hits and climbing," he said gleefully. "Want to tell me again how you're not who I think you are? Because you're in the minority here."

Weariness settled over me like a shroud. Even my reflection stopped moving, which was a relief. My powers are less about concentration and focus to *activate*, and more about concentration and focus to *control*. This little snake was likely to find himself in a world of hurt if he didn't stop pushing on me when I was already off-balance.

"What do you want?" I asked. "I'm just trying to shop. Please, can't you leave me alone?"

"You haven't done a solo interview in a year. Your last public photo opportunity was almost three months ago. Don't you think you owe your fans more than you're giving them?"

We're all required to appear in public every ninety days, to avoid exactly this sort of incident. The guys on the team—all of whom had been given costume designs that included masks, huh, fancy that—said the girls and gender-nonconforming members were exaggerating when we talked about what it was like to go out in public. Why, *they* could go to the movies with their girlfriends and not get hassled at all. They could *have* girlfriends, and not be afraid they'd be raked up one side of the tabloid media and down the other for "slumming it." There had been some discussion lately of upping the appearances to once every sixty days. I'd been against the idea. Maybe there was something to it after all.

"I do my job," I said. "I save the world like, weekly. I don't think I owe anybody anything, as long as I keep on saving the world."

"Wow," said the blogger.

I blinked. "Wow?"

"No wonder your popularity is in the toilet. How does the rest of your team feel about the fact that you're such an entitled bitch?"

My mouth opened and my eyes widened, but that was as far as I got, too stunned by the attack to actually make a sound. I wanted to tell him that gendered slurs are not okay, that people are people and worthy of respect, no matter what. I wanted to ask whether his parents had bothered to teach him any manners. I wanted to do a lot of things, and I couldn't manage any of them. I couldn't do anything but stare.

In the freezer window on the other side of the aisle, my frosted reflection grew stronger, becoming a blue and white sketch of me in my full costume, even down to the Vorpal sword I try not to manifest unless I absolutely have to. She was scowling, reflected face painting disapproval in front of the display of frozen waffles. If I didn't find my voice soon and get this jerk out of here, she was going to step out of the glass, and I was going to have what could charitably be called a serious public relations problem on my hand. Our bosses get *pissed* when we accidentally kill somebody.

"I—" I began.

The front window of the store exploded.

"Whoa!" The blogger covered his head, instinctively shielding himself from the glass.

It was a good, human response to an unexpected situation. It would have been mine, once. Training can conquer instinct. I let go of my cart and whirled around, plunging my hand into the reflection that had been getting ready to make a blogger kabob. The blogger gaped at me, stunned at the sight of a superhero—a superhero he had *pursued* into a private location, which just shows that sometimes curiosity outweighs survival sense—actually doing her job.

"What the fuck?" he demanded.

"You posted a picture of me!" The stupid sword was stuck. Glass doors don't make the best mirrors. If I'd known I was going to wind up fighting, I would have gone to Target or Walmart or someplace with a home goods section and a bunch of good, clear reflections. "You didn't turn off the location tagging, did you? *Did you?*"

The blogger gaped more, not saying a word. The color was draining from his cheeks. Oh, great. *Now* he realized that he'd fucked up. Maybe if we both walked away from this alive, he'd think to take the picture down before I could sic our lawyers on him.

Oh, who was I kidding? I was still going to sic our lawyers on him. Harassment, invasion of privacy, endangerment, whatever they could come up with. Yes, I'm a public figure, and yes, I've had to acknowledge the paparazzi as a part of the job, but there's a big difference between an asshole with a telephoto lens hiding in the bushes and an asshole getting up in my face when I'm trying to buy ice cream. At least one of them has the sense to remember that superheroes are dangerous.

I yanked again. The sword came free. As always, its form had been decided by the environment from which it came: this time, it was a crescent of frost, leaving trails of cold behind it as it whistled through the air. The edge of the blade glowed with the lambent light of the molecules it was cleaving in half. No one knows how that works, myself included, or how I'm not actually the Radioactive Woman. But my sword can cut through anything. *Anything.*

"Come on!" I yelled, and my reflections poured out of the freezer doors, pale frosted copies of me, as translucent as the ice that shaped them. I ran for the front of the store. They chased after me, my icy army of Alices. In the distance, I heard the camera effect on the blogger's phone click several times. Good. He could sell these pictures to pay his legal bills.

The rest of the store was in chaos. Clerks and baggers huddled in the checkout stands, trying to take cover behind their registers, while shoppers scattered in all directions, screaming. The front window of the store was gone, replaced by a pulsing wall of slick purple flesh interspersed with smaller tentacles. I wrinkled my nose and kept charging. If I stopped, my reflections would stop too, and this would end very poorly for the people who'd just been trying to do their shopping.

One of the smaller tentacles lashed out and wrapped itself around the throat and face of a screaming woman. Her screams stopped as she thrashed wildly, and then began to expand into a smaller tentacled horror.

That *did* bring me to a halt. I needed to do some taunting. Get the attention off the shoppers, and onto myself.

"You asshole!" I shouted. Not a corporate-approved battle cry, but there were no camera crews here; no one was going to care if I was family friendly. Even the parents in the store were unlikely to complain, assuming I could keep their kids from being transformed into Venusian squid-creatures. "This is a *grocery store!*"

As I had hoped, the sound of my voice was like a signal flare, attracting the attention—and yes, rage—of the attacker. The wall of flesh pulsed and twisted, until the beaked, squidlike face of the Venusian supervillain appeared. He made a terrible screeching sound, causing several of my reflections to clap translucent hands over frosted ears.

"AT LAST!" he boomed. "I HAVE YOU CORNE—WHAT ARE YOU *WEARING*?"

I scowled, adjusting my grasp on the Vorpal blade. "It's my day off," I snarled. "I just wanted some ice cream."

"YOU'RE A SUPERHERO. SHOULDN'T YOU BE PREPARED FOR THIS SORT OF THING?"

"That's what I tried to tell her!" shouted a voice.

Swell. My blogger buddy was feeling better. "Agreeing with the supervillain isn't a good thing," I muttered.

"I AM NOT A VILLAIN," objected the Venusian. "YOUR STORIES ARE FILLED WITH MANIFEST DESTINY AND THE BEAUTY OF TERRAFORMING OTHER WORLDS. I AM HERE TO VENUS-FORM YOUR PLANET. I AM A HERO."

"You turned that woman into a squid."

"SHE WILL BE A DEVASTATING BEAUTY IN THE WORLD WHICH IS TO COME."

I swallowed the urge to sigh. The main problem with Venusform as a villain is that he'll happily spend hours arguing about the rightness and justice of his plan. Sometimes I want to shake every science fiction author born prior to 1975 and ask them what the hell they had been thinking, telling the universe—thanks to the wonder of television and radio broadcasts—that humanity wanted nothing more than to overwrite all life, everywhere, with ourselves. Venusform believes he's staving off an invasion and giving us a taste of our own medicine at the same time.

He's also a space-bending squid monster capable of transforming whatever he touches, so there's only so much sympathy I can have for his doomed cause. I enjoy the number of limbs I have now and buying jeans is difficult enough without mutating.

"That world isn't coming, and you've got to go," I said.

The other problem with Venusform as a villain is that he's so damn *big*, and his tentacles do his dirty work for him. There's no solution to the danger he presents apart from a frontal assault. So I raised my sword and charged anew, swinging at any tentacle brazen enough to get near me. My reflections joined the fray, glass ghosts darting in to deal damage and distract the waving tentacles. Venusform roared, wrapping a tentacle tight around one of my transparent shadows. She screamed, the screech of breaking glass, and began to swell into an alien parody of my shape. At the same time, the tentacle that held her iced over, visibly freezing.

Venusform roared again, this time in agony. I seized the opportunity. Lopping off the tentacle nearest to me, I leapt, and drove the Vorpal blade right into the closest of his three massive eyes.

The two eyes he had remaining blinked, apparently stunned that I could still do my damn job when I wasn't wearing a blue pinafore. "I WILL RETURN," he intoned ominously, and burst into a putrid green fog that left everyone unlucky enough to inhale it coughing.

Since I still need to breathe, that included me. And since I had been hanging six feet in the air, courtesy of my sword through a supervillain's eye, when Venusform disappeared, I fell square on my famously unpadded ass.

"Oof!" The impact with the floor knocked the sword out of my hands. It flew upward. Before it could come back to earth, potentially impaling someone on the way down, I waved my hands in a quick negation, sending it back to the other side of the mirror. It vanished with a sound that was the aural equivalent of glitter. My reflections vanished with it, even the ones that had mutated in Venusform's grasp. I gasped again as their injuries mirrored into me, drawing bruises and scrapes across my skin. The mutation, thankfully, didn't mirror. Fatal injuries never do.

"Miss!" A man hurried toward me, the name tag pinned to his shirt identifying him as one of the store managers. "Are you all right?"

"Um, yeah." He offered his hand. I took it, letting him pull me off the floor. Pride rarely goes before the fall for me, but it can leave me on the ground for a long, long time. "Sorry about, you know. The window."

"That wasn't your fault," he said, letting go of my hand. "You saved us all."

It was close to the truth. A team would have been dispatched as soon as someone realized there was a problem. It would have taken them at least five minutes to get here, maybe more. The supermarket and its inhabitants would have been reduced to those panels at the beginning of the comic book, the ones where things go terribly wrong for a bunch of nameless civilians who never mattered to the story anyway.

"Not all," I said, glancing at the tangled heap of tentacles that had been one of their patrons. "I'm so sorry."

"You did your best."

"She put you all in danger," corrected a pious voice.

That. Was. It. I whirled on the blogger from before, suddenly grateful for my limitations. If I couldn't draw a sword without a reflection, I couldn't run him through for the crime of being too damn annoying to live.

"What's your name?" I demanded.

His eyes widened. In that moment, he seemed to realize that maybe baiting a superhero for fun wasn't the *best* plan. "I don't see where that's any of your—"

"You incited a supervillain attack by revealing the location of a licensed superhero in civilian form," I said. "Our legal team is already learning your name, your address, and the scope of your personal assets. So why not make me a little less angry, and tell me?"

He seemed to wilt. "Trevor."

"Well, *Trevor*, this is on you. I just wanted some ice cream." It was probably soup by now. Even if it wasn't, it was probably close enough that it wouldn't survive the walk home. "I didn't put anyone in danger. You did."

"You have no business being here, among normal people!"

"Really? That's your story now? Because ten minutes ago, you were all about getting me to smile for your blog." I was starting to get properly angry. My bruises didn't help. They pulsed and ached, making me want a hot shower and some aspirin. "I didn't do anything. I didn't ask you to take my picture. I asked you to leave me alone."

"You *exist*," he said. "You don't get the perks of being famous without the downsides. You're ungrateful. You don't deserve anything you have. You don't—"

The manager's hand landed on his shoulder. He stopped talking, turning to look quizzically at the older man.

"Get out of my store," said the manager calmly. "Do your grocery shopping somewhere else, or I'll call the police on you, and you can explain to them why you think it's acceptable to harass women who're just trying to buy—what was it, miss?"

"Ice cream," I said.

"Ice cream," said the manager. "Go."

Trevor scowled. "I'm within my rights. She's a public figure. I—"

"*Go,*" repeated the manager.

I'm pretty sure Shock Star himself wouldn't have been willing to stand his ground against that tone. Paling, Trevor turned and fled.

"He's going to post about this," I said. I felt light-headed, dizzy with what had just happened. "He's going to tell everyone what a bitch I was."

"He's not the only one who knows how to use the internet," said the manager. "You saved a lot more people than you pissed off."

I wanted to tell him why he was so wrong. I wanted to explain that reality doesn't matter, not really; not when image is for sale on every corner and beamed straight to every smartphone. There's a reason most of us are shut-ins these days, only appearing in costume and when our contracts demand it. Secret identities don't hold up in a world of facial recognition software and constant fan surveillance. We get caught. We always, always get caught.

"Sure," I said softly.

"We knew. About you, I mean. We've known for months."

I hesitated before asking, "Knew what?"

"That you were who you are." The manager shrugged. "We figured you wanted to be left to do your shopping in peace. You save the world when you're at work. We didn't need to get in your way when you were trying to get good food at reasonable prices."

I stared at him. I didn't know what to say.

"I'm guessing you don't like delivery much."

"N-no," I managed, shaking my head. "They never know how to pick the produce."

He smiled. "I think we can fix that for you. If you wanted to take a little break."

Hesitantly, I smiled back.

. . . no way he actually met Alice. She never goes out in public. She thinks she's better than us just because she's got powers . . .

. . . apparently our little diva of the mirrors now has a private arrangement with her local grocery store. They make one of their clerks do her shopping and drive everything to her house—no delivery charge. Guess it must be nice to be famous . . .

. . . what an entitled brat . . .

. . . what a terrible human being . . .

. . . what a shame superpowers are wasted on someone who doesn't appreciate them . . .

. . . isn't Alice one of the ones who was born with her powers? She didn't do anything to earn them. She doesn't deserve them . . .

. . . so lucky . . .

. . . so ungrateful . . .

. . . wish I were her.

Seanan McGuire lives and writes in the Pacific Northwest, in a large, creaky house with a questionable past. She shares her home with two enormous blue cats, a querulous calico, the world's most hostile iguana, and an assortment of other oddities, including more horror movies than any one person has any business owning. It is her life goal to write for the X-Men, and she gets a little closer every day.

Seanan is the author of the October Daye and InCryptid urban fantasy series, both from DAW Books, and the Newsflesh and Parasitology trilogies, both from Orbit (published under the name "Mira Grant"). She writes a distressing amount of short fiction, and has released three collections set in her superhero universe, starring Velma "Velveteen" Martinez and her allies. Seanan usually needs a nap. Keep up with her at www.seananmcguire.com, or on Twitter at @seananmcguire.

As I Fall Asleep

Aimee Ogden

Seventy-eight. Seventy-nine. Eighty—

Cerebrelle came back to herself all at once.

It took her a moment to remember where she was. Shattered glassware and smashed computer parts: a laboratory. Poison Dart's lair? Yes. She remembered the mission now, locked onto the situation at hand before it could slip away again. She ran a quick self-assessment before moving on. Damage? Yes. Her wrist had been badly wrenched. Her vision telescoped inward, and she could see millions of red blood cells flooding into the injured region. No fractured bones, no ligaments stretched or torn.

She let her awareness expand back out to her whole body and flexed the injured wrist once—nothing serious. She looked left, then right, and her eyes fell on the perpetrator of her injuries. She flinched.

Badger Girl's broken body lay across a cracked black laboratory bench to Cerebrelle's left. Cerebrelle closed her eyes and turned away from the too-still face. Should she even think of her as Badger Girl anymore? She doubted the Protectors let you keep your call sign once you took to defending the secret lair of the Coalition's favorite mad scientist. Besides, Badger Girl hadn't even suited up in her black-and-red uniform. She was dressed civilian-style in a denim jacket and T-shirt; only her motorcycle boots would have passed super-heroic muster. Cerebrelle's sidekick—gone rogue.

Cerebrelle squared her shoulders and turned back to Badger Girl. There would be time to deal with the fallout of her sidekick's betrayal later. But for now, she had work to do, and she had to do it fast. Badger Girl had always been more than a physical match for Cerebrelle. Of course, a solid punch wasn't everything—you had to know where it was going to strike, too—but it still meant Cerebrelle had a limited time frame to work. She pulled Badger Girl down from the bench, leaving a smear of red on the broken computer screen where the younger woman's head had been resting. She'd seen a lot of Badger Girl's blood over the years, but this time, she turned her eyes downward to avoid it.

Cerebrelle grimaced as she cinched Badger Girl's hands behind her back with a frayed length of electrical cord and knotted it twice for good measure. As she twisted the cord tight, she could feel the rough edges of broken bones grinding together. She pulled back, but too late: she was spiraling down the black hole of Badger Girl's injuries. Her mind contracted down to count leukocytes and chase platelets through capillary beds, then just as suddenly it was rocketing outwards, assigning numbers to stars never before seen from Earth, let alone from deep underground in Poison Dart's hideout. She triangulated distances, chased the highest prime number. —*Three hundred and twenty, three hundred and twenty-one, three hundred and twenty-two*— She counted the hairs on Craig's head . . .

Craig? Who the hell was Craig?

No time to worry about that now. Cerebrelle rubbed her eyes and dark sparks flew behind her eyelids. Badger Girl would heal; that was what Badger Girl did, after all. And Cerebrelle had work to do. Her gifts were mental, not physical. But it didn't take a powerhouse like Badger Girl or Red Comet to wreak havoc on some helpless technology.

Helpless only until Poison Dart's henchmen showed up, though. Cerebrelle glanced over her shoulder and took in the three access points to the room: door, upper right. Door, lower right. Ceiling duct. Imaginary laser fire trajectories arced through her mind, weaving a perfect spider web . . . or a complex manifold. She blinked and the web folded in on itself, resolving into a Klein bottle.

No. Not now. She lifted a boot and brought it down hard onto an exposed hard drive. Plastic shrieked, wires ripped, the plastic carnations decorating the adjacent desk flew through the air, and suddenly Cerebrelle was translating the complete works of Neruda into Farsi.

—*I love you without knowing how, or when, or from where.*

A thousand and twelve, a thousand and thirteen, a thousand and fourteen—

Wires frayed into a tangle of neurons. Glassware shattered into elaborate constellations. Cerebrelle panted as she stared at her dark, fragmented reflection in the remains of a busted flat screen and tried not to let her heart beat in time with the nearest pulsar star, tried not to count the sodium ions scurrying between action potentials in her brain. Her mask was crooked. She pushed it back into place with a shaking hand. Bring it back. Close it all out. There's a job to do. *—Four thousand three hundred and two. Four thousand three hundred and three—*

"Lian?"

A low blow from Badger Girl. Poison Dart's minions could be here any minute, and Cerebrelle's secret identity would be blown. "I don't want to talk to you right now."

"Oh, no? Because it seems like a damn good time to me." Electrical cords squealed as Badger Girl strained against them, and she grunted in pain. "What the hell do you think you're doing down here? And a better question: why did you smash my head open?" Another groan from the cords. "They pulled me out of a date to come after you. She was cute, too. But they thought it should be me, I guess. Lian, are you listening to me?"

Of course the Coalition thought it should be Badger Girl. A twist of the knife. "Don't use my name." She moved faster down a row of desks. With a sweep of her arm, a cluster of glass bottles shattered to the floor. Under her boots, circuit boards splintered. "And I don't talk to turncoats. How long have you been working for Poison Dart?"

"Turncoat?" The anger in Badger Girl's voice was punctuated by the shriek of the electrical cords as she ripped free. "Is that what you—Lian, stop. Just listen to me. You're going to hurt yourself, or me again, and neither of those options sounds great to me. You don't understand—"

"I understand enough." And Cerebrelle didn't want to understand any more than that. What would make an old friend into an old enemy, what sort of blackmail or leverage would turn Badger Girl against her? She leapt over a silent server bank to put space between them as Badger Girl bore down on her. "Stay back!"

"I'm not going to hurt you!" Badger Girl cried. Her fist pounded down on a wooden desktop, splintering it.

Cerebrelle backed up farther. How much more damage would she need to do before Poison Dart's chances of rebuilding were effectively nil? And she still needed to get out of here before Badger Girl forced her into a fistfight that Cerebrelle couldn't finish. She didn't want to—couldn't end up as the latest addition to Poison Dart's menagerie.

"Will you just sit still and listen to me for a goddamn minute?"

Cerebrelle looked Badger Girl in the eyes. She was the one wearing the mask, really, not Cerebrelle—how had Cerebrelle ever thought she knew that face, knew the person behind it? She watched for the twitch of micro-expressions to betray Badger Girl's true purpose: a pinching of the lips, narrowed eyes, flaring nostrils.

No: she lingered too long, and her viewpoint ratcheted in even closer. Badger Girl's blood was spiked with adrenaline, noradrenaline, and cortisol, and the sinoatrial node in her heart was pulsing an electrical signal nearly twice a second. Millions of glycogen phosphorylase molecules were racing through her muscles, churning glycogen into burnable energy, and her major blood vessels had dilated to a diameter of—

"Stop it!" Badger Girl shook Cerebrelle hard, shattering her trance. Cerebrelle squeezed backward and upward out of arteries and back into the uncomfortably cramped quarters of her own mind. "Damn you Lian, stay with me here!"

"Stop calling me that." A favorite Wing Chun escape twisted Cerebrelle free from Badger Girl's grasp. She darted under Badger Girl's arm and shoved the other woman off balance. A leap and a vault, and she'd scrambled up onto a bench top before Badger Girl's hand locked around her ankle.

"Lian, listen to me. Do you know where you are?"

"Of course I know." Cerebrelle closed her eyes, letting her awareness hang on Badger Girl's muscles and nerves.

"Do you?"

She was no physical match for Badger Girl, but she was more than a mental match. A deep breath in through her nose, then a slow exhale. When Badger Girl pulled her backward, she was ready. Braced against the bench, she shoved herself backward in the direction of Badger Girl's pull, like a tug-of-war combatant suddenly letting go of the rope. Like a compressed coil unwinding. The boot on her free leg clipped Badger Girl's chin, and Badger Girl staggered backward.

Cerebrelle dropped to the ground between Badger Girl's feet but sprang upward immediately. Badger Girl had already recovered her balance—her arm shot forward toward Cerebrelle.

But Cerebrelle was already waiting. She blocked Badger Girl's swinging arm, trapped it over her shoulder, and shot upward as hard as she could.

Badger Girl screamed as freshly-knitted bones snapped anew. Cerebrelle grabbed the broken arm by the wrist and pushed backward. Her heart squeezed at the sound Badger Girl made when the two splintered bone ends smashed together—but she hadn't left Cerebrelle any choice.

Badger Girl arced backward and crashed into a pile of smashed glass bottles and beakers. Cerebrelle ripped the front of the plastic casing off of the server bank and used the broken piece to smash the contents. Surely this much damage would keep Poison Dart too busy to . . .

To do whatever it was that Poison Dart was planning to do? The villain's plan was a dark, dizzying hole in Lian's memory, and she turned away from it. Something dire, something dreadful. It was Poison Dart, and that was all anyone really needed to know. Counting comforted her; numbers had always been a familiar and reassuring place to turn when the universe grew too big or too small around her. —*Five thousand six hundred and seventy-two. Five thousand six-hundred and seventy-three—*

She still didn't hear the sound of jackbooted footsteps marching in lockstep, and a tentative spin of her senses down along the hallways behind both doors revealed nothing untoward. But her luck wouldn't hold out forever. And Badger Girl would heal again before long.

She clambered back up on top of the lab bench and tore the panel out of the ceiling vent. The odds were too good that she'd be spotted—either by one of Poison Dart's minions or a security camera—if she left by one of the regular doors.

How had she gotten in here in the first place?

It didn't matter now, did it? She put her arms up in the vent and braced them on either side. She was about to pull her body up inside when Badger Girl's voice stopped her: "Lian."

That name again. Cerebrelle looked down, jaw set and tight. But Badger Girl was still on the floor, her broken arm cradled against her chest. Her slack face betrayed thin lines and wrinkles far beyond what her age warranted. Working for Poison Dart was hard on more than just the conscience, apparently. A tendril of pity stirred in Cerebrelle's heart, and she couldn't bring herself to choke it out entirely. "Badger Girl, stay down. You were my sidekick once, whatever that's worth now. And I don't want to see you get hurt any worse."

"Badger Girl?" Badger Girl's eyes went wide, then crimped shut. Her head dropped back onto the floor. "Lian, I haven't—this is worse than I thought."

She had an opening to make her getaway, but Cerebrelle couldn't tamp down worry for her former sidekick long enough to convince her body to make a break for it. She took her arms out of the duct and dropped down beside Badger Girl. "What? What's worse?" A thought ricocheted to the forefront. "Are you under deep cover? Badger Girl, are you in danger?" She began constructing escape routes that would let her maneuver Badger Girl's greater weight over a long distance while still minimizing their odds of being discovered and intercepted.

But Badger Girl interrupted her before she could chase down that line of thought. "Lian, no one's called me Badger Girl for ages now." Badger Girl—Evvy—dragged her jacket sleeve across her face. Was she crying? Evvy had never cried, in or out of uniform. Cerebrelle stared at the wet smears under her eyes. "I'm thirty-one years old, Lian. I'm not anything girl anymore. I go by Sun Bear now. I have for, I don't know. Forever."

Cerebrelle was still looking at the teary streaks on Evvy's face. Molecules of prolactin and encephalin spun and collided in every drop, a plain mark of authenticity: real emotional tears, not fakes nor a reflexive response to the dust adrift in the demolished lab. She got caught in the Brownian motion of the particulates suspended in the air around her for a moment before she realized what Evvy was saying. "What? I don't understand."

Evvy gestured to the room around her with her good arm. "What do you think this is, Lian? Where do you think you are? This was Poison Dart's lab a decade ago. We took him down together, but that was—Jesus, that was so long ago. He's not even called Poison Dart anymore." She put her hand over her eyes. "His name is Plasmid, and he's reformed or something. He even works with Alpha Particle and Beta Ray sometimes." A ragged laugh burst out of her, and a bubble of snot burst on one nostril. "God, Lian, he brought frittatas to last year's Protector Christmas party, and you asked for the recipe."

"I don't understand," Cerebrelle repeated. She looked down at the nebula of shattered glass all around her, at the unwoven network of wires and the deep snowbanks of dust. "That isn't right. I had a mission . . ."

"Yeah. You did." Evvy dragged herself to her knees, which brought her nearly to the level of Lian's face. "And you finished it, and you went home, and you did a lot more missions, and you retired. Except you didn't really know how to quit, did you? You had to keep chasing that power trip, until there wasn't any room left in your giant brain for you."

Cerebrelle reached behind her. The heavy black countertop offered support, but the swarms of delocalized electrons in the aromatic rings of the phenolic resin begged her to chase them through probability clouds, and she yanked her hands back. "Evvy, stop it—"

"Sure, I'll stop. As soon as you can tell me my birthday. Or my last name." Evvy's black brows crashed together. "Or your last name, Lian. Come on. Just a word—one word. I'll wait." She folded her arms across her chest, and the broken elbow slipped back into place with a sickening crack.

Lian stared down at her. Inside her brain, neurons fired; rich, oxygenated blood poured into her cerebral cortex. She dug for answers, but came up empty-handed.

Lian staggered away from Evvy, and sat down hard atop the server bank when her knees gave out. A puff of dust went up in her wake. Evvy caught her before she could drop all the way to the floor and crushed her into an embrace. Lian could smell blood and sweat on the shoulder of Evvy's stained jacket. "I don't . . ." she said, "I don't know what to do now."

"I'll take you home." Evvy pulled back, put her arm around Lian's shoulders. It was an odd, backward gesture; Lian had always been the mentor, the leader. An uncomfortable echo of how things were supposed to be. "Does Craig know?"

"Craig?" Lian asked, and Evvy's face fell.

• • •

Evvy parked in front of a little brownstone house. Lian thought it looked familiar and knew, through some blunted instinct, to look under the front leg of the painted Adirondack chair on the porch for a spare key. She stood in front of the door in the civvies Evvy had bought for her and felt the lines of the key cut into her hand. Her face felt too cool without the familiar contour of a mask to cover it.

Evvy offered, not for the first time, to go in with her, but Lian shook her head. "I'll talk to the other Protectors," Evvy said. "And some of the auxiliaries too, especially the Piconauts." She cracked half a smile. "Maybe even Plasmid. One of them will be able to help you, Lian, I'm sure of it."

Lian smiled back, even though she didn't understand the joke. She put the key in the lock, and it turned without a sound.

The house was dark and quiet and cool. Lian slipped off her boots and left them paired tidily on the floor by the door. She paused by the staircase to watch a Jeep drive past the bay window in the front room. Someone she knew drove a Jeep like that, but she couldn't quite put a finger on who it was.

Something she didn't understand drove her up the narrow staircase to the second floor, where the door on the left was cracked just enough to admit her with a tiny creak.

There was a man sleeping in the bed—a man with a broad open face marked by deep furrows between the brows and a fine web of lines framing each eye. On the dresser beside him was an orange bottle of pills, its lid partially ajar, and a half-empty water glass.

When she sat down opposite him on the bed, he rolled away from her, leaving two brown hairs behind on the pillow. She picked them up, then reached out and ran a hand through his curls. —One, two, three— Lian started counting faster. She had a long way to go.

Aimee Ogden is a former biologist, science teacher, and software tester. Now she writes stories about sad astronauts and angry princesses. Her poems and short stories have appeared in *Asimov's*, *Fantasy & Science Fiction*, *Daily Science Fiction*, *Baen.com*, *Persistent Visions*, and the *Sockdolager*.

Meeting Someone in the 22nd Century or Until the Gears Quit Turning

Jennifer Pullen

I
First comes love

The first time Greg asks Sandra out, she doesn't hear a word he says. She works at a bookstore, although "works" might be a charitable term, because what she really does is sit at a desk reading the books she's supposed to be selling. Greg's been coming to the bookstore for weeks, browsing and staring, with a feeling approaching desperation, at her bare feet propped up on the desk. Her perpetually-chipped blue nail polish and the calluses on her heels and her face as she leans back in her chair reading, feel like the sight of land to a sailor. He loves the way she bites her lower lip when she turns the page and, as the hours go by, the way her curly red hair gets progressively more rumpled by her grabbing it and rubbing furiously whenever she gets to a particularly exciting part of the book. She's doing just that when he comes up to the counter with a copy of *Cat's Cradle* in hand and asks if she would mind ringing up his book and also coming to coffee later.

She continues inflicting trauma on her hair. His mouth feels full of saliva. He swallows and sets the book on the counter. He tries again. "Coffee?" She looks up from her book at last and frowns at him. He smiles. She reaches out with one bare foot, hits a button on the cash register, and makes it ding. She says, "Eleven dollars and fifty cents."

He starts to swipe his thumb over the scanner and then changes his mind and takes cash out of his pocket. Maybe she'll touch his hand when she takes the money. She didn't hear him the second time he asked her out, either; he's sure of it. He doesn't even want the book. He already owns *Cat's Cradle*. It was just the first book he saw on the big center display. Back at home, he drank some peppermint schnapps in preparation for this moment, this day, asking her out. She takes his money and then stares at him for a moment. He feels her eyes on his freckles, on his hair with that weird cowlick in the middle he hates. He feels her deciding that he's probably one of those weird guys who plays with action figures and lives in his mother's basement. He doesn't live in his mother's basement.

"If we're going to go out, you should know I'm a cyborg," she says.

"Cyborgs are cool," he says.

She puts his money in the cash register and bags his book. She tells him to pick her up at seven in front of the bookstore, for dinner not coffee, because she'll be hungry. She also tells him to stop staring at her feet—it's creepy. He thought cyborgs were just a myth used to excuse protests against the government. He thought all the fear was just a sort of Uncanny Valley situation. He wonders if she's really a cyborg.

· · ·

Back at home, Greg rearranges his house, including his sock drawer, five times. He doesn't actually expect her to want to come to his house or to look at his sock drawer, but if she does, he wants it to be neat and tidy. He tries to work. He's a comic book artist, and he's supposed to be drawing Wolverine having a nightmare about Jean Gray, but he keeps finding himself giving Jean Gray curls and blue nail polish. He drinks some more peppermint schnapps. Joe at the Marvel offices told him men didn't drink peppermint schnapps, only women and mobsters in cartoons. Greg drinks it anyway because it tastes like gum, and back when he was a kid, before he knew better, he used to eat chewing gum. All that decades-old gum twists in his stomach. He thinks he might throw up.

He shows up at the store twenty minutes before seven and paces on the sidewalk just around the corner so she won't see him and think he's a loser or desperate. He wishes he smoked so that he'd have something to do while waiting. He stares at his watch until all the hands align and goes to wait outside the bookstore. She's already there, tapping her foot. She's put on some improbably-spiked purple heels with her jeans and T-shirt. Those shoes must be why she always goes barefoot.

"You are exactly thirty-seven seconds late," she says.

He tells her he's sorry, but he also can't help but be curious about how she came up with such a precise number. He holds out his arm and she takes it. He leads her down the road to a little American sushi place that serves meatloaf and cheeseburger sushi, among other oddities. At dinner, he talks about his work and she talks about the secret strategy for making sure you always get the books you want (stashing them in the wrong section because no one at the store actually bothers to re-organize things more than once a week) and about her childhood in Seattle, where she used to throw candy at seagulls.

"Are you really a cyborg?" he asks.

"The original," she says.

"I thought 'cyborgs running the world' was just something the anti-government nuts came up with," he says.

"Well, I don't think the men in the big house are cyborgs, but I'm the genuine article." She takes a bite of her meatloaf sushi and washes it down with a swallow of Cherry Coke.

He reaches out and lightly pinches her arm.

"You feel real to me, and I bet you'd bleed if you bit your tongue," he says.

"I'm a cyborg, not an android, silly. A cyborg is just a person who is partially machine." She flicks a wasabi covered French fry at him. He dodges it.

"What part?" he asks.

"My heart," she says.

· · ·

At the doorway of his apartment (she insists on walking him home) he hugs her, and she pulls his head down, pressing his ear to her chest.

"I tick not thud," she says.

He opens his door and she follows him in. He pours her some wine and hides the schnapps. She mercifully stays away from his sock drawer but picks up his action figure collection, manipulating Spider-Man's poseable limbs. She tells him that she was born with a heart problem, that whenever she ran or laughed she could feel her heart slamming itself against her chest like it wanted out. She had to sit still and calm, and never ever have sugar. Her heart got more and more erratic every year, until finally, she had to lie in bed hooked up to a machine as she waited for a transplant small enough for her tiny little body. Her father was a scientist at a robotics lab. He got permission—probably through bribes or something equally unsavory—for the first purely mechanical child-sized heart prototype to be put into her body.

"If life was a comic book, you'd be a superhero," he says.

"Maybe I am," she says.

• • •

Later in the living room she kisses him, and he can feel her pulse in her lips; and it's so regular—not speeding up, not slowing down—but she kisses him hard and fast, and he eases her down onto the couch. He wonders what it must be like to never be able to have your heart beat faster. But she breathes out with a sigh just like any other woman when he bites gently at the nape of her neck. Afterwards, he rests his head on her breasts and thinks about praying a thankful prayer—if only he believed in a god.

"Tick-tock," she says.

II
Then comes marriage

Sandra and Greg move in together six months after they start dating. Greg loves the way she makes sure to beat him home by exactly five minutes every day so she can greet him at the door with a kiss. She makes him throw away all the clocks because she keeps perfect time. It's true. She can put noodles on the stove, take an exactly-ten-minute-long shower, and emerge, dripping and naked, just in time to take the pasta off the stove. He hides the clocks and she breaks the oven timer. He lets her tell him, every day, exactly how many minutes they've been together. When they are in bed together, he imagines that if he touches her just right he'll be able to make her heart skip a beat. He keeps trying. She says she can feel minutes tick by and turn into hours. Greg doesn't know if he should believe her, but he wants to.

He starts drawing his own comic series on the side, one about a woman he calls the Mistress of Time, who throws gears like ninja stars and can stop the world from spinning. Sandra's father, the robotics geek, comes to visit. He's impressed by Greg's drawings, says they show real imagination. Greg feels happier than he should that her father is impressed by him. One evening, Sandra's father pulls him aside and tells him about the cyborg thing, as though it's news. He says no one yet knows all of the long-term effects of a person being part mechanical. He wants Greg to understand. Greg pats his shoulder reassuringly, and then promptly forgets about the conversation. Sandra is magnificent, and that's all he cares about.

• • •

Six months after they start living together, Greg buys Sandra an engagement ring with a heart-shaped stone. He takes her back to the American sushi place and gets down on one knee.

She takes one look at the ring and says, "Wow, I could fry ants with this."

But the second thing she says is yes, and she wears the ring on a chain around her neck. Several times a day, she brings it out to look at, turning it this way and that so it will catch the light. Greg loves the way she smiles softly when she does that, the way she watches the light refracting through the stone like she'll find a secret there. That look is how he knows she really wants to marry him, despite the fact that she'd compared the ring to the tool of a serial-killer-to-be. She says she wants the wedding invitations to have pictures of gears on them—the inside of a clock laid bare. She also wants the invitations to say: *On the 24th of June, Come See the Normal Guy Marry the Amazing Clockwork Woman.* He says no. But then he lets her have everything else she wants.

He goes through the day at work and draws women in spandex who save the world, and every single one of them has Sandra's face. He's spent so much of his life living the ordinary and drawing the extraordinary, and she makes him feel like his two worlds are running together. He decides to create the art for their wedding invitations, to make the invitations look like pages in his comic book, *The Mistress of Time.*

• • •

Two days before the wedding, Greg and Joe are at Joe's apartment talking about the bachelor party, when Greg's cell phone rings. Joe has marvelous plans to take Greg to the video arcade and get really drunk. Greg answers his phone, but Joe keeps talking about vintage pinball and how nothing really compares to touching the machines, to really seeing the wheels spin and the balls fly around. Digital stuff just isn't the same.

"Pinball places never had booze when I was a kid. I wonder if they'll let us call a stripper, too," Joe says.

Greg moves away from Joe, stands in the kitchen, the bare tiles cold on his feet. He tries his best to plug one ear, to close his friend out, because someone on the phone is saying that Sandra's just been rushed to the hospital. A car accident—no, a bike accident, which also involved a car. At first he can't absorb the information. His mind makes old TV static.

"Sir, are you there?" the voice on the phone breaks through the static.

"She's where? Which hospital?" Greg asks.

Slowly, he begins to realize that someone hit Sandra with a car while she was on her bike. Joe hasn't stopped speaking. Now he's rhapsodizing about how he thinks the lady who runs the bar/video arcade looks like Wonder Woman.

"Shut up," Greg says.

Joe obediently shuts up, staring at his friend, who he's never heard angry before. Greg nods his head and says "Okay" a lot into the phone. His hands shake. He turns to Joe and asks for a ride to the hospital. He knows he can't drive himself, and that if he did, he'd probably crash his car, too—and then the only ride he'd be getting would be in an ambulance. He tries not to picture Sandra's body on the pavement, blood across her face, and her intestines like a wet bag of yarn. In the car, images from every violent movie Greg has ever seen torture him. He vows only to watch nice movies—in which genteel British people drink tea while petting cats—from now on. He prays that her heart keeps ticking.

• • •

At the hospital, they won't let him see her. The nurse says Sandra had to be rushed into emergency surgery. They couldn't wait for him; they are so sorry. Sandra's father is there too. He's on a cell phone, making calls, gesturing violently. Greg overhears something about prototypes, something about expensive.

"I don't care what you have to do," her father says.

He hangs up the phone and collapses into the chair next to Greg. The orange vinyl of the chairs squeak as they both shift their weight.

"Do you ever wonder why the chairs in hospitals still look this way? Why hospitals look like a movie from 1990?" Greg asks.

He immediately hates himself for the inanity, but he has to hear the sound of his voice or his ears will fill with other, worse sounds. The sounds of tires. The wet splat of flesh on pavement. His brain insists on creating sound bubbles. *Splat! Boom! Crash!*

"It makes people feel safe," her father says.

"What?"

"Nostalgia. People like it. Would you want this place to be full of hover chairs and holo-displays with the vital signs of our loved ones? Why do you think no one has shit like that in their house? We like old."

Greg doesn't know what to say to that because it feels too simple, although he supposes it has to be right. He lives in a world where people can have mechanical hearts, and last year they started a colony on Mars; yet everyone still drives cars with rubber tires (although the cars do run on animal waste) and wears denim, except for the occasional weirdo who thinks everyone has to wear onesies in the future. Most things people do or don't do ultimately have to do with comfort. He knows this; he learned it in college. Psychology 101.

• • •

Twelve hours later, a nurse says, "You can see her now."

She smiles a red lipstick covered smile. She looks like a nurse from an old movie. Greg can't help but think she might be a clone or an android. He hears they are everywhere now. She looks overly tidy to be quite human. Greg stands up too quickly and weaves on his feet, vaguely nauseated and dizzy, high on caffeine and vending machine sugar snacks. He follows the nurse, Sandra's father right behind him. Greg braces himself for Sandra to be unconscious or covered in stitches, wrapped in a cast. She might be burned, scraped, mummified in bandages, threaded with cords, but she will be there, and that's what matters. He promises himself not to show shock—no matter what. The nurse stops in front of a room and motions them in.

Machines beep and whir, and Sandra rests on the bed, flipping the pages of a book. She turns and looks at them. As her head turns, Greg can hear the sound of gears; it reminds him of the sound of the remote control car he used to have as a kid. She smiles, and her face looks surprisingly whole—just some bandages on her chin. But then he sees one of her eyes. It's blue like the other, but the iris spins and focuses, and he feels like he's in line at the bank, and the camera of the digital teller is zooming in on him. Her father rushes over and hugs her, and she wraps her arms around him. One is silver and metal, and he can see her pseudo-knuckles clicking together. He makes himself walk forward one step at a time. Her father steps away and lets Greg lean in close. He kisses her cheek and feels her cheek bone, hard and unyielding. He wonders how much under there is metal. She whispers in his ear, tells him she was so afraid, she thought she was going to die, or live with one arm, one leg, one eye, some sort of horrible half-person, doomed to stay in bed.

"I'm whole," she says. She grins. Half of her teeth are too shiny, too white, and too perfect.

"Thank God," he says.

He's not religious, but he tells himself he's thankful to whatever deity there might be. He really is. He just has to get used to the way her head turns now, the way her left eye looks like it's recording him. He feels ashamed. He feels even more ashamed when she tears up and looks at him, suddenly, only one eye weeping.

"What about the wedding?" she asks.

"We'll have it here," he says.

III
And then comes baby in a baby carriage

Two years after the makeshift hospital wedding, Greg weeps with Sandra, because she's just miscarried a baby for the fourth time. She's holding the little body, most of the way formed, on her lap. The hospital cleaned the baby girl, wrapped her in a blanket, and made her look almost alive. Greg thinks that hospitals are cruel.

"She could have made it," Sandra says.

"She didn't have lungs," Greg says.

Perhaps he's a little cruel, too, but he can't let her have delusions, can't let her have false hope. With the first baby, he went along with it. He said it was just bad luck and that the little one would have been okay, if only Sandra had carried her to term. But he'd seen the X-rays. He knew that the baby's heart was under-developed, too small to ever support her. He knew that the same way he knew that this baby didn't have lungs and that it was only the umbilical cord that was keeping her alive. All of the babies were missing some part: heart, lungs, brain, liver, stomach . . . something vital every time. Sandra's father comes into the hospital room, pats her shoulder, murmurs something about unintended side effects, the dangers of experimental medicine. Greg tries to get him to leave, but Sandra grabs her father's arm with a too-strong grip.

"You could have saved her," she says.

"Too young," he says.

He doesn't repeat what he's said every time—that Sandra's body part replacements were prototypes, and that infant-sized ones haven't even been attempted yet. He also doesn't repeat what he said once, to Greg, sitting drunk on their sofa. With a glass of brandy in his hands and a bottle between his feet, her father stared at the glass and confessed that he thought the body part replacements—and the genetic manipulation required to make Sandra's body accept them—might be why she kept losing babies, why every infant was lacking. He said he was sorry. Greg poured him more booze and said he forgave him. Which Greg is pretty sure is the truth. He suddenly remembers a long-ago conversation with Sandra's father—one which might have saved them all this suffering. He tries to forget again.

Sandra releases her father's arm. She wipes tears away from her right eye.

"We'll try again," she says.

Greg wants to say no, but he can't bring himself to say that all she's really giving birth to is pain.

· · ·

The hospital makes Greg wheel Sandra out in a wheelchair. There's nothing wrong with her legs, but they seem to think that by taking extra care of her, they are being helpful. The doctor hovers nearby, watching as the nurse helps her into the chair. His hair is dark and dyed red at the tips. Greg thinks it makes him look like an anime character and less serious, but he doesn't say so because he knows he wants to lash out at somebody, anybody.

"Perhaps you should stop trying to have children," the doctor says.

Sandra turns her head and stares at the doctor. Her neck looks bony and frail.

"Piss off," she says.

Greg opens his mouth, but he can't decide if he wants to cheer on her feistiness or say he agrees with the doctor. The two impulses fight within him, and he can't make any words come out, can't bring himself to tell his wife that he'd be okay with adoption or that they could get a cat—twelve cats for all he cares.

The doctor presses his lips together and doesn't say anything. He lets Greg wheel Sandra past him, but Greg can feel the doctor's eyes as they leave.

· · ·

Back at home, it takes Sandra weeks to decide to get up, move around, go back to work.

She lolls on the couch, staring at the television screen projected onto the wall; instead of going outside, she turns on the 3D function of the set and sits, surrounded by a variety of scrolling landscapes equipped with sound. To bring her tea, Greg has to pass through projections of heather-covered Scottish hills, or Antarctic wastelands filled with penguins. He feels awkward stepping through the penguins.

She catches his hand as he hands her a cup of green tea.

"I'll get better," she says.

Greg looks at her matted hair, at her collar bone poking out of the top of her sweater, and wants to believe her.

She grips him tighter, with her mechanical arm, and he cringes. She doesn't apologize.

"I really will," she says.

He leans forward and kisses her forehead. He tells her okay, and she lets him go, grasping the teacup carefully with both hands.

• • •

Eventually, she does get better, and she goes back to work, but Greg can see she's changed somehow. His wife has grown more serious. She jokes less. She lets him keep watches and clocks. She doesn't talk about being a cyborg anymore. Perhaps after the accident her strangeness surpassed her desire to be special. Greg tries not to make her think about it. Most of the time now he can hold her without flinching. They put skin over the metal arm. He's okay, except when she grabs him during sex and holds too tight. Or sometimes, in the night, he rolls over in his sleep and startles awake when he first touches her strangely unyielding flesh.

Sometimes he dreams she's dead, and then he wakes up feeling empty inside. He's still drawing *The Mistress of Time*. He won an award recently, and he and Sandra were in the paper, holding a gigantic poster of the cover of his comic between them. The woman on the cover has a bionic eye and one metal arm. The line underneath the picture says, "Greg Jones and his wife Sandra, his muse."

Her hair is rarely a mess like it used to be when she read at the bookstore counter. Now, when she works at the counter, she sits straight in her chair and never disturbs her coif. Only when she first clambers out of bed in the morning does her hair fall into disarray. The sight of her curls in a riot fills Greg with tenderness.

• • •

The fifth time Sandra gets pregnant, everything seems normal. Greg watches the ultrasounds closely, searching for any sign of missing vital organs. But a little heart beats right before his eyes. He begins to hope. Sandra gleams and glows. She makes him think of a nineteenth century painting, her hair long and luxurious, her body draped in flowing clothes. She's taken up gardening. She sings while she works at the bookstore. She tells everyone to buy poetry.

She starts bringing poetry home, too. She recites it while she cooks. She's trying to memorize all of Yeats. Greg thinks her plans ambitious, but he doesn't say anything. It's Saturday, and she's reaching up to the top of a bookcase to grab a copy of the collected works of William Butler Yeats when her water breaks. She drops the book on the floor and stares down at the fluid pooling by her feet.

She says, "Sorry for the water damage."

She paces around the floor of their home. He draws her, distended stomach, arms braced against her hips, hair loose around her shoulders. He thinks she's beautiful. Hours later, she goes into labor—real labor—on time for once, and she looks positively triumphant. At the hospital, she sweats and she wails and she bleeds, but she also grins in exultation, gritting her teeth.

When the doctor takes the baby from between her legs and cuts the umbilical cord and wipes away the blood and mucus, and the infant starts up a healthy wail, Greg smiles. Until he sees two blank spots where there should be eyes. Smooth skin, no lids. He stares at this healthy but eyeless baby.

The doctor sees his face. "Don't worry, when she gets older and her skull gets larger we can give her mechanical eyes," he says.

Her father nods along with the doctor, says reassuring things, talks about how this one will be okay, nothing vital is missing. By the time she's large enough for new eyes, maybe the technology will be even better. Eyes are easy to replace. Sandra clearly doesn't hear him, her eyes are closed, her head tilted to the side on her pillow, and her lips curved in a smile.

A nurse—who looks identical to the one who talked to Greg after Sandra's accident—comes in and hands him a glass of water. Sandra still hasn't noticed the baby's lack of eyes. She's too high on victory and pain. The nurse smiles her perfect red smile at him. She is most certainly a clone.

"A girl!" she says.

Greg keeps his mouth closed around his words.

"What are you thinking?" asks the nurse, too perkily.

"Tick-tock," Greg says.

Jennifer Pullen received her doctorate from Ohio University and her MFA from Eastern Washington University. She originally hails from Washington State. Her fiction and poetry have appeared or are upcoming in journals including: *Going Down Swinging* (AU), *Cleaver*, *Off the Coast*, *Phantom Drift Limited*, and *Clockhouse*.

Inheritance

Michael Milne

Oliver's classmates locked him with gaping, lidless gazes for a few seconds before the first one screamed. The impulse traveled, then all of them were wailing, and Mrs. Turner quickly led the class out. Alone, Oliver moved to the hole in the wall, a popped blister surrounded by loose plaster. The desk he had thrown lay shattered in the field two stories below, its legs pointed upwards like half of a dead spider.

The principal arrived and silently ushered Oliver off to a stiff blue bench opposite his office, placing his hand close, but never on, Oliver's shoulder. Marooned in the home of kids who smuggled lighters and butterfly knives to school, Oliver's face burned red and hot. Teachers and other sixth graders passed by, keeping a safe distance, whispering as they went.

When his parents finally filed past an hour later, Oliver thought they looked strangely shrunken, that they were his size. Mr. Clark wore his only black suit, still wrinkled from the wedding the family attended two weeks before. Mrs. Clark didn't make eye contact with Oliver, but squeezed her son's shoulder as she passed.

They both spoke in hushed voices, rarely to each other. Oliver could hear his mother shifting in her seat, defeated, each of her sentences trailing off at the end.

"We don't know how much Oliver knows of what's going on . . ." Angie muttered. They were talking about the divorce. Edward asked the principal to recommend a child therapist, someone Oliver could talk to in order to help him manage his anger, and Oliver tried desperately to make himself relax.

"And would either of you mind explaining," Principal Isaacs asked at last, "how he launched a desk through the drywall and across Maple Crest Avenue?" Oliver wanted to burst in and say that the desk had barely cleared the bleachers, that there was no way it could have gotten across the street.

Neither of his parents could or would explain, nor did they explain to Oliver why he could overhear them from three rooms away.

• • •

"Can Dad come to my birthday?" Oliver asked a week before the party.

"You'd like him to come?" Angie asked. Oliver knew he had some degree of leverage—there was a new boyfriend, his name was Craig and he wore loafers and already took the liberty of telling dad jokes. Angie spent the last week seeming deeply apologetic. "It's your birthday. We'll see if he can make it."

In what Oliver hoped to be a carefully negotiated peace, Edward appeared at noon that Saturday. He was out of breath, overdressed. And though this was the first time Edward had entered the new house on Roxborough Street, it seemed totally natural, like he could be walking in, covered in the scent of cut grass or holding a greasy bag of take-out. Oliver moved to meet his father away from the few other press-ganged partygoers, and Edward handed him a gift.

"Open it," Edward said. Under the poorly bound newspaper was a blue monster truck toy, years too young for Oliver. A half-peeled price sticker stained the side, and Oliver pretended not to notice.

"I love it, Dad."

Oliver watched his parents perform a careful dance of evasion, two planets on opposite ends of an orbital path. One in the kitchen, the other awkwardly holding court outside; one leaning over the cake, the other repelled to the outer reaches of the meager crowd. Oliver eyed the assembled middle schoolers, here mostly out of parental decree and the promise of snacks, and was certain they were logging this for gossip purposes.

"Can you stay for dinner?" Oliver asked. He knew the answer, deliberately asking by the fence and far away from prying eyes and ears. He knew that even if it had been yes, it would have been awful. And yet he still wanted it, like the dogged need to rip off a hangnail.

"I don't think I can, Oliver." Edward Clark glanced up to the sky, listening to something far away. "I need to go. Now. I'm sorry. I'll see you soon."

Soon turned out to be nearly two months later, and each subsequent excuse began to feel worn and ragged. Edward rarely told Oliver the truth about where he was—Oliver knew this—but he grew to wish his father had a deeper reservoir of alibis, that he didn't simply cycle through the same two or three. Emergency at work, left the stove on, looking after the neighbor's dog.

Holidays passed. At Halloween, Oliver, newly thirteen, said he felt too old to go out. In truth, he worried that he would see people dressed up in too-familiar masks, juvenile caped heroes shadowed by half-bored but devoted parents.

Edward finally made a token Christmas appearance, taking Oliver to visit his grandparents at the cemetery. They ate limp turkey sandwiches and talked quietly, at the only table in the restaurant occupied by more than one person.

"I'm sorry I've been so busy. You've seen the news," Edward said. Oliver downloaded four different news apps and habitually checked headlines. "I should call more, visit more. I *will* call more." As Edward spoke his eyes kept drifting to the window, assessing every passerby for telltale bulges, aggressive postures. Oliver began to feel like Edward Clark's hobby, an electric guitar stashed in a guest room closet, furtively taken up just seldom enough to lose all previous progress.

"There was an emergency," his mother would always say, half-sincere. She said it through gritted teeth at first—until after months, and then years, she seemed to offer this genuinely. "You know he wishes he could be here." Oliver tallied the number of times he heard these lines from either parent. "You're the most important thing in the world to him."

Other than fires and bank robberies and bus crashes, Oliver would think but wouldn't say. It felt hard to compete with disasters. There were so many of them.

• • •

Oliver read the comics when he was happy and turned them into mulch when he wasn't. Once, with the 24-hour news channel turned to the lowest volume, Oliver watched an ash-smeared boy, freshly rescued from some calamity, receive an affectionate hair scruff from Iron Thunder. Oliver looked down to see that he had shredded a pile of comics into confetti in his lap.

For a long time, he ferreted a pulpy biography around in his backpack, which he read eagerly while only understanding about a third of the words.

"It's almost all fabricated," Edward told Oliver during one abrupt period of familial piety. "Speculation and rumors." He had spotted Oliver's copy of *Behind the Cobalt Cowl*. Peace accords, rising oil prices, and a distracting set of Olympic games kept Edward from being busy, and he now saw Oliver at the divorce-mandated maximum number of visits.

"So then, what?" Oliver asked him. They sat on the balcony of Edward's modest condo on a pair of dining chairs dragged outside for the sunset. They ate delivery pizza, as usual. "How did you—we get this way?"

"Genetic abnormalities, mostly." Edward straightened in his chair, unaccustomed to candor. "Rare recessive predispositions toward strength in both families. Haven't figured out the flight, yet. Maybe there's some raptor DNA in there somewhere." He held his face placid long enough that Oliver couldn't tell if it was a joke.

"So . . . you didn't give yourself superpowers in your lab?" Oliver said it like it was a joke. "When you realized the world needed a hero" This was almost verbatim from the first issue of *The Wrath of Iron Thunder*.

"People always try to write the story that suits them." Edward grumbled often about the comics, about royalties, about how the artists always rendered him suspiciously light-skinned and with a thinner nose. "The truth is hard and rough and rarely poetic." He looked out across the city, and Oliver did too. He imagined it sometimes from above, at night, the millions of lit windows flickering under him. "People like legends. They don't like people."

• • •

Oliver leaned inelegantly on the hood of Mrs. Blakeway's relic Honda in the middle school parking lot. He and Cassandra had stopped to talk after class, and he hoped desperately to give off the impression that he was cool. Or clever, or easygoing. Anything would do.

"So, how do you like Mr. Clavelli for math?" Oliver was desperate for small talk. "I heard Breakfire was playing in town. Have you seen that music video?" Oliver was newish and unpopular, and Cassandra even noticing him seemed like a coup. "Do you like the Pathcrosser series?" It was a gamble to out himself as bookish, but Oliver realized his mouth was moving without his consent.

When Cassandra—long wavy brown hair, two seats back in homeroom and history, scary good at algebra—touched his shoulder, the space under Oliver's palm began to burn. He hoped his blushing wasn't obvious; he hoped she didn't notice how his hands had begun to sweat uncontrollably. The whole car seemed hot, uncontrollably hot underneath his fingers, but he didn't dare look away from the first girl he had worked up the courage to talk to. He prayed that his voice would, for one brief moment, maintain a steady tone (high or low, it didn't matter).

Hey Olli," Cassandra said. No one called him Olli, ever, though he was suddenly awoken to the appeal. "Do you want to go to the movies this weekend?"

The ancient Civic burst into flames.

Classmates would later describe it as an explosion, a massive fiery column of orange belching into sky. A car bomb, maybe; Mrs. Blakeway, surely all of their teachers, had shady pasts.

As Oliver would later emphasize to his father, he was very brave and chivalrous. Cassandra cried out at the fire, and Oliver leapt before her, flinging his tiny frame wide to shield her like a wiry teenaged aegis. They sprinted from the lot, screaming until someone called the fire department. Oliver would never forget the look Cassandra gave him.

The trampled boulevard before the school soon crowded with evacuated students and teachers. Oliver draped his too-small jean jacket over Cassandra's shoulders, as he had once seen someone do on television.

"I'll keep you safe. Take this," Oliver thought he said. "You've got to keep warm." It was June.

His father clapped him on the shoulder ineffectively when he heard the story, told him "good job." He later upgraded to calling Oliver courageous, and Oliver beamed and beamed.

As Oliver would later admit quietly to his mother alone, he had been terrified. The way his fingers tingled with destruction, the danger he posed simply walking around. The shame he felt when, at last as the sirens peeled closer, fear became fuel and he ran faster than any around him could see, his feet eating miles of road and grass, trails of smoke in his wake, scorch marks across the soles of his shoes, wind screaming in his ears like in the engine of a jet, until finally he calmed and slowed and arrived, panting and tear-stained, two hours across town. He took a bus home in bare feet.

Angie did not say a word. She let Oliver tell the whole story before speaking.

"Of course you ran, son." She shook her head and gave Oliver a tissue. "Nobody could blame you." And after all, Oliver thought, running away was in his blood.

• • •

The car fire nearly prompted another move and name change, but these came soon after when Angie remarried and took Craig's last name. Oliver decided to stick with Parker, his fourth surname in two years.

"I need to be trained," he told his mom. "I need Dad. He's the only one who can help me with this." Angie held her hands submerged in the sink, not speaking for a second. He didn't know if it hurt her feelings whenever he asked for this; Oliver, hating himself for being mad and petty, sometimes didn't care if he hurt her feelings.

"I'll try my best," Angie said. "You know how busy he is."

Eavesdropping by default, Oliver heard the phone conversation, the halting stops and starts. His mother so abrupt, giving no quarter, her fingers going white around the phone. His father agreed to meet at sunset (as Oliver had hoped) in a wide-open field two kilometers out of town (as Oliver had always imagined). There was a snide comment about the new husband, which Angie did not reply to until after she hung up.

When the day arrived, Oliver spent nearly an hour preparing. He changed shoes twice, unsure which ones were best-suited to flight. Arm deep in the recycling boxes, Oliver searched for supplies. He had no idea what he was looking for.

"No glass bottles," Angie said. "It'll be too hard to clean up." It would be too dangerous.

"It'll be fine," Oliver grunted. What did she know about flight or his uncontrollable kindling palms? She was attempting to smother him, he decided; she was worried about how he felt with the house and the name and the *Craig*.

When Oliver left the house, declining her offer to drive him, there was a grocery bag near the door. She had packed two sandwiches—one for Oliver and one for Edward, each bag labeled. She packed the lettuce separate. Oliver took them sheepishly, still mad somehow, and at the same time practicing an apology in his head.

Oliver stood in the field where they agreed to meet. His father was never particularly punctual, and so Oliver mentally readied for a lengthy grace period. He searched the field for heavy objects, for the tractor tires and rusting shipping containers he assumed littered all of rural America. Iron Thunder graced so many comic covers with cars and I-beams hoisted above his head, his dark face betraying comically little effort.

He ran as quickly as he could, taking off his shoes to save the soles. He remembered challenging his father to races around their suburban yard when he was younger, speeding between the trees in the nearby woods. Was it once? Twice? Oliver tried to remember if he had merged the details, fusing many memories into one, and was sure there had to be more.

Oliver tried to take flight. The ability had arisen suddenly one day, as Oliver hovered about an inch over his seat in algebra class. He had turned red, glanced around at his classmates, and hoped and prayed that no one noticed him. No matter what he tried, he could not make himself go down. He took deep breaths, he thought about basketball, he thought about having to move again, and then gradually, thankfully, his legs met the cool plastic of his chair. Sheepishly, he had raised his hand and asked to go to the bathroom so he could be embarrassed by himself.

Now he tried to reclaim his accidental lift-off, throwing himself into the air, stretching phantom muscles and clawing skyward. He imagined sprouting wings and soaring across a riptide of wind; he imagined his feet as rockets spraying liquid fire and projecting him upwards.

The sun had long been set, and Oliver allowed himself to recognize that his father was not coming. He checked his phone for news updates: there was flooding in Thailand, a string of bank robberies in New York, a massive disease outbreak in England. Shoes in his hands, the uneaten sandwiches left for the birds, he walked back to the bus stop. He didn't need to check his messages; he knew there would be none.

• • •

"I think it would be good for my self esteem," Oliver said over dinner. He had prepared his arguments formally, writing them first in a notebook and then practicing them before his mirror. "And it would give me a chance to make more friends. You're always saying I should be more social."

"He's using your words against you," Craig joked.

"I know I'm not supposed to attract attention," Oliver said. Oliver was now called Daniel Oliver Swanson, changing names and schools after he was spotted floating around the rafters of the gymnasium. "But I think this would be, you know, good attention. The kind that doesn't get us onto conspiracy websites."

When he managed to visit, Edward often proscribed heroism; he was against Oliver making a name for himself. It would only alienate him from others, it would only lead to more houses and surnames and tabloid photographers. Eyes were dangerous.

"It's weird that you think I'd stop you," his mother said, reaching to take his hand in hers. Was she eager because it might anger Oliver's dad? Had Oliver decided to go for it for the same reason? He hated second-guessing her motives. Or his own. "You'd make a great James. Or a great giant peach."

"You haven't read the book."

"I won't need to, I'll see the play." She smiled.

Oliver managed to take the role of a background insect, and as the understudy for James, he tried not to hope for injury or sickness to befall the lead actor. And on Thursday night, after two thrilling performances, when Darren Pulanski hammed around too close to the edge of the stage and snapped his tibia, Oliver tried not to wonder if his powers extended to predicting the future.

People filled the rickety metal folding chairs that lined the auditorium. Standing below a spotlight, Oliver tried not to hear the skittering drumbeat of three hundred and thirty-six hearts, he tried not to smell the scent of so many breaths coalescing into a gaseous cloud of mouthwash, tooth decay, and barbecue sauce. So many eyes, each pair felt like they were braced against his skin. His mother had suggested focusing on one person in the crowd.

She sat three seats from center, four rows back, hugely pregnant and with Craig grinning and struggling with a camcorder. Five rows in every direction were filled with relatives and family friends, summoned at Angie's call when she put the word out that Oliver would take the lead role for the last show. He willed himself not to notice the empty seat to her right, focusing instead on the seat to her left, where Craig awkwardly fumbled with his recording equipment.

Oliver had come around to Craig—in spite of, or because of, Craig's obvious desperation for Oliver's approval. He had been the one to tell Oliver about the baby, acting like Oliver was the father of the bride.

"Well, I think it's important I tell you something. We tell you something." He had been sweating and wringing his hands. "It's big news, and I will understand if you're not okay with it, or you want some time."

"Spit it out."

"We're pregnant, Oliver." He had looked down, like a dog nervously batting the wet carpet.

"'We?'" Oliver had said, letting Craig off the hook. "So are you going to, like, tag-team the contractions or what?"

Oliver decided he would perform for his little sister, the tiny murmur he heard within his mother, who could not see Oliver and thus would probably not be a harsh critic.

After dinner and ice cream and one illicit, celebratory sip of Craig's beer when Angie wasn't looking, Oliver and the family returned home. He could feel the adrenaline, actually could identify it as it sped his heart and dilated his pupils. More than once, Craig had to pull the car over, so Oliver could take a few celebratory aerial laps above a darkened copse of trees. Old family friends said that Oliver was made for the stage, that his now stably-deep voice had filled the space of the auditorium like warm honey.

Craig's car pulled up the drive. Resting against the front door of the house was a crutch and a greeting card.

I'm sorry. I know you understand.
I hope you broke a leg.

Later that night, after they had all gone to bed, Oliver heard his mother whispering his name from outside of the house. Quiet, but meant to carry. Their own private Bat Signal.

Haloed in porch light against the dark of the street, Angie sat on the swinging bench. She held her abdomen in one hand, and the card in the other. She must have fished it out of the garbage after Oliver had stormed inside.

"I know it's hard to believe it now," she said, "but you might want this one day. He really does wish he could be here."

Oliver wanted to rear back, to shout and wake Craig and the neighbors, but his mother held his gaze. He moved and sat beside her, holding his hands clasped together as they began to redden and steam.

"You can't possibly be defending him. If he wants to be somewhere, he would be there." He moved at the speed of sound when he wanted to.

"I'm not defending him. I'm just saying that maybe it's not fair to compare us. I'm an accountant." She seemed surprised to be saying this; Oliver remembered this as nearly verbatim from the hushed arguments he had tried not to overhear as a boy. "I wish he was here for you." She caught Oliver's gaze. "I wish he had been there for me. Maybe one day he'll be able to be what you need him to be. But until then, maybe don't burn down the whole building, you know?"

She sounded like she was reading from a script, one she maybe believed now, if she hadn't years before. She had Oliver, and Craig, and the new baby. This house was better than the last three. Edward Clark could only disappoint Angie by proxy, and this distance had softened her.

"What if it's already burnt down?"

"Feel what you feel, darling. But maybe trust your mom that it's complicated. Coming from me, you know that's a lot." She took the outside of his hand, Oliver flinching not to burn her, but she didn't move. "Keep the card. The crutch, too, for a couple of days. If you're still mad, throw them out." Angie Swanson hauled herself up and moved to the door. "Porch light on or off?"

"Off," Oliver said. "Please."

He watched as his mother's figure faded up the stairs, trailing into the dark of her bedroom. Oliver opened his hands and lit the porch aglow, letting the light from his palms fade, until he was surrounded everywhere in the dull grays of the night.

• • •

Oliver was summoned just before the end of the school day and stuffed into a taxi. Craig and his mother were already both at the hospital, the principal said.

"Joyous news," Principal McLaughlin had said. "Not to worry. They're both just out of the delivery room and couldn't come by to sign you out earlier."

His hands trembled the entire ride, and Oliver felt small and young as he made his way to the hospital front desk, asking in a croaked hush where to look for his mom. He imagined he would have to wear scrubs and wash his hands up to the elbows. A receptionist took in his expression, rode the elevator up with him, and deposited him in the room.

A strange arrangement—a Frankenstein Christmas card—appeared before Oliver. Mom in bed with a minuscule pink something in her arms. Craig pulled close beside her, his arms laced through the grates. Dad hovering nearby, his face warm and open and strangely paternal. The new family, built on the ashes of the old one.

"Oliver," his mom purred. Epidural or glee? "Come and meet Lorelai."

All of them stared at Oliver, their faces unreadable and adult and weird, and Oliver moved toward the baby, who was simple and easy to decipher. She was red and pinched and delicate, like a paper sculpture of a person, and Oliver declined holding her just yet. He wanted to wait until she looked more solid, like he wouldn't be able to break her.

"She looks a little bit like you," Craig said. He was as sweaty as Oliver's mother. "Same eyes, I guess. Sorry for the age gap, big brother."

"I'm not," Angie sighed. "No arguments, no teasing. Just role modeling."

"He'll be a fine free babysitter," Edward said from across the room. He had moved there silently, as though repelled by the milieu, by the warmth. "I've got to be going. I'll visit again soon, when you're settled at the house. Congratulations, again."

The door closed softly, and Oliver heard his name whispered out in the hall, and again by the stairs. Oliver quickly muttered something about finding the vending machines, and went to follow his father.

Edward Clark sat on the ledge of the hospital roof, gazing outwards into the city. He wore his work lab coat, a frumpy untucked oxford flapping underneath, his bookish glasses tucked into a pocket. His brown, weathered hands were pressed against the concrete, and he seemed to be waiting for Oliver.

"How did you even know?" Oliver asked. He came and sat down beside his father, legs dangling over the side of the building. "You couldn't have heard her." Could he? Oliver noticed they were nearly the same height.

"Your mom included her pregnancy status in the weekly updates she sends me," Edward said. "I did hear her, actually. But I had to deal with Belgrade," he said, referring to some disaster Oliver would probably read about tomorrow, "and couldn't get here until late. Otherwise, I would have picked you up from school. Sorry."

"Sorry," Oliver repeated.

"Yes. Sorry." And Edward twined his fingers together in his lap, looking small in a way Oliver hadn't seen in a long time. "I nearly gave it up, you know. When you were born. I remember you when you were just as small as that little girl." Oliver hated where this was going; he hated that anyone was trying to explain all of this to him. "Your mom told me not to, said the work was too important. We both thought I could balance it."

"So, I should blame her?"

"What? No. Of course not. You shouldn't blame anyone." Edward stood again, his coat billowing out in the breeze. "Or blame me, or blame the world. I don't know. I know it doesn't always seem like it, but I'm trying. I'm not good at it, but I'm trying."

Oliver, too, looked out over the city, trying to hear what his father heard. Hundreds, thousands, millions of voices; glass shattering, candles flickering, guns firing. He tried to hear his little sister, five floors below, or Craig whispering promises to his newborn daughter.

"I got a copy of the play from Craig. Seemed like a full house," he said. "You were amazing. I should have been there." Edward reached out and took Oliver's hand, and Oliver felt his father's hand, hot and angry as his own. Somewhere far away something broke, and Edward's eyes flicked to the horizon. "I've got to go, Oliver. I'll be back. Really." There was a rustle as the white coat moved through open air, and then his father was gone.

Oliver stood for some time on the roof of the hospital, balancing on one foot. Soon he leaned forward and dropped—he felt the air whistle and hiss at his skin as he plummeted through it. Lights illuminated him from each window as he dropped, families drawn close in celebration or despair. The ground vaulted forth to meet him. He could make out gravel, car windshields, puddles in cement. And then something caught within him, his one trustworthy inheritance, and the wind was not buffeting him but moving with him, he climbed skyward and flew.

Michael Milne is a writer and teacher originally from Canada, who has lived in Korea and China, and is now in Switzerland. Not being from anywhere anymore really helps when writing science fiction. His work has been published in the *Sockdolager*, *Imminent Quarterly*, and anthologies at Meerkat Press and Gray Whisper.

Heroes

Lavie Tidhar

Berlin. 1987.

Somewhere, Spit thinks, it's always bloody Berlin, and it's *always* 1987. Big hair, synths, glasnost, Donkey bloody Kong. She hates the whole fucking decade. In the apartment across the street from the Wall, Whirlwind is looking through binoculars at Checkpoint Charlie. Somewhere nearby, by the Reichstag, Bowie is singing "Heroes."

"Oh, do shut *up*, David," Spit says. She hates that song. Bowie had done an entire concept album on the Übermenschen in the early '70s, when he was still wearing his Beyond-Man persona. Beside Spit, Whirlwind shifts, restless.

"Do you like *anything*," she mutters. Spit ignores her. They're having one of their uncommon tiffs. Usually they get on great, but three days inside the flat watching the Wall, they both need a break from each other.

"My God, I *smell*," Whirlwind says. "I mean just look at my hair, it's disgusting."

"You look fine," Spit says. "You look good to me."

Whirlwind grins abruptly. Spit's heart lifts a little when she does that. When did she first see her? She tries to think. Some time during the War, it must have been, though they only met later, here, in Berlin, in the aftermath. But things were different back then. Everything was different, except for them. They never changed. Did they?

"We should have turned down the job," Whirlwind says. She takes Spit's hand in hers. Her hand is warm and dry. Spit can feel the storm trapped inside her, longing to be let out. They should be heroes, she thinks, not . . . *this* again. Clandestine agents at the tail end of a cold war. She misses the War, sometimes. The proper War, the only one that ever mattered. When she knew what she was and what she had to do. When everything was black and white and everything was clear. And she remembers Paris, that long wait in that other cramped apartment overlooking L'Auberge, the restaurant where they'd hoped to finally corner Vomacht.

"That slimy rat fucker and his Nazi bitch daughter," she says, to no one in particular. Whirlwind turns from the window and grins again.

"This whole swearing thing suits you, you know, considering."

"Considering what."

"You being a dainty old English lady and all."

"Fuck you, you're my age."

"And looking good for it," Whirlwind says, preening, until Spit can't help but laugh. They can still hear Bowie's voice, it echoes all over the city and across the wall, into East Germany—from which direction, the Old Man said, the package should arrive.

It's a joint operation, but off the books–hence the two of them, having both left their respective services and gone freelance not too long back. Whirlwind representing the Americans' interests, Spit stepping in once more to cover the Old Man's back for him. It has always been thus, it will always be thus.

And, truth to tell, she can remember Fr. Johann. This might just be a part of it, too.

She remembers the Medicus.

• • •

Berlin, 1946. In the aftermath of the War, the city was filled with ghosts, fleeing. There was something intoxicating about being in Berlin then, being the *victors*, as though the nightmare that was the War had gone on for so long that one assumed that it would always be there, would always encompass the world as we knew it. Then it was over, and we *won*, and it was like waking up from a long, dark sleep, a sleep of death, and in such sleep, what dreams may come, Oblivion says.

"You're drunk," Spit says. Oblivion shrugs. Those long thin fingers, wrapped around a glass. Fogg, off somewhere. Hunting shadows. And Oblivion says, "Do you want to hear a story?"

On the other side of the bar are the Americans, that brash and loud League of Defenders. Tigerman, the Electric Twins, Whirlwind. Tigerman scowls in their direction. On the stage, a woman sings "Rum & Coca-Cola."

"What sort of story?" Spit says.

"A legend," Oblivion says. "What other story is there?"

But Spit isn't interested; Spit is bored with legends. The city is filled with escaped Übermenschen and their legends, all hawking their sad stories, hoping to get picked by the Americans in Operation Paperclip or, if they're not that important, to get a ticket out to somewhere else, even to dreary old Britain. At all costs these refugees want to avoid the Russian bear, and even more, the ongoing trials in Nuremberg. Some have formed into cells. Word is there's an escape route out of Germany for those favored SS, "ratlines" to sunny South America, where every day's a party, like a National Socialist party. So Spit says, "What's this one, then? A bat man? An iron fighter? Gestapo Joe? What sad story has he got? He didn't do nothing wrong? He was just following orders?"

"Sure, sure," Oblivion says. "So young, and yet so cynical, Spit. Can't you ever see the *good* in people?"

"These aren't people," Spit says, shortly. And Oblivion nods that slim head of his, with the secret sorrow in his eyes, and says, "Sometimes, you kind of wish for a miracle."

And it's this miracle that they go see, that night, a little drunk, a little high, and Fogg somewhere else, hunting shadows who knows where–was this before, or after, the whole sorry mess with Fogg? It's somewhere around that time, anyway. And so they go, into the night, into the Russian Quarter, Spit and Oblivion, Oblivion and Spit: to see a miracle.

And they come to a church. It isn't marked as such. It's just a building, miraculously standing, there in a street of rubble. And despite the hour and the curfew, there are people outside, ordinary German citizens, that is to say, the walking dead: men and women and feral looking children, those who survived the bombings and the fall of the city and Hitler's suicide and the Russian invasion and now this, the final humiliation, this occupation by the Allies; the men in hats and the women in shawls and the children with hungry looks in their pinched rat-like faces, and they all wait patiently outside.

There is only a sole lamp glowing within, and it casts long, jagged shadows. And Spit sees one woman, who is holding a baby to her chest, and the baby coughs in a way no baby should cough—the rattle it makes is like pebbles bunched in a fist.

"But what did he *do*?" Spit says, and Oblivion tells her. Then they go inside, into a gutted room and a makeshift altar, and the priest turns and sees them, and he nods: that's it, that's all he does, he nods as though he recognizes them, as though he always knew that they would come.

• • •

But in 1987, Bowie is singing "Heroes." And when they finally do bring out the Medicus, they do so in a coffin. Spit watches, the flashing lights of the police cars, the heavy escort for the hearse, and the people milling outside, beyond the barriers, and there is the Old Man, somewhere down there, with the paperwork, the death certificate and what have you.

"Rest in peace," Spit says, ironically. The Old Man looks from side to side, then up, slowly. As though tracing the flight of unseen birds in the sky. He nods—to himself? to her?—she doesn't know.

Whirlwind says, "Do you think they'll come?"

And Spit says, "They never forget. We could have had him, you know. Oblivion and I. We had him, and we let him go."

"Now why would you do that?" Whirlwind says.

And Spit says, "It was the baby."

• • •

"Welcome," Fr. Johann says. He extends a hand, perhaps hoping for a shake, but it isn't welcomed and he lets it drop. "Only, could it wait?" he says. "I still have parishioners. I would hate to let them down."

Spit glares at him. But Oblivion stays her hand. The priest nods. He welcomes the next in line, an old man with a foot that drags behind him. The Medicus speaks to him, makes the sign of the cross, then lays his hands on the old man's leg. The old man's face is suffused with pain, then something else, a thing one never sees in this time, in this place. An easement, a relief. When the old man stands he does so with his bad leg, he is healed; he thanks the priest but the priest shrugs away his thanks. He turns back to Spit and Oblivion.

"I am making atonement," he says.

Where did he come from, this Fr. Johann? Somewhere in Bavaria, according to his file. Identified and, in due course, recruited to Gestapo Department F. Now in hiding in the wrong quarter of the city, now a priest, though who ordained him, if anyone did but himself, we don't know.

Then the woman comes in, the one with the baby, and the priest takes the child from her, he lays his hands on this tiny bundle, this war time baby, and he does what it is he does, this power, this inexplicable quantum entanglement of the Changed, and the baby *breathes*, the baby starts to cry, a clean, piercing, *healthy* sound, and the woman, the mother, she bursts into tears. And on and on they come, until none are left, and the Medicus, exhausted, just sits down on the floor. Then he raises his head and says, "Now you can take me, if you please."

. . .

"But we didn't," Spit says. She shrugs, a little helplessly. The hearse down below is still stalled. Spit scans the skies. Whirlwind steps onto the windowsill. The storm trapped inside her thrums. She wants to be let free, to take to the air. She can only be still for so long. Down below, the hearse's engine finally starts. If they would strike it would be just beyond, Split thinks. She sees movement, from the corner of her eye. Who would they send, she wonders? Kerach, Ishtar, the Sabra? The hearse glides away from Checkpoint Charlie. The Old Man looks up, gives her a nod. They will come, she thinks.

Then it happens fast and slow. The hearse is lifted into the air, torn off the ground by some terrible, invisible force. Whirlwind, with a sigh of relief, drops into sheer air. She transforms, a storm, a whirl-wind, shooting toward the car and the attackers. Spit looks through the binoculars, focuses. Moving shapes, Israeli Übermenschen, an extraction team. She knows them from other conflicts, other wars. She hawks phlegm. Her special talent. She spits, bullets traveling at ultrasonic speeds, smashing into streetlights, cars, hitting the Sabra in the leg, at least she thinks it's him. He raises his face and bares his teeth in a grin. But his next step is halting, and he grabs hold of his leg, in pain.

She fires mechanically, giving Whirlwind support. The storm leaps from streetlight to puddle. It tears up traffic lights, it rips wheels off cars. It smashes Ishtar—is that her? Spit last ran into her in Buenos Aires, in '71—against the wall of an apartment block. The hearse twists impossibly in mid-air, the metal screaming. Spit glances at the checkpoint, where the Old Man, without much fuss, gets in a small VW Beetle and drives away, and she notes that there's a man, with a hat low over his face, sitting beside him.

Spectators watch the Übermenschen fight. Somewhere, David Bowie is still singing "Heroes." Or perhaps it's only Spit who can hear it now, just the last fading notes as the destroyed hearse crashes to the ground, and the Israeli Übermenschen flee like silent ghosts, and Whirlwind reappears at the window, back in her human shape, and says, "It's time to get out of here."

• • •

It was the baby, it must have been, the baby that shouldn't have lived but did. Later, she heard Fr. Johann came under Bishop Hudal's protection. The pro-Nazi bishop had helped many former SS escape on the Ratlines.

But the Medicus never fled with the others. He stayed on in what was by then East Germany, under the Communists, protected less by the church than by his skills, this miracle he had, this miracle of healing.

And the Communists used him, just the way the Nazis had, just the way, Spit presumes, later, as she and Whirlwind depart the apartment and the police sirens and make their way, anonymously, to the airport, that the Americans would use him now. She saw the photographs, the witness testimonies.

The way he'd kept the prisoners alive, through the worst of it all: the torture, the medical experiments, how he could keep them going long past the point where they would have died, healing them, over and over, with just a touch, to be kept alive, to be kept in *pain*, until their minds couldn't cope anymore and they went gibbering mad, but still healthy, still alive, for all that they wanted by then was to die, to simply not be anymore.

How many had he done this to over the years? Spit wonders. Browsing the newspaper section at the airport, waiting for her flight, she runs into one of the attackers from earlier. The Israeli woman, Ishtar. How many had Fr. Johann kept alive, in Gestapo prisons and the death camps, later in Stasi cells? The Medicus has such a talent it would be a shame to waste, and there are always prisoners who need interrogating, who need to be taken to the edge of death and kept there.

She nods to Ishtar, and the Israeli woman nods back.

"We'll get him," she says.

"I hope so," Spit says.

"He won't get out of Berlin."

"I think he will," Spit says.

The other woman smiles, reluctantly. "We'll get him. If not now, then next time."

"I hope so."

Ishtar nods. Spit fingers a copy of a magazine with a spaceship on the cover.

"Well, it was nice to see you again," Spit says, politely.

Ishtar nods, then she's gone. And Spit doesn't buy anything in the end.

"*The BA flight to London is now boarding.*"

Spit rejoins Whirlwind in the waiting area. "I could have stopped him," she says. "In '46. How many do you think he's kept alive since then? How many for the Stasi's torturers?"

And she says, "How do you weigh the profits and the loss? How many years, how many warm bodies? He did *good*, Whirlwind, when we saw him. I mean, he wasn't one thing or another, he was just a—"

"A tool," Whirlwind says.

"Yes."

"We should board the plane."

"A scalpel can kill, but it isn't what it's *for*," Spit says, stubbornly. "I mean, it's how you *wield* it, isn't it? It's about who does the *wielding*."

"I really think we should go to the gate, Spit."

"It's just that he *was* a war criminal, Whirlwind, I mean, he should have been standing there, in Nuremberg, with the others; it's only that there was this *baby*, and—"

"*The BA flight to London is now boarding.*"

Whirlwind takes her hand, gently. "You can't change the world, Spit," she says. "You can't even change yourself."

"*He* changed it," Spit says, helplessly. "Vomacht. With that machine. He changed *us*."

But Whirlwind leads her, gently but insistently, away. "You think so?" she says. "You really do? The war still happened, people still died, babies are still being born. We don't matter, Spit, not me, not you, not even the Medicus. Leave him to the Israelis. They'll get him, sooner or later; they always do. You and I can't be responsible for everyone, we can't change the world. The best we can do is try to get paid."

Spit nods. On the plane, she plugs in the oversized earphones, while Whirlwind fills in their expenses form. Spit keeps turning the twisty little dial in the armrest, trying to find something, anything other than "Heroes." Tinned music spins round and round until she turns it almost all the way down; until it could be anything, like the sound of the surf on some unimaginably distant shore.

Lavie Tidhar is the author of the Jerwood Fiction Uncovered Prize winning and Premio Roma nominee *A Man Lies Dreaming* (2014), the World Fantasy Award winning *Osama* (2011) and of the critically-acclaimed *The Violent Century* (2013). His latest novel is *Central Station* (2016). He is the author of many other novels, novellas and short stories.

Madjack

Nathan Crowder

Her father died during the second verse of "River to Home," right as Omar hit the flourish that served as a preview for his post bridge solo. She felt it like a sudden swelling in her heart, an explosion of emotion that she almost choked on before instinct directed it out, into the audience. By the time they reached the chorus, everyone within thirty feet of the stage was sobbing.

Atlas McVittie, seasoned rock musician that she was at the ripe age of thirty, didn't drop a note.

The band knew something was wrong. They'd been with her through thick and thin, from the shit clubs and storage unit rehearsal space to the contract with Goblin Records. Eight years of broken promises, collapse, and hopefully a phoenix-like rebirth.

They thundered through the rest of the set and only did one encore, though everyone agreed the crowd deserved two. But Atlas was the linchpin in the band. She was the one people came to see; the tempestuous daughter of the self-styled glam rock "god who fell to earth," the Madjack. If Atlas was off, the band was off. It helped that Frankie, their road manager, was waiting in the wings prior to the encore with the phone call confirming what Atlas McVittie already knew.

Atlas was in a daze post-show. The rest of the band had a few drinks in the green room then went off to an after-hours place that Cleveland, the drummer, knew about. Frankie bundled Atlas up under her heavy wool topcoat, the vintage Russian army thing she'd picked up in a flea market when she was still in high school, back when she and Frankie had met. Atlas let herself be herded out the back and into her friend's toy-like car, shiny and blue like an Easter egg. They drove in silence around the late-night Cobalt City streets, aimlessly, no direction in mind.

When they drifted from the corridors of steel and glass towers in downtown, north toward Moriston, Atlas finally spoke up. "Head up toward Clown Liquor," she said, impulsively but clearly.

Frankie raised one perfectly plucked eyebrow and shot Atlas a curious look from beneath her spider-like bangs. "Where are we going?"

"The Olive."

Frankie said nothing but continued on where Atlas directed, and minutes later they pulled into the lot of a generic Cup-o-Chino coffeehouse where the Olive used to be. Atlas leaned forward in the seat, as if heightened scrutiny would turn back time. Finally, defeated, she sank back in her seat. "Do you remember this place?"

"I remember you," Frankie said. A wistful smile appeared then vanished. "You had never sung for anyone but me. And I convinced you to do karaoke. First time you sang for strangers."

"Ever," Atlas said quietly.

"Ever," Frankie agreed. "And you never stopped. You started writing music and formed the band within a year."

"My dad . . ." Atlas started. Her voice caught in her throat, and sadness filled the car like an invisible wave of force.

Frankie gasped, breath stuck in her chest, a sensation like she was drowning in emotion. She gripped Atlas's arm hard through the coat and the waves of emotion calmed. "Jesus, Atlas."

"I'm sorry. I thought I knew the limits on the emotion thing, but it's like the training wheels blew off tonight. I'm finding that what I thought was ten is more like two or three."

"So that was how you knew?"

"And I saw him," she started. She replayed the memory, the sun behind her father, Brian McVittie, making a halo of his white hair. His hand stretched down to her, and he was speaking. An indistinct, alien garble. Emphasis, quite possibly, on the alien part. "It's pretty confusing."

"Do you want to take some time off? I can shuffle some of the practice gigs. We can bump them back a week or two and no one will mind."

"I never sang to strangers before singing here," Atlas said, tear-rimmed eyes wide, reflecting the streetlights. "I was afraid. I was afraid of how I'd measure up to my dad. Afraid to step in his foot-prints because I didn't think I'd ever get out of his shadow. And I was afraid that I had his . . . gifts. I was afraid I would be different like him, and I didn't want to be different. For the longest time, I couldn't tell if people liked me, liked my music, or if I was making them like it. Sometimes, I still wonder."

Frankie nodded. They'd had parts of this conversation before. Her dad had been a looming but distant figure in her life, all but absent for the last decade. And Atlas went to Jaipur to see her mom on holidays at best. Atlas had lived virtually on her own since the age of sixteen, overseen by a series of executors and housekeepers until she turned twenty-one, and then left to her own devices after that.

It was hard to make friends when everyone believed your father to be an alien.

And when all was said and done, even Atlas couldn't be sure if it were true or not.

"Put the shows on hold for a week." Atlas said. "I'll tell the band myself. They'll understand."

"Of course. Whatever you want to do."

"I want to see my mom," Atlas said. "I want to put my father to rest. And I want to get some answers."

"About the whole alien thing?"

"And why someone killed him," Atlas said. She closed her eyes. There in the darkness, it replayed on a loop. Her father's outstretched hand, a garbled, alien language, a halo of hair backlit by the sun. Then a perfect circle punched through the middle of his head followed by blackness.

• • •

Even in the mountains of Rajasthan, the heat was a living thing. When Atlas stepped off the plane, the wave of heat was an angry fire spirit caressing the fine hairs on the back of her bare arms. At least it was a dry heat, unlike the humid swelter of a Cobalt City heat wave, and her embroidered blue tank top flapped freely in the hot breeze as she disembarked the small jet. She had packed light, just a kit bag with a few changes of clothes, a repurposed Tyvek envelope full of her writing gear, and her trusty acoustic guitar. Customs took its time with her, apparently expecting a certain degree of lawlessness from rock musicians. Her American passport probably didn't help much either. But the exhaustive search of her luggage came up clean.

Atlas didn't waste time or money on drugs. She didn't even enjoy alcohol. One more gift from her father's physiology was a Herculean resistance to chemical substances. She could go through a brick of heroin like it was mashed potatoes if she truly wanted to, and it would have just as much of an effect on her. Once the customs agents were satisfied, they turned her loose into the chaotic swirl of the Jaipur airport where she found a small gentleman in a suit holding a sign reading "McVittie" over his head.

"I didn't ask for a car," she said in out-of-practice Dhundhari.

"Your mother sent one anyway," the driver said. "And if you prefer, I am also fluent in Hindi and English."

She was unsurprised. It seemed it was only English-speaking countries where people were more likely to be monolingual. She'd met so-called primitive musicians in Mali who spoke ten languages and used most of them regularly. "Dhundhari is fine. I need the practice. What's your name?"

"Jasper. Allow me to carry your bags?"

"Bag yes, guitar no." She relinquished the kit bag, which the smaller man slung over his shoulder, crinkling his black suit. "Thank you, Jasper. Lead the way."

Minutes later, as they crawled through the streets of Jaipur in the dusty white sedan, Jasper cleared his throat. "I am very sorry to hear about your father. It is a great loss."

"Were you a fan?" she asked, choosing to direct the conversation toward Jasper rather than her own complicated relationship with the man who was the Madjack.

"Not at first," he said. "When I was in medical school in London, a friend had an extra ticket to one of the Royal Albert Hall shows in '83, so I went with him. I became a fan overnight. It changed my life."

"He had that effect. You went to medical school?"

"Yes indeed. I did my residency at Maidstone Hospital in Kent."

Atlas shifted uncomfortably in the back seat.

Jasper noticed her discomfort and chuckled. "You ask, what is a doctor doing driving a car?"

"The thought occurred to me."

"Your mother leaves the house so infrequently, she felt it was wasteful to employ a driver. I'm her doctor, and I volunteered so she would not try and make the drive herself."

"Her health . . . ?"

"It has been better," Jasper said. "But it has also been much worse. She has not taken your father's passing well. You'll see in a few minutes." He turned the car down the familiar gravel drive of her mother's house, the intermittent shadows of thin fir trees across their path like the dark spaces between cells of a film strip, light then flicker of dark then light again.

The house had been modern once, built in the seventies by a once-famous actor, but now it looked like the abandoned set of a sci-fi movie. Overlapping concrete circles above glass walls, it was like an improbable forest of stone mushrooms about to fall, or a cluster of UFOs in a traffic jam. She supposed that had been the appeal when her parents bought it some time in the late eighties. Atlas had never lived there, though there was a room ostensibly set aside as hers. She had yet to spend more than a few weeks in Jaipur. She loved her mother, but even five days could be difficult in the best of times.

The McVittie family, broken and dysfunctional almost by design. Like the very concept of a functional family was alien to them. And maybe it was.

The small cluster of dusty news vans and ghoulish fans near the gate was new, though not unexpected. Atlas was thankful that the local police moved people back to let Jasper squeeze the cream-colored sedan through the crowd. "How long have they been there?" Atlas asked.

"The first one showed up less than an hour after the news broke. They've been multiplying since then."

"Has mom talked to them?"

"Just the first," Jasper said with an uncomfortable grimace. "She was still shocked. The phone had been ringing nonstop. She answered the door thinking it was her friend Judith coming to sit with her. The reporter was, honestly, less aggressive than I'd feared. I knew they were coming. We both did. He was bright, eager, polite. A big fan, apparently. And very respectful. He just happened to be in the area when he heard and seemed almost as stricken as your mother. But after that reporter, we stopped answering the door. The police have been most generous with their time."

They exited the car in the shaded carport. From beyond the gate, the flash and click of cameras joined shouted requests for interviews or comments, like a localized storm. "And Mom?"

"She's busy writing a statement for the press." They paused, and he watched her reaction to the media frenzy. "Did you have this in Cobalt City before you left?"

"If it was there, I was still in too much of a shock. I didn't notice. Thankful for that, I suppose."

Jasper motioned toward the door at the back of the carport. "Shall we?"

"Give me a minute?"

"Of course," Jasper said. He took her bag and left her with her guitar, leaving the door open a crack.

Atlas approached the gate and felt the complicated swirl of emotions radiating off the crowd like a heat shimmer off Nevada blacktop. She found her own inner calm and let it radiate from her, bringing the forty or so people beyond the security fence to a dull whisper. "We're all very saddened by the unexpected loss of my father, Brian McVittie," she said, her voice carrying cleanly and crisply. "And we're touched that he has meant so much to all of you, as well. We ask that you give us some time, and privacy, to process this as a family. Thank you."

She left them calm and placated, and retreated before they realized the interview was over.

Once inside, Atlas followed the strident *tak-tak-tak* of a typewriter through the cool interior to find her mother where she always did, hunched in a floral house dress over her keys. The position was so adopted, Atlas couldn't be certain her mother could even stand fully erect if she wanted to at this point. An empty cigarette holder dangled out of one corner of her mouth, proof that while the doctor had eliminated cigarettes from her mother's life, he hadn't eliminated the oral fixation.

"How are you feeling, Mom?"

"Dreadful," her mother said, scuttling around her cedar writing table like a beetle to enfold Atlas in her arms. Even that little exertion made her breath rattle in her dry, fragile lungs. "It's like the sun's gone out. I suppose in a way it has, really. The one star we've both orbited for so long certainly has."

Atlas buried her nose in her mother's thinning hair, still black as midnight despite her age. It smelled faintly like mint and brought a smile to her face. "The doctor had me worried."

"Jasper? I swear. A woman blacks out once and he thinks it's the end times."

"Blacked out? What happened? Does he know . . . ?"

Indra McVittie stepped back and patted her daughter's hand with a dismissive tut-tut. "Low blood pressure, low blood-oxygen levels, and exhaustion. Nothing to worry about. Come, sit with me." She tugged Atlas to a long saffron-colored sofa that curved like a smile. Comfortable enough to sit on, but impossible if one wanted a nap.

"Have memorial arrangements been discussed?"

Her mother nodded. "Your father, ever the showman, had his memorial planned out a decade ago, if not more. He is to be cremated when he arrives here, and then packed into fireworks."

"Is that legal?"

Her mother shrugged. She'd been studying Atlas's face, looking for something, some sign of emotion perhaps, some signal of need. Atlas had managed to shut down since leaving her condo in Cobalt City, despite her father's face all over the newspapers and televisions. Behind her dark glasses and zombie demeanor, she had been unassailable. She'd spent most of her life trying to rein in her emotions, and now that practice was paying off. Atlas suspected it must be frustrating for her mother. Finally, one thin hand reached up and isolated a lock of Atlas's hair. "When did this start?"

Atlas's heart froze. "When did what start?"

"The white in your hair."

Atlas stood and walked to the nearest bathroom, her steps more urgent the closer she got. When she looked in the mirror, she saw what her mother was talking about. Her hair had been as dark as a raven's wing two days ago, but now was shot through with so much white that it looked like marbled halvah. If it continued at this rate, it would be completely stark white by the memorial service.

"You didn't know, did you?" her mother said from the doorway.

Atlas looked down into the sink, not trusting herself to look at her own reflection or her mother. "He was an alien, wasn't he, Mother? Really, really an alien."

"Of course, sweetheart."

"I thought it was all a gimmick."

"As your dear father once said, in an industry built on lies and misperceptions, there is no bigger gimmick than the truth."

The lid on Atlas's emotions began to crack ever so slightly, releasing an aura of uncertainty and fear. "Does that mean I'm an alien, too?"

Indra's trembling lip framed her smile. "Only half. Come. Let's have some tea."

. . .

"It was 1968," her mother said. "I was making quite the decent living as a fashion photographer in London, and one summer, my flatmates and I had the wild idea to pack up and go to this big music festival outside of town. Lord, I think we must have been stoned out of our minds at the time, but I figured I might get some good photos I could sell to the newspaper or maybe a magazine or something. Or bed some flaxen-haired buck. Anyway, the three of us bundled up and pissed off to this muddy field to hear a bunch of golden gods break our minds with their music."

"Jesus, you're such a hippie, Mother," Atlas said with a slight smile.

"I would remind you to respect your elders," her mother said, then a sad smile crept into her expression. "But you're not wrong. Anyway, there we were, several thousand of us looking to have our minds blown, and all of a sudden he showed up on stage."

"Dad?"

"Yes. He took a guitar from, oh, Heaton Ransom, I believe, as Ransom was leaving the stage. Looked at it like he didn't even know what it was. A few members of Heaton's band filtered out onto stage, joined by a few members of the next band. It was all quite confusing—Mick and Ryan from Heaton's band, Charles something and Lewton Nash from Gobsmacked. Then your father, he slung the guitar around his neck and struck a chord so pure, so true, it was like the heavens opened. The other musicians on stage stood there, dumbfounded, while the Madjack sang his first song."

"Do you know what he sang?" Atlas asked. She'd never found that information listed in any article about her father.

"I don't even know if they were words, dear. It was just emotion. Like a sound we'd been searching for since we'd been born. By the end of the song, the rest of the musicians on stage were playing with him. He played for half an hour, said he was the Madjack, and that he had come here from the stars. And we believed him. Good god, at that point, how could we not?"

"But there was a birth certificate!" Atlas protested.

"Not until seven years later."

"What? *Seven* years?"

"Yes," Indra said. "A very helpful clerk provided one for him in 1975. He never stopped claiming he was from space. He never lied, dear. Not really."

"Fake. Birth. Certificate." Atlas felt her pulse accelerate. Calloused fingers dug into her legs through her jeans. One slow breath and then another and the wave was past. She looked up at her mother who had waited patiently. "I'm sorry."

Her mother tutted. "I understand your confusion. We were very clear it was a fake certificate. But it was a necessary document so that your father and I could get married."

"Wait. So he went and said, 'Look, I know this is highly irregular, but I need a legal birth certificate saying I'm Brian McVittie, which is totally a made-up name, because who is really named after a brand of digestive biscuit, right? You can pick the birthdate as long as I'm a Leo. And we'll all know it's fake, because I'm really from outer space.' And they just *did* it?"

Her mother bobbed her head, lips pursed. "Well, in so many words, pretty much exactly like that."

Atlas threw up her hands in confusion.

"You had to understand, dear," Indra told her. "The mid-seventies in Britain was a very interesting time. And it was rock and roll. I'm sure you understand that much, at least."

"The world doesn't work like that, Mother."

"Everything is a story, Atlas," her mother said. "Everything. How we got where we are. How we will get where we are going. Who created the tools to take us there. History, science, even math, at its core—all a story. The system of courts and laws, contracts and money, arbitration and legacy—a story. This story needed a birth certificate, so your father procured a birth certificate. And the clerk who furnished him with it went to his grave delighted to have been a part of that story. And now the story passes to you."

Atlas blinked at her mother. For several long seconds, she was no longer monitoring or controlling her emotions, no longer open to the emotions of anyone nearby. For a blissful eighteen seconds, the ache in her head and heart was a void. "I . . . I don't understand."

"While there is much of your father's estate that will be sorted out when we have the reading of his will in two days, his story is yours now. There is no one else to inherit it. No one else he would have *wanted* to inherit it."

"What?"

"The Madjack, dear. You're the Madjack now. Certainly you've felt it."

Garbled alien language in her father's voice.

Halo of white hair in the sun.

A hand reaching down.

"Fuck me."

She was happy she had blacked out before her mother could admonish her over her language.

. . .

The Madjack had been one of the most influential rock musicians of his generation. Social media flooded in the hours after his death with condolences, tributes, and touching personal stories.

The Madjack had been a superhero for a while. He'd fought alongside the Icons in Cobalt City for several years. He'd saved countless lives. Brought peace and hope and love in the most desperate of circumstances. Heroes who had been moved to follow in his footsteps recognized his memory as well.

The Madjack had been an alien.

The stars, bitter and cold in the vault of sky, reserved their judgment.

Atlas lay on the unforgiving mattress and gazed through the skylight overhead, fingers softly strumming random chords in the quiet room. It helped channel her emotion, freeing her brain to process. Sadness that Dad was gone, regret for not spending more time with him, anger at him not trying to spend more time with her, anger at herself for being angry at him, dread at the storm of reporters and ghouls she'd have to deal with because of it, anger at herself again for thinking about how the death was going to affect her, worry about the future set in motion by the tragedy.

Two days ago, she'd been gearing up for something of a comeback tour, rising from the ashes of a toxic contract with Goblin Records. It had been more than a year of fear and uncertainty—that she may never get to record again unless it was for that witch Ruby Killingsworth. Though she could never prove it, Atlas strongly suspected that Dad had intervened behind the scenes to get her released. He never said anything about it, and she never forced the issue, but he'd been unhappy with the Goblin Records contract from the beginning. If she hadn't been so goddamned cocksure and arrogant, she never would have questioned his judgment on the matter.

He had given her a second chance. Now, it seemed he was giving her something else. A legacy that she didn't understand and wasn't sure she wanted. *I'm the Madjack now. And that means, what exactly? I'm a superhero? I get to spend my life like an Elvis impersonator, a constant reflection of a person I never was?*

Things used to be simpler.

She remembered the Olive, the taste of diet cola and lime on her tongue as she took the karaoke mic in trembling hands. The lyrics for "Against All Odds" appeared on the tiny screen in front of her, and she just shut the rest of the world out. The murmur of the bar, the anxiety about her life, expectations that others had saddled her with, her tightly-held fears of inadequacy: gone. She walled it off, replaced it with the memory of hearing the Phil Collins classic as a child at her father's feet. She closed her eyes and she sang.

The die had been cast. The seal broken. She went up on stage questioning everything. She stepped off the stage knowing the only thing that ever really mattered: who she was.

It hadn't been easy going, and more than once she wondered if she'd made a mistake. She didn't need to work. In fact, Dad had tried to talk her out of it more than once with cautionary tales of unscrupulous producers and villainous show promoters, each more garish than the last, until she could almost picture them twirling little cartoon mustaches between fingertips.

She could have lived on her own in Cobalt City, rent free, with a chef and a housecleaner. Could have moved to Jaipur to stay with Mom, though they always ended up getting under each other's feet before too long. Hell, if she'd completely lacked ambition, she could have been a permanent member of her father's entourage, following him around the world on tours and benefits and general frippery. Though God himself only knew what MadJack was doing on most of his travels.

The thought sent a shock wave through her heart and she sat bolt upright.

From a distant room, she heard a gasp and the sharp sound of a dropped glass. Moments later, "Is everything all right in there, dear?"

"Yes. Sorry," Atlas replied. Maybe going to live on a mountaintop with goats was a good backup plan. No messy emotional surges that way. "Surprised myself. It's nothing."

Her mother shuffled to the doorway trailing wet footprints from what Atlas assumed was a doomed glass of water. "Is there anything I can help you with?"

"Where was Dad when he died?"

Her mother's eyes flickered nervously about the room. "Indonesia."

"What was he doing there?"

"Consulting," Indra said. But she didn't sound certain.

Atlas had been conscientious about not trying to pick up on people's emotions. It was an invasion of privacy that she would have hated were someone to do it to her. There had been several frosty years with her father, where she couldn't be sure if he stopped reading her emotions or simply stopped acting on the information it provided. Despite all that, she knew her mother. And Atlas knew how to read her.

"You don't know why he was there, do you?"

"Not exactly."

"Do you know who he was with?"

This Indra did know, telegraphed by the defiant tilt of her chin. "Yes. He was traveling alone."

"You're sure?"

"I spoke with Martzen that morning."

Martzen. Her father's driver at his home in Montreux, Switzerland. "Why was he in Switzerland?"

"Because . . . he lives there," Indra said, reflexively covering her mouth with her hand almost as the words left it. She peered guiltily from behind the hand, reluctant to offer the clarification she needed to tender. "He hasn't lived here for over a year."

Tears erupted from her mother's face. Atlas took her hands and held her until the worst of the tears had passed. "Mom. Why didn't you tell me?"

"We told ourselves it was to protect you. Honestly, I just didn't want you to think less of him. Of me. And I didn't want you to feel sorry for me, like you had some obligation to come ramble around this crypt to keep me company. It was for the best." She patted her daughter's hands. "I'm sorry I've hidden that from you for so long. That was the difficult part, really. I've grown used to him being . . . elsewhere."

"Do you know why he was killed?"

Her mother nodded slightly, her eyes dark. "Yes. It had been a long time coming. He'd failed in his mission. He had been sent to subjugate us. Conquer us. But he changed his mind. They couldn't let that stand."

Atlas had felt her understanding of the world tilt so precipitously since her dad's death, and this revelation threatened to unmoor her. She struggled, trying to find anything concrete to hold on to. Anything that might anchor her to bedrock again. She reached for her guitar, fingertips seeking a melody by instinct.

It took a few bars for her mother to recognize it. "Phil Collins?"

"Dad always liked this song."

Indra placed a strong, soft hand on her daughter's back. To Atlas, it felt like home. "Dear. *Everyone* liked this song."

• • •

The reading of the will was an intimate affair, with just Atlas, her mother, and two dozen of Brian McVittie's closest friends and longtime employees. That was for the best, as far as Atlas was concerned. The emotions were strong in the room, but they were largely of a similar hue, and there were not as many to block out as if it had been a public event like so much of his life had been. Even so, most of her concentration was taken up erecting and maintaining emotional distance from how deeply her Father's life and death had touched everyone present.

Even half-distracted, she heard nothing surprising disclosed in the will. Employees were given a lump payment, as if in apology for their sudden unemployment. Friends were given things of sentimental value. Infrequent writing partners given full share of the royalties.

The bulk of the estate had passed to Indra, just one more part of the story that the fake birth certificate had set in motion. Atlas had been given the condo in Cobalt City, along with enough of the estate to keep it staffed and stocked on the interest payments alone.

The sole surprise in the will was a small recording studio in Mar Vista, California, that Dad had also left in Atlas's care. The unexpected show of support for her music from beyond the grave provoked such profound sadness and gratitude that Atlas had the entire room crying before she knew it. She reigned it in after a minute, but she expected it had made enough of an impression to make ripples on social media. There were too many big names in the room for her to expect anything less.

As people began filing out, the lawyer approached with a sealed envelope. "Your father also left this in my care. I was not informed of what was inside, just told to pass it along in the event of his death. Now if you'll excuse me, I also have one for your mother." With a polite nod, he vanished into a small knot of people giving their condolences to the widow.

The envelope felt heavy in her hands. Cool, like it had been held in an underground vault, waiting. Knowing her dad, maybe it had been.

• • •

"Are you sure about this?" Indra asked, fastening the ivory scarf around her head.

Atlas looked up from her bed, where she was jotting possible lyrics into one of her Moleskine pocket notebooks. "There will be too many people. Too many questions. Too much emotion. Until I have a better grip on this, I should stay here."

"I understand. There is some Kashmiri rice left over. I noticed you didn't eat much. And you'll be able to see the fireworks from the pool. Small display of gold and pink fireworks, then the band will play 'Reign of Hearts,' then we return your father to the heavens. I'm told you won't be able to miss it."

"I always loved that song," Atlas smiled sadly. She wondered if she'd ever be able to enjoy it in the same way again, or if it would always be tinged with this sorrow.

"I loved all of them, I think," Indra said.

Atlas thought of one of her dad's early songs, some loopy thing about a white dog, probably recorded as album filler or as a joke. "Even the bad ones?"

Indra laughed with her. "*Especially* the bad ones. Woof woof."

Before her mom could leave, Atlas stopped her one last time. "Mom. Did you know? Did you know why the Madjack was here?"

"To conquer and enslave the planet?" her mom said. "I figured it out pretty quickly. I am very smart, you know."

"But you loved him anyway?"

Indra crossed to the bed and kissed Atlas on the forehead. "Of course I did, dear. He was your father. Everyone loved him. He changed his purpose once he realized he loved us, too. He belonged to the world. And in, oh, less than an hour, he's going back to the stars. So I should go. Try and eat more. You have a long flight tomorrow."

Minutes later, Atlas watched the taillights as Jasper drove them to the memorial site. For half a second, she almost regretted staying behind. But she meant what she'd told her mother. And things would be stressful enough soon. She'd already received four increasingly frantic voice mails from Frankie back in Cobalt. Recent pictures of Atlas had hit the web, hair now fully as white as her father's, and the internet was exploding with speculation that Atlas McVittie was going to adopt her father's Madjack persona.

Considering she'd spent her adult life trying to get out from under his shadow, it was, at best, a setback. Or she could steer into the skid and own it—outrageous costume and everything. It wasn't a decision one made overnight.

Atlas took her guitar out by the pool and left it on one of the wicker chairs. She came back a few minutes later with a bowl of Kashmiri rice and a bottle of soda. The sun set behind her as she ate, the sky a purple bruise above the famed Pink City. And before her, the first of the stars began to appear.

She opened her father's letter, expecting to find some grand explanation. Maybe some tearful farewell. Instead, she found the deeds to the condo and the recording studio, as well as a concise, handwritten list of fifty-four close friends and their contact information. Allies, should she need them. The letter still smelled like him—sunlight and licorice root.

With a pop and crackle, gold explosions lit the sky across the valley.

She'd promised herself she wouldn't cry, but the world was crying for her father. Who was she to deny him her tears? Atlas exchanged the soda for her guitar, idly checking the tuning, eyes on the glory in the sky before her.

When no more fireworks came, she played "Reign of Hearts," note perfect, just like she'd heard her father, the alien, play so many times in her childhood, on so many scratched vinyl records in house parties, in so many karaoke bars. And she sang. She sang as if there was no tomorrow, because for some, there wasn't. And they'd never know until it was too late. She sang about a better world, as if singing about it could make it real. Because maybe it could.

An unnamed planet had sent a single man to subjugate an entire world. And in his failure, he succeeded in ways they would never understand.

The final note faded, swallowed up by the high Indian desert. Seconds later, her father exploded across the sky in a masterfully engineered sequence of majestic red and blue fire.

The sparks faded, leaving wisps of smoke and a curtain of stars behind. Maybe one of them had been his. They'd been wrong. Brian McVittie hadn't belonged to the stars. He belonged here. He'd been the star around which they'd orbited for so long. And now a new star was needed, otherwise this planet was forfeit.

When Atlas set down her guitar again, she closed her hand into a fist. Somewhere within her grip, on some quantum level, she felt the scepter. It would be there when she needed it. She could learn the rest. After all, it was part of her story.

Nathan Crowder is a Seattle-based fan of little known musicians, unpopular candy, and just happens to write fantasy, horror, and superheroes. His other works include the fantasy novel *Ink Calls to Ink*, short fiction in anthologies such as *Selfies from the End of the World*, and *Cthulhurotica*, and his numerous Cobalt City superhero stories and novels. He is still processing the death of David Bowie.

Quintessential Justice

Patrick Flanagan

9:23AM - HAVE-A-JAVA, CORNER OF MULLANEY AND BROADWAY, DOWNTOWN UPTONVILLE.

Jaleesa found her boss in his usual spot. He liked to sit at the window booth, right below the store marquee, so he could smile and wave to any fans standing outside who were too timid or awed to come in and shake his hand. It never hurt to be optimistic.

He was mumbling his morning litany as she set his breakfast down on the table. "Queen and country, queen and country . . . Ah, good morning." He tore into the Styrofoam container from Quinones' Cantina. "Still piping hot. *Que bonita.*"

She slumped down in the seat across from him. "Just don't get any on your costume."

He smiled around his mouthful of *chilaquiles*. "Because of my generally equable nature," he said, "and because these are so exquisitely piquant this morning, I elect not to quibble over your use of a certain disquieting term."

"Just don't get any on your *uniform*."

"See? That just *sounds* better." He uncapped his bottle of strawberry Nesquik and gulped half of it down. "You really should try this—you're missing out. Good *morning*, fellow citizens!" he shouted at the couple entering the coffee shop, paralyzing them with dread. "Quite a choice you've made today. The service here is without equal."

"Shit, I forgot he comes here," muttered the guy.

"Oh, sorry," said the girl, "actually, I think we don't have time for coffee." They shuffled back out.

"Have an adequate day!" he bellowed at them. "And you can quote me!"

"You know, we," Jaleesa started, but gave up mid-sentence. She didn't even bother trailing off.

"It means 'satisfactory or fair,'" he protested. "It's a perfectly . . . uh, a perfectly *adequate* greeting."

"You really can't hear how sarcastic it sounds? Like you can't be bothered to wish them a great day or a fantastic day?"

Her boss stared at her, unblinking. "No," he said, mildly hurt.

"Oh," Jaleesa said. "Well. You know, it's probably just me then. Sorry."

"No apologies required," he said, his good nature returning.

Quick recovery, she thought, grumbling at the choice of words. After a while, he wore off on you.

"Alright!" he said, wiping the crumbs from his face. "The day's getting away from us. On the double-quick, Ms. Reagan! Let's go serve the people of Uptonville!" He tried hopping to his feet but stopped midway, stooped over. "Hold on, hold on, the cape. Don't say it."

She reached under his seat to free him from where he'd snagged himself. "Don't say 'I told you to take your cape off when you sit down at restaurants'? Don't say that?"

"Yes, exactly. Thanks for acquiescing."

11:01AM - VANDERGELDER CITY PARK, EAST UPTONVILLE.

"My goodness! It's Uptonville's very own superhero, QED!"

Jaleesa ordered her eyes not to roll. At least this guy knew to spell the codename out. Two weeks ago, some lady had called him "Captain Qued."

QED stood and basked in the spotlight, such as it was. The onlookers were more puzzled and curious than adoring and thankful, but he accepted their polite stares with the humility and grace one would afford a throng of fawning acolytes. She smiled without intending to. "Yes, fellow Uptonvillers," he said with a friendly laugh, "in answer to your inquiry, it's me, QED. I'm afraid I've been recognized." He threw Jaleesa a wink. "Just here for a stroll, enjoying the tranquility."

"Yes! Yes! It's the Quixotic Master of Q-Power himself, I knew it!" his fan continued. Jaleesa relented and let her eyeballs react of their own volition. Just terrible. Didn't anyone read these scripts aloud first? "It's such a genuine thrill to meet you, sir!"

QED blushed beneath his masque. She was amazed at how he could summon that reaction at will, even when he was talking to an obvious plant. The hero shook the man's hand vigorously—"Quite a squeeze you've got, citizen!"—and posed for a selfie with him. That seemed to signal to the rest of the crowd that they, too, should probably be asking for selfies. QED dutifully obliged, doling out manly shoulder hugs, handshakes, demure kisses on the cheek, and even posing with someone's golden retriever. "I'm partial to Basque shepherds, personally," he told her owners, "but retrievers are a close second. Top five at least."

"I'm rather surprised you didn't mention the Queensland heeler," an older man with a walker piped up. QED looked at him, his smile frozen on his face. "It's a variety of Australian cattle dog."

"Of course it is!" the hero said, glancing at Jaleesa. She scribbled on her notepad: *Google Aussie dogs.*

QED moved on, trying to corral a few stray park-goers who were trying to make a break for it. Jaleesa edged over toward the planted extra, whose enthusiasm had evaporated.

"Encore, encore," she said to him. He wasn't sure whether to be flattered or embarrassed to be found out, so he split the difference with a smile and a shrug.

"How was I?" he stage-whispered to her.

"I can't talk. I'm too choked up for words."

The actor frowned. "Hey, I thought I sold it pretty well."

"Olivier couldn't have sold it. Although he probably wouldn't have been dropping his lines like they were heavy armloads of firewood."

He shrugged. "Everybody's a critic. As long as I get my SAG voucher for this."

"You've been a huge help," Jaleesa said. The extra nodded and vanished off to wherever desperate actors go. She was trying not to get *too* irritated about this. QED had been stationed here in Uptonville for almost a month now. Planting cheering fans in crowds was the kind of hand-holding you extended to rookies and newly promoted sidekicks on their first day on the job—not seasoned veterans.

The crowd finally managed to break apart and peel away in twos and threes, having fulfilled their civic responsibility to "Be Nice to the Hero." QED bounded over with a hundred dollar smile on his face.

"This community patrolling approach is really starting to pay off! Did you see them queue up?" he said. "I think we're really piquing their interest now. That one guy even knew my complete sobriquet!"

Jaleesa didn't know what to say. She hoped a cheerful thumbs-up would suffice. It usually did with Q.

1:14PM - "GET TO KNOW YOUR HERO" MEET-AND-GREET, SESQUI-PEDALIA COUNTY LIBRARY, LOWER UPTONVILLE.

QED had made Jaleesa promise not to stand next to the fire alarm handle—and she'd consented—but she made sure it was within her line of sight. But so far, her fears had been ungrounded. He was killing it up there.

QED: "—so that brings us to my favorite part of these events: the Q&A." [Polite chuckles.] "The other microphone should be working now, so—yes?—yes, there it is. So, don't be shy, I won't be brusque. No question will be squelched."

Questioner 1: "Hello, sir. Thanks for coming here today. My question is about the time during the Fomalhaut Catastrophe, when you and Dr. Comet were both facing the Titanthrop—"

QED: "Oh, there's a story from antiquity . . ."

Questioner 1: "So my friend thinks you weren't strong enough to take the 'Throp on, because of the Acid Demon's curse still being in effect on you, and that you had to hide while Comet beat him."

QED: "Hmm. A rather oblique account. And your take?"

Questioner 1: "Well, I think you tried to help him but got knocked out, and *then* Comet beat him."

QED: "The Doctor and I are coequals. We conquered the Titan-throp together. Okay, next query."

Questioner 1: "Yeah, but I—"

QED: "Yes, right there, next in queue. What's your question?"

Questioner 2: "Hi there. Thanks for being here. I was wondering what Thunder Lizard was like after he came back to life. Was his personality any different?"

QED: "Uhhh . . . well, that's not really something we frequently discussed. Thunder's fairly opaque; he kept his feelings on the QT for the most part. I mean keeps. Sorry. Present tense again."

Questioner 2: "But was he in heaven while he was dead? And is he alive now or undead? I mean technically—"

QED: "Maybe we could . . . yes, the young man in the red shirt, right behind— Yes, there you go. Hello, young squire. Inquire away."

Questioner 3: "Hi. I . . . um. I was. Um. I was going to ask, do you know Space Leopard?" [Laughter from crowd.]

QED: "Well, yes, I have met Space Leopard before. He's a very nice man. He fights for justice, like I do."

Questioner 3: "Um, yes. I think—I think he's the best of all super-heroes." [Uproarious laughter.]

QED: "I agree, he's a very qualified vanquisher of crime and injustice. But I think I do pretty well, too." [More laughter, somewhat strained.]

Questioner 3: "Space Leopard is my favorite. I think he should come to Uptonville."

QED: "We're making pretty good time here. Next to the podium, please. Yes ma'am, your question?"

Questioner 4: "Thank you sir. Delilah Currie, *Uptonville Universe*. Dr. Quatermain, I'd like to ask about your recent experience with—"

QED: "Whoa. Hold it. Time out. I don't . . . I'm not quite sure to whom you're referring . . ."

Currie: "So you're claiming that you're *not* world-renown quantum physicist Quenton Quatermain, to whom you bear a striking resemblance?"

QED: "Alright. I'll quit pretending to be unfamiliar with the man. The fact is, Dr. Quatermain is an acquaintance of mine who happens to value his privacy. That's obviously why we've never been photographed together." [Laughter.]

Questioner 1: "Come on, everybody knows you're him."

QED: "Please, let's not breach etiquette and speak without the microphone."

Currie: "Mr. QED, I have the phone number for Dr. Quatermain's campus office right here, perhaps we could put him on speakerphone and—"

QED: "He's on sabbatical, actually." [Laughter.] "Wait, wait, if we're friends I *would* know that! Besides—wait, wait—besides, as everyone can see, I have this acquired mole right here on my cheek. And Dr. Quatermain does not. So obviously—"

[Deafening squeal from PA system. Library assistants help escort everyone out through the fire exits.]

• • •

"Did everyone make it out alright?" QED asked. "Hang on, I just want to make a final sweep of the building."

"Q, come on," Jaleesa said. "Do you smell any smoke? I just needed to get you out of there." She had already scribbled on her notepad to nix any future audience interactions until QED got some coaching on public relations.

"Oh." QED's face looked pained. "You don't think it went well? I thought it went mostly well."

Jaleesa bit back a smart remark. "Q, the goal for today is to rein- force the QED brand and get people to see you as a hero. You weren't a hero up there, you were a celebrity, and ripping celebrities apart is the national pastime."

"Well that certainly doesn't square with my experience," QED said. "And I have some real qualms about how you tricked everyone back there. In fact, I find it highly questionable. I request that you never do that again. Quite frankly, I require it."

Jaleesa looked Q in the eye. "Look," she said. "I like you. You're a good guy, and I don't always say that. I've worked for some real prizes in this job. But I don't actually, technically, work for you. I work for the Support Services Division of the Justice Guardian Brigade, LLC." QED looked like he wanted to interject but thought better of it. "And sometimes I have to do things you don't like—not because I want to, but because doing my job means keeping you from becoming a laughingstock. Because when that happens to one hero, it's hard on *every* hero. And that was about to happen back there."

QED looked at her. *Through* her. She could feel what he called his "Q-Power" broadcasting on all frequencies, out of every pore of his body, every atom of his being. "When you misuse safety equipment like fire alarms," he said quietly, "you make people mistrust their efficacy. And that puts people in danger, however slightly. Actions have consequences."

Jaleesa found it hard to maintain her frustration with his Boy Scout mentality. She didn't know if that was due to the Q-Power or not. "Q . . ."

He rested a hand on her shoulder. "I don't care if some cub reporter puts the squeeze on me. I know sometimes I come across as a quavering milquetoast, but I'm hardly quailing at the prospect of Miss Currie's inquisition." Then he tried out a curious and unfamiliar expression. "Besides, if she wants to sell papers by claiming to know my real identity, she'll have to try harder. Who would possibly equate *me* with the likes of Quenton Quatermain? It's absurd. He doesn't have a mole!"

"I . . . you know, I never realized it, but you're right. I was skeptical before, but the mole thing really clinches it."

"Quite right it does!" QED said. "I . . . hold on. I'm picking something up over the law enforcement channels." His eyes darted left to right as he read the incoming message scrolling across his optic LED. "Looks like there's a robbery in progress down at the First Bank of Uptonville. A quintet of hostages. We'd better move."

"Got it," Jaleesa said, switching from conversation mode to work mode. She began striding through the library parking lot toward their car. "I'll check in with Headquarters and let them know you're—" She frowned. "Hang on. I'm not seeing anything here, with either FBI or UPD. Where is it you said—"

She stopped. There was no flapping. Usually, when he took off with a running jump, his cape flapped loudly in the wind. "You really leapt into action there," QED said, catching up with her. "Maybe you should wear the cape and masque and I should drive."

"Oh, but I'm not the Quixotic Master of Q-Power," Jaleesa said sourly.

"My only point was, there are other ways to quit an event early. I'm quick on the uptake, I can play along." He looked at her until she was forced to smile and kept looking until it was genuine. "You really like the sobriquet, don't you? Everyone told me they were too quaintly old-fashioned, but I think they're coming back into style."

He cleared his throat awkwardly. "So, anyway. There's been something I've been wanting to talk to you—wait. Hold on—" His eyes darted left to right.

"Leave it to you," Jaleesa said. "You actually managed your

once-a-year tricking of me and now you blow your accomplishment by doubling down and trying to pull the exact same gag two minutes later. Unbelievable."

"No, no," QED said. "This one's unequivocally legit." His eyes bulged. "*Quetzalcoatl's quincunx!*" he exclaimed.

Jaleesa burst out laughing. "Q, you *cannot* be serious with that one! That's your worst epithet yet! Sweet Jesus."

QED waved her remark aside. "It's the Ruinator. He's tearing up the park. UPD can't quarantine him. Let's go."

"*Ughhhh*," Jaleesa groaned. "We were *just. There.* What a pain."

"No, not Vandergelder," QED corrected. "He's across town at Schuyler Colfax."

"What's he doing, stealing ducks? The Ruinator is strictly a banks-and-jewelry-store guy, what's he looking for in the middle of a public park?"

"Me," QED said. He backed up to get a running start through the parking lot. Jaleesa was already halfway to the car, but she waited to hearing the flapping before calling it in.

4:44PM - SCHUYLER COLFAX CITY PARK, NORTH OF UPTONVILLE.

Jaleesa leaned against the tree, sipping her French roast. She suspected it was almost over now. The Ruinator was looking pretty haggard; her boy Q had ripped his helmet off and pounded on the Ruinator's ghastly orange-green-and-purple armored suit so badly that smoke was pouring out of the vents. QED had blood running down his cheek onto his aquamarine uniform, and he was breathing heavy, but he still looked like he had another five or six rounds left in him.

She checked her wristwatch. They'd long missed the costume contest Q was supposed to judge over at the Uptonville Mall, but that was no big deal. Actually, that was probably a net positive at this point, since Q could not keep his disdain in check when it came to supervillain cosplayers. "I just do not understand the appeal," he'd said once. "They're burlesquing the grotesque. Colorful rogues with chequered pasts is one thing, but some of these guys are literally serial killers. Two or three of them have attempted genocide! Would you walk around dressed as Pol Pot for fun?"

"Maybe if Pol Pot had worn a jetpack and carried a pulse cannon," she'd offered.

Now the combatants were staggering back toward what was left of the park's county-famous grove of vice presidential statues. Most of the nineteenth century had already been decimated during their tussle, but the Ruinator managed to uproot a still-standing Levi P. Morton and swing it like a club at QED, head first. QED summoned a surge of Q-Power and decapitated the former governor of New York with a single punch, then grabbed the torso and tried to wrench it free from his opponent's grasp.

Jaleesa walked over toward an animated cluster of UPD officers. The rookies, who all looked young enough to have arrived at the park via school bus, were watching the battle excitedly; the veteran officers were ignoring it, engrossed in a conversation about their softball league and next week's barbecue party next week. "Beats traffic duty, doesn't it?" she asked the nearest cop.

"Shit *yeah* it does," he said excitedly, then noticed she wasn't wearing blue. "Ma'am, get back," he started to bark. "This area is off limits to civilians. Get behind the barricade—"

She flashed her JGB credentials. "Ma'am? Really? I'm all of 32."

"Oh, sorry," he said, losing interest completely, either because she was allowed to be there or because she was too old to harass. Jaleesa wasn't sure how to feel about that.

"What do you say there, Brigade," said a gray-haired lieutenant. He shook her hand. "Bill Tremaine. Your man's going to town out there. If he demolishes Dick Cheney, the department will buy the two of you dinner."

"I'm hypoglycemic. I can't eat donuts," Jaleesa said.

"Zing," said the lieutenant. "I prefer Italian myself. I'm open to Asian fusion, though."

"Another giant stride for diversity in the police department."

The younger officers groaned loudly in unison; the Ruinator had put Q on his back with a sweeping kick and was trying to crush his skull between the headless torsos of a Democratic-Republican and a Whig. Q rolled up into a kneeling crouch and caught the Whig, crushing it to rubble, but took a Daniel D. Tompkins to the ear and fell back down. "My friend Andrew Jackson thinks GED won't get back up," said one of the kindergarten cops.

"I'll take that," said an even younger-looking one.

"You assholes," Jaleesa said. "This isn't pro wrestling. Show some decorum." No one showed a flicker of remorse or embarrassment. "Besides," she added, "my friend Ulysses Grant here says that QED is going to make Captain Mardi Gras out there eat the rest of the nineteenth century and thank him for the privilege." She made every taker pull out their wallets to show they were good for it.

"Hell, I'll even try the health food thing," said Lieutenant Tremaine. "There's a new vegan café down on Broadway, if you happen to be free one evening this week."

· · ·

"Spirited little pipsqueak, wasn't he?" QED said, still glowing with post-battle exhilaration. "I'll give him credit. Lot of heart. He acquitted himself well."

Jaleesa quickly tucked the wad of cash inside her blouse when QED's head was turned. The Q-Power was rising from him like steam, working overtime to heal his wounds; the cut on his face was already gone. "You did great," she said, trying not mom it up too much. He could be so boyish that sometimes she found herself slipping into that dynamic.

Uptonville's Finest, on their lieutenant's orders, lined up to shake QED's hand with all the enthusiasm of a losing little league team. "I hope I didn't pique them too badly," he said. "I'd hate to squander the goodwill we've built up so far with an internal squabble."

Jaleesa patted him on the arm. "Hey," she said, "in all sincerity, and I mean this, fuck those jealous motherfuckers. Fuck 'em right in the ear."

QED stared at her. "How did one so young acquire such worldly wisdom?"

"Gramma, mainly. She had that one embroidered on a throw pillow."

"A highly quotable woman," he admitted.

"Come on, let's go before Delilah Currie shows up to ask if Quenton Quatermain hates the Vice President."

"I've never discussed it with him," QED said entirely too quickly. "Here, give me the keys, I'll drive."

She let her shocked silence hang there theatrically. "I can *drive*," he said. "I just tend to fly more, that's all."

"Thank you again, QED," Lieutenant Tremaine said. "You as well, Miss."

"I'll follow up with you on that other matter," Jaleesa said. "We appreciate your interest."

QED conspicuously said nothing as they approached the car. He conspicuously said nothing as he started the car and pulled out into traffic. They drove in silence for five blocks before she told him to shut up.

"It's none of your business."

"Quiet as a church mouse here," he insisted.

"Just so long as we're clear," she said. "So. Where are we going?"

6:22PM - 124 QUINCANNON AVENUE, EAST UPTONVILLE.

QED took his hands from Jaleesa's eyes. The first thing she saw was the giant Q of the dilapidated storefront.

"Of course," she said. *QUIC ST P M RKET*, it read. "Pat, I'd like to solve the puzzle."

"I know it's a bit squalid," QED said. "And I suspect the electrical wiring is on the antiquated side. But overall, it was something of a bargain."

"Yeah, but look at this place," Jaleesa said. "There's a reason this store went under, they obviously rerouted the highway away." She paused. "Was. *Was* something of a bargain? Was that past tense?"

QED nodded. There was no containing his excitement at this point. "I'll be eating a lot of ramen this quarter, probably, but I've saved enough during my time with JGB that I was able to make it happen. I signed the paperwork and acquired this property as of yesterday."

Jaleesa's stomach lurched. "Tell me you can still back out. Tell me you can cancel your check."

QED crossed his arms. His posture was equal parts apologetic and triumphant. "I'm afraid not," he said. "*Quod scripsi, scripsi.*"

She held her face in her hands. "Q, come on, you can *not* just blow your entire savings on a money pit like this. It'd be easier to close your bank account and burn the cashier's check. Being broke is better than being in debt up to your eyeballs."

"So you don't think I'm qualified for this?" he asked. There was something different in his voice.

"I can't even believe you're *interested* in this, honestly," she said. "I never figured you for the type. I've seen those before, you know. Second-stringers who decide to retire at thirty-five and live on sneaker endorsements, who end up funneling all that Nike money into a restaurant and a car wash and a mini-mall—or worse, buying a slice of a vaporware casino or hotel, some floundering business deal brokered by their brother-in-law or a jerkoff cousin, and what happens? What happens?" His bemused smile just pissed her off more. "Broke at forty-five! And it's either out on the speaker's circuit, trying to peddle the same book that twenty other guys already wrote, or it's back in the tights. Trying to make a comeback with a spare tire and shot knees. It's pathetic."

QED said nothing. Still smiled that curious little smile. That—*quirky* grin.

Jaleesa sighed. "I know, I know. Overstepping my bounds. Your money, your life. I guess I just . . . just never figured you would . . ." The word stuck in her throat. She opted for the ellipsis this time.

"Go ahead," he said.

"*Quit,*" she blurted out. "And it disappoints the shit out of me." She wiped her hands. "There. That's it, I'm done. You do what you want."

"Well." QED put his arms behind his back and faced the crumbling store. "What I don't want to do is open a grocery store. Or a restaurant. Or a car wash."

"You don't," she said, feeling a little numb. Opening up like this wasn't her thing.

"No." QED turned to face her. "I'm in the justice business. Just like you." He waved his hand at his new not-a-store-after-all. "I'm leaving the JGB, you're quite right about that. It's just . . . it's time. Too much bureaucratic quagmire, too much squad room politics. I'm tired of needing a quorum to pass any team resolutions. I'm tired of having to squash teammates' feuds. I'm tired of *boutique justice*. This shouldn't be a non-stop public relations exercise. I want to help *real* people, not actors paid to recognize me."

She felt her face burn. "I wasn't sure if you knew about that. You never said anything."

He nodded, "I actually thought you might not know either, so I kept quiet. But that's what I'm talking about. I've been in a quandary over this for a while now," he said. "It's time to be my own hero. It's time to leave the JGB and establish my Q-Quarters, here on . . . here on the Quadrangle of Justice."

Jaleesa braced herself to stifle her laughter.

And was surprised when no laughter came.

"Hmm," she said.

QED waited.

"I've heard worse ideas," Jaleesa finally said, to both of their surprise.

"Chief of staff," he pounced before she could talk herself back to earth. "That's your title, but really we'll be equals."

"I can't *really* be a chief of staff before there's any other staff," she demurred.

"Chief of staff-designate, then. Your first assignment is to find people of quality to staff the Q-Quarters. We'll need logistics personnel, security, a communications director . . . definitely want our own R&D division at some point . . ."

"No, first we need to secure funding, *then* we can start hiring," Jaleesa argued.

QED laughed. "I hired you, didn't I? The money will come from somewhere. And if doesn't, the right people will do it for nothing. The way we superheroes *used* to do it."

"Q, come on," she said. "I'm no super—" He stopped her, closed his eyes and exhaled deeply.

"Quenton," he blurted out.

"*Whaaaaaat?*" she gasped.

"Don't be sarcastic. I know you've probably had your occasional suspicions," he said.

"But . . . *the Mole*," she said, pointing insistently. QED cringed a little, then plucked it off his cheek. "Ohhhh," she said, "yes, now I totally see it."

"Right!" he said, breathing deeply. "I just thought there shouldn't be any secrets between partners." He carefully pressed the mole application back onto his cheek and pressed down hard. "What a relief to finally have the truth out in the open."

"I knew the entire time, dumbass," Jaleesa said. "Most of North

America knows. See, this is the kind of ridiculous thing that I'm not going to allow you to do anymore. If we're gonna be partners and all."

"Sure, but . . . I don't know," QED said. "I just thought maybe I could part my hair on *this* side when I'm Quenton, and like *this* when—"

"No. Nuh-uh. *Done* with this foolishness. If you insist on keeping this 'double life' nonsense, then you're gonna be wearing a helmet with a faceplate, or a masque that covers more than 60 percent of your facial features. End of discussion, no arguments. This is Q-Quarters Communiqué 0001. Cover that face."

"Alright, alright," said the Quixotic Master of Q-Power, grinning. "Quit critiquing me."

For security reasons, **Patrick Flanagan** writes from one of several undisclosed locations; either—

1) A Top Secret-classified government laboratory which studies genetic aberrations and unexplained phenomena;
2) A sophisticated compound hidden in plain sight behind an electromagnetic cloaking shield;
3) A decaying Victorian mansion, long plagued by reports of terrifying paranormal activity; or
4) The subterranean ruins of a once-proud empire which ruled the Earth before recorded history, and whose inbred descendants linger on in clans of cannibalistic rabble

—all of which are conveniently accessible from exits 106 or 108 of the Garden State Parkway. Our intelligence reports that his paranoid ravings have been previously documented by Grand Mal Press, Evil Jester Press, and Sam's Dot Publishing. In our assessment he should be taken seriously, but not literally. (Note: Do NOT make any sudden movements within a 50' radius.)

The Fall of the Jade Sword

Stephanie Lai

"NEW HERO OF MELBOURNE" the *Times* announces—tales of a man stopping runaway airships and helping people burned by wayward pipes. He sounds magical: flying from airship to anchor and onto roofs, unscathed.

There is a little more information to be gleaned from a single page Chinese broadsheet. It's pasted up in teahouses and slipped under the doors of certain homes. They call their hero the Jade Sword for the green band on both arms and the character one old auntie swears she saw.

Mok-Seung isn't so sure of the name. She pushes the paper aside and allows it to wrinkle on the floor where Auntie Hong will frown at it later. She rises to her feet and sinks into the opening form of the *Tai Gik*—imagines the knife, or the wheel.

How useful can a jade sword be? It would shatter upon impact. She prefers fast sword or jade spirit. Sturdier, stronger names. Names of which one can be proud.

• • •

Mok-Seung watches a young boy ride on one of the new augmented bicycles, which are so popular in this place. He cruises past the window, his feet still but for the occasional push, steam billowing from the pipes at the back. She longs for such a vehicle, fast as a horse but much more useful, and far less likely to bite her.

"Mok-Seung," she hears, and turns back to Auntie Hong.

"I wager I could ride a bike," Mok-Seung says, hinting. Auntie Hong shakes her head.

"I wager you could fall off. They're not as easy as you think they are."

Mok-Seung latches on. "Have you—" she starts, but Auntie Hong shakes her head again.

Mok-Seung could try suggesting that Auntie let her go outside, but she knows her own schedule perfectly well and knows Auntie Hong is firm, like bamboo. Resisting the urge to sigh dramatically, Mok-Seung picks up her brush and tries again to focus, to get the flow of the ink and the shape of the characters right.

Outside, the sounds of the augmented bicycle fade into the street noise and the sound of birds at dusk. She thinks she hears the cry of a kookaburra in the distance, and she frowns that it would laugh at her.

• • •

Jade Sword's form is fast and expert. There are rumors of Jade Sword carrying children to safety, Jade Sword stopping robbers in their tracks, Jade Sword rescuing the crew of an airship as it tangled on one of the new skyscrapers in Melbourne.

The *Times* reports him as a hero; it draws sketches of him tall and lean and white, with a full brown beard and a long, *gwailo* face. The *Times* declares he is there to assist the civilized people of Melbourne; from the Chinese, they mean, and from the Indigenous, those not yet sickened or stolen or pushed away.

In the teahouses, the *huaren* know a practitioner of *wushu* when they see one; they claim Jade Sword as one of their own, and they are proud.

• • •

Mok-Seung trails behind Mama as they step from the tram onto the cobblestones. The stones are rough beneath her feet, and as she glances down alleys and keeps her eyes peeled for augmented bicycles and other new technologies, she falls farther and farther behind. Mama snaps when she notices, and Mok-Seung has to hurry to catch up.

The white ladies frown disapprovingly at her as she dashes past them.

She's grateful they're so far away from home, that her feet are her own, and she can dart as she sees fit, despite Mama's frown.

Mok-Seung grins, and Mama's frown widens.

"Be calm of face, little flower," Mama says. "You will give yourself away."

• • •

Mok-Seung sits by the window, a book in her lap. She's reading *The Art of War,* a highly suitable text for a young woman growing up in a foreign land. Though she understands its benefit, she finds her mind drifting, and the book, newly printed for use outside the Middle Kingdom's wide borders, drops from her hand.

She contemplates the shape of the land she's on instead, contemplates the Australians who own the building and the rumors of sandstorms in the desert; if the gwailo can be so wrong about the Chinese in their midst, she wonders, surely they are all wrong about those who have come before.

She wonders how bikes work in the desert.

She starts drafting a bike on the corner of a page, pauses when she realizes she's going to need a closer look if she's going to have any ideas.

"Mok-Seung," Auntie Hong says, and Mok-Seung looks up to meet her eyes with a guilty look.

"I'm reading!" Mok-Seung says, and holds *The Art of War* up as evidence. Auntie Hong nods.

"You will find that book very useful in the years to come," Auntie says, hinting toward things they don't talk about, "but for now, perhaps it is time for a break, and a different kind of training."

Mok-Seung allows herself to hope, follows Auntie Hong into the courtyard, and squints into the setting sun.

They drop into the opening form and begin to breathe.

• • •

As Mama selects the tea for expected guests, Mok-Seung stands beside her. Yong Taitai likes an Oolong, but Ye Taitai prefers something more pungent, something you would never dream of serving an Australian guest. Mama's hand hovers over a Pu-er, six months old, from a bush back home, as she says, "Auntie Hong tells me you seem restless. Is something wrong?"

Mok-Seung presses her lips together. She knows this is her chance. "Melbourne is very interesting," she says. "I thought if I had one of the new bikes, it would be easier to explore."

"Ah," Mama says. "The technology could be better. What you have will do you adequately." She wraps her hand around a tin and continues talking, doesn't notice the face Mok-Seung pulls and quickly hides. "This Pu-er will go well, I think, but Can Sin-Man is always the most unknown of us."

"Can Sin-Man is coming?" Mok-Seung doesn't know why Mama continues their association; Can Sin-Man is austere and serious, uninterested in what Australia has to offer, and always asks Mok-Seung detailed questions about her studies and her forms. She's sure Can Sin-Man would never approve of the new bikes.

Actually, maybe she does know why Mama has her over for tea.

There's a knock at the door, and Mok-Seung pulls a different face: she greets Yong Taitai with a smile.

• • •

The eucalyptus is old, and it takes her weight with ease. Mok-Seung crosses into its branches, and after carefully closing her window and peering through the branches onto the street below, she scales its trunk to the top and onto the roof, disappearing into the dark.

Clad in loose *ku*, her traditional pants, with a green band across her brow, she runs over the rooftops lining Little Bourke; she stretches herself to leap out over Exhibition Street and keeps running. Mok-Seung nearly misses a couple of jumps, but she's getting better, and she makes it across town without too many mishaps.

From atop the roof, she sights one of the new augmented bikes leaning against a terraced house. She jumps down to the road and drops to the ground inside the house's high front gate. The generators beside the house are working overtime, pressing steam into the sky, so the house is still awake. She hopes they won't notice that she longs for this contraption, sleeker than the new steam carriages with their gears and the constant need for fire, ceaseless in comparison with horses, which plod and clop through the streets. This one has red and white streamers tied to the handlebars and around the pipes. She wonders if, perhaps, that's less than wise, but she wraps the streamers around her hand and admires them all the same.

Mok-Seung sits on the bike, imagines cycling it through Little Bourke, imagines its potential when coupled with the airship technology.

She blinks, suddenly awash in bright light. "Get off!" she hears. "Jeremy, there's a Chinese on your bike!" She looks up in confusion, and the woman at the door screams. Mok-Seung reaches for the fence, balances on its pointiest peak as she reaches for the balcony of the townhouse, and then pulls herself onto the roof. She feels a scratch against her ankle, but doesn't pause as she starts to run.

She sprints across the roofs, hears a clatter as she jumps onto the English-style tiles. She curses them for their difference and keeps running, her footsteps not as light as she might hope. She sees the curve of an airship rising to her left and turns suddenly, making a leap like the photo captured by the local newspapers.

The skin of the balloon is too smooth beneath her hand, and she loses her grip. She scrabbles for purchase but it's to no avail—she loses her hold and starts to free fall off the side of the airship, bounces on its edge, and brushes past the edge of another roof. Mok-Seung continues to plummet and panics, looking for anything to break her fall, when she is stopped, suddenly, a hand grasped fast around her wrist. She looks up and meets bright brown eyes and an unrelenting stare under a green band. The real Jade Sword!

"Pay attention," says the familiar voice, not unkindly. "You need to know where to throw your weight." She flicks her wrist and the figure releases her, letting her drop painfully the final few feet to the ground. Mok-Seung pauses, her hand resting on an augmented bicycle; she lets herself breathe for a moment, the shame of being caught out curling in her gut. She admires the lean build and smooth pipes of the bicycle. One day she'll have one.

A shout behind her spurs her back into action. Ahead, "Yong's Chinese Laundry" is monogrammed in red above a brick building. She speeds up, darts through the red door, past the uncle at the counter and into the steam of the pressing room. The auntie emits a yell, "Out, out!" as another clasps her heart. "Jade Sword!" the second auntie yells, in what Mok-Seung hopes is awe and pride, even though she's not who they think she is.

"Sorry," she says as she trips over a steamer. "Sorry, sorry." She bows to each auntie as she passes them and heads straight for the back window she knows opens onto a narrow laneway. At the last auntie, she pauses. "Lou Yap," she says. "Your *pau* at festival last week was the greatest I have ever eaten."

As she climbs through the back window, there is silence in the usually chatty laundry, broken only by the hiss of the press. She peers back through as the front door clangs open. Suddenly, the laundry swings back into action, and a number of large trolleys are completely accidentally wheeled into position between the door and the window. Lou Yap waves cheerily, and Mok-Seung ducks out of sight, running down the alley.

She leaps up onto a roof, delightfully low placed. She puts some distance between herself and her pursuers, until all she can hear is the city settling down.

• • •

Mok-Seung pulls the ribbon down from across her forehead and sweeps her hair away from her eyes. She smooths the fabric of her top and begins to unwrap it from her body. She hisses as she pulls it away from her arm. There is a gash across her skin, and a similar slash through her shirt. She grimaces, wonders if her embroidery skills are strong enough to hide such a mark.

She washes the blood from her arm and winces at the sting. The door swings open; Auntie Hong gasps. "You are not Jade Sword!" she declares, unsurprised, after looking around for anyone who might overhear. She closes the door.

Mok-Seung nods her head. "I'm not," she agrees. As she sits through Auntie Hong's admonitions and ministrations, she wonders if the real Jade Sword would have been caught out by her old *Ayi*.

• • •

(Auntie Hong already knows the real Jade Sword's identity, because the real Jade Sword isn't stupid enough to hide from her old friend.

But if the real Jade Sword hasn't told Mok-Seung that—well, it's good for Mok-Seung to have to wait. Patience is a virtue she's always lacked.)

• • •

The Chinese broadsheet reads "JADE SWORD FALLS OFF ROOF." The *Times* reads "CHINESE BICYCLE THIEF THWARTED."

• • •

Mok-Seung begins to read the papers—not only the Chinese broadsheets but the local English-language ones, too, and the papers brought down from Sydney and across from the gold fields. She engages in gossip on the streets and pokes her head into every restaurant, every sporting club, every place that doesn't have a sign over the door banning her entry.

She looks for anything she can find, but she isn't quite sure what she's after. She finds breaths of shapes in the desert: wagons that run using sand, not horses; white deaths that find no retaliation, left with nothing but dust and the land; riots and thefts and gold and fire; and she wonders, why they have come to this place.

She hopes there's something for them to learn all this way from home. She fears that there is not.

• • •

"NEW HEROES FOR A NEW TIME" declares the *Times*, beside a picture of the Mayor of Bendigo and a tall, strapping white man with a firm grip. The article text includes details: a tragic accident by one white worker and the completely reasonable retaliation resulting in native deaths and Chinese deaths, and maybe some other deaths; and they had not disrupted mining any further.

"PERMISSION TO TRANSPORT BODIES HOME FOR BURIAL RESTRICTED BY AUTHORITIES" reads the Chinese broadsheet.

Mok-Seung's stomach turns.

• • •

She sneaks out into the night, careful of running into Auntie Hong, careful of her shiny, dark hair reflecting in the moonlight.

It's a warm night, and she sweats beneath her layers. An Australian summer is nothing like the summers of her childhood, but she struggles all the same.

She eyes the steam rising from generators and is careful to weave around them as she leaps from roof to roof, across to the edge of town and back again, watching for traces of the Jade Sword, of some hero, of the desert of which she hears and reads but has never seen.

In the distance, she hears a half-choked scream. She cocks her head, then takes off without pause and leaps fast, with surety, mindful of the advice of the Jade Sword.

She lands—her left foot light on the cobblestones, her right heavy on the hand of a large man. She shifts all her weight onto her left; she kicks, her right foot pointed.

Mok-Seung lifts the girl and her purse off the ground. Her arms are just strong enough. She really should increase her training, she thinks, as she pants and increases speed, dragging the girl with her.

• • •

"MINERS TERRORIZED BY COLORED VIGILANTES!" says the *Times,* followed by mention of a slow in production and meetings broken up in migrant camps.

The Chinese broadsheet is no less excited. "JADE SWORD SAVES TWO MINERS; MAY BE WORKING WITH LOCALS." She wonders how the Jade Sword travels between Melbourne and Bendigo, what secrets are being harbored out beyond the city.

• • •

Mok-Seung sits at her table, *The Art of War* pushed as far away as her arm can push it. She's stuck on Pian Ten, unsure how to move forward. She has her atlas before her instead, mapping the route from Melbourne to the gold fields of Bendigo. She considers how one fortifies such a town in such terrain. She looks for more available information on inhabitants and history and threats. Mok-Seung considers the indigenous population and the possibility of their ghosts and spirits and *bunyips*, and hopes she's making the right leaps.

She knows she's making excuses, but she tells herself it is a useful real-world application of her studies, and no tactician could disapprove.

It's with relief that she hears the sounds of the front bell heralding the arrival of some visitor. In the absence of Baba and Mama, she must set aside her studies and greet the guest.

Can Sin-Man is short and firm, plainly dressed as if she were a monk or a scholar. Although Mok-Seung thought such people kept themselves to the mainland, she wonders if perhaps Can Sin-Man might be both monk and scholar, here in this place.

Can Sin-Man bows and takes the proffered seat facing the door with a contented smile. She directs a sharper smile to Auntie Hong, who hovers by the door with a smug grin on her face.

"Oh, you've come for a visit, have you?"

Can Sin-Man's smile widens before she turns to Mok-Seung.

"Mok-Seung *mui mui*," Can Sin-Man says after inquiring after her parents, after the business. "I have brought you a present."

Mok-Seung is confused by this gesture from Can Sin-Man, friendly and well-known by name but ultimately still a stranger. Confused, that is, until she unwraps the red fabric to find green fabric within: a ribbon with the character for jade embroidered on it. "Oh," Mok-Seung says, with a start. "This isn't mine."

"It is mine."

Mok-Seung looks up, meets Can Sin-Man's eyes. She glances back at the empty door where Auntie Hong was—and from which she has silently disappeared.

Can Sin-Man smiles and picks up *The Art of War* from where Mok-Seung dropped it on the table. "Pian Eight is my favorite," she says, turning the pages. "I have read it many times, though it feels unusual to read it now, in this place." She reads aloud, "If, on the other hand, in the midst of difficulties we are always ready to seize an advantage, we may extricate ourselves from misfortune."

Mok-Seung thinks upon the words, familiar from frequent encounters but sounding so new from Can Sin-Man's presence. Can Sin-Man smiles welcomingly as she returns the book to the table.

"It is time for this old Jade Sword to take an apprentice. You know some of the old styles, but you're adapting to these new ones. I think you will flourish with me. And your encounter with the airship tells me that you need a teacher." Her hand rests lightly on her tea cup, and Mok-Seung hastily reaches for the pot.

"You're mistaken," she replies mildly. "I have a teacher." Can Sin Man touches her finger to Mok-Seung's wrist, and for a moment, Mok-Seung thinks Can Sin-Man is taking her pulse, but she shakes the thought and leans forward to pour.

"Auntie Hong has taught you all she knows." She pauses significantly, brings her tea to her mouth and sips politely, carefully. "I know, because she was my teacher before she retired. But there is more for you to learn."

Mok-Seung shakes her head. "What Auntie Hong has taught me serves me well."

"But will it serve you further?"

Mok-Seung will not be pressed, not even in the face of Auntie Hong's silent disappearance and Can Sin-Man's knowing smile, and she refills Can Sin-Man's teacup in lieu of an answer.

They speak a little longer, but here it is, the point Can Sin-Man has come here to make. She is blunt, as is their way, elder to youth: Mok-Seung is adaptable and keen, and Can Sin-Man wants to impart and, unusually, wants to learn, too. Mok-Seung thinks of the hints of the desert, of the Jade Sword's technique, of giving meaning to their presence here in this place.

Can Sin-Man soon takes her leave, gathering her skirts around her as if she always wears them and is never leaping across the roofs and bounding lightly between rising airships. She stops at the door.

"We are in a different country," she says, "and there are always new advances to make. What kind of warrior would you be if you were to stop here, where you are? There is no room for us here if we cannot adapt."

Can Sin-Man's words—and her smile—sit with Mok-Seung through the fading afternoon, twisting around the shadow already in her heart, until Lou Kong comes to light the lamps, and Auntie Hong tells her she will be late for dinner.

• • •

The summer rains fall and bring with them a sudden chill and the smell of petrichor, staining the cobblestones red as they mix with the dust blown in with the wagons.

The broadsheets report nothing.

• • •

Mok-Seung climbs out of her window and scales the eucalyptus up onto the roof. She keeps climbing higher, until she can climb no further. If she had the skills, she could scale the side of the Darrods building and keep on going, but she knows Can Sin-Man is right. She can go no further.

She sits above Melbourne, watches a night officer ride past testing his new augmented bicycle, watches airships floating high as points of light that dull into shadows as the sun rises over the city.

She looks out toward the city's edge.

• • •

Mok-Seung rests her hand on the brush, its bristles long and clean. She imagines it as an extension of her body. Imagines a fountain pen in her hand instead. Imagines a paint brush. Imagines using her finger. "I should pay Sin-Man *cheche* a visit," she says. "I enjoyed her company."

Auntie Hong hums. "I'm sure she would appreciate it. Your Mama always enjoyed her visits."

Beside Mok-Seung sits *The Art of War*, a note in Pian Ten. "If you know the enemy and know yourself, your victory will not stand in doubt; if you know Heaven and know Earth, you may make your victory complete." She knows nothing about her terrain and the situation she is in, and she knows very little about herself.

She pauses her brush; when has Mama ever visited Sin-Man cheche? She turns to ask Auntie Hong, but her Ayi's grin is beatific, and she merely pushes Mok-Seung back to her work.

And so she writes, focusing on the brush strokes, breathing slowly as the sun fades to red.

Stephanie Lai is a Chinese-Australian writer and occasional translator. She has published long meandering thinkpieces in *Peril Magazine*, the *Toast*, the *Lifted Brow* and *Overland*. Of recent, her short fiction has appeared in the *Review of Australian Fiction*, *Cranky Ladies of History*, and the *In Your Face Anthology*. Despite loathing time travel, her defense of Dr Who companion Perpugilliam Brown can be found in *Companion Piece* (2015). She is an amateur infrastructure nerd and a professional climate change adaptation educator (she's helping you survive our oncoming climate change dystopia). You can find her on twitter @yiduiqie, at stephanielai.net, or talking about pop culture and drop bears at no-award.net.

Origin Story

Carrie Vaughn

Living in Commerce City, odds are you're going to get caught up in something someday—pinned down in the crossfire of some epic battle between heroes who can fly and villains with ray guns, held captive in a hostage crisis involving an entire football stadium, or even trapped by a simple jewelry heist or bus hijacking.

When my turn came, I got stuck in a bank robbery.

I was waiting in line to make a deposit when a hole opened up in the ceiling. A glowing green laser light traced a perfect circle, and that section of ceiling dropped to the floor, scattering the line of people underneath in a cloud of dust and noise. I was too far back to really see what was happening, just that there was debris and screaming, some of which might have been mine. Then Techhunter rappelled through the hole, wielding a laser pistol and shouting at everyone to get down and lie still. We did.

He was just one guy. No henchmen, no partners. That was Techhunter's M.O. in the news stories I'd read. He worked alone, with only his machines as backup. This time, he had a swarm of hovering metallic balls zooming down the hole in the ceiling with him. They fanned out around the room and trained tiny cannons on everyone. They probably shot lasers or tranquilizer darts. Surely in a place like Commerce City, with so many vigilantes and criminal gangs battling each other, bank tellers would be trained how to handle situations like this, but the ones here all stepped back from their counters, arms in the air, staring at Techhunter with trembling gazes. As if they didn't live in Commerce City, where this kind of thing happened on a monthly basis at least.

Techhunter didn't ask for the manager to open any safes; he just drilled through the locks with his laser pistol, collected cash and emptied a pair of safety deposit boxes into a hard-sided case. He wore wide goggles that hid most of his face, and a headset with all kinds of wires and antennae sticking from it, probably what he used to control all his devices. His suit was made of some slick material, supple as leather but appearing to be much stronger, probably armored. Pants, tall boots, padded shirt, and a fitted trench coat, all in a midnight blue so dark it looked black, except when the light caught it right.

Everyone cowered. Except me. I couldn't help it, because by that time I'd had a chance to really look at him. The superhero stalker website Rooftop Watch had posted a half dozen or so pictures of Techhunter over the last couple of years, blurry action shots in semi-darkness, and I hadn't paid much attention because he was just another guy in a mask. Now, seeing him in person, the way he moved, smoothly and urgently; the way he studied the room and pursed his thin, slightly chapped lips—it was all familiar. I should have thought it was just a coincidence, but I was sure. Even under those face-obscuring goggles, I knew him.

Then he looked across the room at the one person not cowering in his presence. Through the goggles, he caught my gaze. His lips parted and he froze, just for a second. *He* knew *me*.

Before I could call his name—or think that maybe I shouldn't call his name, or find any way at all to ask what the hell he was doing here, a masked villain with a super-high-tech armory—the guy next to me reached out. While I'd been staring at Techhunter, this unassuming young businessman with a goatee and a red tie had very slowly and carefully drawn a gun out from inside his jacket. Was he an undercover cop or just paranoid? Didn't know, didn't care, because he proceeded to take aim at my old boyfriend.

I grabbed the gun out of his hand and threw it across the room. He wasn't expecting that, and he stared at me in consternation, stammering out, "What—"

And I was kneeling there, shocked at what I had done, wondering if this made me a bad guy now. Again, Techhunter and I looked at each other, and I started to call out, "Jas—"

But he shouted me down. "You—get up!"

I knew that voice. It was definitely Jason. I stood, and then it all happened very fast. Police sirens blared—the whole incident had only started a couple of minutes ago—and some guy on a megaphone shouted at him to stand down and lower his weapons, and someone else yelled that Techhunter had a hostage. Remote gun spheres altered course to zoom toward the front of the bank and aim their weapons outward.

Techhunter—Jason?—went into action, hauling the case's strap over his shoulder as he wrapped his arm around my waist and pulled me close. He clipped himself to the rope, then clipped me, and at some command the thing wound up on a winch and carried us to the roof of the bank and then into his stealth hovercraft. The floating gun spheres swarmed back up with him. A dozen police cars surrounded the bank now, and cops poured out of them with weapons drawn, ready to fire until they saw me, the hostage. The hatch at the bottom of the ship closed, Jason went to the cockpit, pulled back on a control stick, and I fell over as the thing tipped back and zoomed away.

Techhunter was not known for kidnapping, but I must have been special.

I wasn't hurt, wasn't even scared. I was just waiting for him to stop being busy so I could ask what the hell was going on. The ship was small. The cargo area, which held the rope winch and a few equipment cases, wasn't any bigger than the back of an SUV. The cockpit was one bucket seat surrounded by control panels, looking out through panels of a wraparound windshield.

We flew for what felt like a long time.

* * *

The last time I saw Jason Trumble was the week before high school graduation, right after he found out he wouldn't be allowed to graduate because he had too many unexcused absences from gym class. He punched his hand through the window between the principal's office and reception, shattering the glass with the sound of ringing bells, and marched out, right past where I was waiting for him, dripping blood along the way and not caring. I called after him, and he turned around to look at me. My heart fluttered a bit, thinking, he really does care, he really does like me. But then he scowled and kept going out the front doors, never to return. I got a birthday card from him a few months later. He said he was joining the army, which sounded like a bad idea to me, but he didn't give me a return address, and he hadn't answered his e-mail since he left, so I had no way to tell him that.

I decided maybe he didn't care after all, and I moved on.

• • •

That was eight years ago. Sometime between then and now, he'd become a supervillain. On reflection, I wasn't surprised, not exactly.

I waited for Jason to say something.

The ship finally came to rest on something solid, street or helipad or garage or something. I was able to sit up and arrange myself more comfortably. The engine whined to silence, the hum of electricity ceased, and in the cockpit Jason flipped a last few switches before turning around. He seemed to take a deep breath, as if steeling himself, before crouching to enter the cargo hold.

He took off the goggles and headset, and it really was him, his sharp nose and thin eyebrows, spiky brown hair and scowling expression.

"Sorry about that," he said. "You okay?"

"Jason, I—" For just a second, I teared up, but the moment passed. "I thought you died or something. What happened to you?"

He looked at me for a long time, his expression distant, thoughtful, before saying, "It's good to see you, Mary."

And just like that we fell against each other, hugging, like none of the time since high school had passed. After that long, impossible hug, we sat side by side, knees pulled up, and he explained.

"I tried to join the army. Washed out of basic. I guess I should have known that wasn't going to work out. I . . . kicked around for a while. Here and there, this and that. Picked up some things." He glanced around the ship, regarding his gear with a pleased, proud smile.

"Why didn't you write? Why didn't you tell me what happened to you?"

"I didn't want you to worry," he said, deadpan.

"*Jason.*"

"Do you . . . um . . . want a drink or something? I only have water and coffee and a couple of energy drinks. Can't really *drink* drink while I'm out in the ship. You know."

"Coffee, I guess."

We drank coffee he poured from a thermos into Styrofoam cups. I had another flashback of us in high school, at the diner after an all ages show or late movie, sucking on coffee and planning to take over the world.

It had been a joke, I thought.

"Um. I never expected to run into you like that," he said. "I thought I was seeing things, but you just kept staring at me."

"I'd recognize you anywhere."

"Yeah, but what were you *doing* there?"

"Making a deposit. Going to the bank, like a normal person."

A bit of the light went out of his eyes. "So that's what you are, now? Normal?"

He said it like I was the one who'd been committing crimes.

I'd been doing really well with my own tailoring and dressmaking business. I was designing, making custom evening gowns and wedding dresses. A couple more high-end gigs like that, and I'd be on my way. I was proud of myself, but I couldn't read Jason's expression, which seemed blank, uncomprehending. Old high school Jason would have accused me of selling out, making cocktail dresses for society bitches, hustling for their dime like some peasant. But old high school Jason had left me behind. I spent a lot of months—years, maybe even—missing him and wondering where he'd gone. Then I just couldn't, anymore. Would new Jason, with his unreal gear and flashy persona, understand that?

"Well," I said. "And look at you. You're famous. Techhunter, one of the archvillains of Commerce City."

"Yeah. Who'd have thought?"

I always figured he'd either take over the world or die in a gutter, and since I never heard what happened, I figured it was the latter. I should know better than to make assumptions.

For the next minute or so, we drank coffee in silence. We never had a problem coming up with things to say in the old days. The old days—as if we were really that old, as if it really had been so long. It hadn't, on the scale of things, but it sure felt like it.

"I'm sorry," he said finally, abruptly. I stared at him, not sure what to say. "For not letting you know what happened to me. For not telling you where I was. I figured . . . I just figured you were better off without me. That it'd be better if I left you alone."

I wanted to punch him. I had to think about it, but then I did it, slamming my fist into his shoulder. My knuckles banged against the armor plate protecting his bicep.

"Ow," he muttered, rubbing his arm, just as I hissed and studied my skinned knuckles.

"Jerk," I said. I looked around his ship, gray and sleek, like something from outer space, with levers and monitors, winches and crates holding who knew what, hatch covers and control panels. The hovering gun spheres nested in a rack on one wall, lurking ominously. Had he built all this? Found it and co-opted it for himself? And why did he rob banks, when he could use all this to be a hero?

"I didn't do it for the money," he said, when he caught me staring at the case of loot he'd taken from the bank. "I don't need money, it's just to confuse them. But the safety deposit boxes—"

"I don't think you should tell me," I said, gesturing for him to stop, closing my eyes, as if I could unsee it. I should have waited until tomorrow to drop off that deposit. But no. I wouldn't have missed this for anything.

"Right. You're right."

More silence. Too much to say, rather than too little, maybe.

"And I'm not really trying to take over the world," he said, as if he had to explain himself. "I'm not that ambitious. Not yet, anyway." He showed that sly grin again.

A beeping alarm drew him back to the cockpit, where he checked a monitor. "Police band," he explained. "They'll sweep the area soon. I have to get moving." He swallowed, licked his lips. Just like he had when he asked me to prom. "Would you—do you want to come with me?"

He'd said later that asking me to prom was the most difficult, bravest thing he'd ever done, not because he was afraid I'd say no, but because he was afraid to go to prom at all. He was sure he wouldn't be welcome. He didn't think it would even be fun. No matter what he did, he'd be made fun of, pushed to the fringes, like he always was. But he wanted to show that they couldn't keep him out, either. So just for once, he did the normal thing and asked a girl to prom, and of course I said yes, because I'd been waiting for him to ask, and we hatched a plan together. I made our outfits, his tuxedo and my knee-length cocktail dress, out of leather scavenged from thrift store handbags and biker jackets. We looked wicked, in patched-together leather in a dozen different shades of brown and black. He found a black lily for my corsage, and I made a boutonniere from old resistors and wires. God, did people stare at us, but once we got to the hotel ballroom we behaved ourselves so no one could kick us out. We even had a good time.

I thought—I'd thought back then—that things could only get better, but then came that meeting in the principal's office, and that was the last straw for Jason, who must have decided that not only were the rules not fair, they weren't worth dealing with at all.

I wished I'd known what to say to him, then. Or that he might have thought then of asking me to run away with him. I'd said yes to prom, hadn't I?

Shaking my head was hard. My neck felt stiff, and I wondered if I pulled a muscle when he winched me up on the rope. Or if this was just hard.

"I can't," I said. "My business is taking off. I've worked too hard. I can't leave all that. Even if it is *normal*."

He nodded as if he really did understand, as if he hadn't really expected me to say yes. "Yeah, okay. So . . . you must have a boyfriend."

That was his problem. He made too many assumptions.

That anxious-sounding beeping from the police monitor sounded again. All serious, he went to check, flipped a couple of switches and held a hand to his ear—listening to a signal coming in through an earbud.

"They're getting close. I'll let you out, but I should probably tie you up. They'll treat you like a victim then, and not an accomplice—"

"No," I said, the word just bursting out of me like a gunshot.

He stopped, his expression neutral. "No, what?"

"No, I don't have a boyfriend." I had never really wanted one, after he left.

He had this look in his eyes, hungry and angry, and I didn't know if I'd given him the right answer, or the wrong one. He moved back to the cargo compartment, was just a few inches away from me, a length of rope in hand. He smiled apologetically. "Then can I maybe see you again?"

I nodded, and by some mutual signal that I didn't recognize, we came together. His hand pressed around my waist, the length of our torsos fit together, my hands on his shoulders, our lips, kissing. A slow, careful, melting kiss. Both his arms wrapped around my back, me clinging to the slippery fabric of his trench coat. Then we came up for air.

Just like the old days, except so much sadder, because we knew now what we'd lost.

We had to let go when we heard the police sirens through the hull of his hovercraft.

In addition to tying nylon cord around my wrists and ankles, he blindfolded me, explaining carefully what he was doing as he did it, tying the cloth over my eyes, securing me to the rope and winch, gently setting me on what felt like a concrete sidewalk. Giving my hand a squeeze as he released me.

The hatch hissed as it slid shut, the engine whined as the ship climbed away, and I listened until I couldn't.

The police arrived just a minute later.

• • •

They were very nice to me, because I was the victim. Jason had been right about that. I sat in an empty conference room at the police station, a blanket over my shoulders and a paper cup of bitter coffee in my hands, waiting for someone to arrive to take a statement. I was assured it wouldn't take long, that it wouldn't be difficult. They asked if I wanted a social worker or victim rights advocate with me. I said no.

A pair of detectives arrived, a man and a woman, both in their thirties and looking haggard, like they'd been working for a long time without sleep. They sat across from me, and the woman set down a manila folder stuffed to bursting with records.

They asked the standard questions. My name, why I was at the bank, what happened there, why Techhunter had picked me, and what had happened after. Did I know where he'd taken me? Did he say anything about where he was going? About what he stole from the bank and why? And so on, and I didn't know anything, and I said so. The detectives nodded, resigned.

"Did he tell you his name? Who he really is under the costume?" the man asked, and I knew I was in trouble. I could feel my face blush and my stomach turn over. They must have heard my stomach turn over.

"No," I answered truthfully, because Jason hadn't told me. I'd just known.

"Can you tell us anything about him? Anything that might lead to identifying him?" he asked, and again I didn't really feel like I was lying when I said no.

Then the woman pulled a photo from the file folder and slid it across the table to me. "Do you remember this, Mary?"

It was our formal picture from prom, the two of us side by side in the patchwork leather outfits I'd made, only Jason was snarling and flipping off the camera with both hands, and I was hanging on his arm and laughing. The photographer didn't bother trying to get us to stand still and be nice, just snapped the picture and took our ten bucks for copies. Mine was in my scrapbook back home, which meant this was Jason's copy, and I wondered how they got it. Or maybe the photographer had saved an extra proof or something. I wasn't going to ask.

We looked so young. So bony and new, and I wouldn't say we looked particularly happy, but we were something, and it was good.

"Yes, I remember that," I answered, and the catch in my voice made me sound vulnerable and worthy of sympathy, I hoped.

The woman spoke kindly. "Mary, what would you say if I told you that we suspect that Techhunter may be Jason Trumble? That he may have taken you hostage because he knew you?"

"I would say that makes a lot of sense." I hoped my watering eyes made my story sound more true.

"Did he reveal himself to you? Give you any sign that he was Jason and that he knew you? Did he say anything that made you suspect?"

Everything, I didn't say. I shook my head and touched the edge of the picture, like I was mourning him. I could have told them anything, that he didn't look anything like that skinny kid in the picture anymore, that he used a machine to disguise his voice, that I couldn't recognize anything under his goggles. But they assumed all that, so I didn't have to say anything. And that's how I became a bad guy. Henchwoman to a supervillain, and weirdly that was okay.

"If Techhunter contacts you again, you'll let us know?" the woman said, and I nodded. The man handed over a tissue, and I scrubbed my eyes.

• • •

They let me go. I assume they're watching me, and that my phones are tapped and my computer hacked and all that. I'm not really even angry about it, because of course, and if it were any other former girlfriend of any other supervillain I'd think it was the right thing to do. But I also can't stand the idea that they'll use me to catch Jason. So I mostly don't talk about him at all, and I hope he doesn't contact me. At the same time, I hope he does. I constantly watch for little flying drones, buzzing as they follow me, and wait for him to make his move.

But he's too smart for that, so he hasn't.

Yet.

Carrie Vaughn is best known for her New York Times best-selling series of novels about a werewolf named Kitty, who hosts a talk radio show for the supernaturally disadvantaged, the fourteenth installment of which is *Kitty Saves the World*. She's written several other contemporary fantasy and young adult novels, as well as upwards of 80 short stories. She's a contributor to the Wild Cards series of shared world superhero books edited by George R. R. Martin and a graduate of the Odyssey Fantasy Writing Workshop. An Air Force brat, she survived her nomadic childhood and managed to put down roots in Boulder, Colorado. Visit her at www.carrievaughn.com.

Eggshells

Ziggy Schutz

What's stupid is it doesn't even happen while she's masked up.

She's gotten plenty of bumps and bruises as Mayhem. That's what she's there for, to take damage. Tough skin and a pain tolerance that just won't quit. Their tank.

What about this is any different from all the other times?

It's a question she'll ask later. Right now, there's nothing in her head but static. She's looking up at a sky that is bright enough to sting. She's on the ground but has no idea how she got there, and she's not in uniform, which means it wasn't some big bad.

"Penny?" A face she knows hovers over her, concern obvious in her eyes. Pen knows her name, but when she goes to reach for it, it's not there. She closes her eyes against the light and makes a grunt of acknowledgment.

"You alright, Penelope?" That's another person she knows. Moses. A classmate. She feels a moment of pride for remembering his name before frustration chases that away. Remembering the name of a boy who's been in her class since kindergarten is no triumph. What's wrong with her?

"What happened?" Pen's voice sounds funny—slurred and slow. A scowl makes her face crumple as she tries again. "Why am I on the ground?"

Still not right. She goes to push herself up, and immediately there's a helping hand on her back. With gritted teeth, she allows it, because she still doesn't want to reopen her eyes, because something's obviously happened, and because she's not actually sure she can do it on her own.

"You slipped on the ice. It looked like you hit your head."

"We called Davie, he says he's coming to pick you up."

"Do you need to go to the hospital?"

Her protests come out just as garbled as the rest of her words, which they take as a yes. Davie must have told the team, because it's Kieran's car that rolls up, Davie in the passenger seat. Their leader drives them to the hospital while Moses and Davie switch, her brother keeping her head steady while Moses fills the two in on what happened. The girl doesn't come with them. She says she can't stand the smell of hospitals, they make her ill, but demands they keep her updated.

Pen doesn't remember the girl's name until they reach the emergency room.

The thing is, it's not even a super serious concussion. She was only unconscious for a second or so. It means she needs supervision, that she shouldn't participate in anything physical until the symptoms—the headache the doctor assumes she's feeling, the way bright lights are making her eyes water, the slurred speech—go away.

"Probably won't be longer than a few weeks," the nurse says.

A few weeks will be the longest she's taken off from her heroing since they all started—almost two years ago now. Her little brother promises the nurse that he'll make sure she takes it easy, and then they're headed back home again. Moses promises he'll collect her class work and bring it over tomorrow, which means that not even the threat of missing stuff in school can save her from the doctor's orders.

Pen is not good at taking it easy. She mumbles her protests to Davie about how boredom isn't restful, but it's all for nothing. The minute she gets home, she falls into bed and sleeps for sixteen hours. She wakes up groggy and exhausted and proceeds to spend the next week hardly able to leave her room at all.

"Must have caught a cold at the hospital," her mother muses. Pen can't remember the last time she got sick. Davie keeps looking at her with wide, worried eyes, a look she isn't used to and quickly grows to hate. By the third day, he's gotten himself banned from her room. Not that it matters much. He's not the one grounded from physical activities. He can still spend every day after school with their "study group," the one that dons masks and costumes and goes out to save the city.

She'd watch them on TV, but the screen makes her vision swim.

Still, by the end of the week, she is feeling a lot better. She goes back to school wearing sunglasses like armor. Pen isn't exactly known for being talkative. If she still can't get out vowels quite right yet, no one needs to know.

Faking being okay shouldn't be this easy, she thinks.

• • •

Six months down the line, and still no one has noticed. She's made sunglasses her thing, doesn't even get questions about them anymore. If she makes her words frosty and scornful, no one will think their lack of speed is anything but intentional. The team doesn't even fuss over her when she takes a hit anymore.

The problem is that the only time she can properly pretend she's okay is when she's in her suit. When her mask hides the way her pupils sometimes don't quite react at the same time. When she leaves the speaking to her chattier teammates. It doesn't matter that she finds herself forgetting simple words (Warehouse. Fastidious. Sneaky). It doesn't matter at all.

Outside her suit, she feels like she is falling. Like the impact she doesn't remember is still just about to hit. Without the pressure of her helmet, the cracks in her head threaten to rattle apart. This is a problem, because Pen is already a girl of few words. Pen is the one you come to when you need a door kicked in. Even before she went and scrambled her brain, she did not have the vocabulary to talk about feelings or ask for help.

So she doesn't.

"Penny? Are you listening to me at all?"

"Hmm?" She isn't, really. Jenny's been going on about something for almost ten minutes now, and Pen tried to pay attention at first, she really did, but nothing was really making sense anyway. "Sorry, no."

Jenny's face crumples into an expression somewhere between annoyance and hurt. "What is up with you lately? You're always grumpy. You never wanna talk. Are you fighting with your boyfriend or something?"

Pen doesn't have a boyfriend, but people assume things about her and her team leader when they see them out of costume, and she doesn't correct them because it's easier for them to fill in the story than for her to tell it.

Maybe it's no surprise: her approach to this concussion. She keeps her mouth shut and lets others assume her story, assume she's okay, assume whatever they want. She has never really cared about what other people thought, has always been secure enough in her own skin that she doesn't mind what people see when they look at her. She's too busy saving lives, fighting supervillains.

She never really cared. But all of a sudden, the thought of pretending to have a boyfriend (the thought of pretending at all) is exhausting.

"We were never dating."

Jenny scoffs. "You've been dating for ages; don't try to pull that. You're together all the time. Unless you guys were faking it . . . Oh my god, are you coming out to me? Is this what's happening?"

Pen has been open about her sexuality since she was seven. It's just that people look at her long blonde hair and her soft curves and they don't ask. They don't get close enough to realize that under every bit of fat is muscle hard as steel. They don't wonder about the days she paints her nails rainbow. They see what they want to see.

"I'm going home," she tells Jenny, and leaves before Jenny can splutter a response.

• • •

"Do you think lying runs in our family?"

Davie is hiding in her room because their parents are having an argument again. It's not that they'll do anything to hurt them, it's just that if their parents spot either of their children lingering around the war zone, they'll try to pull them into the conversation, ask them what they think of whatever topic they've decided to throw down over this time. Some parents fight with raised voices and thrown objects. Their parents fight over the dinner table in low, lofty tones, sometimes with the help of a tablet between them to bring up relevant studies and statistics. Lawyers, even out of their courtroom suits.

Davie snorts. "How should I know? I'm adopted."

"Careful!" She reaches over and slaps a hand over his mouth. "Say that too loud and they'll decide it's time to revisit nature vs. nurture."

He promptly licks her hand.

Because she is a veteran superhero with hundreds of hours of training under her belt, she does not shriek.

But it's a near thing.

Jenny pulls Pen aside the next day to tell her not to worry, that she does forgive her. She gets that Pen is under a lot of pressure right now because her grades aren't as good as they usually are, and besides, Jenny was reading something about how families with adopted kids can sometimes start to struggle when the children all hit puberty.

Pen doesn't hit her.

But that's a near thing too.

• • •

"Okay, here's a question for you, Pen." Sandhya, no-you-cannot-call-me-Sandy, has a way of cornering people without ever really getting close. That's how Pen feels right now. Cornered, even though Sandhya is across the table fiddling with a piece of machinery Davie put together, not even looking at Pen. It's a game the two like to play: Davie puts little machines together and Sandhya finds the perfect way to make them fall apart. Sometimes they use their powers and sometimes they don't, but they never seem to get tired of it. Still, it seems rather unfair that Sandhya can do this and interrogate Pen all at the same time.

"Hit me," says Pen, and savors how sharp the T is, how the M doesn't linger. She's been practicing quick mutterings in front of the bathroom mirror. She feels a little worn thin and can't remember ever talking so much, even if no one is around to hear it, but the results are starting to show.

It's been seven months since her slip, and she's starting to feel like her lips, tongue, teeth are her own again.

"Did something happen? You've been acting different."

"I got a concussion." The topic sends her right back to soft consonants, vowels tangling together. "Remember?"

"Oh, that was ages ago." Sandhya waves a delicately henna'd hand covered in grease dismissively. "I meant like this week."

Pen can't think of anything she's been doing differently, especially not within sight of her team. She shrugs, but that's avoiding the question, isn't it? That's letting Sandhya make up her own reasons.

Pen's really tired of other people telling her story.

"I'm not getting along with my friends at school," she says, and Sandhya actually looks up from her project to smile at her, surprised at the straight answer.

"Good thing you've got us, right? Remember, if they're dragging you down, they're probably not worth it."

Pen lets the words sink into her, because drag was a word she misplaced the other day, and she wants to remember the way Sandhya smiled at her.

The next day, Pen sees Jenny and opens her mouth to say hello, but something entirely different spills out.

"I don't like the nickname Penny," she tells Jenny, and she doesn't stumble. "It was cute that we matched when we were kids, but it doesn't really fit anymore."

Jenny gapes at her, and it takes her a good beat to recover.

"Um, alright. What should I call you, then?"

"My study group calls me Pen."

"And you prefer Pen?" There's disbelief in Jenny's tone. Pen thinks the question might be less about the name and more about the company she prefers.

"Yes. I do."

Pen sits with Moses during math, and the numbers only swim a little.

• • •

It's been ten months since Pen's concussion, and she's pinned underneath some concrete. Her helmet and mask are gone—must have been knocked off when the giant lizard thing they were fighting flung her several blocks with its surprisingly quick tail. The sun is at just the wrong angle, or maybe that's her head, because no matter how she twists, it's still shining right in her eyes. Her head is already feeling strange, like it isn't attached to her body quite right, and if Pen could feel pain, she's pretty sure she'd be hurting right now.

Well, her body *is* getting crushed by the remnants of what looks like a wall of the library, so she'd be hurting regardless. That's beside the point.

It takes her longer than it should to find her voice, and her chest clenches at the thought of having to start over, of new holes in her vocabulary when she's just started to patch the old ones. But after a few moments of struggling, a strangled "Help!" leaves her lips, and within the minute, Davie is standing over her.

"Pen?" He's shaken enough that he forgets to use her codename. It's okay. There's no one around. "Don't worry, we'll get you out of there, okay? Hold on."

Whether by accident or design, Davie stands in the light as he works, grabbing gears and other bits of metal from the various pockets hidden in his suit. Pen loves watching technopaths work, and Davie's the best she's ever seen. Her panic fades away, leaving her more than a little embarrassed, because this is nowhere she hasn't been before. Just not since the injury.

"I didn't realize it was you at first," Davie says as he guides his creation to where it will have the best leverage to lift the rubble enough for Pen to get out from under it. "I wasn't aware that 'help' was in your vocabulary."

Privately, Pen didn't think it had been, either. She can't ever remember saying it out loud before. It doesn't feel as shameful as she thought it would.

Out loud, she groans, "Less talking, more lifting, little brother."

But her mask is gone, so there's nothing to hide her proud grin.

The fight does make her lose a few things. But no more than the sirens and flashing lights did that night she walked home without her shades. It's predictable: this two steps forward, one step back. Aggravating, but it no longer feels like her world is falling out from under her every time she has a bad day. That's what progress feels like, right? Like finding balance in a mess. Like finding new words under the rubble.

Pen stops thinking about "getting things back to normal" and starts thinking about what she can do to feel better, what she can do to be better. Even if better looks different than it used to.

• • •

It's been eleven months since her head hit that ice, and Pen still can't spell like she used to, but she's better at remembering to spell-check now. She still keeps shades on her at all times, but she's finding that she needs them less and less.

"Maybe it's because it's winter now. You've got cloud cover."

"Could be."

She and Sandhya are early for weekend training, sitting on the bench outside of the shut-down school they use as a makeshift base. They don't technically have a key, because that's a thing the leader has, and although neither of them would have any trouble breaking in, they let Kieran have this faux victory. Anyway, it's one of those late-in-the-year days that is just cold enough to make you feel like you're more awake than usual, and the two of them both want to soak up as much of it as they can. Pen's mind feels clearer than she can remember it feeling in a long time, and she closes her eyes, wanting to commit the feeling to memory, so she can come back to it when the clouds leave the sky and take up residence in her head instead.

"It's good to see you looking so happy."

Pen blinks, and opens her eyes. Slowly, because that's something she does now, giving her eyes time to adjust. "Was I not happy before?"

"You might have been." Sandhya shrugs, drawing little symbols into the frost beside her. "You just never told anyone one way or another."

"I'm not saying anything now, either."

"Yeah, but I can see it, silly." Sandhya reaches over and tangles a hand in her hair, probably because she knows how long Pen took getting it untangled this morning. Her friends know her better than she ever really gave them credit for. "You let yourself smile, now."

Pen can't think of any response, but that's okay. Her smile should be enough.

She's still barely passing math. She asks Moses to tutor her, and he has the decency to not look too shocked at her request for assistance.

"Of course, I can," he says. "But don't you already go to a study group every day after school?"

"I can make time for this. Anyway, we're all more like a group of friends than anything productive."

Moses laughs. "Fair enough. It's good to hear you have some of those, Pen."

He must have overheard Davie using the nickname. He's always had a good eye for details. His way of learning math is completely different than hers, but that's okay. That's what she needs. Sometimes, when a tunnel collapses, you're better off foregoing clearing it out in favor of digging an entirely new one. She thinks of her brain as an ant hill, or a subway network, and writes down everything Moses is telling her. The dirt shifts. The tunnel holds.

• • •

"I was really worried, you know," says Davie, in a surprising moment of sincerity.

It is almost a year to the day since Pen slipped and cracked her head against the icy pavement. She thinks about looking for her hospital bracelet to find out the exact date but decides she doesn't care. What she cares about is this: she and her brother are playing some convoluted card game that she's pretty sure is just a bastardized version of Go Fish, expertly ignoring the world past the bedroom door. At least for the evening.

"Because you know I'm ruthless when it comes to card games?"

He rolls his eyes. "In your dreams. No, I mean when you hit your head. You were always quiet, but for a while there, I thought I was going to forget what your voice sounded like altogether."

"Oh." She looks down at the cards in her hands, but the numbers are starting to be unreadable, and she's much more interested in what is going on across from her. This is a conversation she's been expecting for months now. She's honestly shocked Davie lasted this long. She owes him her full attention.

His over-expressive face looks almost cartoonish in the low light of the candles they've been playing by, and Pen takes a moment to take him in. People used to wonder about them, opposites in every way. Davie with his dark skin and tight curls, Pen with her bright blue eyes and pale blonde hair—long even then.

She's thinking of cutting it. Sandhya offered to do it for her–she thinks she's going to take her up on the offer. Pen wants to know if it will make her feel lighter, shedding it all. Wants to see who looks back at her from the mirror.

It wasn't just looks that had people talking, either. Davie, despite being the younger by eight months, despite his dramatic origin story (abandoned on a doorstep like a comic book hero, small enough to barely count as a baby at all, adopted more out of a sense of duty than anything) was talking a full half a year before Pen got around to saying her first word. He spent their shared childhood charming everyone he came across, while Pen hung back. Not shy, like people always guessed, but barely knee-height and already distant. Already weighing each word she said like she only got so many.

"It's a good thing she took to school as well as she did," she remembers overhearing her mother tell one of the other moms. "Otherwise we were going to have to start getting her tested for things."

It was her brother who was initially approached by Kieran, too. She was only brought on board because of Davie. Davie who somehow knew he could trust this strange, focused boy at face value when he said he was putting together a team of superheroes. Davie who whispered like a proud secret, "Oh yeah, my sister can't feel pain and her skin doesn't break."

Pen owes a lot to her little brother. She's not sure if she's ever said that out loud before.

"Sorry for worrying you." She watches his mouth twist, probably preparing to protest against her apology. She doesn't let him get there. "And thanks."

"You don't need to apologize. And you don't need to thank me either, Pen."

"No, I do." She puts her cards down so she doesn't distract herself with them, then regrets doing it. This would be easier if she had something to fiddle with. "You're always looking out for me, even though you're the younger sibling—"

"Pen, you've been protecting me from big bad bullies since we were six."

It's her turn to make a face. "That's not . . . That's not what I'm talking about. That's different."

"Why?"

"Because I'm trying to thank you for helping me with . . . everything. You're just talking about how I used to punch people for you."

"I don't think those two things are as radically different as you are implying."

"Yes, they are. You're just trying to derail this now."

Davie drops his own cards to grab her hands. It reminds her of how they were as children, walking hand in hand, pretending not to notice the people staring. Back when their parents were still playing at being some power couple—their perfectly imperfect family standing still for the photographer's flash. Pen remembers smiling until her cheeks hurt.

She wonders what her parents would do if they found out their two children were part of the team of superheroes that keeps their city safe. Would they be proud? At least for the cameras? It wouldn't stop them from fighting. That would take more than superpowers. That would take a miracle.

"I am not trying to derail you, Pen. I'm just saying you've been there for me when I've needed you, too." He smiles. He's never had to force a smile for any camera. Smiling is his natural state. "And it's actually you who changed the subject first. I had a nice speech about how I was so concerned, but then you learned to be a big girl and ask for help from your friends, and how we're just so truly blessed that you learned to use your words, after all these years—"

"Shut up," she says, and shoves him back into their card game, barely missing the candles. They're both laughing, louder than Pen has laughed in a long time, and it goes on longer than Davie's tumble warrants, like it was just waiting for an excuse to escape.

"Cheese aside, I mean what I said." And he's beaming at her, like she's gone and done something incredible.

"I know. And I do, too. The whole thanks thing. I don't . . . I don't have the words to explain exactly what I'm thanking you for, but I am."

"Don't worry. I'm awesome. There will be plenty of things for you to thank me for in the future."

That earns him a punch in the arm.

From the dining room comes the unmistakable sound of a very large file slamming against their dinner table.

"When do you think is a good time to tell them they should get a divorce?" Pen muses.

"I'm hoping they buy us a car, first."

She snorts, "You would be a terror behind the wheel."

Terror is a word she couldn't think of for over three weeks. She remembers searching for the word that would describe what she felt when she would turn her head and the world would tilt. What it felt like to forget the address of the house she had lived in all her life. Now it comes to her with only a slight moment of hesitation. She's not as good as new. Not back to normal. But she's relearning what her world can look like.

Pen was never normal, even before the concussion. She just didn't have the words to deal with that before. Those words are all new.

Ziggy Schutz is a young queer writer living on the west coast of Canada. She's been a fan of superheroes almost as long as she's been writing, so she's very excited this is the form her first published work took.

When not writing, she can often be found stage managing local musicals and mouthing the words to all the songs. Ziggy can be found at @ziggytschutz, where she's probably ranting about representation in fiction.

Salt City Blue

Chris Large

"Skyball did *what*?" I said, unable to believe my ears.

My logistics manager took a deep breath. "He seriously damaged our lunar transit depot. It was an accident, Ms. Marshal. I believe he was trying to defend it. But you know how he loves to grandstand."

"And what have you done about it, Martin?"

I was going easy on Martin. He was the closest thing I had to a friend.

"What *could* I have done?" Fine beads of sweat had begun to form on his furrowed brow. "He's Skyball!"

Genevieve, my personal assistant, and Laura, a pale young graduate she'd recently hired, stood by the conference room's floor-to-ceiling windows, gazing out on a typically gray Salt City afternoon.

"You're my second in command, Martin," I said. "I expect you to manage situations like this."

"Ms. Marshal," said Martin. "With respect, no one could have managed this . . . including you."

Martin realized his mistake the moment the words were out of his mouth, but it was a moment too late. I rarely tolerated excuses, and even rarer were the times I admitted to being personally incapable of doing my job.

"For Chrissakes, Martin!" I cried. "What the hell am I paying you for?"

Martin sighed. "I really don't know, Ms. Marshal. You seem perfectly capable of running the company without advice from me . . . or anyone, for that matter." He glanced toward Genevieve and Laura, who continued to studiously ignore him. Beyond the windows, neon-colored mist crawled sluggishly between the city's edifices of glass and steel.

"This isn't about them!" I cried. "I'm talking to you. You're *gutless*, Martin. You're a plodder. You wouldn't recognize a hot prospect if it sat on your fat, fucking face! Now get out of my sight. I never want to see you again. You're fired!"

Martin's eyes snapped wide. He'd expected a tongue-lashing, but he clearly hadn't expected to lose his job. Neither had I intended to fire him. That's just the way it goes sometimes.

Martin's face drained of color. "You mean . . ."

"I mean *get out!*" I screamed, thumping the table with a clenched fist.

I waited for the sound of his departing footsteps to die a slow death then swiveled toward Genevieve and Laura.

"Now Laura, can you *please* remind me what the hell it is you do here? And why I shouldn't just fire your ass right now as—"

But something caught my attention beyond the bulletproof window-glass. A small, man-shaped speck shot soundlessly through the dark mist in the distance, lit intermittently by spotlights from the towers above.

"Jesus," I said, jumping from my chair. "It's the man of the hour. Look at the sonofabitch go."

I pushed past the two women and stood with my face so close to the glass it began to fog over, anger radiating from my skin in waves. "I wonder who he's going to bankrupt this time?" I muttered. "Thank God we don't have any material assets downtown."

As he cut through the rain and clouds, a vapor trail billowed out from a point behind his feet, a ghostly after-echo in the evening air. We'd all seen Skyball survive lightning strikes, rocket strikes, and meteor strikes on news vids. He had no known weakness, except perhaps Crimson Reign, Salt City's perennial enemy and Skyball's arch nemesis.

News media had linked the pair romantically. Some went as far as to suggest Skyball and Crimson Reign were the last of their kind, survivors from a dying planet who'd escaped and found their way to Earth, destined to be together, doomed to be apart.

"One of Crimson Reign's giant robots is causing havoc at the Mendelsohn Center," said Genevieve, touching her earpiece. "Twenty stories high with death-ray vision."

I sighed. No matter what Salt City's inhabitants thought of them, Skyball and Crimson Reign were the real players in town. The rest of us were just supporting cast.

"Um . . ." Laura's eyes were huge behind wire-framed glasses.

"What is it, Laura?"

"Ms. Marshal, your skin. It's . . . glowing."

• • •

"I've taken a blood sample," said Doctor Singer. "I'll run it overnight and have the results tomorrow." She dropped the vial into her bag and snapped it tight. "If you have any further symptoms, call me."

"But glowing skin? Have you ever heard of that before?"

Singer was well into her sixties and not given to fancy. She'd rushed to my offices because I was a woman with significant demands on my time and because I paid her a substantial retainer.

"Ms. Marshal, I can't diagnose what I can't see. Genevieve said you were standing by a window?"

"Yes," I replied. "In the conference room, watching Skyball fly downtown."

"Skyball doesn't interest me, Ms. Marshal. For how long did your skin 'glow'?"

"Twenty or thirty seconds. I didn't even know it was happening. Laura noticed."

"Laura? Who's Laura?"

I sighed deeply and put my head in my hands. "Christ, Doc. I don't know. I think I'm losing it."

"Hey, look at me." Doctor Singer fixed me with her gray, watery eyes. "Is it possible someone shone some type of ultraviolet light through your office windows?"

Sure, it was possible. That must have been what happened. Who ever heard of glowing skin?

• • •

Fuse was the most exclusive nightclub in town. From the bar, I caught a glimpse of a blond-haired kid with thick-rimmed glasses. I'd picked him up a few weeks back. God, I'd been drunk that night. All I could remember of the encounter was that he had a scar running the length of his abdominals down to his groin, and that we'd broken the headboard of my bed that night. The kid quickly disappeared into the crowd with a young brunette on his arm.

I didn't care. I came to *Fuse* to get laid, not find a life partner. I was a thirty-eight-year-old career businesswoman. If I'd ever wanted kids—and maybe once I had—the opportunity was rapidly slipping away, but in my current role as a ball-busting bitch, my life-expectations no longer extended to a loving husband and two point three kids.

A guy sat beside me and bought me a drink. He was tall, balding, and had a small paunch marking the beginnings of middle-age spread. I'm sure he told me what he did for a living, but between the music and the booze, I didn't much care. He earned enough to buy me three shots of scotch in the most expensive club in town. That was enough. Some nights you *won* the prize, some nights you *were* the prize. So long as everyone understood who the prize was, things generally worked out okay. That night, I was definitely the prize and Kevin knew it. I'll call him Kevin. He *looked* like a Kevin.

Kevin was all over me in the back seat of the limo as we sped across town to my apartment, taking a detour at Deakin and 41st to avoid the inner-city carnage caused by Crimson Reign's Robot of Death. The robot hadn't been messing about. If Crimson Reign and Skyball had been a couple in the past, he'd clearly done something to piss her off.

I was eager to see footage of the fight. Skyball's costume was often blasted, blown, or burned away, his skin being far stronger than any material known to man. He might have been a prize douchebag, but that was no reason to pass up an opportunity to catch a glimpse of an amazing body. Those abs—my *God!*

The driver's eyes strayed regularly, but we were close to my apartment, and I honestly didn't care. Kevin was getting playful. He'd unbuttoned my top and was kissing and biting my neck and ear. I liked it. Perhaps there was something to be said for a homely man after all.

At my apartment, Kevin had my shirt off before the DNA-locks had cycled open. As we tumbled into bed, Kevin panting like a hyperactive puppy, it was all I could do not to laugh. I wasn't expecting much in the way of foreplay but Kevin surprised me again, his long, slender fingers stroking me slowly, until I was well and truly ready.

"What the . . . ?" said Kevin.

I opened my eyes. Kevin's horrified features were bathed in a soft, aquamarine glow.

"Holy shit!" he cried, jumping out of the bed. "What the hell are you?"

I cast about for the source of the light.

Kevin bolted from the apartment, clothing bundled in his arms, muttering, "Oh my God," and "Let me out of here," over and over, becoming increasingly hysterical.

I lay unmoving on the bed, staring down at my naked body, my skin crawling with softly pulsating light.

"You are freaking kidding me," I muttered.

• • •

"There *wasn't* any light on in the bedroom, Doc, just me and my shiny blue butt." The telephone felt strangely insubstantial in my hand.

I'd had a rough morning, having woken up to a cross between a hangover and the worst case of the munchies in human history. For breakfast I'd inhaled a plate of eggs and leftover Madras curry "lite," before going back for beans and bacon. The bowl of banana yogurt had tasted a little tart before I'd washed it down with an entire pot of coffee. Not bad for someone whose average breakfast consisted of a slice of gluten-free toast and a skinny latte.

"I have some news for you, Helen," the doctor said eventually. Her voice sounded even drier over the phone, if that was possible

"Helen?" I replied. "You never call me Helen."

"Just shut up and listen for a moment," said the doctor in a stern voice. Doc Singer was probably the only person on Earth who could speak to me like that without getting an earful in return. I took a deep breath and braced myself for the worst.

"Are you calm?"

"Yes," I said. "I'm calm"

"Helen, you're pregnant."

"*The hell I am!*"

"All the symptoms are there," the doctor said. "Increased appetite, cravings, mood swings. Helen, you're *glowing* for crying out loud."

"Are you out of your mind?" I was on my feet in the middle of my bedroom, holding the phone in front of my face and shouting into the microphone. "Pregnant women have a healthy glow, Doc. *They don't light up like a fucking radioactive smurf!*"

"The human body is bioluminescent, Helen—usually at levels well below the ability for the human eye to detect. Your luminescence may have temporarily increased due to your condition. The blood test I conducted on you yesterday confirms pregnancy," the doctor said firmly. "I'd guess three weeks based on what I have in front of me right now."

It was possible. Three weeks back I'd picked up the blond kid with the thick-rimmed glasses and stomach scar—the one I'd seen the night before in *Fuse*. Even so, I wanted to argue. What I was going through was bizarre and frustrating and freakish, but it wasn't pregnancy.

Oddly though, I also wanted her to be right. If I was honest with myself—a rare enough occurrence, but not unheard of—this was the news I'd been secretly hoping to hear. Perhaps, looking back, it was the culmination of a plan I'd been subconsciously attempting to execute for years. I'd gone off birth control long ago, citing pill-induced hormone rage.

A tinkling sound caught my attention. Clenched in my white-knuckled fist were the shattered remains of my phone.

No matter, I had three more.

I dropped the mess of glass, aluminum and circuitry into the trash on my way to the recently-raided fridge. After a quick scan of its dismal contents, I pulled out a bottle of tomato juice and drank the lot. Footage of Skyball's battle with Crimson Reign's Robot of Death was playing on a news panel over the breakfast bar. His suit had been shot to tatters by bolts of energy blasting from the robot's single, ruby-red eye, and as usual, his rock-hard abs were on display for womankind to ogle the world over. But the news presenter's hysterical, yet unremarkable commentary barely registered. My head was spinning.

I was glowing, I was starving, and I appeared to have developed enough strength to crush small electronic objects with my bare hands. *I was pregnant.* The knowledge was like a little bead of happiness deep in my chest. Something no one else could see or touch or detect in any way. This baby was going to be mine to raise the way I wanted—to be the person I wanted it to be—without interference from some deadbeat dad who would likely just run off when things got too . . .

When things got too . . .

I snapped up the remote and hit the pause button.

It couldn't be. I stared at the news panel for a good couple of minutes, tomato juice dribbling down my chin.

In a daze, I rummaged through a drawer and pulled out a thick, black marker. The frozen, high-definition image was of Skyball grimacing determinedly at the robot. I swished my finger across the screen to center him and expanded the image.

I raised the marker and drew a pair of glasses onto Skyball's glaring eyes.

"Oh no," I muttered. "No, no, no."

My fingers tracked down the screen toward a faint scar running the length of his abdominal muscles, down into his fuzzed-out groin.

I tasted bile and ran for the toilet, into which I proceeded to vomit the contents of my stomach.

Welcome to pregnancy Helen Marshal. Tears ran freely from my eyes and I had more spit in my mouth than any woman should have to cope with, but I wasn't done. Once I'd finished throwing up breakfast, I moved on to dinner from the night before, along with a few of the more colorful cocktails Kevin had bought me.

When I was done with dinner there was wasn't much left in the tank, but my body appeared to be enjoying the sensation of vomiting so much that I continued dry retching for another few minutes, at which point I discovered the first disadvantage of a solo pregnancy.

There's no one to hold your hair.

• • •

"You look pale, Ms. Marshal," Genevieve said as I brushed by her toward my office.

"I *feel* pale," I answered without pause.

"You've had urgent calls from Tony Marsden."

Marsden wanted me off the board of directors. I didn't have time for small-minded pricks like him. "I'm busy today, Genevieve. I don't want to be disturbed. Martin can deal with Tony Marsden." I hung my coat on the rack and collapsed into my chair.

"Ms. Marshal, you *fired* Martin last night," my assistant reminded me, having followed me into my office from reception. "Don't you remember?"

I should never have fired Martin. I liked him, and I needed him at his desk. "Of course I remember, Genevieve. Please don't stand over me like some kind of anorexic praying mantis. Call Martin and get him back in here."

The look on Genevieve's face was one of open-mouthed disbelief. "B-But . . ." she stammered, wide eyes blinking behind her large glasses. "You were so adamant."

I switched on my desktop terminal and tapped in my passcode. "And I'm just as adamant now, if not more so."

"I'll call him right away," Genevieve replied, finally getting the message.

"Good girl," I said. "Oh, and while you're at it, I want you to get in touch with Skyball and arrange a meeting."

"I'm not sure Skyball does meetings . . . as such."

I sighed. Was I being unreasonable? "Genevieve, you came to me very highly recommended—"

"I'll do it now, Ms. Marshal," she said, turning and scurrying back to her desk.

The daily report flashed up on my screen. Production was down. Only forty thousand pounds of salt had been delivered to the lunar depot Skyball had damaged the day before, meaning I'd lost the company around three million dollars in a morning. And we'd lose another three million every day until repairs were complete. Clock one up for Skyball, our friendly neighborhood super-dick.

I hit the comm. "Genevieve, where's Laura? I have a job for her."

"I'm sorry Ms. Marshal, Laura hasn't come in today."

I literally saw red as my blood pressure hit the bell. "Genevieve!" I screamed. "*What kind of Mickey Mouse operation are we running here?* I mean, how much am I paying that tarted-up scarecrow to decide she'd rather not come to work today? *How much?* Get her on the phone. No, wait. *I'll* get her on the goddamn phone. You just . . . do whatever it was you were doing. Have you managed to get hold of Skyball yet? I mean, he must have a manager or something. How do the police communicate with him?"

"I'm speaking with the police now, Ms. Marshal," said Genevieve. "They say he just comes when he pleases."

"Comes when he pleases," I muttered. "Should be his *fucking byline!*"

I picked up the phone, intending to ring Laura and fire her on the spot, when I realized I had no idea what her number was.

It was the last straw. Without thinking, I leaped from my chair and upended my three hundred pound, solid mahogany desk like it was a child's mattress, shattering my vid-screen and sending files and newsprint flying in the process.

As paper fluttered down around me, I decided I'd had enough. Skyball owed me an explanation. If he was an alien, and I was pregnant with his child, I damn well wanted to know what kind. But even more importantly, my body was going haywire, and he was going to give me some answers. That, or there was gonna be one hell of a bar fight at the club tonight.

• • •

Dark rain fell hard in the lane outside *Fuse*. Water overflowed from rooftop gutters, tumbling in waterfalls to the sidewalk before gushing furiously into litter-clogged drains. I huddled in the shadows, watching clubgoers hurry in and out of *Fuse*, grouped under umbrellas or scurrying for cabs, designer label jackets tented over their heads for shelter.

A cluster of neon signs further down the lane cast an ominous, bloody hue across the shimmering pavement. I waited for forty minutes before finally catching a glimpse of him. Three cabs were backed up outside the entrance, and from the last stepped a young man: athletic build, blond hair, and thick-rimmed glasses.

While he was paying the cabbie, I abandoned my umbrella and raincoat and skipped across the road. After a few short seconds, my dress clung to my breasts, thighs, and butt. I wiped my eyes, deliberately smudging the eyeliner like a dark, rain-smeared mask.

Skyball was still leaning into the window of the cab waiting for change or making a joke as I approached from behind.

He straightened and stepped away from the cab. The collision was firmer than I'd intended. His body was hard—like crashing into concrete—the blow softened only by the sheath of his suit.

I landed, splay-legged, on my ass. The look of shock on my face only partly feigned.

"I'm so sorry," said Skyball, rivulets of rainwater running down his glasses. "Here, let me help you up."

His grip on my elbow was gentle as he brought me to my feet. "You're soaked," he said, looking me up and down. His eyes lingered on my torso slightly longer than was strictly necessary, but no longer than another man's would have.

"Are you hurt?" he asked eventually. He didn't recognize me at all.

I shook my head and crossed my arms over my chest, hugging my shoulders. "Just wet."

A true hero, Skyball drew me close, protecting my frail body from the driving rain. "Come on," he said. "Let's get inside. I owe you a drink."

Fuse was buzzing. Those who'd come early were loath to leave while the rain was so heavy outside, and those who'd come late were cold and wet and in need of a drink. Skyball found us the last corner booth, beside a six-foot-high vid-screen of a raging hearth fire.

"I'll get us something," he said, without asking what I wanted. I liked a man who wasn't afraid to make decisions. I made decisions all day at the office and didn't need to be making them after-hours as well.

Skyball was a smooth operator. He slipped in and out of the crowd around the bar as though they weren't even there, and returned with a scotch for himself and a shot of luminous yellow liquid for me.

"To warm you up," he said. "A shot of Lady Luck."

I knew perfectly well what it was, but sometimes it's nice to let a man think he's in charge. The drink was irrelevant. I was pregnant. No happy-juice for me. I lifted the glass to my lips and pretended to sip.

"I'm sorry," said Skyball. "But in the commotion, I didn't catch your name."

"Helen," I said. "Yours?"

"Gene," said Skyball. "Gene Prendergast."

"Ah yes," I said, recognizing the name and kicking myself for not making the connection sooner. "Gene Prendergast, of Prendergast Shipping. Your freighters carry quite a bit of my cargo to the lunar colonies."

Skyball looked momentarily confused. "My God, you're Helen Marshal." He laughed nervously and took a sip of his scotch. "What are the chances, eh?"

"Oh, pretty good I'd say," I replied, a little dryly perhaps.

Skyball's eyes narrowed, darting around my face, over my straggly, wet hair. "I'm sorry. Have we met before?" he asked, a little less certain of himself.

"Three weeks back, yeah." I replied.

Skyball's smile dropped a little but snapped back into place in the blink of an eye. "You must have me confused with someone else. I flew into town on Wednesday three weeks back to meet up with friends here. I left with . . . I left with . . . Oh shit."

Cue sardonic smile.

"Look, Helen," said Skyball, and I could see him preparing to run. "I'm really sorry I didn't recognize you, but that was just a one-night thing, right? It was fun. I had an appointment early the next morning. You know how things are . . ."

I smiled. It was genuinely amusing watching Skyball squirm. "More than you know."

His teeth were white, his hair gorgeous. I'd always been a sucker for natural blonds.

"I hope this won't affect our business arrangement," he said. And it was all so chummy, so mundane. Here I was talking to Skyball—a man whose body was literally the most lethal weapon on Earth—and I was discussing business.

"Skyball, I'm pregnant," I said, dropping a huge double bomb on him without the slightest misgiving.

Skyball froze for ten full seconds.

"Skyball?" I said.

"Shh!" he snapped. "Stop calling me that. I mean, I know I look a bit like him but Skyball has super vision, right? Why would he wear glasses?"

"So he can hang out in *Fuse* and get laid?"

"I'm afraid you're barking up the wrong tree, Helen."

"Take off your glasses."

"I'm getting up and walking away right now."

"You do and I'll tell everyone in this place who you *really* are."

"You think they'll believe you?"

"Take off your glasses and we'll see."

Skyball cursed under his breath. Then: "Wait!" he said, gripping my arm, too tightly. "What did you say just now?"

It was dark in *Fuse*, but fear glittered in Skyball's eyes.

"I said, take off your glasses and—"

"No!" he hissed. "Before that."

I sighed deeply, and without warning there were tears in my eyes. I didn't know where they came from, but I wasn't ashamed of them.

"Skyball," I said, and it was hard to breathe. "I'm pregnant."

"But, you can't be," he said. "I mean, it's not mine. I'm not even . . . I'm not even human. Crimson Reign said it could never happen."

I didn't dwell on the fact he'd admitted to being Skyball. There were more important matters at hand. "That's why I need to talk to you. My skin glows blue, I'm breaking everything I touch, and I'm eating like a fucking elephant. What *are* you? Some kind of alien? Will the child be human? Or . . ."

Skyball fixed me with ice blue eyes. "I can't tell you, Helen," he said. "I'm truly sorry, but my enemies . . . If they knew about this . . . about you . . . and a *child*, my God. You can't possibly give birth to it. You've got to get rid of it."

"What?" I said. "Get rid of it? Are you insane?"

"It's a liability."

"Screw you, Skyball!" I cried. "Try anything and I'll go straight to the papers."

There was a wild look in Skyball's eye when he said, "You *do realize* if Crimson Reign got wind of this, she would tear you apart to get the child. Literally rip you *limb from limb*."

"She can try. I have a few tricks of my own."

"I'm sure you do," he muttered. "My home planet is harsh. A fetus imbues its mother with strength and agility in order to allow her to survive the pregnancy."

"Like I said, I can protect myself."

"You don't understand, Helen. You may have developed a few minor abilities, but I know Crimson Reign. We were together for a while. *She's fucking nuts.* You saw the scar on my stomach. Who do you think gave me that? My skin's ten times harder than diamond! You wouldn't stand a chance. She's *obsessed*."

"Obsessed with what?"

Skyball paused ominously. "It doesn't matter," he said, grabbing me by the arm. "Jesus, your skin's glowing. We have to get out of here. The child's a danger to you, to me, to everyone on this planet. Let's go."

"Don't touch me, you asshole!" I cried, and pushed him away.

To my astonishment, my angry shove sent Earth's mightiest super-hero sailing across the club, crashing through the bar and into a back room. Bottles rained down around the terrified bar staff, who threw themselves under what cover they could find. A moment of silence followed, during which all attention turned to me. I stood unashamed, glowing so brightly some onlookers were forced to cover their eyes.

Skyball eventually emerged from the wreckage, and with his glasses cast aside, he was instantly recognizable. A few idiots cheered at the sight of him, but the smart ones, knowing a deadly situation when they saw one, grabbed their coats and bolted for the nearest exit.

"You shouldn't have done that, Helen," said Skyball.

"Get over yourself, Skyball," I replied. The power coursing through my limbs felt incredible, like having an orgasm in every part of my body at once. "You can't tell me what to do, especially when it comes to my child."

Skyball came at me, faster than anything I'd ever seen. Somehow he shot behind me, pinning both my arms.

"That's enough," he said in my ear. "Let's go for a little trip." We blasted though the wall of the club and shot high into the night sky. The rain had eased and Salt City glimmered below. We were moving incredibly fast. The city lights whirled around us and for a moment I was too disorientated to fight back.

"See that down there? That's my home. Everyone in Salt City knows I'm the good guy, Helen," Skyball said. "Choosing to fight me makes *you* the villain."

I tried to kick at his legs, but it was no use, and his grip around my arms was vice-like. "No one thinks you're a good guy, *Gene*," I cried above the sound of wind blasting past my ears. "They're all just too scared of you to tell you to fuck off!"

Skyball chuckled. "You just don't get it at all, do you?"

I'd heard enough. I thrust my head back with everything I had and butted his face with the back of my skull, which had the immediate effect of shutting him the hell up and the secondary effect of suddenly finding myself in free fall.

Cold air buffeted my face, and I could barely see through my narrowed, watering eyes. I tumbled over and over, arms and legs flailing, reflexively grasping for purchase where there was none. Skyball's blurry outline rapidly grew smaller, while below, an office tower loomed murderously into view. I pictured myself skewered on one of the antennae jutting from its roof, or crashing through floor after concrete floor until I was nothing but a battered mess of torn flesh and broken bone.

That wasn't how Helen Marshal was going to die. I couldn't let myself down like that, *let alone my child*. At the thought of my unborn child being killed by its idiot father, my body pulsed so astonishingly brightly I was momentarily blinded.

When the glare faded, I was no longer falling.

I was flying.

• • •

I scanned the story in the *Chronicle* with interest the following day while sitting outside a small café far from my usual haunts. I was pregnant, I was financially secure, and I'd just kicked Skyball's ass in front of hundreds of witnesses. It didn't get much better than this, which was why I was preparing to resign.

Tony Marsden wanted my head over the diving production figures, and I was in no position to argue. Shit had happened and I'd allowed myself to become distracted. But distractions didn't come any bigger than the fulfillment of a dream that for years had seemed out of reach. I hadn't been distracted by a fling, a better job offer, or some crazy mid-life crisis. I'd been distracted by the next phase of my life, and it was clear to me that to move forward I was going to have to jettison baggage—my job being the first bag out the door.

I had a billion in cash, property, and shares. I was well placed to be a mother, stay-at-home or otherwise.

"Excuse me ma'am," said a very young-looking waitress. "May I take your order?"

"Yes," I said. "A skinny latte please."

"Won't be a moment," she said, turning to go.

"Oh, and a bowl of summer berries, two Dutch waffles, hash browns, four poached eggs, raisin toast, and a jug of maple syrup on the side."

When the waitress failed to respond, I looked up from the newspaper to find her staring at me blankly. "Are you expecting someone to be joining you later, ma'am?"

"No," I replied, irritably.

"Actually, she is expecting someone." Laura, my personal assistant's personal assistant, slid her skinny backside onto the chair opposite.

"Oh, Laura," I said. "FYI? You're fired."

"Nonsense," Laura said. "You need me now more than ever."

"Hey, do I know you?" the waitress asked Laura.

"No," Laura answered, removing her sunglasses and dropping them into her handbag. "But you should go now."

Intrigued, I put my paper aside. Laura had not made much of an impression on me when I met her, but looking at her now, she was a striking woman, with wine-dark hair and bright healthy skin.

"I just fired you," I said. "Why are you still here?"

"You fired Martin," Laura countered. "He's still around."

"I *like* Martin," I replied.

"You're not the hard-nosed bitch you pretend to be, Helen," said Laura, cocking an eyebrow. "You met Skyball last night. What did you think?"

"The man's a *total asshat*," I said—the words were out of my mouth before I could lock them down.

There was true joy in Laura's laughter, and it made me realize how long it had been since I'd heard the sound of genuine delight. "Couldn't have put it better myself," she said. Her green eyes literally sparkled in the crisp morning sun.

Everything fell into place. "You're the ex."

Laura gave a curt nod. "Don't call the cops or do anything stupid. I don't want to have to start breaking things. You know they're calling you Salt City Blue?" she said. "Has a certain ring don't you think?"

Despite her reputation as a degenerate supervillain, I felt an instant camaraderie with Crimson Reign. Her enthusiasm was infectious. "Hmm. Three word title, it's a bit of a mouthful."

"At least it doesn't sound like a euphemism for a heavy period," she said, lightly touching my wrist. "I mean seriously. *Crimson Reign?*"

We both laughed.

"You know, Skyball told me you were going to tear me limb from limb," I said.

"Because you're pregnant?" said Crimson Reign. "*Please.* I knew right away when I saw you glowing in the office. Sorry for stalking you like that, but it's kinda my thing when it comes to Skyball's partners. Congratulations on your little girl."

"How do you—"

"The color," she said. "Blue for a girl, red for a boy. It's how I got my name, actually. Three years ago, Skyball and I . . . Well, I fell pregnant with a boy. Some reporter saw my skin glowing and came up with the name."

Her smile faltered and she looked briefly into her lap. "I lost the child."

I wasn't used to offering sympathy to strangers. I didn't know how, and I didn't think Crimson Reign would've accepted it anyway.

"Skyball and me," she said, and I felt she was pushing through a tough moment. "We're the only ones of our kind who made it to this world. Our planet was roasted by a series of solar flares so intense, nothing could survive. Those who could leave, fled to all corners of the galaxy. There was no time to develop a plan. It was chaos.

"So you see we aren't ambassadors for our race, or diplomats, or even very nice people. In fact, we're so far from the best our planet had to offer, it's just embarrassing. In the scramble to evacuate, we were forced to leave all traces of our former lives behind. I guess I thought having a child with Skyball would be like regaining a little bit of home.

"My pregnancy was a surprise, and he wasn't interested in having a child. Then you come along and *BAM*, fully knocked-up. From what I read, you've already got some badass moves."

I shrugged. "I can hold my own."

Crimson Reign nodded. "When I fell pregnant, the extra speed and strength felt amazing. The changes to our physiology are permanent, Helen. We're never the same again. When he dumped me, I guess I went off the rails. I've been raging against that sonofabitch so long now I don't know how to live any other way. But you know what? I'm gonna take some time out."

"Hey," cried the waitress, coffee in hand. "I *do* know you. You're Crimson Reign!"

"Not anymore," Laura replied, slinging her handbag over her shoulder and standing to go. "I'm taking a long overdue holiday, and when I return, I'll be a new woman."

The waitress looked from Laura to me.

"You can thank Helen, here," Laura said. "Vanquished me over morning coffee." She winked at me. "See ya 'round, Blue."

Laura turned and sauntered away, her long, beautiful hair lifting in the morning breeze.

"Holy cow!" the waitress cried. "You're Salt City Blue? You know everyone's talking about you, right?"

I wrested the coffee from her trembling fingers and took a sip. "My name's Helen," I said. "This is good coffee."

"Best in town," said the waitress as she watched Laura walk away. "So, whatcha gonna do now?"

It was a fair question. "Me? I'm going to have a baby." The words had a warm feel. I couldn't help but smile.

The waitress looked at me as though I was some kind of simpleton. Disappointed, perhaps, that her exciting new super wanted nothing so much as to become a parent.

"Really?" she said. "That's *all*? You're not going to be . . . awesome?"

I took another sip of coffee. "Oh, I'm gonna be awesome," I replied, and Salt City air had never smelled so good. "You can count on that."

Chris Large writes regularly for *Aurealis Magazine* and has had fiction published in Australian speculative fiction magazines and anthologies. He's a single parent who enjoys writing stories for middle-graders and young adults, and about family life in all its forms. He lives in Tasmania, a small island at the bottom of Australia, where everyone rides Kangaroos and says "G'day mate!" to utter strangers.

Birthright

Stuart Suffel

The bombs weren't strictly neutron bombs, but they were built upon a similar idea. They were nicknamed the Darwin bombs because they only targeted women, changing their DNA, rendering them infertile. The idea was to wipe out a nation by stealth. But it hadn't quite worked out that way. Some women became infertile, some didn't. Some became different. Some gave birth to the different.

Sara's difference was "a kiss from the sun," her mother had once told her. "Bite" was probably a more accurate word. Two thin shining rivulets sprang upwards and outwards from the dip above her breast bone and curved over her shoulders before expanding across her back into a wide burbling lake—enraged waves of discordant frenzy set loose upon her soft flesh. The lake began at the base of her neck and ran all the way down to the tip of her pelvis, stretching wide to each side of her back. *Lupus Ammorsa,* the doctors told her. Named after the wolf.

The doctors hadn't mentioned the true cause of the bite. Sara's mother was well-known, and even so, Sara was hardly the first birthwrong—the name the tabloids used to christen those changed by the radiation poisoning inherited from the corrupted genes of their mothers.

• • •

Sara pulled back the heavy curtain and peered out of her bedroom window. There was no sign of the flash flood from last night, not here in the soft ground of the lowlands. But up higher where the ground was harder, the rain would fill the playas, creating small desert pools—a brief and welcome relief from the arid air.

She washed at the sink in her bedroom rather than use the main bathroom—the noise of the electric shower would only wake her father. She told herself it was a kindness not to rob him of his much-needed sleep. But the truth was, she did not want to see him.

It was clear the anti-radiation therapy hadn't worked. They both knew that meant a return to the treatment unit at Ridgecrest, but neither of them could broach the subject.

She toweled herself off then sank down onto her bed. Her head slumped into her hands.

The nightmares were getting worse. She had awoken earlier, sure that the wings of a giant insect were mashed across her back. She had even run naked to the hallway mirror, sure she would find a piece of matted wing crushed into her skin—but there was nothing.

The desert and its fucking insects. Black stiletto-limbed monsters.

Sara rubbed her temple, took a deep breath, then another. She pulled on her jeans and a crumpled T-shirt then reached under the bed for her tennis chucks, but her hand met something else—the satchel she'd specially packed sometime ago. She pulled it out from under the bed and opened it. The bright new rock chisel gleamed up at her. She snapped the satchel shut and flung it with force against her bedroom wall. The world had given her nothing. She owed it nothing.

• • •

Sara lifted the sash window up and a gust of heat met her face. The day was as hot as ever, the street as empty as ever. Some people used to call Randsburg a ghost town. She'd never liked the description, but maybe they were right.

As a young girl, Sara had liked the quietness. A lot of the dwellings in Randsburg had been empty back then, and she had visited most of them. Just a "howdy" to the walls. To the ghosts.

Not anymore, now that the army had requisitioned every empty building for a hundred square miles. After the last bombings, short land attacks had followed. Brief sorties, assessing damage, adding confusion and despair to an already disoriented population. The army hadn't managed to stop the bombs last time. But they "sure as hell" would respond to any more ground assaults.

Sara pulled on some tennis chucks, grabbed her bike jacket, and hopped out her bedroom window. The yard was the same as always: bits of broken vehicles, her father's half-finished mechanical gizmos strewn about the place. She picked up a piece of chrome fender and looked at her face. Her eyebrows were disappearing gradually—the wolf bite on her back sending invisible tendrils to the rest of her body. She had, on occasion, rubbed a little black oil across them with her thumb. The result was not so good—two dark streaks above her pale blue eyes, like some freaky cartoon character. It had made her grin. Someone who carried a giant boil on their back had no truck with beauty.

As she lifted the helmet off the handlebar of her bike, the cabin door swung open. Her dad filled the door frame.

"Breakfast?" he asked.

Sara shook her head no. "I didn't wake you, did I?" she asked.

"Nah. Been awake an hour or so." He glanced at her for a moment. "No satchel today?"

Sara gestured another no.

"You be back for supper?" he asked.

"I guess," Sara answered, but her eyes flickered to the ground. She mounted her bike and waited until she heard the door swing closed before sliding her helmet on and starting the ignition. The bike purred to life.

• • •

Sara traveled down the highway for ten miles then exited off onto a track for another five. When she reached the playa, she eased the bike to a halt.

The *bajadas* had fed the dry lake bed well. Joe's place was a half hour south, but there was no rush. She would take a quick swim, then ride over. She hadn't been there for three months. A while longer would do no harm.

She'd found the playa some years ago and had told no one of its existence. It was all hers, until the sun claimed it back later in the day. As Sara stripped off her clothes, the memory of her first, and final, swim in her high school pool came to mind.

The PE teacher had insisted she join the others. And for some unknown reason—maybe because it was a new school and she'd made a few friends and felt at ease—she conceded. Her sense of ease and her friendships all ended as soon as she had entered the pool area. For the following four years, until the day she graduated, she'd been known as "Scabby Sara."

She winced. Where had that come from? She shrugged the memory away and walked to the edge of the playa. Working with her dad the five years after high school had fine-tuned her arm and leg muscles. She dove gracefully into the water and swam to the far side. There she glanced at her watch—she'd reached it in record time. Flipping over onto her back, she powered back the way she had come. Again in record time. Sara toweled off her hair and sat at the edge of the natural pool, taking in its serene tranquility, allowing her body to dry in the sun.

Finally dry, she put her clothes back on. Mounting her bike, she glanced back at the pool and another memory came. She and her mother watching Sara's father swim in a local creek, his strong laughter echoing back from the nearby rocks as he reached the far edge with impressive speed. Sara would have been around seven or eight. She remembered laughing back at her father, then looking expectantly at her mother. Her mother didn't laugh. Instead, she was looking at the glistening expanse of water with an aching sadness.

Birds don't swim.

• • •

Sara continued up the track. Sometimes Joe stayed out in the desert for days. Sometimes for weeks. A growl sounded to her left. Two quad bikes roared into view, cutting across her path. She dropped her speed just in time. The soldiers were dressed in shiny neon shell-suits, indicating they were nuclear specialists. One of them waved an apology as they sped off-road again, scattering the desert dirt like a mini-Moses parting an insolent sea.

Sara watched them go. The new Conquistadors. The inhabitants of Randsburg and most of the villages around it had depended on tourists when the gold ran out. Now they fed off the army's largesse, such as it was. Even she had succumbed. The pieces of volcanic glass she chiseled out of Copper Mountain were sold to the Curious Curios shop for pocket money. The glass was almost as sharp as a surgical knife, so the shop in turn added a handle to each one and sold them for a hefty mark-up to the many new recruits who had been pouring into the San Bernardino Valley since the bombs.

As she rode, she thought about that first day she had met Joe and watched his crazy tomahawk ritual—the tomahawk adorned with feathers almost as colorful as the soldiers' shell-suits. She'd seen it as she drove by, a flurry of color dancing into the air, then turned back, pulled right up to his shack, and sat there on her bike, watching.

Joe had been standing on open ground, eyes closed. He hurled the two-headed tomahawk straight up into the air. It came tumbling down at a goodly speed, straight for his head. With his eyes still closed, he caught the weapon by the shaft, the blades inches away from splitting his skull in two. "What happens if you miss?" she'd shouted out.

Joe answered without opening his eyes or turning his head. "Then my prayers will have been answered." Then he threw the axe up in the air again.

Sara thought about this as she watched. "Can't you just miss on purpose then?"

He turned toward her, eyes a sparkling greenish-brown sheen. The axe came tumbling down. He caught it deftly in one hand. "Can't never deny the gifts we're given, little one."

• • •

When she got home later that day and told her dad about the crazy Indian, her father's face turned dark. It wasn't until much later that she found out why.

Joe's wife had been one of the early victims of poisoning when the first bombs had landed. It was through his wife that Joe had met Sara's mother at the Ridgecrest Treatment Center. But unlike her mother, Joe's wife died soon after the radiation exposure.

When Sara's mother became the first Bird, Joe left his job in the local mining company and followed her around day and night. Her father reckoned if it hadn't been for Joe, her mother might not have gained the notoriety she did, might not have sacrificed herself so selflessly. Sara doubted this—Joe wasn't the only worshiper who followed her mother and the other Birds around like drug-crazed lapdogs.

Joe's parents were both Cahuilla Indian. Though he was born and raised in a suburb of Bakersfield. When Sara's mother died, folks said Joe went crazy. He went into the desert to return to his roots and lived there as a hermit in a makeshift hut. Everyone pitied him. Strange thing was, within a few years folks from all around went to see him. Turned out Joe had become a medicine man of sorts. For a time at least—then he'd stopped making his concoctions, as abruptly as he had started.

That first day, when Sara asked her father if it was okay to visit Joe again, her father didn't answer. She took that to mean it was her choice.

• • •

Sara glanced at the fresh rattlesnake skins adorning the frame of Joe's hut. Beside them were a few skins from ground squirrels—Joe was still paying no heed to the government warning about killing them. He appeared in the doorway, grinning as usual. "Flood brings out all the wildlife," he said. "Even the lizards."

Sara grinned. Joe called her Tikka, meaning "little lizard"—or at least, that's what he'd told her. "Even the lizards need to bathe now and then," she laughed.

"You want some stew?" Joe asked.

Sara glanced over Joe's shoulder to see steam rising out of a small cooking pot. She shook her head no. She had tried Joe's squirrel stew only once. It was delicious—but now the thoughts of the once-living ingredients turned her stomach. Funny, really. Snake soup she could eat forever. Sara guessed snakes were too far removed from humans to see a connection. Joe saw no difference between the two, except maybe taste-wise. "Some water'd be good," Sara said, and Joe beckoned her inside his hut.

Joe's hut had holes everywhere. A mishmash of desert goods were hung along the walls: drying bean pods, bundles of bark, stripped creosote bush, herbs, bits of cactus, sharpened stones, bird feathers. Interwoven with these were a range of store bought goods, gaudy and loud, but somehow fitting right in with the desert stuff. Sara found something comforting in that. The walls were of deadwood and salvaged logs. Joe liked to hang things up—there was nothing on the ground but a bed roll and a stool. The stool was for visitors, the few there were. Joe squatted on the bedroll. Sara sat on the stool.

"How's your Pa?" he asked.

"He's . . . the same."

"You still having visions?" Joe asked.

He meant her nightmares. Sara laughed. "Visions? Guess that's one word for 'em."

Joe frowned a little. "The only word."

Sara flushed. A feather came loose from the wall, floated toward her, landing at her feet. She picked it up, twirled it in her hand. "Joe, why did you stop helping people? I mean, the medicines. Folks say you helped a lot of people."

The hermit looked to the ground for a minute, then he looked at Sara. "You remember the first day we met?"

Sara nodded. "Your prayers are still not answered," she joked.

Joe grinned. "My prayers were answered the day you stepped into my world." His expression became more somber. "That was the same day I laid aside my medicine bowl."

Sara got to her feet. "I'm not my mother!" she snapped. "My mother . . ." Sara said, then stopped.

"I thought she was the one," Joe said. "But she was only the first."

"The first to die."

"The first to live, Tikka. The first to live."

Sara frowned, looked to the ground. She suddenly felt tired and sat back down. Neither spoke for a time, but then Joe noticed something. "You don't have your satchel? You stopped breaking off God's fingers?"

God's fingers was the local name for obsidian rock, the volcanic glass she dug out of Copper Mountain. Sara had convinced herself she had harvested the glass to make some extra income. Now she knew differently. She had to tell him about the rock she had found—and left behind. That's why she was here. She had to tell him. Maybe then the nightmares would stop.

"I found a piece Joe. Sliver of sparkling gold through it. I think it's . . . the best I've seen."

Joe shifted in his stance. "Sharp?"

Sara nodded. "Have to pry it out fully yet, but I can tell. Sharpest so far."

"When did you find it?"

"A while back."

His eyes flickered around the cabin, then settled on her. "You thinking maybe this one should stay in the cave?" Sara heard the quiver in his voice. She looked out through a gap in the hut, eyes drifting off into the distance. "You afraid, Tikka?" Joe asked.

"I ain't afraid, Joe. I just don't see why my mother . . . died. For a bunch of—" She stopped.

Joe held his gaze on her as he took a slow spoonful of the piping hot stew, grimacing a little as it touched his lips. "You ever see her?"

Sara didn't understand for a moment. Then she realized Joe meant in her visions. Her nightmares. She shook her head.

"Your Pa does," Joe said. "Every night."

Sara dug her fingers into her knees. "She shouldn't have left us."

Joe nodded. "Maybe." He swirled his spoon around the bowl to cool the stew. Quick as a flash Joe's hand hit the ground. Sara jumped. When Joe slowly lifted his hand away, a small scorpion lay dead on the hardened dirt. Joe deftly lifted it up by the middle of its tail and flicked it outside. Joe grinned. "I don't like killing the little 'uns. But I don't like getting sick, neither."

Sara nodded. She looked out to where the scorpion lay on the desert ground. A couple of ants were already running across the scorpion's soft translucent corpse. Soon there were more.

"Breakfast," Joe quipped. Sara gave an absentminded nod as she continued to watch the ants swarm over the dead scorpion.

"Life and death, Tikka. Life and death."

• • •

Sara stalled her bike and parked on the side of the road some miles away from Joe's place. She took a slim book from inside her jacket and opened it to a photo, which acted as a bookmark. It was the only photo she had of her mother.

In the photo, her mother was wearing dungarees and had her hair tied back. She was half-concealed under a cottonwood tree, her face and neck speckled with the blotches of shadow from the tree's many leaves. She was smiling, but without showing any teeth.

As a child, Sara had thought that one had to smile with no teeth visible in order to be elegant. She'd practiced it herself for many hours in front of the mirror, until she'd come across the newspaper clipping that detailed her mother's radiation poisoning—complete with graphic illustrations of tooth loss.

The photo was dated June 3, 2025, exactly five years after the start of the war—four and a half years after Sara was born. Her mother's stance had a juvenile awkwardness, like a polio victim who had never stood before—likely to collapse at any time. It wasn't just the radiation. The wings were heavier than they looked. They affected her mother's balance when she was on solid ground. In the picture, the wings weren't visible: They were folded back, like hair tightly brushed. Sara had sometimes wondered if her mother had been ashamed of her "blessing."

Lily, her mother, was the first to get the poisoning. Soon others turned up at the medical center in Ridgecrest, their backs and shoulders bubbling like hot soup, yet none felt any pain. If anything, they each claimed to have felt healthier than they'd ever felt. Finally, one of the specialists sliced open her mother's back to see inside. He and the other surgeons recoiled in horror as the two blood-wet wings unfurled before them. Not long after, her mother and the others were hailed as the salvation of the free world. In truth, they were the sacrificed.

In other parts of the world, it wasn't wings. In some countries, it was dragon horns and a tail; in others, the legs and torso of a horse; in still others, multiple heads or arms. The scientists had said it was an "inverted psychosomatic manifestation of culturally inherited representations of the archetypical good or powerful."

Each to their own crazy, Sara had once heard someone quip.

But growing up, Sara, like so many others, saw them as heroes. Real life heroes come alive from the comic books of old. Fearless, invulnerable superhuman creatures born from deep within the human psyche. Our childhood fantasies made flesh.

Some said the bombs were a blessing. There were even new comics made—*graphic novels* her father always corrected her—of the Birds, the Minotaurs, the Dragons, the Kali.

She had collected all of the Bird novels. They were heroes. Superheroes. Unbeatable. Impenetrable. Invulnerable.

But it turned out they weren't any of these things.

• • •

Her mother and the others had saved many lives during the land attacks, but the price of every death denied, was the birth of a new cancerous cell. The others stopped when they realized the price they were paying and so gained an extra few decades of life. But her mother didn't stop.

When Sara first realized that her mother could have lived longer, she'd hated her. Hated her for leaving her and her dad. Hated her for her selfishness. Hated her for putting strangers before her own flesh and blood. Her mother was no superhero. She was a fool. A selfish fool.

And now Sara had the poison, a gift from her mother. Only this time, there was a cure. The surgeons weren't allowed to release the wings anymore. Too many crazies getting riled up. Now anyone with the altered gene pool had to undergo treatment, have the poison removed. Better for everyone, they said. It would all be over soon, they said.

Her hand clenched around the photograph. It began to crease, collapsing inwards. But when her mother's face became distorted, she stopped, flattened out the photo, and returned it to the book.

• • •

Sara's father was sitting in the middle of the sofa, watching TV, and for a moment she thought she might be able to slip by him unnoticed. "Hi," she said softly, hoping he wouldn't hear.

He turned his head. "Made some popcorn." He lifted up a plastic bowl, as if proof were required.

Sara smiled. It'd been a while since they'd sat together. She flopped into the armchair near the sofa, taking the proffered bowl. It was still hot. She ate, hungrier than she'd realized. The news was on. Almost always news, now. A clip of a former president giving a speech. The text at the bottom gave the date as 2021, a year after the first Darwin bombs had hit.

The clip changed to a funeral procession in the present. The members of the Committee of Six were aligned along a raised platform; some saluted the passing coffin, some did not. Sara guessed the former president must have died. The volume was low. She was glad of that.

"He reckoned it would all be over by Christmas," her father said. He gave a mocking grunt. "Problem is, he didn't say *which* Christmas." He winked at Sara.

She grinned back. This was good, she thought. This was . . .

"You been up to Joe's?"

She held her popcorn in midair for a moment, then popped it into her mouth. "Uh-huh," she murmured.

"He still think I hate him?"

Sara rested the plastic bowl in her lap, cradling it like it was a baby. "Don't you?"

Her father glanced at her, then back at the TV. "Too much hate goin' round these days. You see him again, tell him I'm sorry."

Sara ran her hand through the popcorn, swirled it around a bit. She noticed a feather stuck to her arm. It was the one she'd picked off the ground at Joe's. She released it from its prison and slipped it into her jeans pocket. "You think it's true, Pop? That there's another bomb coming? I mean, didn't they say they could blow them up before they landed?"

Her father shrugged. "All I know is this madness ain't stopping anytime soon."

Sara turned to look back at the TV. Another clip of the former president addressing a crowd of supporters after his election. Many in the crowd were dressed in long, multicolored robes. They punched the air every so often in response to the president's speech. The screen flashed to the present again—everyone wearing black. Sara put the bowl of popcorn on the ground, pulled her knees up to her chest, and locked her hands together. After a while, her father spoke again. "It wasn't for them, Sara. You know that."

Sara's body tightened. Her father hadn't referred to their mother's sacrifice in years. He turned to face her. "It wasn't for them. Yes, we marched with them. We believed with them. But it was never for them. The bombs don't choose sides. Neither did she."

Sara felt her lips tremble, her body start to shake. Her father leaned forward, stretched out his hands, and placed them on hers. She stopped shaking. He spoke softly. "I think of her every day. Just like you do. And every day, I love her more and more. I don't want to lose you Sara, and I know you don't want to lose me." He gave her hands a gentle squeeze. "But this ain't about us."

He smiled briefly, then went back to watching the TV. Sara failed to stop the tears that now coursed down her cheeks.

After a while, her father spoke into the distance. "They were called angels at first, you know. Before they started dying."

• • •

The tunnel was known as Burro's Tunnel, named after William "Burro" Schmidt, the madman who'd spent thirty-three years of his life carving it out of Copper Mountain with nothing but a pickax. Burro was the name for a Jackass. "Jackass Schmidt" became "Burro," when folks knew more of his story.

He had traveled from Rhode Island in the late 1800s, after burying six of his tuberculosis-riddled siblings under the wet northern soil. He came to the sun to dry out his lungs, make sure the dampness never crept back in.

Sara had heard the old-timers in Randsburg say that Schmidt had found strong veins of gold, silver, and copper along the tunnel, but that he'd passed them by like they were shale. They said he had sought greater riches.

Burro's Tunnel was big enough to walk upright in most places and taking her bike was no real difficulty. When she was halfway through, she opened her satchel and the gold-lined volcanic glass gleamed in the half-light. It hadn't taken her long to pry it free from Copper Mountain with her new chisel. She closed the satchel again.

It took another hour to get to the end of the tunnel. She didn't want to damage the bike—puncture a tire or scrape the fuel tank—so she took her time. The tunnel led out onto a narrow ledge: a four-thousand-foot-high balcony overlooking a majestic Mojave kingdom.

The shimmering Saltdale Plains stretched for miles below. In the distance, she could make out the ragged town of Randsburg, and a little farther on, the perfectly aligned box that was Johannesburg.

She took a deep breath, relaxed her mind and closed her eyes.

Can't never deny the gifts we're given, little one.

An image of Joe loomed before her, then her father's face. She took off her jacket and T-shirt as her back bubbled.

Reaching into her satchel, she took out the volcanic glass. It sparkled a golden hue. She used the leather strip to grip one end of the glass, and then she knelt down, arched her back forward, and bowed her head.

She stretched the hand that held the shimmering glass up and over her back. With an instinctive movement, she lightly danced the blade of glass across her back.

She crouched further forward, breath held tight, then moments later two wings unfurled, stretching forth from her back. It didn't take long for their shadow to spread across the valley below.

Sara rose from her kneeling position and gradually steadied herself. She opened the fuel cap of her bike to make certain the tank had not leaked and that she had enough gas. There was enough gas. She glanced at the tires and the foot throttle for any dirt or snags. All clear.

There was no need to check the brakes.

The rev of the engine hummed across the plains, and the desert rocks hummed the same tune back. The desert was ready.

And so was she.

Stuart Suffel's body of "work," includes stories published by *Jurassic London*, *Evil Girlfriend Media*, *Enchanted Conversation: A Fairy Tale Magazine*, *Kraxon Magazine*, and *Aurora Wolf* among others. He exists in Ireland, lives in the Twilight Zone, and will work for chocolate sambuca ice cream. Twitter: @suffelstuart

The Smoke Means It's Working

Sarah Pinsker

"The smoke means it's working," Ms. Frazier told Dora.

Dora eyed the machine, which eyed her back. Not really. Lifeguard Inc.'s RescueBot 4 didn't have eyes, only a sensor array designed to detect signs of life in debris and a dozen assorted limbs a Swiss army knife would be proud to possess. Dora had learned them all in training over the last two days: a scoop for sand or muck, a spike for large pieces of lumber, a pick, a claw, a grasper. Its backside was a padded forklift, and it had no legs. When it traveled, it hovered above the ground on an air cushion; it had a heavy-duty steel tripod to anchor it when it needed traction. It was about her height, resting dormant on its truck-tire base, but it gained a foot on her the second it powered up. It wasn't really very anthropomorphic at all, but Dora still felt like it was judging her. Another day, another new job, and she was still no closer to her goal of becoming a superhero's sidekick.

"Why would anyone design a rescue robot to smoke on purpose?"

"Don't ask me," Ms. Frazier said. "I just work here. But I haven't met one yet that doesn't smoke, so I have to assume it's deliberate."

"But, um, what about if you're trying to rescue people from a subway tunnel or a catacomb or something? Wouldn't it asphyxiate the victim? Hell, we're standing in a glorified supply closet with it right now."

Ms. Frazier waved the concern away. "It works fast. If we start to choke, it'll dispense oxygen. Anyway, I find it reassuring. Even when it's out of sight, I can still tell where it is by the plume."

"Hang on. Help is on the way," the RB4 said to Dora. Its fan whirred like it was working overtime. Contrary to what Ms. Frazier said, she didn't find the smoke reassuring.

"Hang on. Help is on the way." It advanced on her.

"Back off," she said. "I don't need your help. I'm not injured or trapped."

Ms. Frazier sighed. "RB, recalibrate. That's Dora. She's your new handler."

The RB4 scanned Dora. "Emotional distress detected. Elevated heart rate detected."

"Yours would be too if you were trying to learn a new job and a robot came at you with a pickax."

"I will relay your concern to a fellow human. Help is on the way."

A moment later, a distress beacon lit up Dora's tablet. First coordinates, then "Emotional distress detected. Elevated heart rate detected. Victim reports, 'Yours would be too if you were trying to learn a new job and a robot came at you with a pickax.'"

Ms. Frazier peered over her shoulder. "Hit 'acknowledge,' then 'dismiss.'"

"I know," said Dora, swiping past various icons. "It's just taking me a minute to remember where all the commands are. I'll get faster once I'm used to the interface. It's one thing in a classroom simulator and another when I've got the real thing in front of me."

She found the icons she'd been looking for, then pressed "continue scan." The RB4 turned to assess the entire room, running its non-eyes over the dormant forms of a dozen other RescueBots and assorted computing supplies. It gave a smoky little belch.

Ms. Frazier nodded her approval. "You're doing fine. Speed picks up with experience. Ready for a trial?"

"I am if it is. Where to? Is there a practice grounds?"

Ms. Frazier waved her phone. "Who needs practice grounds? It's nearly noon. Somebody's got to be destroying a building somewhere nearby. Hero, villain, some combination thereof."

"Seriously? We're going straight to a real emergency?"

"People need help. Why waste time? It's not like you can do any more damage than has already been done." Ms. Frazier looked down at the screen, then grinned. "Winged Victory Avenue and 18th Street. What's over there? The Opera House? Shouldn't have been too many people in there at this time of day, but let's go make sure, shall we?"

Dora gave the RB4 another glance. "If you say so. Isn't there an assignment list or something?"

Ms. Frazier shrugged. "You'll be getting assignments from Dispatch, but if you want to know the truth, they just make it up using the Roadz app and a police scanner, and the scanner isn't even necessary half the time. You can impress Dispatch by being there before they even make the call. If it's not rush hour and an intersection is glowing red, some villain is probably starting a fight or launching a cyborg army or hacking the traffic signals."

"Couldn't it just be a fender bender?"

"Have you seen an ordinary fender bender since the Air Bag moved to town? I haven't. Now show me how you get the RB prepared to travel. I'll grab the keys to the van."

$$\bullet \bullet \bullet$$

All Dora wanted on the drive was to watch the action out the window, but Ms. Frazier seemed intent on getting to know her. "What sparked your interest in RescueBot operation, Dora?"

"I, uh, I like the idea of rescuing people. Whoa! Was that the Patron who just flew by? I didn't know she was that fast! Uh, I'm not powered myself, and I haven't found a special skill or calling, so this felt like the best way." That was pretty close to the truth, without implying this was a stepping stone. Unless you were lucky enough to be an orphan adopted by a superhero and trained up to it, you needed experience to be a sidekick. But how do you get experience when no hero would hire you without experience? It wasn't a lie to say the Rescuebot program felt like the best way to learn how to rescue people, even if the ultimate goal was a different gig.

If she craned her neck, she could see police helicopters circling something in the distance. A line of squad cars shot past their van. More heroes joined the Patron in the sky, though Dora still couldn't see what or who they were fighting.

"Do you think they're heading where we are?"

Ms. Frazier shook her head. "The 'copters are too far north. And this one still hasn't hit Dispatch. You'll see."

They exited the highway. As Ms. Frazier had predicted, the intersection of Winged Victory and 18th was total chaos, with no sign of anybody official. Nobody to spare for this emergency, Dora guessed, given whatever was happening to the north.

This emergency: something had flattened the opera house and all the cars in the lot opposite. Two pillars still stood upright near what used to be the entrance. The rest was fallen beams and upturned seats, and a dusty velvet sea that must have once been the stage curtains. Still, something about this rubble looked different from most rubble she'd seen around the city. Dora tried to put her finger on it.

"City Building Code 17.3," she said, remembering it from a class the previous semester. "What's with all the glass shards and splintered beams? This looks really dangerous!"

Ms. Frazier put her hands on her hips and surveyed the scene. "17.3 only applies to new construction. Any building built since it took effect fifteen years ago is required to use safety materials. Shatterproof glass, underground wires, beams that turn to powder instead of splinters. Older commercial buildings had to do a certain amount of retrofitting—mostly replacing old glass—but historic buildings are exempt. And of course, when they do inevitably get stomped or smashed or blown up, they have to rebuild using the new materials."

"But I could swear the Opera House has been hit before. Six or seven years ago?"

"The Craw targeted it. She wanted to do a Phantom of the Opera revenge deal, but the Patron stopped the bomb with thirty seconds to spare. They had to redo the stage and the first ten rows after the fight, but the structure itself wasn't damaged."

Dora remembered now. She had still been in high school then. Nobody would fault her for drawing a blank on stuff that happened while she was in high school, and in college that all fell into the gap between History of Silo City and Contemporary Issues in Superheroism.

Ms. Frazier interrupted her thoughts. "So, before the police and EMTs get here and start thinking they're in charge, do you want to get working? What's the first step?"

"Assess the safety risks. That's what I've been doing."

"Do it faster. Remember, you're not going in, the RescueBot is. As long as it's turned on, its armor will protect it. You're not liable for anything, as long as you're acting within your training. The main things you should be asking in your safety assessment are 'Is the threat going to return?' and 'Is there a safe place from which to operate the RB?'"

"That's what I'm doing. Um, it looks like the 'copters aren't circling back this way, so maybe whoever did this has moved on. And yes, I think we can operate the RB from across the street, without worrying about those beams hitting us."

"Good. I agree. What's next?"

"Assign the RB parameters." Dora pulled out her control tablet and zoomed the city map down to this particular intersection. She set boundaries at the corners of what used to be the Opera House, a ceiling of ten feet above the ground, since that was the largest pile's height, and a floor of twenty feet below ground, since there seemed to be a basement. "Then I power up the RB. Then I hit 'activate.'"

"One step missing."

Dora squinted at the tablet, hoping it would give her a clue. "I power up the RB. Then I choose between 'survivors' and 'bodies.' Then I hit 'activate.'"

"Good. And which are you choosing here?"

"Survivors."

"Why?"

"Because the scene is fresh."

"And?"

"And?" Dora repeated.

"And because there's at least one person shouting for help in the rubble. Hear 'em? Get moving already."

Dora got moving. She followed the steps she had just recited. The RB4 belched some smoke. She pressed "activate, " then leaped aside as the bot whirred off across the street. She followed its progress on her tablet, with quick glances up at the actual scene.

"Scanning," reported RB4.

"Direct it toward the shouting, so it doesn't go quadrant by quadrant," Ms. Frazier said.

Dora pulled the map up again and tapped a spot on the site's rear wall.

"Hang on. Help is on the way," the RB4 said.

"Life signs detected. Physical and emotional distress detected," it reported back to Dora. A heat signature flashed on her screen.

She toggled from heat to camera. All she could see was rubble. The wall had caved inward.

Ms. Frazier looked over her shoulder. "Good. Now?"

"Assign a tool. I'm thinking the shovel first? It looks like a lot of crumbled brick."

"That works. Make sure to shift to something finer before you get close to the victim."

The RB4 shoveled quickly, and she switched it over to the scoop, on a setting between "gentle" and "archaeology."

A deep voice spoke from beside her. "Oh, goody. Amateur hour."

Dora looked up to see that an ambulance had arrived. Two EMTs stood surveying the area. The deep voice belonged to a statuesque black woman. Her muscled shoulders and back strained her uniform. Dora thought she looked a lot like the First Responder, but if she were a cape, surely she'd be here in that capacity, not her civilian identity.

"Are you—"

The woman glared at her. "Am I pissed our city has subcontracted rescue operations to a group of software operators and their pet robots? Yes."

Ms. Frazier glared back. "Our pet robot is keeping you from getting beaned by a beam or zapped by a live wire. You can still do all your medical magic after we do the hard work. You aren't benched. This is a relay, not a team sport."

The RB4 feed interrupted them. "Victim identified: human male. Adult. Spinal injury: negative. Puncture wounds: negative. Open fractures: negative. Move? Yes/No?"

"Say yes, Dora," Ms. Frazier said.

"Y'all are going to get sued one of these days," the second EMT said. He was half his partner's size, but looked equally tough. "You've got the order of things all wrong."

Dora pressed "yes," then engaged the forklift.

"Broadcast, Dora! Give the poor guy some warning." Ms. Frazier grabbed the tablet and hit the microphone. "Hello. This is Brenda Frazier, operating RescueBot 4. We've come to get you out. Sorry for grabbing you without warning, there, but we wanted to get you to a safer location as quickly as possible."

She handed the tablet back to Dora, who tried to hide her embarrassment.

The tall EMT snorted. "Trainee software operators, no less. This gets better and better."

Dora pushed the RB4 up to ten feet to clear the debris, then put it on high speed to cross the street. She thought maybe the EMTs were a little impressed at how fast she had given them someone to work on. They busied themselves with the victim, who was shaken but not badly injured.

"I'm the janitor," she heard him say.

"Was there anybody else in the building?" Dora asked over the big EMT's back.

"The office manager, maybe. She's usually there at this hour, but I hadn't seen her yet."

More people were gathering now. Some wandered into the rubble to help with the search.

"Where are the police? They should be cordoning this off," said Ms. Frazier. "One of these amateurs is going to fall through to the basement any second."

Dora wasn't counting, but she guessed it was forty seconds later that an amateur fell through to the basement. She sent the RB4 down after that person. He had managed to impale his calf on some rebar. After sawing off the rebar, the RB4 brought the man and his new piercing back up to the EMTs. They were more enthusiastic about this injury than the previous one.

She also noticed they weren't mocking the RB4 anymore. Either one of them could have wound up like the rebar guy if they had gone climbing into the rubble. The ambulance left with the second victim, leaving the first with a blanket, an oxygen mask, and a promise to send someone else for him.

Two police cars arrived and another ambulance. They started taping the area off, yelling for the civilians to clear out of the wreckage. "We've got robots for that," they said, as if they weren't half an hour late to the party.

Dora sent the RB4 back in again. There weren't any other voices calling for help, so she set it back to its default quadrant search.

"Can you tell me what happened?" A police officer asked the janitor.

"No clue. I waxed the stage first thing when I got in this morning. I was heading out to the loading dock for a smoke when the building came crashing in."

"Anybody else see it?" the officer asked the gathering crowd. Most shook their heads.

"I did," said a man in a polo shirt with "Parking King" emblazoned on the pocket. "It was some kind of sound wave. Brought the whole building down. Knocked me off my feet."

"How did a sound wave flatten the cars in your lot?"

"Oh, it didn't. That was something separate, maybe two minutes before. A giant leapfrog. Landed right in my lot, then leaped again. Then a whole bunch of police cars and choppers, then Power Star and the Patron flew by. I was watching all that when BOOM! Down goes the Opera House. Unrelated, I'm pretty sure."

"So it could have been an ordinary gas explosion?"

"You heard me say sound wave, right?"

"An ordinary sound wave?"

"Sure. I'm just glad my lot got hit by the frog. We've got insurance for giant animals, and Acts of Villainy. Never heard of BOOM insurance."

"Did you hear anyone monologuing before or after? Were there any ultimatums?"

"BOOM. That's it."

Dora hadn't realized she wasn't paying attention to the RescueBot until Ms. Frazier called her attention back. "Dora. Respond?"

Dora glanced down at her tablet. Emotional distress detected. Victim identified: humanoid. Scan: malfunction.

"It says there's a malfunction in the scan, Ms. Frazier. What do I do?"

"Sometimes non-human humanoids mess with the sensors. Switch to camera and take a look for yourself."

That made as much sense as anything. The RB4 had reached what used to be the stage. Its sensors were aimed at the piled curtains and the fallen lighting scaffold. The camera showed a large form pinned beneath. Dora deployed the anchor tripod to get enough traction, then used the claw to shift the scaffolding and peel back the curtain.

Underneath, a blonde woman.

"Manual scans, Dora."

Dora switched to manual. She had the robot scan for breathing.

"Breathing: affirmative."

Broken bones?

"Negative."

"Spinal injury?"

"Negative."

"Head injury?"

Dora read out loud. "'Indication: positive. Move? Yes/No?'"

She looked at Ms. Frazier for reassurance, then gave RB4 the go ahead. This time, she remembered the broadcast, even though the woman appeared to be unconscious. "Hello. This is Dora Silver, operating RescueBot 4. We've come to, um, to get you to a safer location as quickly as possible. Sit tight and the RescueBot will carry you to safety."

She engaged the forklift.

"Warning: over load capacity," the RB4 reported.

That didn't seem possible. The RB4's load capacity was two thousand pounds. It was designed not to body shame anybody. It should have been able to lift a Clydesdale. Dora glanced over at Ms. Frazier, who was talking to an EMT. Getting them ready for their next patient, maybe. She could handle this.

She switched to manual. The RB4 was already in position, so all she had to do was override the warning and order it to lift. She glanced up from her screen: a smoke plume wafted from the stage's general direction. Smoke meant it was working.

"Attention, citizens!" A powerful soprano voice boomed across the street.

Dora watched as the smoking RB4 rose haltingly from the rubble, carrying a tall blonde woman with two long braids and a helmet. It sank a few inches, then stuttered again toward its ten foot cruising altitude.

RB4 broadcast to the tablet. "Health update: victim has regained consciousness."

Dora could see that. The woman was definitely not unconscious. She stood astride the RB4's wobbling forklift, looking suspiciously like she was about to monologue, or at least disclaim.

"Attention, citizens!" she said again, in a Scandinavian accent. "You may be wondering what happened to your opera house. I, Sigrdrifa, happened to your opera house. I have happened to opera houses all over the world. I bring down the house because—"

A policewoman started advancing on Sigrdrifa. Sigrdrifa interrupted her own monologue with a short burst of song. It blew the officer back ten feet. "You dare interrupt me? I will lay waste to your entire city!"

Dora scanned the skies. Where was the Patron? Where was Power Star? First Responder? Were they all dealing with the giant frog? This was obviously a powered individual. Or a god, maybe? That might explain the weight warning. Gods were often denser than their mass suggested; she had learned that in Introductory Superphysics.

"Warning: load capacity exceeded," the RB4 messaged Dora again. "Warning: fan overheating."

It was already on manual override. The smoke turned black and dense, nothing like the plume that reassured Ms. Frazier. Dora wasn't sure what else she could do, and the scene looked like it was becoming less safe by the second. She had a feeling Lifeguard Inc. wouldn't approve of whatever she did next. She flipped through the icons looking for a command to fix things.

And there it was: emergency shutdown. She pressed the button.

"Emergency shutdown? Yes/No?" flashed on her screen.

She pressed "Yes".

"Warning: RescueBot 4 unit is airborne. Armor will disengage in emergency shutdown. Emergency shutdown may cause damage to the RescueBot 4 unit. Proceed? Yes/No?"

She hesitated a moment. If a broken RB4 came out of her wages she'd be paying for it for the rest of her life. Still.

Yes. Proceed.

It was instant. The RB4's air cushion died, and it dropped like a rock—no, really, like a rescue robot that had lost its air cushion while carrying a Valkyrie. Its gyros must have been compensating for Sigrdrifa's mass, because as it fell, it tipped forward on its forklift, dropping her and pinning her beneath it.

A moment later, the Patron dropped down from the sky. She was covered in some kind of slime and was more than a little out of breath. "Wherever the arts are threatened, I am there," she panted.

"You're a little late!" called one of the onlookers.

She looked around and fell to her knees before the remaining pillars. "Too late, too late. But this is only the edifice. The arts cannot be killed. They will rebuild, better than before!"

When she was done, an officer pointed her to the spot where Sigrdrifa had fallen. It took the Patron, Ms. Frazier, Dora, and two others to lift the smashed RB4. The Patron took charge of the unconscious villain, and Ms. Frazier spotted a handcart in the rubble. They levered the RB4 onto it.

"That was a pretty clever thing you did back there, Dora," Ms. Frazier said as they wheeled the RB4 back toward the van. "I think you're going to get fired for it, but it was clever anyway."

"I'm sorry," Dora whispered to the RB4 when she had a chance. "You were a very nice robot."

She wondered what its scans would say if it read her now. Emotional distress? Some part of her was distressed; she was definitely getting canned. But on the plus side, she had totally taken down a powered villain all on her own, maybe even a minor god. This was going to look great on her resume.

Sarah Pinsker is the author of the 2015 Nebula Award winning novelette "Our Lady of the Open Road." Her novelette "In Joy, Knowing the Abyss Behind" was the 2014 Sturgeon Award winner and a 2013 Nebula finalist. Her fiction has been published in magazines including *Asimov's*, *Strange Horizons*, *Lightspeed*, *Fantasy & Science Fiction*, and *Uncanny*, among others, and numerous anthologies. Her stories have been translated into Chinese, French, Spanish, Italian, and Galician. She is also a singer/songwriter with three albums on various independent labels and a fourth forthcoming. She lives in Baltimore, Maryland with her wife and dog. She can be found online at sarahpinsker.com and twitter.com/sarahpinsker.

Torch Songs

Keith Rosson

Scorched Madam, seared Madam, melted Madam Glass—the townies file past her while she sits on her tin throne, a line of men and women and their children all wide-eyed and awed and lusciously sickened, lusciously frightened as they shuffle past her little roped-off section of the tent, as she sits in her sequined gown and gazes for hours at a spot above their heads, her eyes hidden behind their dark lenses, the goggles riveted through scarred flesh to the orbital sockets of her skull, moored to the very bone—Madam Glass.

"Good Lord," says a man in line. He spits, and a dark thread of tobacco juice arcs to the straw floor. "Gal straight got smacked with the ugly stick. All melted and shit, Jesus."

The woman with him, heavyset and holding a cup of soda emblazoned with the carnival's logo, says, "Looks like someone's dinner what got left on the stove, is what."

His eyes crawl across Madam on her chair, horrified and enrapt. "Her face, you mean?"

"Yeah, her face. All over."

"Makes me want a chili dog, honestly," says the man, and winks.

The woman laughs, swats him playfully on the arm, and casts a wistful, almost sad glance at Madam. "Does it hurt?" she asks.

Madam sits silent on her throne.

Madam gazes at a point on the far wall.

Madam stoic. Madam charred.

"Ah, she ain't gonna answer you, Eileen," says the man. "They just supposed to sit there and look messed up, is all."

"Let's go then." The woman sighs. "I wanna go ride on that ride where they throw you upside down and whatnot. The Frightenator or whatever it is."

They move further down the line, past Madam (though with their necks craned back, taking one last deep sip at the ruined river of her face), and then they are on to the monstrosities beyond her: Ernie the Lizard Man, and Two-Mouth Tina, and the Raptor, and Mister Fog. Oddities all.

More people—a ceaseless, trundling line of people. Madam Glass on her beaten tin throne, a half-melted wax dummy for all the liveliness she gives them. All the movement. They can't see her eyes behind the dark lenses of the goggles, of course.

That's the whole point, isn't it?

If they could see her eyes, if she *looked* at them, it would all be over, wouldn't it?

• • •

Five days they'll stay in one spot, usually, then two off for breakdown and travel. Sometimes it fluctuates; maybe the next town is farther away, or the crowds just can't sustain five days worth of tickets and concessions and game play. And monsters. But all things end, and eventually the hands break down the tents, the games, the booths, the Ferris wheel and the Frightenator, the Demon House and, for the little ones, the slaloming teacup ride with the faces of beavers and mice and puppies and kittens on the front. Five days on, then two of travel, and right now they're in the middle of their stretch and somewhere in the middle of America, as well. Missouri? Oklahoma? Impossible to tell exactly where, and pointless besides—the carnival forges its own country. Forms its own borders, crafts its nation from arcing mazes of power strips and gurgling generators, cotton candy and cigarette smoke, grease-spotted paper trays and the clang of bells, the stink of diesel, the shriek of children—both happy and not. The great tidal sound of the carnival. Indiana? Iowa? It doesn't matter. Only the light of the sky ever changes, the heaviness of the air. All else is the same—the tide of people and Madam Glass on her throne (they all have their beaten tin thrones, a half-handed nod at supposed royalty, save for Mister Fog, who is neither liquid nor solid, really, and either way is wholly incapable of sitting on anything). Five days a week she sits, her face like gleaming meat, her goggles covering her eyes like two discs of black smoke.

The oddities and their scant families sleep in Airstreams and campervans and VW buses; part of Madam's deal had included an off-the-showroom-floor Ford F-250 and a 30-foot Sportsmen 3052 camper, and it's this that she walks to as the night takes hold, as the floodlights bracing the carnival begin to clack and shudder off behind her, as her shadow grows longer and longer before her scissoring legs. The Department of Justice had dragged their feet at buying the trailer, but Sergeant Liberty, all cleft chin and sparkling blue eyes and gleaming bandoliers of .50 cal ammunition, had surprisingly agreed to her demands. Though maybe not that surprising after all. She remembers him as unable to meet her gaze, even though they'd already drilled the lenses into her face, rendering her powerless. Guilt singing through him like a river crying out through a tuning fork.

• • •

She can't sleep. That night, the air is too close in the trailer, the rain on the roof too loud. A warm rain; she knows it. Unsatisfying. Wet, and little else. On the roof of the Sportsmen, on the gravel lot they've parked in, the rain sounds like oil sizzling in a pan. It's a sound that invites merciless introspection, and it seems likely she'll spend the rest of her sleepless night immersed in her past. The unspooling images: the vat of toxic waste Sergeant Liberty had knocked her into, the green haze that fell over her eyes, the terrible screaming agony of it all.

There are nights when she does not think about it, of course, does not think about that night at the missile silo (the secret laboratory hidden deep beneath the missile itself, the barrels of toxic waste flanking one entire wall of the lab, and what kind of half-assed operation had they been running there? Who stores *barrels of toxic waste underneath a missile?*), the kick to her stomach that sent her reeling into the barrels with their bright yellow radiation symbols.

Madam yawns, rises from her bed. Rain sizzles. Nights, alone, mirrorless, she feels mostly whole, feels no need to trace the rippled contours of her face, or gaze upon the back of her suppurating hands. Nights alone in the trailer, where she feels not the nubs of her yellowed teeth, her smoked-char curl of tongue. Her wig unpinned hours ago, beneath a robe she hides from herself her warped, melted breasts, the burn-swathed valleys of her thighs. There are nights where she watches game shows and sitcoms on the sixteen-inch television in the Sportsmen's kitchenette. Listens to soul records, gospel, the bitter, loving lamentations of long-dead blueswomen on her turntable, the ache of them stilling something inside her.

But tonight? No. Tonight she is awake and not alone, because even over the hiss of rain and a dim chorus of frogs somewhere—and this is a first—she can hear Two-Mouth Tina moaning in her own trailer, crying. They park the oddities ("freaks" being no longer an acceptable term in this day and age, even in a show as decrepit and nearly-run-down as *Mr. Hara-Sobanza's Good Tyme Carnival!*) far away from the rest of the crew, with the trucks and trailers and the few remaining sad and bedraggled show animals as a buffer.

Madam Glass steps out of her trailer into the warm night, those three steps down to the gravel, and the rain is very loud. Wigless, in her pajamas and robe and her green galoshes with the blue raindrops on them, she walks along the gravel. The sky above is a grim, featureless blanket, a low-slung thing. Falling threads of rain are lit like spider silk from the few sodium lights that line the edge of the lot. The rain darkens her robe at the shoulders, falls warm on her scalp. (The wig, black as lacquer and resting now on her bedside table, is her one concession to her old, cold beauty.)

Two-Mouth Tina's trailer door is dented and pocked, the trailer itself significantly older than Madam's. The outside of it has been buffered and caulked many times, panels of siding are coming undone, and there are swaths of paint with old graffiti ghosting through. Hinges are stripped, molding busted off. A cracked window is laced in a veering roadmap of silver duck tape. The camper rests above an old tomato-red GMC, the whole setup at least a generation past new. A hand-me-down affair, she knows, from a retiring contortionist, given to Tina long before Madam's arrival. She can hear Tina crying through the door. Her knock is clipped, precise, measured; it's only when her plans are foiled, when she is denied her wishes at the last moment after so much hard work and plotting and calculation, that she explodes. Otherwise, she is distant and measured. And with her life the way it is now, there is nothing left to wish for. No reason to *feel* anything. That was the trade: give up your ways, Madam, fold on the leaders of the Viper Clan, *confess*, and you may live your days quietly among the monsters of the carnival. Given the way you look now, you'll fit right in.

Madam, in her robe and galoshes and a body like half-melted plastic, has finally been culled of desire—be it vengeance or otherwise.

Tina answers the door, sniffling, holding a crumpled tissue to her nose. "Hey, doll," she says from her upper, more dominant mouth. Tina: pink sweatpants and a T-shirt, blond hair in a lank ponytail, eyes puffy from crying. Two mouths tiered on top of each other, the lips of both knit in bloodless lines. "I'm making a lot of noise, huh?"

"I couldn't sleep anyway," Madam rasps.

"Come on in," she says, and Madam hoists herself up into the tiny camper. "You want a beer? I got soda too, but that'll probably keep you up."

"I'll have a beer, Tina," and then, like dislodging a stone from the ground, like working a strange new muscle: "Thank you."

Tina walks to her tiny kitchen, just a few steps away. She opens the half-fridge and pulls out a Budweiser. Hands it to Madam, gets one of her own. They sit on opposite sides of the narrow space, Tina folding her legs under her on a loveseat built into the wheel well, Madam Glass on the other. She coils, unconsciously, her damp robe around her like a cloak. Her boots look ridiculous in here, and she asks if she can take them off.

"Totally," Tina says mid-swallow, the word glottal and strange as one throat simultaneously does the work of two mouths.

Madam sets her galoshes at her feet. Out the open door she can see the rain falling. The beer is chilled and metallic—terrible in taste and yet strangely thrilling for the camaraderie it implies. This is, of course, a different kind of fellowship than she is used to. She and Tina have seen each other almost daily in the two years since Madam was placed in the Good Tyme Carnival as part of her plea deal with the Department of Justice. They have parked their campers next to each other on a hundred different lots, used the same picnic tables and rest stops, sat for hours in the same tent as the townies shuffled by and stared. But never once has she been in the woman's camper, her home.

The walls are faux-wood, the carpet is worn to tread in the middle. There's a warped circle on the small wedge of kitchen counter where a hot pan was once placed. But it's homier than her own place: Two-Mouth Tina has actual pictures on her shelves, for one. Above Madam's head rests a photo of a pair of smiling blond children, a boy and a girl in swimsuits, sunburned and squinting at the camera. On another wall, there is a poor painting of a desert, cactus and lizard and turquoise sky, the brushmarks blunt and brutal and joyous, Tina's name at the bottom. Her own home is antiseptic in comparison.

They watch television with the sound down low. An action film, men in blood-smeared shirts shooting at each other. Mayhem and cursing and smoke, the slow-motion architecture of bodies being dismantled in graphic detail. If there's a plot, Madam can't discern it. She still, after all this time, understands little about the machinations of supposed "evil." Rage seems so frequently to be at its root, but rage has been burned out of her. The thirst for power was always there, always the bedrock of her plans, but she still cannot reconcile the notion that she was truly evil.

After a while, Tina says, "As far as me crying goes, I was just mad." She looks over at the picture above Madam's head. "I just get so mad, and then that always turns into a crying-type situation, you know?"

"I know," Madam says in her coarse whisper, her vocal cords atrophied from her acid bath, though of course she has never cried, not once, not even after Sergeant Liberty pulled her howling and smoking from the laboratory floor, and some military stooge knocked her unconscious with his rifle butt. Not even after all that was done to her afterwards. Fourteen rivets surround each lens, driven into bone. Her powers robbed of her, and a dark veil thrown over her world. Even on the brightest days, her world is dim.

Tina says, "Some customer flicked a cigarette at me today. A lit cigarette. You believe it? It's cruel is what it is. People are shitty, ain't they?"

Madam looks at her, but Tina's gaze is locked on the TV again, the screen's movement reflected in her eyes.

Madam says, "You should tell Mr. Hara-Sobanza."

"Ha," Tina says dryly. "Like that'll happen."

"They aren't even supposed to be smoking in the tents."

And now Tina looks at her, and there's a flat, languid challenge there in her eyes—not toward Madam herself, but toward the notion that she would even bring up the idea of fairness here, the two of them being who they are.

"Doll," Tina says, "if I put my foot down every time someone did something they weren't supposed to, I wouldn't ever get to move a damn inch." And then she laughs, bitterly, and from both mouths.

• • •

Is evil born or cultivated?

Jean-Baptiste Devereaux had been a French physicist, a drunkard, a womanizer, an eventual double-agent for the Axis, and one of the spearheads of the Infinity Project, which after the end of World War II would ultimately—and *here* was irony—provide Sergeant Liberty with his powers and near-immortality. This, of course, was after Jean-Baptiste had been detained by the Americans after the fall of the Nazis, and after he was found guilty at his Nuremberg trial, and after the Office of Strategic Services—the CIA before it was the CIA—offered him a deal: work for us or die by the sword.

Jean-Baptiste, a fan of drink and women and a continuing heartbeat, took the deal.

The Infinity Project took countless lives before it was smoothed out, successful. By the time Madam Glass was born—she could think of herself as Simone Devereaux in only the most distant, self-conscious way—the project was going well, on its way to converting dozens of young test subjects into super soldiers. Jean-Baptiste, old by then, had fathered her with the same offhanded contemptuousness he held for physics, the government, his long-lost France, for everything save the bottle. Her mother had been a lab assistant, one who was quickly shuttled away to another laboratory after Madam's birth, and her father became little more than a cipher for her as she grew. He took his own life the day of the Tonkin Gulf Resolution, a man intimately familiar with the velocity of war.

But Madam often wondered—had he been evil? He had worked for fascists, certainly, but it had been under threat of death, yes? She herself had vied for world domination, the power inherent in it. Granted, her attempts were haphazard, frayed, half-mad. But the intent had been there—might through chaos.

Had her father been evil, his face lit in strobing flashes, experimenting on poor, frightened boys, lights curling along the walls of his lab, machines humming and groaning? Or had he merely been an opportunist? More importantly, was evil transitory? Was it inherited, like her double-jointedness?

Had she grown up not knowing her father's history, would her own story have been different? Would she have formed the Viper Clan? Would she have released the nanobots in the Prime Minister's nightcap? Orchestrated the Seoul Blackout? Lashed the President's son to the warhead? Would she have freed the Tornado Feet Gang out of prison and loosed them on the streets of New York?

It was not an issue of vying for her father's love—God, no, the man was long dead and she hardly knew him to begin with—but had she felt that it was the only avenue afforded her?

Was evil, in this case, just a matter of a girl being diminished by her own expectations? Her lack of self-worth?

And now that she was here, among the other oddities, in this cruelest of guises—who was she now?

Was she, like her father at the end of his life, simply exhausted?

Was there anything left of her to reclaim?

· · ·

Indiana to Missouri to Kansas. The oddities making up their own condensed convoy along the highway. In a little town called Burnt Grass, right between Topeka and Kansas City, the carnival stops, breaks ground, builds itself up. The Ferris wheel climbs the sky, screams echo from the Demon House, the children wail and chortle in their teacups, their hair fanning out behind them. Romance blooms, fights erupt and calm, up and down the midway. The oddities sit alone in their roped-off squares, and now that Tina has mentioned it, Madam can't avoid seeing the way they are treated. The gagging noises the townies make when they see her, the leering taunts they make at Tina. The jeers at the Raptor, and one day someone threw *salt* on Ernie the Lizard Man, as if he were a slug. Madam feels some old vestige stirring inside her, something long-buried. Like seaweed wavering in an underwater current. Like sparks whirling in a funnel. It's a dangerous feeling, she knows, but she welcomes it anyway.

• • •

Dusk in the badlands. Prairie grass and the plains stretched out, the limned spikes of power lines the only thing vertical out there in the twilight. The days lasting longer, getting warmer. They are in Tina's trailer; she has made soup and sandwiches, and they are watching a rom-com DVD on her television, their plates in their laps.

When the two characters kiss, they both busy themselves with their sandwiches. Had they expected something different? Madam is still so awkward around people. There is a world of difference between talking to someone in a room and ordering a Clan squad to storm a laboratory. Madam smiles down at her plate. Then, grown brave with their closeness, she nods toward the photo on Tina's shelf and says, "Your kids look sweet."

Tina nods, chewing, a cigarette parked in the lips of her bottom mouth. "I miss those guys so bad. Oh man, do I."

"Where are they?"

Tina sighs, rolls her eyes at the ceiling. "With their dad. It was a, you know—it was a freak show every time I left the house. No pun intended. We were broke. Like *bad* broke. Nobody would hire me." She ashes her cigarette into a Coke can and smiles, but it's a private smile, rueful and closed off. "Reporters camped out everywhere, coming out of the bushes, peeking in the windows, taking pictures for those newspapers. People calling all the time, saying awful things. It was real hard for them."

"That's terrible."

Tina shrugs, long inured to the cruelty of her situation. It's only Madam that is wounded, only Madam that is new to the repercussions of *otherness* extending beyond the body, the self.

"I'm pretty used to it," Tina says. "I was born like this, so I've never . . . you know. This is how it's always been."

Madam thinks, *I was beautiful once, beautiful and merciless,* but realizes how this would make Tina feel if she spoke it aloud, and simply nods.

"Hey, listen," Tina says. "I've been meaning to ask. I don't—I don't really know what to call you."

It's true: Only Mr. Hara-Sobanza himself knows Madam's true identity, having accepted a significant cash payment from the Department of Justice to allow her to join the carnival. The other oddities are civilians themselves, though she supposed a few of them—the Raptor, perhaps, and certainly Mister Fog—could've made a decent go as supervillains. Hara-Sobanza, a wizened, happy man of eighty-four who still traveled with the carnival, had asked her during her first week on the crew, and somewhat apologetically, if they could bill her as Toxic Girl. Numb to her new situation, she'd allowed it.

"Simone," she says now, her voice hoarse. "Call me Simone."

"Ah, that's pretty. That's real nice."

"Thank you," she says, her eyes on her plate again, suddenly bashful. "This is a good sandwich." Her heart flutters like a bird loosed in her chest.

A friend, she thinks. *I have a friend.*

• • •

The foothills of the Rockies now. Summer in full bloom, hot, depthless blue skies and the bright coin of the sun hanging above them all. The tent is a tinderbox, Madam sweat-slicked in her sequined outfit.

It's unclear how long he has been there—she has been staring at that familiar spot on the far wall above the heads of the customers—but she looks down, and there he is. Gaunt and pale and hollow-eyed, packed between two families, a beanpole among summer squash. He nods and nods at her, presumably unsure if she is looking at him through her dark lenses. His smile is a dark, curling thing. When her posture stiffens, when her hands grip the armrests of her throne so hard some distant part of her can hear the sinews creak, he salutes her. It is a movement rich, she thinks, with contempt.

She recognizes his face, but can't place it. Jutting cheekbones, purple bags beneath the eyes. Wearing a pale yellow T-shirt dark at the armpits. Where does she know him from? They are on the outskirts of a town called Dumbell, in Wyoming. It has been over two years since Sergeant Liberty and the arrest, the operation, since this new brutal chapter of her life began. And where does she know this man from? Is he a member of the Viper Clan? From some other crew, out to seek revenge? If only she could look at him without these lenses, she would demand he tell her everything.

He winks at her and moves past the others, farther down the line, out of her sight.

• • •

That night Tina invites her over for dinner and a movie, but Madam begs off, claiming illness. Her eyes are hidden, and Tina can't see her confusion, the apprehension at play there. Today's events unfolding again and again behind her eyes.

She sits at the table in her little kitchenette, Simone Devereaux and Madam Glass and Toxic Girl, all of her lives enveloped in the slow crackling burn of old torch songs from Etta James and Edith Piaf spinning on the turntable.

And so she is alone when the knock comes at the door. The inevitable knock.

Weaponless, powerless, Madam rises and opens the door of her camper in the only armor afforded her: her wig, her robe, her blue galoshes.

It's the gaunt man, though she sees that even under the harsh illumination of the lot lights he looks more a boy. The moment unfolds in silence.

Finally she says, "What do you want?"

A sea of crickets out beyond the scrim of light, the distant tidal roar of traffic on the highway.

"Can I come in?" He speaks with a familiarity that borders on insouciance. Years ago, it would have driven her to pin him against a wall, gaze upon him, and order him to *do* something—to walk a thousand miles, or wash his hands until they bled. He'd have been powerless against it. She'd done that and more to those who had failed to treat her with the subservience she deserved.

Now, she pulls tight the collar of her robe, lets him in.

He steps up the Sportsmen's stairs, ducking against the low ceiling, folds his long legs into the kitchen booth.

"You were here earlier today. In the tent."

He seems more timid now that he's inside, nervous about gazing upon her ruination, her lenses and sloughing skin. She slides in to the other side of the booth, considers taking off her wig. Leaves it on.

"I know who you are," he says simply, his hands folded in front of him. Not accusatory, like a proffering.

This, strangely, comfortingly, seems to carry no impact. She feels nothing. She is pleased to find that she is unafraid. "And who might that be?" she asks.

"You're the Madam," he says.

"And who are you?"

"Well, my name's Dan."

"Dan? How did you find me, Dan?"

"It's one of my . . . that's a gift I have. Finding people."

She nods—she's hardly surprised to find that he has powers of some kind—and rises, goes to the refrigerator and takes out two Budweisers, sets one before him.

He grimaces. "This is shit beer. We don't even sell this at my store."

Madam sits. A hiss as she twists off the cap. A lifetime ago she would have told him to run his head through a window. "Your store?"

"I work at Nature's Table."

"Ah."

Acidly, snapping his fingers, Dan croons, *"Like nature's fable straight to your table."*

"Yes," Madam says.

Dan opens his bottle, and they drink in silence.

The record stops and she rises, takes the few steps to the record player. She flips the record, drops the needle, and thinks, *Now. I will turn around and he will be standing before me, and whatever is going to happen next will happen.*

But she turns and he is still there at the table. The music starts, solemn and smoky, and she walks over and grasps her beer. Walks over to the camper door, opens it. Hears the wind shirring the grasses outside.

"I'm not anybody," she says.

"I was a lieutenant with the ground forces in Seoul."

"During the blackout?"

He nods. Of course. This is where she knows him from—if not by face, by the way he carries himself. A member of the Viper Clan, a foot soldier, nameless. One among thousands. "I was arrested," he says, "with the rest of my platoon after Sergeant Liberty filled the streets with Slow-Gel. We were stuck. Easy pickings."

"So that's what happened. I always wondered."

"You and Professor Smart and Mister Fist all escaped."

"We did," she said.

"I did three years in Lewisburg."

Madam says nothing.

"They're not big fans of the Viper Clan in Lewisburg, Madam."

She holds tight her robe with one hand, gazes out at the fields beyond the parking lot, the Rockies cragged and impenetrable beyond.

"They're winning, you know," he says.

"You need to leave," she says.

He snorts—a sound that conveys disappointment, contempt, incredulity—and then he stands. Walks out into the night without brushing past her, without touching her at all.

• • •

The next day brings a still, crushing heat and short-tempered, sweat-lashed crowds. The tent is stifling. She sees a father yank a child and swat her behind after the girl takes one look at Madam and begins bawling. She sees a fight nearly break out between two families over who was in line first. The heat itself seems nearly malevolent, alive. She thinks of the fan in her trailer, the beaded condensation on a beer bottle.

The customers gaze at her sullenly, fanning themselves with their Hara-Sobanza handouts, when she hears Tina farther down the line, in a voice bright with fear, say, "That's *enough*. Stop it!" People murmuring, jagged caws of laughter.

Madam Glass rises from her throne, her knees protesting after sitting for so long, and then she is over the rope, threading her way among the crowd. Past Ernie, past the ululating vapor-shape of Mister Fog.

And there is Tina, half-standing before her own throne, crouched, and there are two boys, young men, inside her section, having stepped over Tina's rope. One is holding a phone, filming, and the other holds a . . . newspaper? The front page of a newspaper that he's showing

Tina, who stands curled at the waist as if she's been punched, and maybe she has, or maybe it's simply that the newspaper shows a grainy, blurred image of Tina being walked to a police car in handcuffs, her irises glowing red from the camera flash, the kid holding it before her crowing, "This is you right? I *knew* I knew you! You're the hooker freak that got her kids taken away!" and the ghost of movement in Madam's muscles is like any other ghost—always present, always coiled in memory—and she cups the two boys' skulls, one in each hand, and drives them together. There is a clack like a bowling ball dropping on a wooden floor, and they tumble like de-stringed marionettes. She clutches Tina, who wraps herself in Madam's arms, sobbing, sobbing.

Still holding Tina, she drives the heel of her stiletto into the outstretched hand of one of the boys. Bones break as delicate as filigreed china.

• • •

A knock on her camper door later that night. She drops the needle on the record—Peggy Lee—and opens the door, expecting Mr. Hara-Sobanza to tell her she is fired. Expecting an angry mob of carnival-goers, or a phalanx of DOJ agents to take her into custody.

But it's Dan. Dan in his pale yellow shirt, his bowl haircut, his simmering rage.

"I want to show you something," he says.

She follows him, their feet crunching on the gravel, a mosquito whirring past her ear, the flit of bats overhead among the lights.

Dan has parked his sedan—an old rust-eaten thing—at the edge of the lot. As they walk, she catches a whiff of the tiger cage, dank and sweet with the rot of dead meat, the animal's own ineffable fug. The light as they continue grows buttery and vague.

He opens the trunk and there, accordioned among the trash—a tire jack, a bottle of motor oil—is Sergeant Liberty. He is wrapped in chains, gagged. He wears chinos and a polo shirt. Laddered in veins, his arms are mapped in burn scars, exit wounds. His blue eyes glitter in the scant light. Of all the things she sees at play on his face, surprise is not one of them.

"You have a choice to make," Dan says to her, his hands on his hips, gazing down at the man in the trunk.

Scorched Madam, seared Madam, melted Madam Glass, she can hear a torch song drifting low and mournful from her camper, a testament to all things lost, gained, lost again.

Keith Rosson is the author of the novels *The Mercy of the Tide* (2017, Meerkat Press) and *Smoke City* (2018, Meerkat Press). His short fiction has appeared in *Cream City Review*, *PANK*, *Redivider*, *December*, and more. An advocate of both public libraries and non-ironic adulation of the cassette tape, he can be found at keithrosson.com.

The Beard of Truth

Matt Mikalatos

I figured out my superpower at the drive-through window of Columbo's Burgers A-Go-Go when I handed over my wadded-up five and the burger jockey said, "My girlfriend is manic depressive. Mostly depressed is what it feels like, though, you know? I don't want to leave her because it will depress her more." I said something noncommittal, something like, "Oh." Then he gave me my change.

After my burger, I went by the post office and waited in line as the twenty people in front of me handed over packages and cash. When I got to the window, I couldn't get the clerk to stop telling me about her relationship with her dad. He left when she was a kid, and now he was dying and wanted to get to know her, but she didn't think she could handle another loss like that. She started weeping and they had to send another clerk, and then he started telling me how he had been overcharging people for postage and pocketing the difference.

That's when I knew for sure my power had finally kicked in. I dialed my girlfriend. She said hi and I said hi and I said, "I got superpowers today."

She laughed. "That's amazing, Jimmy! What did you get?"

"Some sort of truth serum thing. Try to tell me a lie."

She paused, then said, "I'm leaving you."

I cleared my throat. "Um. Please tell me my truth serum isn't working."

She laughed for a long time. "Must not work over the phone, dummy. I just started dinner, so buy some wine and get over here."

When I got to her place, she flung open the door, pulled me in by the shirt and shoved me down on the couch. She had her hair pulled up, a black tank top and khaki shorts on, and her long brown legs and her strong arms set my heart racing. She had a ballerina's grace and a runner's body— balanced, lean, and fit. She gave me a kiss and said, "I've always worried you were just a rebound for me. I was so messed up after my break-up with Brad."

"Hey!"

She frowned. "I guess it works in person. Sorry."

I met Lindsey when we were both working as servers at a restaurant called Pizza the Action. Her boyfriend-at-the-time, Brad, was away at grad school. They had a messy breakup, and we fell in love three days later. I'm always worried I'm not enough for her because she's amazing and I'm only okay. But getting powers—that could change everything. It could bring us money, fame, influence.

"On the other hand," she said, "it's really hot to have a boyfriend with powers. I still think about going back to Brad sometimes." She clapped her hand over her mouth and scrunched up her nose, like she always does when she regrets what she just said. She smoothed the frown off my face and kissed me. "Brad doesn't have powers, that's for sure." She took a big swig out of the bottle of Prosecco I'd brought. "You are about to have a very active evening." She pulled her shirt over her head, then started unbuttoning mine. "I hate your shirt," she said. She pulled her shorts off, then her bra. "I've always hated it." She yanked me down on the floor. "You need to shave and your breath stinks and I hate it when you frown like that, and get ready for something amazing." I started to roll her over, but she pushed me back down. "I'm in charge tonight. When you don't shave you look old and sad." She put her mouth over mine, and from then on we didn't say much, which was probably for the best.

Later, she told me it was good for her, too, and I knew she wasn't faking. I hoped maybe my new powers worked as an aphrodisiac, not just a truth serum.

• • •

In the morning, after I'd shaved and showered, Lindsey told me she hadn't meant it when she said she still thought about Brad sometimes.

"Wait, Lindsey. Is that true? Because that means my powers didn't work on you."

She sighed. "No, I lied just now. I still think about Brad. I guess your powers stopped working."

"That hurt my feelings, you know."

She threw her hands up in the air. "You're the one with truth serum powers."

"Oh, this is on me?"

"Yes! We've been together for a year, and I've never said anything stupid like that before."

"You've been thinking about going back to Brad since we first got together?"

She bit her lip. "It's not like I think about it all the time. Just once or twice when you're driving me crazy. Like right now."

I sighed. "You're lying to me, aren't you?"

"Maybe a little."

"Dammit, my powers aren't working anymore!" I yanked on my jeans and threw on a shirt. I'd heard of people whose powers only lasted a couple of hours, and if that was the case, I wasted them listening to my girlfriend tell me her doubts about our relationship.

She put her arms around me. "You know, they say the powers are triggered by weird things sometimes. Maybe your powers turn off after you have amazing sex."

I laughed. "Or maybe they only work the first hour I'm near someone."

She smiled at me and said, "Maybe they'll turn back on if I turn *you* back on."

"I'm going to be late for work," I said.

"Yes. Yes, you are."

• • •

On my lunch break I called the Powers Reporting Line. A woman with a pinched voice answered and asked for my name. I told her.

"Are you reporting your own manifestation or someone else's?"

"My own."

"I am required by law to tell you that if your manifestation inadvertently caused the harm or death of someone else, you have the right to a lawyer, and any prison time may be commuted to time served in the Military Powers Program."

I choked. "People get killed by new powers?"

"Yes, sir. Just last week we had a call from a man who accidentally turned his gardener into gelatin."

"That's horrible."

"Actually, sir, our scientists think it's possible the gelatin is still sentient, so it is being kept under observation at our facilities here in town. Perhaps it will turn back into a gardener."

I cleared my throat. "That's, uh, good news. And I'm relieved to hear the gardener might be okay."

"We had a woman last week who causes people's livers and brains to trade places." I didn't know what to say, so I didn't say anything. She waited a long time before saying, "Those people are dead."

"Uh. Yeah. Well. Either way, I didn't hurt anybody. My powers just make people all . . . truthy."

"And where are these extraneous teeth growing, sir? Please stop me when I reach the appropriate location. Mouth. Eyes. Forehead. Fists. Knees. Belly—"

"Not toothy. Truthy."

"Truthy?"

"Yes."

"As in 'honest.'"

"That would be another word for it," I said.

"That would be the correct word for it, sir. Please hold while I transfer you."

I had no idea why she would need to transfer me. The Powers Act required that anyone who manifested powers had to report it within twenty-four hours, but I was unclear what happened after that. There were rumors, of course, of people being drafted or locked up or becoming politicians. But I just figured those were all things that could happen to you, powers or not.

Another voice came on the line, crisp and authoritative. "Mr. Stevens, I am Special Agent Sam Travis."

"How did you know my name?"

"I have limited telephone-lepathy, which only activates when I am filling out forms. If there's a blank on a paper in front of me and you know the answer, I can fill it out. But only if we're on the phone."

"That's amazing."

"I suppose. Nothing like a truth serum, though. I can see from your paperwork here—"

"I haven't filled out any paperwork yet."

"Telephone-lepathy, sir. Try to keep up. As I was saying, your power has gone dormant, probably because of some change in your person. It's unlikely to be the sex thing—"

"I put that on the paperwork? My girlfriend would kill me for sharing that!"

"Sir, I can see it from your mind. While we're on the telephone. I'm going to go ahead and round your IQ down, I think you may have exaggerated it. In any case, yesterday was Tuesday, so I've set up an appointment for the two of us for next Tuesday in case your power only works then. Do everything you did yesterday. Wear the same clothes, do the same errands, eat the same breakfast. When your powers start to kick in again, drive directly to my office. I've sent you an email with these instructions, my phone number, and our address. Any questions?"

I hadn't really followed all of that, but I figured I could read the instructions off the email. "Which email address did you use?"

"The one on the form, Jimmy."

I tapped my fingers on the table. "Yeah. Okay." I hung up. I asked one of my coworkers how his day was going and he said fine, so I knew my powers hadn't kicked back in yet.

• • •

That whole week, Lindsey and I got along better than we had in months. Lindsey felt bad about the things she said when she was being honest. I felt bad my powers had introduced this weird thing into our relationship. Both of us were worried about my powers, whether they would come back, and what would happen when I went to the meeting with Special Agent Sam Travis.

Tuesday came. I woke up early but didn't get out of bed, just like the week before. I had crumpled my shirt on the floor the night before. I hadn't shaved in a couple of days. I checked my email on my phone, then got up and played some video games. At eleven I went to Columbo's Burgers A-Go-Go, and when I pulled around the corner and that little window opened, I held out a crumpled five and held my breath. The burger jockey hung out the window, took my money, and said, "Buddy, if you keep eating here, you're going to have a heart attack."

I took my change. "Thanks, pal."

"Also," he said, "I think my girlfriend is cheating on me, probably because she doesn't think I make enough money. We don't even get tips at this restaurant. I make most of my money selling pot on the side."

"I thought you were going to leave your girlfriend."

"That was last week, man!"

I nodded, grabbed my burger, and drove straight to Special Agent Travis's office. The secretary told me she hated all the freaks and losers who came through the door, and refused to shake my hand. She also told me she had just moved to town a couple of months ago and wished she could go back home, but she hated her sister, who had just moved there with her husband and kids. I nodded dutifully and took my seat.

She frowned. "You're the truth serum guy, aren't you?"

"Yeah."

"You're supposed to go straight back."

Agent Travis's office looked surprisingly like a dentist's—cold waiting room with magazines on the tiny tables, a stark hallway, and then a room with a weird chair and lots of scary looking lights and tools. There was also an office chair facing the dentist and/or torture chair. No way was I getting in the dentist's chair.

Agent Travis walked in, eating something out of a small paper cup. He noticed me sitting in his chair and promptly sat down in the dentist's chair. He felt the arms experimentally, wiggled around a bit, and said, "It's more comfortable than I thought it would be." He took a bite of whatever was in his cup. "This is the worst Jell-O I have ever eaten." He spit into the cup and tossed it aside. "Really, that was horrible." He smiled at me. "There's a whole bathtub full of the stuff. I don't know why they would be making it in the lab. Must be for a party or something. Yuck."

He stood up, leaned over the desk and shook hands with me.

"My powers are back," I said.

"Oh yeah? Wow, that's an awful shirt you're wearing. Think you can get me to say something I shouldn't?"

"Sure." I tapped the desk with my fingers. I couldn't believe he hated my shirt, too. "Does the government have any idea why all these powers are flaring up?"

He shrugged. "Six months ago the Earth went through some cosmic debris. We think the powers are linked to that." He rubbed his eyes. "Um. That's classified, by the way. Don't mention it to anyone else."

"So you have a whole bunch of powered individuals on government strike teams or something?"

"Those with interesting powers. Believe me, a lot of them are useless. We had a guy come in who could heal paper cuts. We released him back into society."

Suddenly, I found myself wishing for the power to heal paper cuts. "You mean some people don't get released?"

"Most of them get locked away. We had a guy last week who is the world's strongest telepath. Can't have him wandering around. The telepathy only activates when he's peeing, so that makes it easier to keep him under wraps. The poor guy wasn't going to be able to use a public restroom in peace again, anyway."

"You locked him up?"

"More or less." He pointed at me. "That's classified, now, Jimmy, don't forget."

"Right. Are you going to lock me up?"

He sighed, moved some metal arms around the dentist's chair. "We'll give you some choices, I suppose. First choice would be to have you join the military and work as an intelligence collector."

"A what?"

"An interrogator."

"And if I refuse?"

"Oh, probably vivisection." He grinned. "Wow, your power is really strong. That whole vivisection thing, Jimmy, that's classified."

I choked. "Vivisection? Are you kidding me?"

He laughed. "I don't think I can when your truth serum is working! It's better than dissection though, right?"

I shook my head. "I guess. Depending on how you look at it. Not really."

Agent Travis slapped a folded paper into my hand. "Listen, here are your marching orders. When to show up, all that stuff. And

Jimmy, I've got a guy who can tell what activates powers if he sees them functioning. He observed you when you arrived and says your truth power comes from your beard."

"From my beard?"

"Yeah. If you shave, it will go away completely. We're going to ask you to shave for boot camp, incidentally. We'll grow your beard back when you report as an interrogator."

I stood up, holding the papers. "So that's it, then?"

"Yeah. Don't worry, Jimmy, it could be worse."

"How could it be worse?"

"We've got a guy right now who is invulnerable but only when he's sleeping. You wouldn't believe the missions we give him."

I shook my head. "I have to get home and talk to Lindsey."

"His sergeant always says, 'I hope you don't wake up during this assignment!' Ha ha ha."

"Hilarious," I said, and walked past him and the dentist's chair.

"Jimmy," he called.

"Yeah?"

"That whole sleeping soldier thing, that's classified."

"I figured."

"Jimmy?"

"What?"

"If you don't show up for boot camp we're going to kill you. Or catch you and vivisect you, whichever is cheapest."

I sighed. "I assume that's classified."

"Yes. Please don't mention that to anyone."

I waved and headed out the door.

• • •

When I got home, Lindsey had a strip of duct tape over her mouth and a pad of paper in her hands. On the paper she wrote, "The agent called and explained about your power and boot camp and everything."

I nodded and gave her a hug. "You don't have to wear that tape."

She wrote, "With you leaving tomorrow, I didn't want to say anything that would hurt your feelings or make us fight."

"Tomorrow?" I pulled the paper out. I figured I had a couple of weeks, at least. But no, she was right, I had to report the next day, freshly shaved, and no need to bring personal belongings.

"Well," I said, "I guess you can go back to Brad now. I'll probably be gone for months, maybe years."

She mumbled angrily behind the duct tape and wrote furiously on her pad of paper. She slapped the paper against my hand until I took it. She'd written, "Sometimes things are true but it's only part of the truth. Sometimes it's not everything that needs to be said. I think of Brad sometimes, but not because I want to be with him, not really."

I put my hand on her shoulder. "I shouldn't have said that. I'm just upset about tomorrow, and I'm scared."

Her pen flew across the paper. "What are you afraid of?"

I ran my hand across my beard. "I just . . . it seems likely that a few weeks after I'm gone you'll find some new guy, and I'm going to get a letter saying that you're sorry, but you've met someone, and you're going to be—I don't know—a trapeze artist in your boyfriend's circus."

She rolled her eyes and wrote, "Seriously? A carnie?" She underlined carnie five times.

"Circus performer," I said. "You always twist my words."

She wrote, "You're being a jerk. I wanted us to have a nice night together."

"Whatever." I went into the bathroom and closed the door. I couldn't believe it. Tomorrow I was joining the military with a bunch of powered freaks, and who knew where that would lead? I looked at my beard in the mirror. It really did make me look old and sad. I knew I was acting like a petulant teenager. I sighed, and lathered shaving cream on my face. I planned to shave and shower so Lindsey and I could speak the obligatory lies shared between loved ones when one of them is leaving.

She opened the door and grabbed my hand just before the razor took its first swath down my cheek. She yanked the tape from her mouth and said, "Jimmy, I'm going to be here when you get back. Because that's my superpower. Loving you. You're stuck with me."

And then she held me for a long time, and I didn't shave until morning, just before I left to catch my bus for boot camp. As the bus pulled away, the sun shone through the dust on the road. The guy next to me said, "I can see the future. What's your thing?"

"My beard is a truth serum."

He nodded. "You and Lindsey are going to be all right, you know."

Even though my face was smooth, I believed him.

Matt Mikalatos is the author of four novels, the most recent of which is *Capeville: Death of the Black Vulture*, a YA superhero novel. You can connect with him online at Capeville.net or Facebook.com/mikalatosbooks.

Over an Embattled City

Adam R. Shannon

The people sway and sway, their heads bobbing to the train's tuneless clicks.

A woman in the row ahead bounces a fussy baby. I can see him in the gap between the seats, struggling as if taken captive by a giant. He fastens his cloudy blue eyes on mine, and I make a wild face, blowing out my cheeks and raising my eyebrows. For a moment, he goes quiet. Then his face collapses, and his wail fills the train car with unfiltered anguish. He weeps huge, adult-size tears.

Nice job, Emma. Frightener of Babies, Ruiner of Train Rides.

• • •

Grand Central has been rebuilt since I moved from the city. Only it wasn't rebuilt; it was always here. The Unmaker never brought it down on top of thousands of morning commuters, reducing it to shrieking rubble, before Outsider subdued him. From its soaring ceiling to its urine-scented lower corners, it has remained unchanged, reliable. For everyone but me.

Two Hyde cops are leaning against the wall at the end of the platform, bullshitting and watching the disembarking commuters. I resist the urge to pull my hoodie tighter around my face. Try not to look like a criminal, Emma. There's no way they're looking for me.

Well, it's possible.

As soon as my parents discover I'm missing, they'll know where

I'm headed. They might call the cops. And, of course, I'm carrying a gun in my messenger bag, which I basically stole.

Emma, Fugitive from Reality.

They're not Hyde cops anymore, I remind myself. They're New York City cops. I'll never get over that. Of all the insults I've endured in sixteen turbulent years, the worst—well, the second-worst—was waking up to find someone had renamed my city.

When I meet the man responsible, I'm going to demand an explanation.

• • •

No one knew Outsider's exact origin story, but you could always detect in him a restless sorrow, a weariness, even when he streaked through the skies over Hyde on his way toward danger, rattling the skyscrapers with sonic booms.

He broke a few windows in the early flyovers. He was frightening: a man stumbling around in blind grief. He once careened through a flock of Canada Geese, sending lifeless birds spiraling down onto rooftop decks. He was sloppy, but in his carelessness, we saw sadness.

Outsider came from a distant future, a dying Earth. He was the first to step through a painstakingly-constructed wormhole designed to carry the last surviving humans to the safety of the past. They hoped to live out their lives under cover of false identities, refugees scattered in the confusion of our age. Like all of his people, he was augmented at the molecular level, possessing abilities far beyond those of his human ancestors. They planned to conceal their natural advantages from the inhabitants of the time.

There were some amongst his kind who implored him not to go, arguing that humanity's lifespan was simply at an end. The human story was over, they said. You only do us a disservice by prolonging it.

His mate and two children planned to join him on the other side.

He entered the blinding tunnel and was swept into history.

• • •

What I love about Hyde—or New York—is that in a hundred steps I can pass the apartments of dozens of interesting people. Where we live now, a hundred steps only take me as far as the home of a distracted broker and a "concierge travel specialist," whatever that is. Together they drive a sleepy, flaccid child between play dates.

I miss Hyde. I can tell my parents do, too, although they think it was always called New York City.

"It was too crazy there," my mom says. Meaning: *you* were too crazy there, Emma. You and your stories about Outsider, and the Unmaker, and battles that demolished places you loved. Your frightening insistence that they were real and not the stuff of comic books. "Hasn't the city been through enough?" my mother would ask. "Do you have to pretend it was worse?"

• • •

Focus, the last surviving hero, lives in a tightly-guarded penthouse atop a metallic modern building. He seldom descends to street level, but my research tells me he's going to attend a meeting of global financial bodies this afternoon. With no supervillains to fight, Focus campaigns against the evils of corruption.

He's a shadow of the hero I remember, but he's the only person who can help me.

I'm not prepared for the throngs of people outside Focus's building. The street is cordoned off, with New York cops keeping people on the opposite sidewalk. A limo idles at the curb. Many of his admirers hold up signs, appealing for his help: *Please find my daughter. Missing since June 1997* and *What happened to Flight MH370?* They fidget and peer over the heads of the others.

The doors open, and a sigh passes like a breeze through the crowd, but it's only two hefty men in dark suits, who regard us through mirrored sunglasses. Then I feel the crowd urge forward, and he's there, wrapped in a hooded black cloak like a monk's robe, his face obscured. He's being hustled forward by a female guard in a suit and identical sunglasses, and he seems frail, harried.

"Focus!" people call out. "Focus! Over here!" They hoist their signs, begging for recognition.

If I'm right, I won't have to shout. If I'm wrong, and he won't listen, the last superhero is probably a dead man, and I'm on my own.

"Focus," I say, making no effort to raise my voice. "I believe you're in danger from Martin Tucker, the comic book writer."

All at once, the people around me slow and blur, their voices dialing down to mere whispers. The entire world fades—everything except me and the stooped man in black across the street.

"Why do you say that?" he asks. His voice is as clear as if he were standing directly in front of me.

I begin to perceive a web of filaments, a forest of glowing fibers stretching in all directions, connecting everything in a complex lattice. A woman, brandishing a sign with glacial, agonizing slowness, ate at the same table in a diner as the man who is yelling in extreme slow-motion at a taciturn cop. The cop's neighbor once bummed a cigarette off the man who sold the magic marker that the woman used to make her sign.

This is the power Focus wields: to perceive and make plain the patterning behind the skin of the world.

The people between us move incrementally forward, their details blurred. Here goes nothing.

"He's somehow related to the disappearance of several dozen superheroes—and villains—over the last ten years," I say.

The skein of filaments reaches out beyond the city. I see a woman in Malaysia making my shirt, a stooped man strolling the beach somewhere along the Indian Ocean.

"There are no other superheroes," he says. "I'm the only one." His face is hidden behind wraps of dark cloth, the eyes barely visible.

"You are now."

"Please get in the car," Focus says.

• • •

Outsider's passage through the wormhole produced an electromagnetic pulse that fried networks within sixty miles of Hyde. He awoke under dark streetlamps and darker buildings, breathing the unfamiliar stink of burning fossil fuels. People began filtering out of doorways, congregating in the streets and talking to strangers in the way you only see during a disaster.

The wormhole inverted and closed with a thunderclap. His children never appeared. Outsider's passage had led to the total collapse of the timeline he knew as his history. He had erased everyone he loved from existence.

He was alone, angry, and powerful in ways unimaginable to the people around him.

But almost immediately, he began to weaken.

The quantum-level alterations in his mind and body were powered from extra-dimensional realms created in his timeline. When his universe collapsed, this energy source began to fade.

That was Outsider's great secret. With his powers faltering, he was constantly forced to improvise, to push harder, to discover new capacities within himself. He became more than he ever might have been, had he remained in his own time. But he sometimes wished he had stayed behind with the people he loved to watch the world die.

Everyone knows that story now. They read it in the comic books, now that Outsider is just a fictional character. But I remember when he rattled the windows of Hyde, and no one knew exactly why. Back then, that little quantum of knowledge in the hands of the Unmaker might have leveled a city.

• • •

Everything speeds up again. The female guard, following whispered instructions, crosses the street and points me out to a cop, who waves me through the cordon tape.

Resentment shimmers through the crowd. "What's so special about her?" I hear one woman say. A man shouts to the dark, hooded figure, "You only help little girls?"

I duck inside the limo door, and I'm with the last living superhero.

The filaments reach out from me and weave into those growing out of the seats and unraveling like vines from the ceiling. Only Focus remains untouched by the pattern. The fibers bend around him, moving slightly as if to avoid his touch.

"You've been found to be . . . delusional," he says. "I see two—three?—protective orders that forbid you to contact individuals in the comic book industry."

"There were more," I admit, "but those people don't exist anymore.

I was trying to get in touch with the Glass Samurai and Fidget. Their people got a little jumpy."

"Those are fictional characters."

"They are now."

He sits back. The filaments fade a bit, retreating into the world. I wonder if he's about to kick me out of the car. I can't let it happen. "I *remember*," I tell him. "I remember when Outsider was a real man, when New York was called Hyde, and there were villains who nearly leveled the city. One by one, they vanished, and no one else knows they were ever real. Right about the time a superhero disappeared, they showed up for the first time in a comic book."

"By Martin Tucker," he nods.

He's not going to kick me out. Inside my chest, I feel a spring uncoil, the loosening of a tightness I'd forgotten was there, and all at once I'm afraid I'm going to cry. No one has ever believed me. For years, I've been sitting across from nodding therapists, who listened intently without rolling their eyes, and just when I began to think they understood, they'd say "I believe you believe it's true," and smile as if that was the same thing as "I believe you."

Emma, Sufferer of Delusions.

"He's killing all the heroes," I say.

Focus looks out the window. I wonder if he can perceive the city the way I do, unmade and remade, its near destruction flattened into inked pages in a comic book.

He speaks with little moments of hesitation, as if holding up and discarding all the words that don't quite fit his meaning. "I've seen . . . flaws in the patterns around him. Every time a new comic series comes out, there's a strangeness to the world, like pieces of a blanket were cut out and . . . patched back together."

"Do you remember when the other heroes were real?" I ask.

"No. Whatever he does, it affects me, as well."

"He's changing everything. I think I'm the only one who sees it."

Focus turns back and nods slowly.

"So go after him!" I say, a little too loudly.

He regards me from deep under the dark hood. "I can't."

"Why not?"

His voice is strained and surprisingly young. "For months now, I've been aware of him . . . studying me. Trying to trace my connections, discover my identity, my story."

That's how all the comic books start: with the secret identity. No one knows Focus's origin story.

He continues. "My privacy is my only defense. I believe if he can . . . discern my personal history, he can do me harm."

"You can stop him first."

He leans in, so close I can hear him breathing through the dark wraps that encircle his face. "Tucker is surprisingly . . . disconnected. If he's rewritten history, then he's written himself out of it. I know his location, nothing more. And he has . . . influential friends."

"Other supervillains?"

"No. People who are very . . . connected. People I need as partners . . . in my work."

What's he talking about? The excitement I felt at being believed is already draining. "I need your help," I plead.

He shakes his cowl. "No, you don't. Go home. You should—" He angles his head, sensing something in my pattern. "You brought a gun."

I'd almost forgotten about it myself.

"I didn't know what else to do," I admit.

"That was—"

Filaments shoot from the seats, passing through me. Something is wrong. They reach out for Focus, lightly at first, like a mother touching her newborn, then wrapping his arms and legs in glowing shackles.

"No!" He howls. "Please!"

A shimmering fiber bursts through the wall of the limo and enters the back of his head. His body jerks as if electrocuted. More filaments encircle and bind him. With visible effort, he pulls the fabric wraps from his face. He's handsome. I could see talking to him longer, on a train or somewhere normal, in a normal world.

"He found me," he gasps. As the threads cocoon him, he blurts out an address and apartment number.

Then he's gone.

"Where you going?" the driver asks. I'm not in the limo anymore. I'm in a New York taxi.

I swallow, trying to dispel the violence of what I've just seen. "Have you ever heard of a superhero called Focus?" I ask.

"You mean like a comic book guy?" the driver asks.

"A real man. Focus. He perceives patterns."

The man hesitates. "I don't know what you're talking about. You mean a DJ or something?"

I think about looking for a bookstore, so I could see if Martin Tucker's latest creation has hit the stands yet.

I direct the driver to the address Focus gave me.

I have a gun, I remind myself. I don't have super strength, and I can't fly or perceive underlying patterns, but I have a gun, and that passes for a superpower among normal people like me. I can kill Martin Tucker if I want to.

• • •

They say that every time you remember something, you open up the memory and repack it again, like viewing a painting and making a perfect copy of it, over and over. With time, the details smear and change, until the picture is something entirely different, not a transcription of the way the world was, but your own creation.

But my memory of the Outsider feels perfect, untouched.

Dust blew around me. Not like a sandstorm, but an unspeakable darkness, the pulverized remains of people, buildings, and dreams. Blocks of debris impacted nearby, like the footsteps of an approaching giant.

My mother, somewhere in the dust, was screaming my name.

Then he was there.

He never bothered with an extravagant costume, never indulged in theatrical capes or high collars. He wore the same simple shirt and pants he had on when he came back to our time. When his feet settled on the cracked sidewalk beside me, I felt the solid, reassuring thump through the bottoms of my shoes.

"And what are you doing here?" he asked. There was a faint accent, an endearing lilt he never quite shed when he learned our language.

I knew him by sight. Everyone did. I'd watched him in videos, on the news, and listened to my parents debate whether he was a hero or something else.

I stared.

"Do you have a name?" he asked.

I nodded. "Emma."

A man ran out of the swirling dust, his face contorted in panic, and vanished back into the storm.

Outsider smiled. Caked dust cracked at the corners of his eyes. "Emma the Brave," he said.

• • •

"We're here," the driver tells me.

It's one of those buildings where you need a key or someone to buzz you in. I wait a few minutes, hoping to slip in behind another resident, but no one comes along, so I pick an apartment and ring the intercom.

"It's Sara from down the hall," I say to the buzzy voice in the grill. "I forgot my key."

"What apartment?" the voice demands.

"Uh, 503?" I can't keep the lie out of my voice. Emma, Master Criminal.

Click.

It will be pretty pathetic if my quest to meet Martin Tucker ends on the front stoop of his building.

Chin up, I tell myself. There are lots of apartments up there, full of different kinds of people. Smart people, suspicious people, gullible people. I just need one of the latter.

After a few more tries, I find one, and I'm in.

On the long, clacking elevator ride to the top floor, I slip my hand into my bag and touch the gun. I have no idea how one confronts a supervillain. Should I put the muzzle in his face as he opens his door? As a villain, he probably won't show any emotion, but he'll be looking to outwit me as soon as he can. I have to act fast.

And by act fast, I guess I mean shoot him.

I've never fired a gun in my life. I'm not cut out to kill someone, supervillain or not.

If there were a reverse button on the elevator, I would press it, go back to ground level, and start the long walk back to Grand Central right now. Maybe I could stop by a few places I remember being destroyed, a tourist from another world.

The clattering of the elevator rises to a crescendo, then falls silent. The doors open.

I never had a master plan. I thought if I could enlist the help of Focus, we might have a chance at stopping Martin Tucker before he erased everything amazing from the world. This is utterly, stupidly hopeless.

Speaking of hopeless, I'm going to be in more trouble back home than I've ever imagined. I swiped my parents' credit card and stole a gun from their safe. I'm not compliant with my useless medications and not cooperating with my psychologists. I've been told that if I continue with my obsessive behavior toward certain figures in the comic book industry, I'll be confined to a rehabilitation facility against my will. Being in Martin Tucker's building with a stolen firearm probably qualifies as my last strike.

On the other hand, I really want to know why he renamed my city.

The elevator doors start to close. I put up my hand to stop them. Emma the Brave steps out.

I leave the gun in my bag and knock on the apartment door. From within, there's a mousy scurrying, then silence. The peephole darkens.

"Who is it?"

I utterly failed to plan for this phase. "Are you Martin Tucker?"

"Who are you?" he asks.

"I'm here to ask you what you did to Outsider!" I yell.

A pause. "I'm sorry," he says. "I don't know how you got in here, but I suggest you leave."

He sounds nervous.

"I'm not talking about the comic book," I say, leaning in. "I mean the real Outsider."

He doesn't answer, and I begin to wonder if he walked away from the door. "And I want to know why you changed Hyde to New York!"

There's no sound. Maybe I should have led with the gun. At last, he speaks. "Step back and let me see you."

I comply, looking directly into the peephole until I lose my nerve and stare at the carpet.

"Are you the one who's been hassling my agent?" he asks. There's no anger in his voice. He actually sounds curious.

"Uh, probably," I answer. "I was trying to get in touch with you."

The door clicks and rattles as he draws back the locks. "Well," he says. "I'd hate to disappoint a fan."

I was expecting someone more . . . villainous. He's wearing a ratty gray T-shirt with a cartoon manatee on it and cargo shorts that reach below his knees. He's mostly bald, with a scruffy goatee. He might be my dad's age.

"Place is a mess," he mutters, gesturing me inside.

His apartment is lit by huge windows full of sky, and it's a dump. The red couch and three mismatched chairs look like furniture rescued from a sidewalk. They're stacked with books, papers, and magazines, and there are more piles on the floor. The walls are bare. The sink overflows with grimy dishes. The only clear spot is a wooden stool and a space on the kitchen counter for his laptop.

It's about the furthest thing from a villain's lair that I can imagine.

I have the disconcerting feeling that I'm supposed to say something nice about the apartment. My parents used to say that was what everyone in Hyde did when they went over to each other's places. "Nice windows," I say.

"Thanks." He doesn't make eye contact.

We pause, as if uncertain who is supposed to speak first.

"Please," he gestures to the stool. "Have a seat."

"I'll stand," I reply, because I'm pretty sure that's what you're supposed to say to the villain. Then I feel foolish and sit. "Fine."

Martin Tucker leans against a dirty counter. "How much do you know?"

No point in being coy. "You've been making superheroes vanish."

"Villains too," he points out. "But continue."

"They vanish, and some time later, they show up in a comic book. Everyone thinks they're fictional."

"Except you, it appears."

I nod. He seems nervous. "How do you do it?" I ask.

Martin Tucker shrugs. "It's just a matter of unearthing their secrets." He meets my eyes for just a moment before again letting his gaze wander the room. "I discover their secret identity. I get the origin story. I write it up, hit 'send' to my publisher, and—poof! They're long gone before the edition ever hits the stores. Thirty-two total, so far. Today will be the last, number thirty-three."

"Yeah," I reply. "It already happened. I was there."

He looks shocked. "What?"

"I was asking Focus's help to defeat you."

Tucker laughs. Not a villain's laugh—certainly not the laugh of an evil genius with a plan to rule the world from a gross apartment. It's more like the tired way you laugh when someone else steals your cab. "And how did he weasel out of it?"

I don't try to hide my annoyance. "He wasn't weaseling out."

"But he wouldn't help."

I shake my head.

"He's corrupt," he says. His hands ball up and relax. "Like all of them. Someone got to him. A criminal group, or a government, or a company with deep pockets. They found something he cared about, and they applied pressure. No one is immune."

"He was fighting to stop corruption."

"No, he was fighting to stop *some* corruption, so that other people could sweep in and take a bigger piece of the pie. Those same people have been trying to find me, too, for several years."

"That's not an excuse to kill him," I say.

"Well, technically, he's just a fictional character now. You can't murder someone who never existed." He waves a hand in front of his face, as if swatting at flies. "But that's arguable—I get it. What I want to know is this: do you miss the time before I started cleaning things up? When this city was almost destroyed?"

"That's not—" I begin, and don't know how to answer. Because, yes, I miss it a little, and I don't know what that says about me. I was terrified at the time. I had to sleep in my parents' bed because I had nightmares in which buildings fell on them and they cried out to me from under the rubble. I hated it, and now I miss it. I feel wrong even admitting that.

He picks up a pile of leather volumes from another kitchen stool and steps gingerly around the apartment, looking for a place to put them down. "I see. After all I've done to make it safe. Well, the least you can do is make a better argument than 'it's wrong to kill people,' because that ship has sailed."

"You took something from me," I say. "From everyone."

He drops the stack atop another pile on the couch, a little more noisily than he needed to, and returns to sit.

"When I unmade the Unmaker? Spare me. Were you in the city when he fought Outsider?"

I'm surprised how nonthreatening Martin Tucker appears. You'd think he would be sort of stiff, like a Bond nemesis, showing off his plans to irradiate the earth or drop the Hoover Dam on Washington. It occurs to me that he's probably never had anyone he could talk to about his power. "I was outside Grand Central," I admit.

He opens and closes his mouth and seems to forget what he meant to say for a moment. "It's just . . . guys like that embodied something I've always hated. He thought his anger and specialness entitled him to run the world. I really hate people like that."

"But you took away all of them. Even Outsider."

He shrugs. "Yeah, that was a tough one. Hard to write about a villain without including a superhero, too. And once I found out that Outsider's power was fading, I knew he would eventually be corrupted, too. He was already showing signs of caring too much. It was only a matter of time before someone used it against him. To borrow a phrase: he was too big to fail."

I think about the dust caking the Outsider's clothes, the way it broke around his eyes and in the corners of his mouth. He could have just picked me up, flown me to safety, and gone back into battle. But he paused.

"Emma the Brave," Outsider said. "Would you like to take a ride?"

He squatted down and offered me his back. I wrapped my arms around his neck, hiked my legs over his hips. His back felt warm—solid but yielding, like my dad's.

"Are you ready?" he asked, standing and supporting my legs with his hands. I nodded into his hair, and we went up.

"Why do you care, anyway?" Martin Tucker asks. "The world is getting along just fine without him."

"He saved me," I explain.

I clung to Outsider's back as we rose through the swirling gray storm. Without warning, we shot into bright sunlight, and I saw the embattled city below. Dust ran in furious rivers between the buildings, darkness shot through with bright electrical flares. A bridge swayed, flinging its cables skyward like an enraged squid.

It was terrifying and awful. And it was something else—something I barely understood and could not then admit. It was important. It *mattered*.

I held on to Outsider and flew.

"*I* saved you," Martin Tucker says.

"The hell you did!"

"You're not quite old enough to grasp this," he says, "but the only thing we love more than revering our heroes is destroying them. We wait for them to sell out for money or fame, or say something that conflicts with our values, or fail to agree with us on who the real enemy is. Then we trash them and move on."

I think about the angry people outside Focus's building. "That's what you think you saved me from? The disappointment of growing up?"

"No—that of living. Most people would rather live in one of my story lines than the real world. You obviously wish you were still there. Despite the fact that many people died before I intervened."

"At least we had someone to look up to!"

"No, that's what *I* gave you. That's the importance of fiction. People will always love Outsider now. We tolerate imperfection in our fictional creations. We root for flawed and damaged characters, people utterly unlike ourselves. Fiction is the new secret identity. It's a refuge from which damaged heroes can continue to do good."

"Well, it wasn't your decision to make," I say.

"Yeah, it was," he barks a laugh, as if amazed by my stupidity. "Because I have the power. Like you. We run the show, until the last one of us is gone."

Us?

I shouldn't have come here. I've made a mistake.

He nods, reading my thoughts. "Only we remember the alternate timelines. That's a superpower."

"It's not a power," I counter. "Everyone thinks I'm nuts."

"Please," he holds up a hand, "spare me the story." He gets up and opens the fridge. It's full of soda bottles. He pulls one out, offers it to me. I shake my head, wondering if he intends to erase me, too. What will it feel like to vanish? One moment, walking or riding the train—the next, nothing. A girl in a book. Emma the Nonexistent.

"I'm not special," I go on, the words coming fast. "I really can't *do* anything. I just remember things. When I was a kid—"

"I told you I *don't want to know!*"

That's it, I'm dead.

At least I won't have to face my parents.

He twists the cap off his soda, and I jump at the hiss of escaping gas. I'm overwhelmed by the urge to run, as if I can flee my own undoing, outdistance the transformation of my life into paper and ink.

"I have to go," I mumble. I slide off the stool, and my messenger bag upends. The gun clatters out, skitters across the wooden floor, and comes to a stop between us.

"Well," Martin Tucker's soda bottle freezes halfway to his mouth, "that's a thing."

"I came to kill you." It comes out more like a question that I would have liked.

"You're certainly taking your time."

I should leap for the gun, but I don't.

He takes a drink. The sound of him swallowing is surprisingly loud.

"But I don't think I can do it," I admit.

He looks down the neck of his bottle. "I don't think I can, either. Not to someone in my kitchen."

"I don't understand."

He regards the floor. "Your appearance today is an opportunity for me. All the other superheroes are gone. I'm out of material. If I know your story, I can write another comic."

"I'd rather you not do that." Emma, Master Negotiator.

He smiles, and his eyes wrinkle the way I remember Outsider's did. A sad smile. "Don't worry, I've already written my last work."

"The story about Focus," I say.

"No. That's already done. I'm talking about one more tale, just waiting for me to hit 'send.'"

I begin to understand why he hasn't tried to grab the gun.

"You?" I ask. "You're erasing yourself?"

"I think the fans will really love this one. It's about an unlikeable man who discovers how to spin reality into fiction. He's revered by fans, called a genius by people much smarter than he is. He soaks it up, and all the while he despises himself for it, knowing himself to be the worst fraud imaginable. Corrupted by his desire to be loved, of all things. Eventually, he tells the truth, and vanishes."

He slumps, wrinkling the cartoon manatee's face in a way I might find funny under different circumstances. The room seems darker, although the sky outside the windows is as bright as ever.

"I'm sure there's another way," I offer.

"There is," he nods. "But I'm not the one to write it. Outsider's people were right about one thing. All stories end." He looks at his watch. "Speaking of which, don't you have somewhere to go?"

"Uh, yeah." I hesitate. "No. Not really. Just home."

He arches an eyebrow. And, without planning it, I decide to tell him how I'm probably going to get arrested, sent to an institution, and disowned by my exhausted parents. He holds up a hand as if to stop me, but I go on with the story. I might be giving him enough information to fictionalize me, but I tell him anyway.

"Why did you share that?" he asks when I'm done. "You know what I could do with it."

I wait until he meets my eyes. "I think you want one person to remember you."

He nods, retrieves the gun, and hands it back to me. "It was nice to meet you. I have to put some finishing touches on my story before I send it off."

He walks me to the door.

"You never answered my question," I remind him, "about renaming the city."

"Oh, that. Reality and the story sometimes switch places," he says, leaning against the doorframe. "While the main character's life becomes fiction, little details from the story become true in the real world. I've used it to alter my identity a few times."

I shake my head. "Not *how* you changed it. *Why.*"

"I was on a tight deadline. The publisher suggested setting the story in a fictional city. I forwarded some ideas for names to my assistant. She misunderstood, put New York into the draft, and the rest is, literally, history."

"Wait," I hold up a hand. "Are you telling me you changed the city's name by *mistake*?"

"Something like that."

"Why didn't you change it back?"

"People seemed to like it."

"Well, *I* don't."

He points at me, suddenly serious. "It's not a vote. You don't get a say. That's the way it will always be while people like us are around."

It's awkward for a second.

I have a strange thought. "So if you become fiction, who will be the author of the comic book in the real world?"

He nods and smiles, as if he approves of the question. "I don't know. Do you want it to be you?"

I shake my head. "No way. Leave me out of it."

He pushes the elevator button.

"Come back by the building when I'm gone," he says. "It *would* be nice to be remembered."

"I'll say hi to whoever lives here."

"Oh, I was going to have the character's apartment remain empty after he disappears. The fans like the suggestion of a sequel."

The elevator rattles like an approaching train.

"You should have a name," Martin Tucker says.

"Emma," I say.

He rolls his eyes. "No, a superhero name. Something befitting your powers. You alone remember how the other heroes fell to human weaknesses and were destroyed by a lesser man. You could be the Storyteller."

"No." I shake my head. "Just Emma."

The doors open, and I leave him standing, like Outsider on the verge of his wormhole. I descend into the streets of a changed city, walking halfway in memory.

I'm back on the train when I notice that my bag feels lighter, almost weightless. The gun is gone.

Of course it's gone, because I never took it. It's back in the safe where it belongs, and only I remember any differently.

Martin Tucker has changed the story. When the comic comes out, I suspect his character will be visited by a mysterious stranger. No name, no backstory—and no gun.

Something jingles in the bottom of the bag: two keys on a plain metal ring. The apartment will be waiting for my return, its wide windows regarding a mundane and beautiful sky.

For now, I watch the people sway to the long, slow song of the train, letting myself move with them, enjoying, for now, my secret identity.

Adam R. Shannon is a career firefighter/paramedic, as well as a fiction writer, hiker, and cook. His work has been shortlisted for an Aeon award and appeared in *Morpheus Tales* and the SFF World anthology *You Are Here: Tales of Cryptographic Wonders*. He and his wife live in Virginia, where they care for an affable German Shepherd, occasional foster dogs, a free-range toad, and a colony of snails who live in an old apothecary jar. His website and blog are at AdamRShannon.com.

Origin Story

Kelly Link

"Dorothy Gale," she said.

"I guess so." He said it grudgingly. Maybe he wished that he'd thought of it first. Maybe he didn't think going home again was all that heroic.

They were sitting on the side of a mountain. Above them, visitors to the Land of Oz theme park had once sailed in molded plastic balloon gondolas over the Yellow Brick Road. Some of the support pylons tilted back against scrawny little opportunistic pines. There was something majestic about the pylons now that their work was done. Fallen giants. Moth-eaten blue ferns grew over the peeling yellow bricks.

The house of Dorothy Gale's aunt and uncle had been cunningly designed. You came up the path, went into the front parlor, and looked around. You were led through the kitchen. There were dishes in the kitchen cabinets. Daisies in a vase. Pictures on the wall. Follow your Dorothy down into the cellar with the rest of your group, watch the movie tornado swirl around on the dirty dark wall, and when everyone tramped up the other, identical set of steps through the other, identical cellar door, it was the same house, same rooms, but tornado-tipped. The parlor floor now slanted and when you went out through the (back) front door, there was a pair of stockinged plaster legs sticking out from under the house. A pair of ruby slippers. A yellow brick road. You weren't in North Carolina anymore.

The whole house was a ruin now. None of the pictures hung straight. There were salamanders in the walls and poison ivy coming up in the kitchen sink. Mushrooms in the cellar, and an old mattress someone had dragged down the stairs. You had to hope Dorothy Gale had moved on.

It was four in the afternoon and they were both slightly drunk. Her name was Bunnatine Powderfinger. She called him Biscuit.

She said, "Come on, of course she is. The ruby slippers, those are like her special power. It's all about how she was a superhero the whole time, only she didn't know it. And she comes to Oz from another world. Like Superman in reverse. And she has lots of sidekicks." She pictured them skipping down the road, arm in arm. Facing down evil. Dropping houses on it, throwing buckets of water at it. Singing stupid songs and not even caring if anyone was listening.

He grunted. She knew what he thought. Sidekicks were for people who were too lazy to write personal ads. "The Wizard of Oz. He even has a secret identity. And he wants everything to be green, all of his stuff is green, just like Green Lantern."

The thing about green was true, but so beside the point that she could hardly stand it. The Wizard of Oz was a humbug. She said, "But he's *not* great and powerful. He just pretends to be great and powerful. The Wicked Witch of the West is greater and more powerfuller. She's got flying monkeys. She's like a mad scientist. She even has a secret weakness. Water is like Kryptonite to her." She'd always thought the actress Margaret Hamilton was damn sexy. The way she rode that bicycle and the wind that picked her up and carried her off like an invisible lover; that funny, mocking, shrill little piece of music coming out of nowhere. That nose.

When she looked over, she saw that he'd put his silly outfit back on inside out. How often did that happen? There was an ant in her underwear. She made the decision to find this erotic, and then realized it might be a tick. No, it was an ant. "Margaret Hamilton, baby," she said. "I'd do her."

He was watching her wriggle, of course. Too drunk at the moment to do anything. That was fine with her. And she was too drunk to feel embarrassed about having ants in her pants. Just like that Ella Fitzgerald song. *Finis, finis.*

The big lunk, her old chum, said, "I'd watch. But she turns into a big witchy puddle when she gets a bucketful in the face. Not good. When it rains does she say, Oops, sorry, can't fight crime today?

Interesting sexual subtext there, by the way. Very girl on girl. Girl meets nemesis, gets her wet, she melts. Screeches orgasmically while she does it, too."

How could he be drunk and talk like that? There were more ants. Had she been lying on an ant pile while they did it? Poor ants. Poor Bunnatine. She stood up and took her dress and her underwear off—no silly outfits for her—and shook them vigorously. Come out with your little legs up, you ants. She pretended she was shaking some sense into him. Or maybe what she wanted was to shake some sense out of him. Who knew? Not her.

She said, "Margaret Hamilton wouldn't fight crime, baby. She'd conquer the world. She just needs a wet suit. A sexy wet suit." She put her clothes back on again. Maybe that's what she needed. A wet suit. A prophylactic to keep her from melting. The booze didn't work at all. What did they call it? A social lubricant. And it helped her not to care so much. Anesthetic. It helped hold her together afterward, when he left town again. Superglue.

No bucket of water at hand. She could throw the rest of her beer, but then he'd just look at her and say, Why'd you do that, Bunnatine? It would hurt his feelings. The big lump.

He said, "Why are you looking at me like that, Bunnatine?"

"Here. Have another Little Boy," she said, giving up, passing him a wide mouth. Yes, she was sitting on an anthill. It was definitely an anthill. Tiny superheroic ants were swarming out to defend their hill, chase off the enormous and evil although infinitely desirable doom of Bunnatine's ass. "It'll put hair on your chest and then make it fall out again."

• • •

"Enjoy the parade?" Every year, the same thing. Balloons going up and up like they couldn't wait to leave town and pudding-faced cloggers on pickup trucks and on the curbs teenage girls holding signs. We Love You. I Love You More. I Want To Have Your Super Baby. Teenage girls not wearing bras. Poor little sluts. The big lump never even noticed and too bad for them if he did. She could tell them stories.

He said, "Yeah. It was great. Best parade ever."

Anyone else would've thought he was being one hundred percent sincere. Nobody else knew him like she did. He looked like a sweet-heart, but even when he tried to be gentle, he left bruises.

She said, "I liked when they read all the poetry. Big bouncy guy / way up in the lonely sky."

"Yeah. So whose idea was that?"

She said, "*The Daily Catastrophe* sponsored it. Mrs. Dooley over at the high school got all her students to write the poems. I saved a copy of the paper. Figured you'd want it for your scrapbook."

"That's the best part about saving the world. The poetry. That's why I do it." He was throwing rocks at an owl that was hanging out on a tree branch for some reason. It was probably sick. Owls didn't usually do that. A rock knocked off some leaves. Blam! Took off some bark. Pow! The owl just sat there.

She said, "Don't be a jerk."

"Sorry."

• • •

She said, "You look tired."

"Yeah."

"Still not sleeping great?"

"Not great."

• • •

"Little Red Riding Hood."

"No way." His tone was dismissive. *As if*, Bunnatine, you dumb bunny. "Sure, she's got a costume, but she gets eaten. She doesn't have any superpowers. Baked goods don't count."

"Sleeping Beauty?" She thought of a girl in a moldy old tower, asleep for a hundred years. Ants crawling over her. Mice. Some guy's lips. That girl must have had the world's worst morning breath. Amazing to think that someone would kiss her. And kissing people when they're asleep? She didn't approve. "Or does she not count, because some guy had to come along and save her?"

He had a faraway look in his eyes. As if he were thinking of some-one, some girl he'd watched sleeping. She knew he slept around. Grate-ful women saved from evildoers or obnoxious blind dates. Models and movie stars and transit workers and trapeze artists, too, probably. She read about it in the tabloids. Or maybe he was thinking about being able to sleep in for a hundred years. Even when they were kids, he'd always been too jumpy to sleep through the night. Always coming over to her house and throwing rocks at the window. His face at her window. Wake up, Bunnatine. Wake up. Let's go fight crime.

He said, "Her superpower is the ability to sleep through anything. Origin story: she tragically pricks her finger on a spinning wheel. What's with the fairy tales and kids' books, Bunnatine? Rapunzel's got lots of hair that she can turn into a hairy ladder. Not so hot. Who else? The girl in Rumpelstiltskin. She spins straw into gold."

She missed these conversations when he wasn't around. Nobody else in town talked like this. The mutants were sweet, but they were more into music. They didn't talk much. It wasn't like talking with him. He always had a comeback, a wisecrack, a double entendre, some cheesy sleazy pickup line that cracked her up, that she fell for every time. It was probably all that witty banter during the big fights. She'd probably get confused. Banter when she was supposed to *POW! POW!* when she was meant to banter.

She said, "You've got it backward. Rumpelstiltskin spins the straw into gold. She just uses the poor freak and then she hires somebody to go spy on him to find out his name."

"Cool."

She said, "No, it's not cool. She cheats."

"So what? Was she supposed to give up her kid to some little guy who spins gold?"

"Why not? I mean, she probably wasn't the world's best parent or anything. Her kid didn't grow up to be anyone special. There aren't any fairy tales about that kid."

"Your mom."

She said, "What?"

"Your mom! C'mon, Bunnatine. She was a superhero."

"My mom? Ha *ha*."

He said, "I'm not joking. I've been thinking about this for a few years. Being a waitress? Just her disguise."

She made a face and then unmade it. It was what she'd always thought: he'd had a crush on her mom. "So what's her superpower?"

He gnawed on a fingernail with those big square teeth. "I don't know. I don't know her secret identity. It's secret. So you don't pry. It's bad form, even if you're archenemies. But I was at the restaurant once when we were in high school and she was carrying eight plates at once. One was a bowl of soup, I think. Three on each arm, one between her teeth, and one on top of her head. Because somebody at the restaurant bet her she couldn't."

"Yeah, I remember that. She dropped everything. And she chipped a tooth."

"Only because that fuckhead Robert Potter tripped her," he pointed out.

"It was an accident."

He picked up her hand. Was he going to bite her fingernail now? No, he was studying the palm. Like he was going to read it or something. It wasn't hard, reading a waitress's palm. You'll spend the rest of your life getting into hot water. He said gently, "No, it wasn't. I saw the whole thing. He knew what he was doing."

It embarrassed her to see how small her hand was in his. As if he'd grown up and she just hadn't bothered. She still remembered when she'd been taller. "Really?"

"Really. Robert Potter is your mother's nemesis."

She took her hand back. Slapped a beer in his. "Stop making fun of my mom. She doesn't have a nemesis. And why does that word always sound like someone's got a disease? Robert Potter's just a fuckhead."

• • •

"Once Potter said he'd pay me ten dollars if I gave him a pair of Mom's underwear. It was when Mom and I weren't getting along. I was like fourteen. We were at the grocery store and she slapped me for some reason. So I guess he thought I'd do it. Everybody saw her slap me. I think it was because I told her Rice Krispies were full of sugar and she should stop trying to poison me. So he came up to me afterward in the parking lot."

Beer made you talk too much. Add that to the list. It wasn't her favorite thing about beer. Next thing she knew, she'd be crying about some dumb thing or begging him to stay.

He was grinning. "Did you do it?"

"No. I told him I'd do it for twenty bucks. So he gave me twenty bucks and I just kept it. I mean, it wasn't like he was going to tell anyone."

"Cool."

"Yeah. Then I made him give me twenty more dollars. I said if he didn't, I'd tell my mom the whole story."

That wasn't the whole story, either, of course. She didn't imagine she'd ever tell him the whole story. But the result of the story was that she had enough money for beer and some weed. She paid some guy to buy beer for her. That was the night she'd brought Biscuit up here.

They'd done it on the mattress in the basement of the wrecked farmhouse, and later on they'd done it in the theater, on the pokey little stage where girls in blue dresses and flammable wigs used to sing and tap-dance. Leaves everywhere. The smell of smoke, someone farther up the mountain, checking on their still, maybe, chain-smoking. Reading girly magazines. Biscuit saying, Did I hurt you? Is this okay? Do you want another beer? She'd wanted to kick him, make him stop trying to take care of her, and also to go on kissing him. She always felt that way around Biscuit. Or maybe she always felt that way and Biscuit had nothing to do with it.

He said, "So did you ever tell her?"

"No. I was afraid that she'd go after him with a ball-peen hammer and end up in jail."

When she got home that night. Her mother looking at Bunnatine like she knew everything, but she didn't, she didn't. She said: "I know what you've been up to, Bunnatine. Your body is a temple and you treat it like dirt."

So Bunnatine said: "I don't care." She'd meant it, too.

• • •

"I always liked your mom."

"She always liked you." Liked Biscuit better than she liked Bunnatine. Well, they both liked him better. Thank God her mother had never slept with Biscuit. She imagined a parallel universe in which her mother fell in love with Biscuit. They went off together to fight crime. Invited Bunnatine up to their secret hideaway/love nest for Thanksgiving. She showed up and wrecked the place. They went on

Oprah. While they were in the studio some supervillain—sure, okay, that fuckhead Robert Potter—implemented his dreadful, unstoppable, terrible plan. That parallel universe was his to loot, pillage, discard like a half-eaten grapefruit, and it was all her fault.

The thing was, there *were* parallel universes. She pictured poor parallel Bunnatine, sent a warning through the mystic veil that separates universes. Go on *Oprah* or save the world? Do whatever you have to do, baby.

The Biscuit in this universe said, "Is she at the restaurant tonight?"

"Her night off," Bunnatine said. "She's got a poker night with some friends. She'll come home with more money than she makes in tips and lecture me about the evils of gambling."

"I'm pretty pooped anyway," he said. "All that poetry wore me out."

"So where are you staying?"

He didn't say anything. She hated when he did this.

She said, "You don't trust me, baby?"

• • •

"Remember Volan Crowe?"

"What? That kid from high school?"

"Yeah. Remember his superhero comics?"

"He drew comics?" "He made up Mann Man. A superhero with all the powers of Thomas Mann."

"You can't go home again."

"That's the other Thomas. Thomas Wolfe."

"Thomas Wolfman. A hairy superhero who gets lost driving home whenever the moon is full."

"Thomas Thomas Virginia Woolfman Woman."

"Now with extra extra superpowers."

"Whatever happened to him?"

"Didn't he die of tuberculosis?"

"Not him. I mean that kid."

"Didn't he turn out to have a superpower?"

"Yeah. He could hang pictures perfectly straight on any wall. He never needed a level."

"I thought he tried to destroy the world."

"Yeah, that's right. He was calling himself something weird. Fast Kid with Secret Money. Something like that."

• • •

"What about you?"

She said, "Me?"

"Yeah."

"Keeping an eye on this place. They don't pay much, but it's easy money. I had another job, but it didn't work out. A place down off I-40. They had a stage, put on shows. Nothing too gross. So me and Kath, remember how she could make herself glow, we were making some extra cash two nights a week. They'd turn down the lights and she'd come out onstage with no clothes on and she'd be all lit up from inside. It was real pretty. And when it was my turn, guys could pay extra money to come and lie on the stage. Do you remember that hat, my favorite hat? The oatmeal-colored one with the pom-poms and the knitted ears?"

"Yeah."

"Well, they kept it cold in there. I think so that we'd have perky tits when we came out onstage. So we'd move around with a bit more rah-rah. But I wore the hat. I got management to let me wear the hat, because I don't float real well when my ears get cold."

"I gave you that hat," he said.

"I loved that hat. So I'd be wearing the hat and this dress— something modest, girl next door—and come out onstage and hover a foot above their faces. So they could see I wasn't wearing any underwear."

He was smiling. "Saving the world by taking off your underwear, Bunnatine?"

"Shut up. I'd look down and see them lying there on the stage like I'd frozen them." *Zap.* "They weren't supposed to touch me. Just look. I always felt a million miles above them. Like I was a bird." *A plane.* "All I had to do was scissor my legs, kick a little, just lift up my hem a little. Do twirls. Smile. They'd just lie there and breathe hard like they were doing all the work. And when the music stopped, I'd float offstage again. But then Kath left for Atlantic City to go sing in a cabaret show. And then some asshole got frisky. Some college kid.

He grabbed my ankle and I kicked him in the head. So now I'm back at the restaurant with Mom."

He said, "How come you never did that for me, Bunnatine? Float like that?"

She shrugged. "It's different with you," she said, as if it were. But of course it wasn't. Why should it be?

"Come on, Bunnatine," he said. "Show me your stuff."

She stood up, shimmied her underwear down to her ankles with an expert wriggle. All part of the show. "Close your eyes for a sec."

"No way."

"Close your eyes. I'll tell you when to open them."

He closed his eyes and she took a breath, let herself float up. She could only get about two feet off the ground before that old invisible hand yanked her down again, held her tethered just above the ground. She used to cry about that. Now she just thought it was funny. She let her underwear dangle off her big toe. Dropped it on his face. "Okay, baby. You can open your eyes."

His eyes were open. She ignored him, hummed a bit. *Why oh why oh why can't I.* Held out her dress at the hem so that she could look down the neckline and see the ground, see him looking back up.

"Shit, Bunnatine," he said. "Wish I'd brought a camera."

She thought of all those girls on the sidewalk. "No touching," she said, and touched herself.

He grabbed her ankle and yanked. Yanked her all the way down. Stuck his head up inside her dress, and his other hand. Grabbed a breast and then her shoulder so that she fell down on top of him, knocked the wind out of her. His mouth propping her up, her knees just above the ground, cheek banged down on the bone of his hip. It was like a game of Twister, there was something Parker Brothers about his new outfit. There was a gusset in his outfit, so he could stop and use the bathroom, she guessed, when he was out fighting crime. Not get caught with his pants down. His busy, busy hand was down there, undoing the Velcro. The other hand was still wrapped around her ankle. His face was scratchy. Bam, pow. Her toes curled.

He said up into her dress, "Bunnatine. Bunnatine."

"Don't talk with your mouth full, Biscuit," she said.

. . .

She said, "There was a tabloid reporter around, wanting to hear stories."

He said, "If I ever read about you and me, Bunnatine, I'll come back and make you sorry. I'm saying that for your own good. Do something like that, and they'll come after you. They'll use you against me."

"So how do you know they don't know already? Whoever *they* are?"

"I'd know," he said. "I can smell those creeps from a mile away."

She got up to pee. She said, "I wouldn't do anything like that anyway." She thought about his parents and felt bad. She shouldn't have said anything about the reporter. Weasel-y guy. Staring at her tits when she brought him coffee.

She was squatting behind a tree when she saw the yearlings. Two of them. They were trying so hard to be invisible. Just dappled spots hanging in the air. They were watching her like they'd never seen anything so fucked up. Like the end of the world. They took off when she stood up. "That's right," she said. "Get the hell away. Tell anybody about this and I'll kick your sorry Bambi asses."

. . .

She said, "Okay. So I've been wondering about this whole costume thing. Your new outfit. I wasn't going to say anything, but it's driving me nuts. What's with all these crazy stripes and the embroidery?"

"You don't like it?"

"I like the lightning bolt. And the tower. And the frogs. It's psychedelic, Biscuit. Can you please explain why y'all wear such stupid outfits? Promise I won't tell anyone."

"They aren't stupid."

"Yes, they are. Tights are stupid. It's like you're showing off. Look how big my dick is."

"Tights are comfortable. They allow freedom of movement. They're machine washable." He began to say something else, then stopped. Grinned. Said, almost reluctantly, "Sometimes you hear stories about some asshole stuffing his tights."

She started to giggle. Giggling gave her the hiccups. He whacked her on the back.

She said, "Ever forget to run a load of laundry? Have to fight crime when you ought to be doing your laundry instead?"

He said, "Better than a suit and tie, Bunnatine. You can get a sewing machine and go to town, *dee eye why*, but who has the time? It's all about advertising. Looking big and bold. But you don't want to be too designer. Too Nike or Adidas. So last year I needed a new outfit, asked around, and found this women's cooperative down on a remote beach in Costa Rica. They've got an arrangement with a charity here in the States. Collection points in forty major cities where you drop off bathing suits and leotards and bike shorts, and then everything goes down to Costa Rica. There's a beach house some big-shot rock star donated to them. A big glass and concrete slab and the tide goes in and out right under the glass floor. I went for a personal fitting. These women are real artists, talented people, super creative. They're all unwed mothers, too. They bring their kids to work and the kids are running around everywhere and they're all wearing these really great superhero costumes. They do work for anybody. Even pro wrestlers. Villains. Crime lords, politicians. Good guys and bad guys. Sometimes you'll be fighting somebody, this real asshole, and you'll both be getting winded, and then you start noticing his outfit and he's looking, too, and then you're both wondering if you got your outfits at this same place. And you feel like you ought to stop and say something nice about what they're wearing. How you both think it's so great that these women can support their families like this."

"I still think tights look stupid." She thought of those kids wearing their superhero outfits. Probably grew up and became drug dealers or maids or organ donors.

• • •

"What? What's so funny?"

He said, "I can't stop thinking about Robert Potter and your mother. Did he want clean underwear? Or did he want dirty underwear?"

She said, "What do you think?"

"I think twenty bucks wasn't enough money."

"He's a creep."

"So you think he's been in love with her for a long time?"

She said, "What?"

"Like maybe they had an affair once a long time ago."

"No way!" It made her want to puke.

"No, seriously, what if he was your father or something?"

"Fuck you!"

"Well, come on. Haven't you wondered? I mean, he could be your father. It's always been obvious he and your mom have unfinished business. And he's always trying to talk to you."

"Stop talking! Right now!"

"Or what, you'll kick my ass? I'd like to see you try." He sounded amused.

She wrapped her arms around herself. Ignore him, Bunnatine. Wait until he's had more to drink. *Then* kick his ass.

He said, "Come on. I remember when we were kids. You used to wait until your mom got home from work and fell asleep. You said you used to sneak into her bedroom and ask her questions while she was sleeping. Just to see if she would tell you who your dad was."

"I haven't done that for a while. She finally woke up and caught me. She was really pissed off. I've never seen her get mad like that. I never told you about it. I was too embarrassed."

He didn't say anything.

"So I kept begging and finally she made up some story about this guy from another planet. Some *tourist*. Some tourist with wings and stuff. She said that he's going to come back someday. That's why she never shacked up or got married. She's still waiting for him to come back."

• • •

"Don't look at me like that. I know it's bullshit. I mean, if he had wings, why don't I have wings? That would be so cool. To fly. Really fly. Even when I used to practice every day, I never got more than two feet off the ground. Two fucking feet. What's two feet good for? Waiting tables. I float sometimes, so I don't get varicose veins like Mom."

"You could probably go higher if you really tried."

"You want to see me try? Here, hold this. Okay. One, two, three. Up, up, and a little bit more up. See?"

He frowned, looked off into the trees. Trying not to laugh. She knew him.

"What? Are you impressed or not?"

"Can I be honest? Yes and no. You could work on your technique. You're a bit wobbly. And I don't understand why all your hair went straight up and started waving around. Do you know that it's doing that?"

"Static electricity?" she said. "Why are you so mean?"

"Hey," he said. "I'm just trying to be honest. I'm just wondering why you never told me any of that stuff about your dad. I could ask around, see if anybody knows him."

"It's not any of your business," she said. "But thanks."

"I thought we were better friends than this, Bunnatine."

He was looking hurt.

"You're still my best friend in the whole world," she said. "I promise."

• • •

"I love this place," he said.

"Yeah. Me, too." Only if he loved it so much, then why didn't he ever stay? So busy saving the world, he couldn't save the Land of Oz. Those poor Munchkins. Poor Bunnatine. They were almost out of beer.

He said, "So what are they up to? The developers? What are they plotting?"

"The usual. Tear everything down. Build condos."

"And you don't mind?"

"Of course I mind!" she said.

He said, "I always think it looks a lot more real now. The way it's falling all to pieces. The way the Yellow Brick Road is disappearing. It makes it feel like Oz was a real place. Being abandoned makes you more real, you know?"

Beer turned him into Biscuit the philosopher-king. Another thing about beer. She had another beer to help with the philosophy. He had one, too.

She said, "Sometimes there are coyotes up here. Bears, too. The mutants. Once I saw a Sasquatch and two tiny Sasquatch babies."

"No way."

"And lots and lots of deer. Guys come up here in hunting season. When I catch 'em, they always make jokes about hunting Munchkins. I think they're idiots to come up here with guns. Mutants don't like guns."

"Who does?" he said.

She said, "Remember Tweetsie Railroad? That rickety roller coaster? Remember how those guys dressed like toy-store Indians used to come onto the train?"

He said, "Fudge. Your mom would buy us fudge. Remember how we sat in the front row and there was that one showgirl? The one with the three-inch ruff of pubic hair sticking out the legs of her underwear? During the cancan?"

She said, "I don't remember that!"

He leaned over her, nibbled on her neck. People were going to think she'd been attacked by a pod of squids. Little red sucker marks everywhere. She yawned.

He said, "Oh, come on! You remember! Your mom started laughing and couldn't stop. There was a guy sitting right next to us and he kept taking pictures."

She said, "How do you remember all this stuff? I kept a diary all through school, and I still don't remember everything that you remember. Like, what I remember is how you wouldn't speak to me for a week because I said I thought *Atlas Shrugged* was boring. How you told me the ending of *The Empire Strikes Back* before I saw it. 'Hey, guess what? Darth Vader is Luke's father!' When I had the flu and you went without me?"

He said, "You didn't believe me."

"That's not the point!"

"Yeah. I guess not. Sorry about that."

• • •

"I miss that hat. The one with the pom-poms. Some drunk stole it out of my car."

"I'll buy you another one."

"Don't bother. It's just I could fly better when I was wearing it."

He said, "It's not really flying. It's more like hovering."

"What, like leaping around like a pogo stick makes you special? Okay, so apparently it does. But you look like an idiot. Those enormous legs. That outfit. Anyone ever tell you that?"

"Why are you such a pain in the ass?"

"Why are you so mean? Why do you have to win every fight?"

"Why do you, Bunnatine? I have to win because I have to. I have to win. That's my job. Everybody always wants me to be a nice guy. But I'm a good guy."

"What's the difference again?"

"A nice guy wouldn't do this, Bunnatine. Or this."

• • •

"Say you're trapped in an apartment building. It's on fire. You're on the sixth floor. No, the tenth floor."

She was still kind of stupid from the first demonstration. She said, "Hey! Put me down! You asshole! Come back! Where are you going? Are you going to leave me up here?"

"Hold on, Bunnatine. I'm coming back. I'm coming to save you. There. You can let go now."

She held on to the branch like anything. The view was so beautiful she couldn't stand it. You could almost ignore him, pretend you'd gotten up here all by yourself.

He kept jumping up. "Bunnatine. Let go." He grabbed her wrist and yanked her off. She made herself as heavy as possible. The ground rushed up at them and she twisted, hard. Fell out of his arms.

"Bunnatine!" he said.

She caught herself a foot before she smacked into the ruins of the Yellow Brick Road.

"I'm fine," she said, hovering. But she was better than fine! How beautiful it was from down here, too.

He looked so anxious. "God, Bunnatine, I'm sorry." It made her want to laugh to see him so worried. She put her feet down gently. The whole world was made of glass, and the glass was full of champagne, and Bunnatine was a bubble, just flicking up and up and up.

She said, "Stop apologizing, okay? It was great! The look on your face. Being in the air like that. Come on, Biscuit, again! Do it again! I'll let you do whatever you want this time."

"You want me to do it again?" he said.

She felt just like a little kid. She said, "Do it again! Do it again!"

• • •

She shouldn't have gotten in the car with him, of course. But he was just old pervy Potter and she had the upper hand. She explained how he was going to give her more money. He just sat there listening. He said they'd have to go to the bank. He drove her right through town, parked the car behind the Food Lion.

She wasn't worried. She still had the upper hand. She said, "What's up, pervert? Gonna do a little Dumpster diving?"

He was looking at her. He said, "How old are you?"

She said, "Fourteen." He said, "Old enough."

• • •

"How come you left after high school? How come you always leave?"

He said, "How come you broke up with me in eleventh grade?"

"Don't answer a question with a question. No one likes it when you do that."

"Well, maybe that's why I left. Because you're always yelling at me."

"You ignored me in high school. Like you were ashamed of me. *I'll see you later, Bunnatine. Quit it, Bunnatine. I'm busy.* Didn't you think I was cute? There were plenty of guys at school who thought I was cute."

"They were all idiots."

• • •

"I didn't mean it like that. I just meant that they were really idiots. Come on, you know you thought so, too."

"Can we change the subject?"

"Okay."

• • •

"It wasn't that I was ashamed of you, Bunnatine. You were distracting. I was trying to keep my average up. Trying to learn something. Remember that time we were studying and you tore up all my notes and ate them?"

• • •

"I saw they still haven't found that guy. That nutcase. The one who killed your parents."

"No. They won't." He threw rocks at where the owl had been. Nailed that sorry, invisible, absent owl.

"Yeah?" she said. "Why not?"

"I took care of it. He wanted me to find him, you know? He just wanted to get my attention. That's why you gotta be careful, Bunnatine. There are people out there who really don't like me."

"Your dad was a sweetheart. Always tipped twenty percent. A whole dollar if he was just getting coffee."

"Yeah. I don't want to talk about him, Bunnatine. Still hurts. You know?"

"Yeah. Sorry. So how's your sister doing?"

"Okay. Still in Chicago. They've got a kid now. A little girl."

"Yeah. I thought I heard that. Cute kid?"

"She looks like me, can you imagine? She seems okay, though. Normal."

• • •

"Are we sitting in poison ivy?"

"No. Look. There's a deer over there. Watching us."

• • •

"When do you have to be at work?"

"Not until six a.m. I just need to go home first and take a shower."

"Cool. Is there any beer left?"

"No. Sorry," she said. "Should've brought more."

"That's okay. I've got this. Want some?"

• • •

"Why don't you leave?"

"Why go wait tables in some other place? I like it here. This is where I grew up. It was a good place to grow up. I like all the trees. I like the people. I even like how the tourists drive real slow between here and Boone. I just need to find a new job or Mom and I are going to end up killing each other."

"I thought you were getting along."

"Yeah. As long as I do exactly what she says."

"I saw her at the parade. With some little kid."

"Yeah. She's been babysitting for a friend at the restaurant. Mom's into it. She's been reading the kid all these fairy tales. She can't stand the Disney stuff, which is all the kid wants. Now they're reading *The Wizard of Oz*. I'm supposed to get your autograph, by the way. For the kid."

"Sure thing! You got a pen?"

"Oh, shit. It doesn't matter. Maybe next time."

• • •

It got dark slow and then real fast at the end, the way it always did, even in the summer, like daylight realized it had to be somewhere right away. Somewhere else. On weekends she came up here and read mystery novels in her car. Moths beating at the windows. Got out every once in a while to take a walk and look for kids getting into trouble. She knew all the places they liked to go. Sometimes the mutants were down where the stage used to be, practicing. They'd started a band. They were always asking if she was sure she couldn't sing. She really, really couldn't sing. That's okay, the mutants always said. You can just howl. Scream. We're into that. They traded her 'shine for cigarettes. Told her long, meandering mutant jokes with lots of hand gestures and incomprehensible punch lines. Dark was her favorite time. In the dark she could imagine that this really was the Land of Oz, that when the sun couldn't stay away any longer, when the sun finally came back up, she'd still be there. In Oz. Not here. Click those heels, Bunnatine. There's no home like a summer place.

She said, "Still having nightmares?"

"Yeah."

"The ones about the end of the world?"

"Yeah, you nosy bitch. Those ones."

"Still ends in the big fire?"

"No. A flood."

• • •

"Remember that television show?"

"Which one?"

"You know. *Buffy the Vampire Slayer.* Even Mom liked it."

"I saw it a few times."

"I keep thinking about how that vampire, Angel, whenever he got evil, you knew he was evil because he started wearing black leather pants."

"Why are you obsessed with what people wear? Shit, Bunnatine. It was just a TV show."

"Yeah, I know. But those black leather pants he wore, they must have been his evil pants. Like fat pants."

"What?"

"Fat pants. The kind of pants that people who get thin keep in their closet. Just in case they get fat again."

He just looked at her. His big ugly face was all red and blotchy from drinking.

She said, "So my question is this. Does Angel the vampire keep a pair of black leather pants in his closet? Just in case? Like fat pants? Do vampires have closets? Or does he donate his evil pants to Goodwill when he's good again? Because if so then every time he turns evil, he has to go buy new evil pants."

He said, "It's just television, Bunnatine."

• • •

"You keep yawning."

He smiled at her. Such a nice-boy smile. Drove girls of all ages wild. He said, "I'm just tired."

"Parades can really take it out of you."

"Fuck you."

She said, "Go on. Take a nap. I'll stay awake and keep lookout for mutants and nemesissies and autograph hounds."

"Maybe just for a minute or two. You'd really like him."

"Who?"

"The nemesis I'm seeing right now. He's got a great sense of humor. Sent me a piano crate full of albino kittens last week. Some project he's working on. They pissed everywhere. Had to find homes for them all. Of course, first we checked to make sure that they weren't little bombs or possessed by demons or programmed to hypnotize small children with their swirly red kitten eyes. Give them bad dreams. That would have been a real PR nightmare."

"So what's up with this one? Why does he want to destroy the world?"

"He won't say. I don't think his heart's really in it. He keeps doing all these crazy stunts, like with the kittens. There was a thing with a machine to turn everything into tomato juice. But somebody who used to hang out with him says he doesn't even like tomato juice. If he ever tries to kidnap you, Bunnatine, whatever you do, don't say yes if he offers you a game of chess. Try to stay off the subject of chess. He's one of those guys who think all master criminals ought to be chess players, but he's terrible. He gets sulky."

"I'll try to remember. Are you comfortable? Put your head here. Are you cold? That outfit doesn't look very warm. Do you want my jacket?"

"Stop fussing, Bunnatine. Am I too heavy?"

"Go to sleep, Biscuit."

• • •

His head was so heavy she couldn't figure out how he carried it around on his neck all day. He wasn't asleep. She could hear him thinking.

He said, "You know, someday I'm going to fuck up. Someday I'll fuck up and the world won't get saved."

"Yeah. I know. A big flood. That's okay. You just take care of yourself, okay? And I'll take care of myself and the world will take care of itself, too."

Her leg felt wet. Gross. He was drooling on her leg. He said, "I dream about you, Bunnatine. I dream that you're drowning, too. And I can't do anything about it. I can't save you."

She said, "You don't have to save me, baby. Remember? I float. Let everything turn into water. Just turn into water. Let it turn into beer. Tomato juice. Let the Land of Oz sink. Ozlantis. Little happy mutant Dorothy mermaids. Let all those mountain houses and ski condos go down, all the way down and the deer and the bricks and the high school girls and the people who never tip. It isn't all that great a world anyway, you know? Biscuit? Maybe it doesn't want to be saved. So stop worrying so much. I'll float. I'm Ivory soap. Won't even get my toes wet until you come and find me."

"Oh, good, Bunnatine," he said, drooling, "that's a weight off my mind"—and fell asleep. She sat beneath his heavy head and listened to the air rushing around up there in the invisible leaves. It sounded like water moving fast. Waterfalls and lakes of water rushing up the side of the mountain. But that was some other universe. Here it was only night and wind and trees and the stars were coming out. Hey, Dad, you fuckhead.

Her legs fell asleep and she needed to pee again, but she didn't want to wake up Biscuit. She bent over and kissed him on the top of his head. He didn't wake up. He just mumbled, Quit it, Bunnatine. Love me alone. Or something like that.

• • •

She remembers being a kid. Nine or ten. Sneaking back into the house at four in the morning. Her best friend, Biscuit, has gone home, too, to lie in his bed and not sleep. She had to beg him to let her go home. They have school tomorrow. She's tired and she's so hungry. Fighting crime is hard work. Her mother is in the kitchen, making pancakes. There's something about the way she looks that tells Bunnatine she's been out all night, too. Maybe she's been out fighting crime, too. Bunnatine knows her mother is a superhero. She isn't just a waitress. That's just her cover story.

She stands in the door of the kitchen and watches her mother. She practices her hovering. She practices all the time.

Her mother says, "Want some pancakes, Bunnatine?" She waited as long as she could, and then she heaved his head up and put it down on the ground. She covered his shoulders with her jacket. Like setting a table with a handkerchief. Look at the big guy, lying there so peacefully. Maybe he'll sleep for a hundred years. But more likely the mutants will wake him, eventually, with their barbaric yawps. They're into kazoos right now and heavymetal hooting. She can hear them warming up. Biscuit hung out with some of the mutants at school, years and years ago. They'll get a kick out of his new outfit. There's a ten-year high school reunion coming up, and Biscuit will come home for that. He gets all sentimental about things like that. Mutants, on the other hand, don't do things like parades or reunions. They're good at keeping secrets, though. They made great babysitters when her mom couldn't take care of the kid.

• • •

She keeps her headlights off, all the way down the mountain. Turns the engine off, too. Just sails down the mountain like a black wing.

• • •

When she gets home, she's mostly sober and of course the kid is still asleep. Her mom doesn't say anything, although Bunnatine knows she doesn't approve. She thinks Bunnatine ought to tell Biscuit about the kid. But it's a little late for that, and who knows? Maybe she isn't his kid anyway.

The kid has fudge smeared all over her face and her pillow. Leftover fudge from the parade, probably. Bunnatine's mom has a real sweet tooth. Kid probably sat up eating it in the dark, after Bunnatine's mom put her to bed. Bunnatine kisses the kid on the forehead. Goes and gets a washcloth, comes back and wipes off some of the fudge. Kid still doesn't wake up. She's going to be real disappointed about the autograph. Maybe Bunnatine will just forge Biscuit's handwriting. Write something real nice. It's not like Biscuit will care. Bunnatine would like to crawl into the kid's bed, just curl up around the kid and get warm again, but she's already missed two shifts this week. So she takes a hot shower and goes to sit with her mom in the kitchen until she has to leave for work. Neither of them has much to say to the other, which is normal, but her mom makes Bunnatine some eggs and toast. If Biscuit were here, she'd make him breakfast, too, and Bunnatine imagines that, eating breakfast with Biscuit and her mom, waiting for the sun to come up so that the day can start all over again. Then the kid comes in the kitchen, crying and holding out her arms for Bunnatine. "Mommy," she says. "Mommy, I had a really bad dream."

Bunnatine picks her up. Such a heavy little kid. Her nose is running and she still smells like fudge. No wonder she had a bad dream.

Bunnatine says, "Shhh. It's okay, baby. It was just a bad dream. Just a dream. Tell me about the dream."

Kelly Link is the author of four short story collections: *Get in Trouble*, a finalist for the 2016 Pulitzer Prize in Fiction, *Pretty Monsters*, *Magic for Beginners*, and *Stranger Things Happen*. She lives with her husband and daughter in Northampton, Massachusetts.

About the Editors

Tricia Reeks lives in the bear-infested mountains of Asheville, North Carolina with her mountaineer husband and her two ferocious French bulldogs. She is the founder of Meerkat Press and the editor of *Love Hurts: A Speculative Fiction Anthology*.

Kyle Richardson lives in the suburban wilds of Canada with his encouraging wife Michelle, their rambunctious son Kai, and a staircase that Kyle seems to be constantly tumbling down. He writes about shape-shifters, superheroes, and the occasional clockwork beast, moonlights as an editor at Meerkat Press, and has been working on his first novel for so long now, his wife has resorted to ultimatums. He made his short-fiction debut in *Love Hurts: A Speculative Fiction Anthology* and has since sold stories to *Daily Science Fiction* and his enthusiastic mother, at exorbitant rates.

CPSIA information can be obtained
at www.ICGtesting.com
Printed in the USA
LVOW12s0840140417

530637LV00004B/5/P